M O ...
MUSIC

MOON MUSIC

a novel

FAYE KELLERMAN

William Morrow and Company, Inc. New York

It is the policy of William Morrow and Company, and its imprints and affiliates, recognizing the importance of preserving what has been written, to print the books we publish on acid-free paper, and we exert our best efforts to that end.

Library of Congress Cataloging-in-Publication Data

Kellerman, Faye.
    Moon music : a novel / Faye Kellerman.—1st ed.
      p. cm.
    ISBN 0-688-14369-5 (alk. paper)
      1. Indians of North America—Mixed descent—Fiction.   I. Title.
    PS3561.E3864M66   1988
    813'.54—dc21
                                                                                     98-6735
                                                                                       CIP

Printed in the United States of America

First Edition

1   2   3   4   5   6   7   8   9   10

BOOK DESIGN BY BERNARD KLEIN

www.williammorrow.com

For Jonathan, Mom, and the children: my celestial beings

Special thanks to Phillip Roland, Community Partnership Coordinator, Sharon Masada, Senior Law Enforcement Official, and Detective Sergeant William Keeton (Ret.) of the LVMPD for their invaluable help, and for being so generous with their time. Any inaccuracies in place and procedure are mine, *not theirs.*

MOON
MUSIC

PROLOGUE

It was a land—hostile and unforgiving. Vast stretches of savage, alkaline desert where the wind blasted grit in the winters and summers were relentless hours of sweltering heat. Deep into August, the wasteland surfaces withered and cracked, producing deep fissures to a fiery hell. An area so seemingly without heartbeat that it had once been used for atomic bomb testing.

But to the chosen few—like herself—it was a place called home. Because she knew this barren topology as well as she knew every cell in her body. She knew its crevices, its caves, its rocks, and its shelters. As she surveyed the area from above, a tear formed in her eye.

Once, the mesas had held flourishing greenlands—wild grasses and flowers fed by natural artesian springs. So beautiful the Indians had referred to the land as The Meadows, translated into Spanish as *Las Vegas*. But the White Man grew greedy and raped the ground's precious resources—the oh-so-righteous Mormons with their all-knowing God, the silver prospectors with their debauchery, the Department of Energy shooting off bombs, the gaudy gangsters bringing crimes and corruption, and the billionaires with their lifeless corporate empires.

All of them—parasites. They may have built the desert, but they couldn't make it bloom. Because they never gave a thought to the land's indigenous inhabitants—the majestic bighorn sheep, the powerful rattle-

1

snakes, the playful rabbits, the ancient desert tortoises, the clever coyotes, and the beautiful, athletic birds which soared in the open sky as if gliding to heaven.

Still, she smiled. There was hope. Because the land rapers had been all take and no give, they were in the dark about the true power of the land, unaware of its deep mystery and magical forces. Mired in tunnel vision, they were ignorant that the land and its creatures had power.

But she knew the secret.

The desert could fight back.

ONE

Ignoring the subtle vibrations under his pillow because he was just too damn comfortable. Warm and sated, inhaling the rich sensuality of musky sex. With force, Jensen opened a rebellious lid, his vision assaulted by the Strip's strobic neon. Outside the winds moaned, pushing everything in their paths. Grit crackled against the picture window as his eyes swept over the vista. A panoply of garish colors nonexistent in nature.

Looking away from the glass, back down at his covers. Beside him, Gretchen slept—young and lithe—beads of sweat lining the crack of her small, round ass. He wanted to take a bite out of it. His breathing became pronounced, audible.

Then his pager went off again.

Jensen swore to himself, then, with resignation, lifted his head from the pillow. He'd never realized how much a cranium could weigh. Digging his palms into the mattress, he hoisted his large frame forward until he was sitting. He tried to make out the number in the dark, but gave up and flicked on the light.

"Hmmm," she grunted. "Turn it off."

"In a minute."

"What time is it?"

Jensen's heart jumped as he read the number. Rom's mobile phone. How long had he been beeping in?

"What *time*—"

"One-thirty," he snapped back.

"*One*-thirty?" She was whining now. "C'mon, baby. Bebe says we got the room until three. Turn off the light."

Jensen already had his pants on. "I've got to go."

"But it's so *nasty* outside."

"Nasty" was an understatement. The wind was howling dust and sand. Jensen slipped on his shirt and socks and tied his size eleven shoes. Brought up the hotel's outside line and punched in Rom's numbers. Static over the wires like lightning. Still he could make out a terse "Poe."

"It's Steve."

"Lemme go inside my car. If we get disconnected, call me back."

The line managed to keep as whooshing sounds, like tidal waves, came through the receiver. Jensen knotted his tie, then stroked Gretchen's ass. She purred, then rolled over and made a little snoring noise. Just as well. No sense starting what couldn't be finished. He heard the pop of the car door closing, the gusts die down. "What's up?"

"You turn your pager off, Stephen?"

"Why? How many times did you beep me?"

"Half a dozen."

Jensen knew Poe was exaggerating. "Must have slept through it."

Not a total lie, but one Poe wasn't about to buy. "You know, I almost broke down and called your house."

Jensen's heart started hammering. For once, he paused before speaking. Rom had said *"almost."*

As if Alison didn't know. Yet she chose to play dumb. After fifteen years of marriage, he still hadn't figured her out. In the early years, she had kept him at arm's length. He had put it down to her youthful shyness . . . their difference in age. Later on, her mental state made her impenetrable, her mind blocked by a steel-trap door of undiagnosed illness.

Jensen was all professional now. "What's going down, Rom?"

"Single desert dump off West Charleston."

"In Red Rock?"

"Before." Poe gave directions. "And, in answer to your unasked question—how someone came upon the body by happenstance at this time of night and in this weather—*no,* it doesn't make any sense. The call came through a public phone outside Big Top.'' A beat. ''Where are you, by the way?''

''Big Top.'' Pause. ''Want me to go downstairs and check it out?''

''You have a print kit on you, Steve?''

''I meant to guard the phone.'' Jensen's voice rose a notch. ''You got a problem with me tonight, Rom?''

I've got a problem with you every night, Stevie. Instead, Poe said, ''I've already sent someone down to dust. But sure, go down and take a peek if you think it'll do some good.'' A hesitation. ''I've got to get back, watch the corpse to make sure the sand doesn't totally bury it before the ME gets here.''

''Stiff a male or female?''

''Female. One of her breasts was partially exposed. I can't tell if her entire body is nude, because the rest of her is coated with sand. I couldn't find a purse or any ID. Useless to search now. Tomorrow we'll go on a treasure hunt to look for things tossed and blown.''

''Who's we?''

''You, me . . . probably Patricia.'' Poe swiped limp, dark hair from his black eyes, stared out the windshield of the Honda. Darker than syrup and about as thick. Even the moon was having trouble breaking through. ''After you check out the phone booth, get down here. And bring some light. The grit is so thick I can barely make out my shadow.''

Over the line, Jensen said, ''Why don't you hammer down a stake and go home?'' A pause. ''Body'll keep till morning.''

Poe could picture Steve's flip smile as he caressed the backside of his latest mistress. What was her name again? Greta? Something like that. ''I'm hanging up.''

And he did.

To prevent hair from blowing into his eyes, Poe had attempted a ponytail. But the lank tresses were too short and kept coming loose, tickling his eyes, making them red and irritated. He blinked repeatedly, wishing he had brought his protective goggles. His disposable face mask did little to cut the sting of the grit. He snapped his fingers through gloves, then caught himself and dropped his hands at his sides. A makeshift tent had been erected around the stiff, an attempt to give it and the pathologist some protection. Inside, flashlight beams shimmied in strobic fashion. Jensen was standing a few feet away, hands tucked into his pockets, coat collar turned up. Poe sensed the burn from the big man's suspicious eyes. Jensen was ten years older than he, a good six inches taller, outweighed him by fifty pounds of muscle. But circumstances had dictated that professionally the younger would rule the elder.

Poe shouted to him, "You can wait in the car."

"You sure?"

"Yeah, go ahead. We'll take shifts."

"Thanks." Jensen lumbered over to his latest four-wheel-drive—an Explorer. He slipped inside and shut the door.

Poe remained restless. He jogged over to the tent and stepped inside. The body had been photographed, its current position outlined by three-foot stakes. Although the desert floor held a top layer of loose sand, a foot or two below lay pure clay. He knelt beside the pathologist.

Calmly, she remarked, "You're blocking my light."

Rukmani's hot breath was laced with Indian spices—not unlike his own. Their quiet dinner of *baigan masaledar* had been rudely interrupted by the page from the Bureau. Under a coat, she wore regulation scrubs. But her face was framed in a traditional Hindu veil—this one was green silk to match her working clothes.

"Sorry." Poe stood up, then backed into the shadows. He stood outside the canvas and bounced on the balls of his feet. He shivered. Miserable and cold and exposed. Even after six months of somewhat steady dating, Rukmani was a hard woman to read. Attentive when they were together, yet she insisted that they take separate cars to the crime scene. Take separate cars almost *everywhere,* unless he made a point of picking her up. Poe supposed that was telling of something.

Rukmani called out, "You know, Rom—"

"Can't hear you." Poe came back in, knelt in front of the blanketed body. "What?"

"I've done all I can out here. I took her temperature, but I doubt it's accurate, the liver being exposed to the wind. I dare not open her up further, pollute the body with more flotsam and jetsam. As it is, she's in bad shape. Did you get a good look at her?"

"No."

Pulling back the tarpaulin, she uncovered the dead face. Poe felt his stomach lurch. It took him a moment to find his voice. And when he did, it took the form of old malicious speech patterns. "Wha . . . what . . . ha . . . happened to her face?"

Rukmani ignored his stutter. "You mean what happened to half of it. Could you push up my glasses? They're falling off my nose again."

Poe complied, feeling his gut jerked once again. How could that woman be so placid? Maybe it was seeing all those bodies float in the Ganges during her childhood. "Wha . . . what happened to her?"

"Offhand, it looks like someone gouged her." Rukmani's dark eyes peered at the visage. "Raked her clear down to the bone. He also scooped out the left eyeball—"

"Enough, Ruki!"

The pathologist was taken aback. "What's wrong with you? You're acting like a rookie."

"She looks so . . . *grotesque.*"

"That she does." She studied the mutilated face. "I fear someone was proving a point. Look at the perfect bilateral symmetry . . . right through the tip of the nose. Ruler-straight. Right side of the face is completely untouched, the left completely destroyed. Know what it reminds me of?"

"I don't want to hear this."

"*Phantom of the Opera.* Wonder if your killer is an Andrew Lloyd Webber fan." She threw the tarp back over the face. "I'll get my guys. Take her down to the morgue and finish her up indoors."

"Could you call Steve in?"

Rukmani snapped off her gloves. "Be glad to, Sergeant."

Technically it was detective sergeant. Poe smiled back without meaning it. As soon as she left, he pulled back the sheet, eyes immediately focusing on her face . . . on the lone eye. It had been blue. Now the pupil was fixed so that it appeared black. Using extreme imagination, he could picture her pretty once upon a time. A nice complexion, a high cheekbone, thick lips—half of them. Gently, he pulled the blanket away from her body, then winced and backed up.

Her upper torso mimicked the face. One half was totally intact. Delicate bones. A large breast, no doubt with the help of implants. The side held smooth skin, a flat abdomen, a swoop of waist . . . shapely legs. The other side of the rib cage was shredded hamburger. Loose tendrils of muscle had remained attached to exposed bones, dancing with each blast of air.

At that moment, Jensen chose to make his entrance. Open-mouthed, he stared at the half-mangled corpse. Instinctively, he retreated, groped for one of the tent panels, and stuck his head outside. He felt his dinner bubbling up until it erupted with volcanic pressure. Hot molten lead in his mouth, spewing into the wind. Heaving until he was empty. When he was done, he ejected the last chunks from his mouth, then wiped his eyes and lips with a handkerchief. Shakily, he returned his focus to the body, then looked away.

"Sorry about that."

"Who was she, Steve?"

Jensen licked his sour lips. "What are you talking about?"

"You know her. Why else would a vet like you puke—"

"Did you get a look at her *face*?"

"Yes. It's an abomination. Who was she?"

Trapped. Jensen rubbed his face. Better to head Rom off before he dug too deep.

Jensen coughed. "I think her name is . . . *was* . . . Brittany. Brittany Newel."

"You think?"

Jensen was quiet.

"Age?" Rom asked.

A big sigh. Jensen said, "Maybe twenty-two . . . twenty-three."

"Nice legs." Poe stood up, brushed his pants off. "Dancer?"

"Yeah, I think she danced."

"Show or lap?"

"Maybe both."

"Remember which hotel?"

"God, it was so long . . . maybe Havana."

"Is that where you met her?"

"Does it matter?"

"Now that she's dead it does."

Jensen's eyes narrowed. He straightened his spine and loomed over Poe. "Are you *questioning* me?"

Poe shrugged off the intimidating body posture. "About her, yes. Not about her murder."

Not yet.

The explanation did little to mollify Jensen's anger. "I picked her up in a bar, Poe. Around a year ago. A quickie thing. Nothing long-term."

"Long-term," Poe repeated. "Aren't you married?"

Jensen glared, then stormed out of the tent, bumping shoulders with Rukmani, spinning her sideways. He stopped instantly, turned around, came back inside. "God, I'm so sorry. Are you okay?"

Rukmani rubbed her sore shoulder. "What's your problem?"

"Are you okay?"

"Yeah, yeah, I'll live."

Poe bent down, covered the body. "Are your guys coming, Doc?"

"Yes, of course. Takes a moment to unload the gurney, Rom."

Jensen said, "What can you tell us about this, Doc? Other than the fact that the guy who did this must have lots of shit under his fingernails."

"You think someone did this with his fingernails?" Poe asked.

Jensen said, "As opposed to . . ."

"A tool," Poe answered.

"Not a sharp tool," Rukmani said. "Too many jagged edges. Maybe a rake of some sort. Lots of parallel lines. You look at the tissue shreds under a microscope. If it was done with an implement, we'll find bits of metal or plastic . . . or bits of fingernail. Someone very strong, with *sharp,* strong nails. Ah . . . the gurney cometh." Rukmani smiled at Rom. "It's kind of crowded in here."

Poe cocked his head at Jensen. "Let's go."

Immediately, their faces were hit with gravel.

Poe shouted, "Talk in the car."

They broke for the Honda. Once inside, they took a few moments, wiped sand and dust from their faces and mouths. Poe said, "You shouldn't be on this case."

"C'mon—"

"Steve, you have a problem. You fucked her!"

Jensen winced, brushed blond hair from his face. "You take me off now, it makes me look bad. C'mon, Rom. Toss me a bone."

"Like?"

"Suppose I just get the basics. I'll go over to the apartment and talk to her roommate." A pause. "I really don't know anything about her. Things like who her friends were, who her enemies were. You know. Just . . . the basics."

Poe thought over the proposal. Pulling him off would point the finger. And then there was Alison. . . . "Call up Patricia. You two can go together—"

"Oh, for Chrissakes, Rom—"

"For your own welfare, Steve." *To make sure you don't rifle through her personal effects and pull incriminating evidence.* "She's your backup."

Jensen spoke through clenched teeth. "Nothing personal about Fat Patty. I love Fat Patty. But I *don't* need backup."

"I'll determine that," Poe said. "Call up Patricia or go home. The choice is yours."

Steve glared with irate eyes, trying to throw daggers into Poe's orbs. A midget with a motherfucking Napoleon complex. Unfortunately, Poe sat in the catbird seat.

A moment passed.

"Go pick up Patricia," Poe said. "Stop wasting time."

Angrily, Jensen bolted from the car, slammed the door. Poe watched as Jensen's Explorer skidded out from the sand, then tore down the road.

Minutes later, Rukmani knocked on the car window. She opened the door, slid inside the passenger seat. "He's acting awfully pissy."

"He knew her. The dead girl—"

"Wha—"

"He fucked her."

Rukmani was quiet. "So maybe he's acting guilty."

Poe started snapping his fingers. "Nah, he didn't do it."

"You're sure?"

"Well, I'm not *positive* of anything." Still snapping. "But it doesn't look like Steve's style. He likes his meat young and *alive.*"

Rukmani took his hands, held them in her own. "You've got more tics than a clock. You really should be on Prozac."

Poe remained serious. "I should have pulled him off the case."

"Why didn't you?"

He shrugged. "Don't know."

"It wouldn't have anything to do with Alison, would it?"

He jerked his hands away, but hesitated before he spoke. "Maybe . . . probably."

Alison.

Poe said, "I figure let him run loose for a day or two. He'll be watched. If he's guilty, it'll lead to something. If not, why screw him up prematurely? The man does have a wife and kids."

A wife and kids.

"Despite what he thinks, I'm not out to ruin him." A beat. "He does a decent number on himself without my help."

Rukmani straightened her jacket. "Well, I'm off to the morgue. How about you?"

"Guess I'll dig up a ghost named Brittany Newel." He scratched his aquiline nose. ''She might have been a dancer for the floor show at Havana. Might as well start there.''

Rukmani gave Poe's long, lean face a gentle pat. ''Evil critters out there, Rom. Watch your back.''

He nodded. Living in a city that never slept, her words were good advice.

TWO

It was well past three, so Alison knew Steve was working a legitimate case. Which didn't surprise her, given the circumstances of the evening.

No matter how many times she bathed, it still remained with her. The smell of sweat, the taste of blood, the adrenaline rush that appeared from nowhere. Scratches scored her arms, chest, and back. Superficial. They didn't hurt . . . would probably disappear in a day or so. But they looked suspicious. If Steve saw them, he'd ask questions. Like how did they get there.

As if she knew.

What was *happening* to her?

Washing and scrubbing. First with soap, then with alcohol, lastly with bleach. Burning and stinging her until she had to rip and tear at her skin to make it stop.

She thought a moment.

Maybe *she* had put the scratches there. With her nails. Or with her loofah. Or her bathing sponge. Or the thick tufts of steel wool.

Why was she doing this?

And still she felt horribly dirty . . . contaminated.

That was the key word.

Contaminated.

Thinking it over. Trying to make sense out of it all.

Which was a dangerous thing to do. To think. Instead, she should be doing her research. She should try to discover. Because there had to be reasons for everything.

Her research. It grounded her. All the information in the green book. It was *all* there. If she could just piece it together, she'd have answers.

She stood at the bathroom sink, her body covered in Steve's oversized Turkish terry robe. Standing bulky and fluffy, like a snowdrift. More like the yeti of Las Vegas. Her wet blond hair was still knotted, her red-rimmed hazel eyes shelved with dark circles. Turning the cold-water tap on and off.

On and off. On and off. On and off. On and off.

Quietly . . . so as not to disturb the boys.

Trying to think it through.

Like when she was little.

All the rituals. They had started after Mom had died. Everyone agreed on that. The tragedy had been the triggering factor. At first, the rituals had been harmless enough—silly, childish obsessions. Checking windows before she went to bed. Opening and closing dresser drawers before she pulled out an article of clothing.

But then they had progressed into lengthy codes of unstoppable behavior. Kissing her bedpost a thousand times before she went to sleep. Closing and opening the curtains for a full hour. Constantly checking her closet for hidden burglars. Straightening her desk so many times that she fell asleep before she could study. Her native intelligence had kept her afloat—an A/B student without even trying.

Years of therapy had followed her mother's death. Dad carting her to every psychiatrist in the city. Yes, the gambling mecca boasted shows and entertainment. But go past the casinos, past the stars, the glitter and glitz. That Las Vegas—the city of her youth—had been a small, naive town with little to offer except heat and sand.

This medication, that medication. This therapy, that therapy. All of it rooted in *the tragedy*. Because no one had dared to speak the word *suicide*.

Still, something must have taken hold. Because during her adolescent years, when most of her classmates had gone off on fanciful flights of psychosis and self-destruction, she had become model teen. Calm, cool, very popular, because she had been smart, classy, pretty, and experienced in all the right places. No, never had problems attracting boys . . . more like keeping them away. She had treated them like playing chips—discarding or hoarding them at will. Somehow, her compadres had magically forgotten about that weirdo, psycho little girl who sat by herself and never spoke a word.

Not Rom, of course. Rom was different. Rom had eyes in the back of his head—saw and heard everything. Honoring her request, he had left her alone in high school. Yet, he had always been there . . . lurking in some corner . . . completely at ease with himself and his geekiness. Nothing had ever bothered him . . . not the insults, not the taunts, not the rejections. Slings and arrows had bounced off him as if he were protected by chain mail. She had admired him for it. Told him so when they had turned adults.

But back then, she hadn't been able to accept him. Because she had been popular. And popular girls didn't say such things to geeks.

Shame suddenly coursed through her veins. Feeling the heat in her face. But it wasn't *her* fault. Because she had no one to guide her. Besides . . . it was all working out. Everyone *loved* Alison.

Gliding through high school because she had managed to condense her routines into one or two tidy rituals.

Like handwashing. Infinitely better than kissing bedposts. Now, at least, her hands were always antiseptic.

Ten minutes had passed.

Water on and off. On and off. On and off.

Then she took the plunge. Forced herself to turn off the water and pick up the hairbrush. Major anxiety—an accelerated heartbeat, jumpiness in her stomach, light-headedness. But she talked herself through it.

I'll be okay, I'll be okay, I'll be okay.

Running the hard nylon brush through her shoulder-length locks. Combing out the knots. With each successive stroke, her agitation lessened. By the time she was done, she only needed to turn the water off and on a couple of dozen times. Then she told herself to *leave.*

Practicing an exercise she had learned years ago. To literally take her own hand and guide herself out of the high-frequency-behavior area. Tugging at her own fingers until she was back in her bedroom.

Now lie down!

An order.

She always listened to orders.

Except when the voices told her not to.

But that didn't happen very much. No, not too much anymore. Because she knew they weren't real, and often she talked back to them. Of course, when she did, it made her feel like she wanted to wash her hands again.

Longing to go back to the bathroom.

To run the tap.

On and off.

On and off.

On and off.

No, no, no. Better to do research.

You have a brain, Alison. Just learn to use it. Steve's pithy encouragement to his young, new wife.

It had been right after they had been married. About a month after their fabulous honeymoon in Hawaii. She had burned something in the oven . . . probably a chicken. She figured that if it took a chicken two hours to bake at 350 degrees, why not cook it for one hour at 700? Except the oven didn't go up to 700. So she had turned the sucker on the highest temperature—broil—and waited.

The small wooden house had been moments away from becoming tinder. The firemen had said she had been very lucky.

She hadn't felt at *all* lucky.

It hadn't been her fault. What had she known about cooking? Her dad's idea of homemade grub had been picking a grapefruit from their backyard tree. Poor little thing . . . languishing in the clay soil. Still, Daddy had been persistent. He had fed it, nurtured it. And eventually it had given fruit . . . beautiful sweet, pink fruit.

Just like her.

Two beautiful boys. Daddy loved them so.

Her boys.

Have to stay sane or else they'd take away her boys. She knew that. Not that anyone ever said that to her *explicitly*. But she knew the score.

She had to stay sane.

It really wasn't that hard to fool them. She could be sane when she had to be. It was just staying sane . . . as in all the time. Who could stay sane *all* the time?

Her research kept her grounded.

To read and write. To write and read.

Anything.

So long as the mind was occupied.

Because when the mind was occupied, there was no room for voices.

THREE

"I'm not telling you to spy on him. Just keep him out of situations that could come back to haunt us."

There was a long beat over the line. Patricia asked, "Am I supposed to play dumb? I don't feel comfortable with that, Sergeant."

"No, you can tell him I called . . . tell him what I said verbatim. Knowing Steve, he'll do a true confessions as soon as he sees you . . . get all the garbage out of the way." Poe raked his hair with his fingers. "Probably'll say some choice words about me. So be it. Let him rant. Just keep an eye out."

"All right."

But she sounded wary. Poe knew he was putting her in the middle. Not a choice assignment, but since he had kept Steve on, someone had to watch him. He said, "Jensen should be there any moment."

"He's pulling up now."

"I'll be at Havana. Beep if you need me. After that—unless I get some hot lead—I should be back at the Bureau to finish up paperwork. Let's all plan on meeting in a couple of hours."

"Fine."

"Bye." Poe cut the line, started the car, let it idle in neutral. Before he jerked the stick into reverse, he took off the plastic protective slicker he'd been wearing and slipped on a lightweight ebony blazer he kept in the trunk for emergencies. It wouldn't keep him warm, but it gave him a look.

Black jacket, black turtleneck, black jeans, black socks and shoes. All-purpose clothes. He'd fit in anywhere. Again, he combed his droopy locks with his fingernails. Checked himself in the mirror. He needed a shave, which gave him the appearance of pulling an all-nighter. Casinos like that image.

West on Charleston, he headed back into town, making it to Main in under five minutes. A few more blocks, then Poe merged onto Las Vegas Boulevard. Some cars and cabs were still on the road, but the Strip was essentially deserted. Things slowed down as night inched toward dawn. People calling it quits, roosting in their hotel rooms, licking their wounds or sleeping off a bender. Besides, the weather wasn't conducive to strolling.

A pleasure to drive the boulevard empty. Devoid of life but not light. He had spent most of his life in this fabulous city—a bizarre combination of horse town friendliness and metropolitan frenzy. For Poe, the tacky street spectacle held comfortable familiarity. Like his own dysfunctional family—hard to be around, but it *was* home.

Gaudy Day-Glo colors still sparkling at three in the morning. Silly but actually much tamer than the Vegas of his youth. Yes, hotels continued to erect idols in the neon wilderness. There was the Hard Rock Cafe's electrified Gold Top Les Paul pointing up toward the all-powerful Guitar God in the sky and an emulsified hologram of King Tut floating in the night air at the Luxor. But since the eighties, the city had tried to class up its act. Instead of eighty-foot pink clicking champagne flutes, the hotels opted for the more corporate marquee look. Besides being perceived as better behaved, the signs provided free advertising for Vegas acts—a Madison Avenue integration of form and function.

Passing the thousand-foot-tall Needle in the Sky—more of a space station than a hotel—then the dowager Sahara, which had once been the hottest showgirl of the Strip, and the Big Top, a tangible homage to P. T. Barnum's adage "There's a sucker born every minute." A family-oriented place replete with theme park, circus acts, RV hookups, and cheap rooms and food. Keeping the kids stuffed and occupied with roller coasters and high-wire acts, allowing Mom and Dad free time to squander away the college tuition. Four separate casinos providing everything and anything—from penny-ante slots on up. Lest the homey facade fool the innocent, old Steve had found Brendon, AKA Bebe—Mr. Connected Bellman. Jensen had been using the hotel for his second bedroom for over three years. Bebe gave him hourly rates in the city's off-season.

Like now.

Tourism had been especially light the past couple of weeks. April blues. With Mr. IRS Man waiting in the wings, disposable cash was suddenly scarce. Poe had yet to file himself. This year, as in the years past, over half his income had come from gaming wins. Blackjack. He'd been kicked out of most of the big casinos. But there were always ways to work around it.

Poe loved the pits, loved to play. It provided him with a place to sit, cards to hold, and a set of rules to follow. It prescribed his life for a couple of hours, warding off urges to bounce off walls. Just like the job, cards kept him occupied.

Driving past the Stardust, the Mirage, and Treasure Island—the brain-child of the Golden Nugget's onetime wunderkind Steven Wynn. On warm summer nights, the sidewalks were jammed with gawkers watching buccaneers battle on grounded galleons. Others piled up to stare at a fifty-four-foot fiery volcano complete with spewing lava. Once, Poe happened to be in one of the hotel rooms overlooking the smoking mountain. Peering into the bowels of the man-made Vesuvius . . . seeing all those gas jets and pipes . . .

Past the Hilton, past Bellagio, Monte Carlo, Caesars, MGM, Excalibur, the Luxor . . . to the last few dirt lots before McCarran International.

Havana had recently been constructed as a joint venture by two major hotel moguls. Its grounds were densely planted with coco palms and hundreds of tropical fruit trees and banana bushes. During the summer, the landscape was kept lush and green by a zillion different sprinkler and spray systems. The place was low-rise for the city, and catered to high rollers who wanted old-time decadence and privacy.

The main lobby and hotel emulated a Cuban plantation—a four-story building of vanilla stucco, with green-and-white-striped awnings and red roof tile. Lots of balconies and verandas—unusual because most Vegas hotel fronts were pressed as flat as asphalt. Behind the main structure lay the more expensive—and very personal—bungalows. The rock pool was actually a series of man-made lakes, streams, and waterfalls rimmed with rain forest housing an imported parrot population. But the lodging's biggest draw was the smoke shop. Though Cuban cigars were illegal to buy and sell on Uncle Sam's turf, Havana boasted its own line of smokes made from Cuban-stock tobacco. Apparently the leaves were grown on the hotel's own private land down South. No one had ever verified if the fields really did exist, but word of mouth had been sufficient. The inn's humidifier was as big as Phileas Fogg's ballroom.

Pulling into the multilane circular driveway, Poe drove up to the entrance. A valet peered inside the window of the Honda and opened the car door, pausing a nanosecond before giving him a laser-light smile. Poe knew the footboy was sizing up his tip. Poe's straight black hair, large, almond-shaped dark eyes, and café-au-lait complexion coupled with the cheap car suggested a Southern Paiute Native American—a lowly cigarette-hawking Digger who'd probably stiff him. On the other hand, the straight black hair, dark eyes, and dark complexion *could* mean Italian and therefore "connected." Actually, Poe's lineage held both bloodlines plus pinches from other nationalities. He was a true mongrel. Flashing his badge, he smiled, then tipped generously, told him to keep the Honda out front.

Havana's lobby was three stories tall and held a half-dozen atria of exotic birds and squawking wildlife, including macaques, which were Asian, not Central American, monkeys. But so far, few if any demanded absolute authenticity. Animal rights activists had tried to stop the construction, but the hotel had preempted them by bringing in the Las Vegas Zoo and designing the cages to simulate natural animal habitats. Poe admired the hotel's ingenuity.

He had to walk through the Cuban-themed casino—through the flashing lights and an aural assault of bells, whistles, and bongs—to get to the check-in desk. The dealers wore white double-breasted suits and linen shirts, white loafers on their feet and broad-brimmed Panamas on their heads. Cocktail waitresses were garbed in ruffly midriff blouses and multicolored sarongs, flowers tucked in their coifs. When business was hot, they often wore fruit hats à la Carmen Miranda. Poe followed the floral carpet walkway past seas of slots dinging out monotone mantras as coins were absently dropped into ever-hungry mouths. They held no interest for him, no magic allure. Just money down the toilet.

The pits were a different story—the crap games, the wheel games, regular poker, pai gow poker, and blackjack. If a half-shredded face hadn't been torturing his soul, Poe might have stopped. Instead, he moved on, leaving behind the hushed and genteel action of baccarat. Roped-off

area. Very high stakes. There the dealers wore white tailcoats. At three
in the morning, there were a half-dozen tables to service a lone player,
the ladderman hovering about his charge like a mother hen.

Finally making his way up to the front desk. A long walk. Not too
many people could resist the urge to drop a quarter. And once you were
hooked . . .

The receptionist wore a white skirt suit and a blouse fabricked with
pink and purple hibiscus against a yellow-and-green jungle backdrop. She
was under thirty with creamy skin and blond hair pulled back into a braid.
But there was something hard about her face—steely eyes that appraised
unsparingly. She gave him a practiced smile, asked how she could be of
service. He pulled out his badge, and she frowned, her eyes turning gray.

Her name tag pegged her as Noel Goddard. Poe said, "Night manager
around, Ms. Goddard?"

His using her name threw off her rhythm. She stammered, said, "Can
I ask what this is all about?"

"Routine investigation."

"About what?"

"Could you call the manager for me please, miss?"

Noel paused. "Casino manager or hotel?"

A smile. "Whoever's around."

She hesitated, then disappeared behind a secreted door in the back of
the desk area. Five minutes later, she came out with a can of muscle
wearing a white linen suit over a peacock-blue Hawaiian shirt. He was
in his mid-fifties, bald, with biceps as big as wrecking balls. No name
tag, but Poe had known Peter Delatorre for years.

Poe gave him a smile; Delatorre returned it with a glare. He muttered
a thank-you to Noel, then crooked a sausage finger to Poe. Noel opened
a swing door and Poe followed Delatorre into a series of backroom mazes.
Several minutes later, the manager unlocked the door to a hidden niche.

The room was done up plush in a tropical color scheme. Thick teal
carpeting, soft multicolored sofas and slouch chairs, a wet bar with cut
crystal holding lots of rum and scotch. A ceiling fan buzzed overhead.
In the corner stood a small caned desk with a phone and a fax. The
quarters were apparently a suite, because Poe noticed a connecting bedroom. Delatorre shut the common door and pointed to a chair.

Poe rocked on his feet, looked around. No outside windows, but plenty
of one-way mirrors. A video camera was mounted in one of the corners.
"How's it going, Pete?"

Delatorre paced. "What the hell you doing, Rom? Flashing muscle like that?"

"What are you talking about?"

"Cramming your badge down that poor girl's throat—"

"I didn't cram anything. I showed her ID. I'm a police officer. We identify ourselves. It's not only procedure, it's polite."

Delatorre sneered. "Sit down." A beat. He stopped pacing. "Or don't sit. Do I even want you around?"

Poe said, "When did you start working here?"

"Six months ago."

"What happened to Potetsky?"

"You don't want to know." Delatorre waved him off. "So what good cheer do you bring me tonight, Rom?"

"I'm looking into a dancer named Brittany Newel. Heard she worked the floor show at the Copa Room here."

"Wanted as a suspect, or is she your latest corpse?"

"In the morgue as we speak."

"Jesus!" Delatorre made a face. "Does this mean I gotta get the keys to the records room?"

"I'd sincerely appreciate it, Pete."

"You stay outta my pits, I'll make the effort."

"I'll stay out of your pits in any case."

"Yeah, yeah. Why don't I believe you?"

"Because I'm untrustworthy."

"Yeah. I forget. You're part Digger."

"I'm part dago, too. It's three-twenty in the morning. Can we get this show on the road?"

"I thought you were a night owl."

"Age is catching up with me."

"Yeah, you look pretty bad." Delatorre started pacing again. "And you're only what? Thirty?"

"Thirty-five." A pause. "I can't look that bad if you thought I was thirty."

"I must need glasses."

"Thanks. I needed a boost."

Delatorre raised his eyebrows. "You want a boost, I can get you a real boost."

" 'Fraid I'll have to pass."

"Just trying to keep the good boys at Metro happy."

"Thank you. We're very happy. The keys?"

Delatorre laughed. Again the beckoning finger. "C'mon."

They exited through a back door, went through a hallway dimly lit and stone silent. Their footsteps were muffled by the thick carpeting. Poe had no idea where they were going, but Delatorre navigated the twists and turns like a conditioned rat. An old-timer, Pete had worked his way up from mopping floors at the Flamingo, to dealing at the Stardust for Lefty Rosenthal, and finally to pit boss at the Riviera and Tropicana. Apparently he finally passed muster and became casino manager at Havana. A big step up in pay and prestige. Well deserved. Delatorre knew gambling. More important, he knew gamblers.

When they reached his destination, Delatorre pulled out an employee identification card, stopped in front of a red panel light, then held the card up to a scanner. Moments later, the panel light turned green. Then he punched a code into a number panel. He turned to Poe.

"Smile at the birdie, Rom."

"Where?"

Delatorre turned him ninety degrees. "Look up."

A video camera. Poe gave a little wave. "You'd think you were taking me into the counting room."

"I trust no one. Especially the police." Delatorre then pulled out a ring of keys, pushed two of them into the corresponding keyholes, and finally opened an electric security door. "You aren't packing, are you? Don't want you to set off any bells."

"I don't even have my keys. I left them with the valet."

"Go ahead. You first."

Poe walked into a plain room stacked with hundreds of file cabinets. Enough to hold tens of thousands of Pendaflex folders. In the center stood several computer terminals and keyboards atop a bolted-down round metal table. Three bolted-down chairs were positioned around the table.

Delatorre followed, shut the door. A pneumatic seal locked out air and brought on a fan. He explained, "Ever since Wynn's daughter was kidnapped, management's been squirrelly, you know. Everything's nailed down so you can't use it as a weapon. More security codes than the Pentagon."

He put a key into one of the monitors and turned it on.

"Not that it does crap if you're dealing with pros. Hey, they want you, you're dead meat. But it's a deterrent. What's her name again?"

"Brittany Newel." Poe spelled it.

Delatorre clicked the computer keys. "Got a picture of her?"

"No."

"Not even a postmortem?"

"She wasn't pretty, Joe."

Delatorre grimaced as he punched in words and the computer spit back her name, rank, and serial number. "Yeah, she worked here for about a year. Looks like she was terminated about two months ago."

"Why was she fired?"

"Uh . . . let's see . . . number fifteen dash four two A. Nowadays everything is coded and double-coded."

"Keeps you all honest."

"Nah, just makes smarter thieves. Uh . . . here we go. She was canned for missing performances. How many?" He shrugged. "Havana's policy: if you miss two workdays without explanation, you're out."

"Anything else of interest on her record?"

Delatorre scanned the file. "Nope . . . nothing."

"Can I see her initial employment paperwork?"

"Not policy." Delatorre looked up. "Confidentiality."

"Pete, she's dead."

He pointed a stubby index finger in Poe's direction. "Good point." He scanned the computer, looked up the corresponding file number, wrote it down on a slip of paper, then walked over to a file cabinet. A couple of minutes later, he pulled out Newel's file, scanned through it.

Poe said, "May I?"

"First I gotta scan it for black marks . . . see if anything in it concerns our current employees—'cause that could be construed as breaking confidentiality. Gotta keep it kosher."

"Is there a picture of her?"

"Several." Delatorre pulled one out, eyed it for a moment. Just enough time for Poe to see another photo of Brittany resting in the file.

"Cute little thing," the manager pronounced. "Here you go."

A full-color portfolio head shot. Draping honey-blond hair nestled around soft, nude shoulders, crystal-blue eyes full of wonder, pouty lips daring to be kissed. A graceful neck and the smooth skin of youth. Very beautiful. And very nondescript. Typical L.V. dance fare. Completely unoriginal.

Completely Steve.

A miracle how he'd snagged Alison.

A pause.

Not so, Rom old boy. Alison wanted to be snagged. Back then, she had wanted something mainstream . . . something very, very normal.

Delatorre was still scanning the file.

Cagily, Poe turned his back to the video camera, and with sleight of hand, slipped the photograph into his pants, moving it down until it sat between the upper part of his thigh and pants. Helped that he was wearing snug jeans.

Delatorre was talking. "'. . . can't see the rest of the file, Rom. Sorry. Confidential information in here that could affect others. You want to look at it, I'll need a subpoena."

"S'all right." He pulled out a notepad and pen. "Can you give me her vital statistics?"

"Uh . . . yeah, I suppose—" Delatorre's beeper went off. He looked at the pager, read the number. "Trouble, Sergeant. I gotta go."

"Real quick job for me, Pete? You don't want another one of your girls to end up like she did."

"She wasn't one of my girls."

"She ended up a mess, Pete. It's bad for everyone if this isn't solved quickly."

Delatorre muttered, but quickly scanned through her application.

"Born in 'seventy-five, five-eight, one-ten, blond hair, blue eyes . . . seven years of dance training in L.A., worked as a secretary before taking this job. Recommendations from her dance teacher, her former boss, some friends, and some state senator in California. Bet she sucked him to the root to get that. Found out about the job through her boyfriend. It's local. You want the address?"

Poe sighed inwardly. Guess where he was now headed at four in the morning. "Shoot."

Delatorre gave him numbers, closed the chart. "Oh, I'll need that picture back."

"I returned it to you."

"No you didn't."

"Open the file. It's the one where she's resting her head on her hand."

Delatorre opened the folder. Sure enough, there was a picture of Brittany Newel leaning her head against an open palm. "I didn't give you this one. I gave you a head shot."

"I don't have it, Pete." He held his arms out straight from his waist. "You want to frisk me, be my guest. I'm a captive audience."

Delatorre studied Poe's face, closed the file, and put it back in the

24

cabinet. Licking his lips and saying nothing, he punched some numbers on a wall panel and the door opened. He whispered, "After you."

"Thanks."

Delatorre led Poe back through the maze, back out to reception, walked with him halfway through the casino. Then he stopped. "I still think you owe me a picture, Rom."

Poe grinned. "I promise I won't play in your pits."

Delatorre stared at him. "Fucking Digger."

Poe ignored the insult. "I'll keep in touch."

"Fine," Delatorre said. "Only next time, use a phone."

FOUR

At twenty-three, Brittany Newel had hit the skids—a bargain-basement whore whose rapid descent from high-priced showgirl/call girl to ten-buck-a-pop blow jobs had been made possible by Mr. Crack. Her address led Jensen to a seedy bungalow apartment complex in the north side of town. Brittany had lived with a roommate named Ria—a pale wisp of a woman also running on a fast track to nowhere.

To Jensen's surprise, the place wasn't a total sty. Sure, there were some dirty dishes in the sink, sticky counters and gummy tabletop. But the couches, though old, were cleared of debris. The carpet was an odd fluorescent green weave that looked like Astroturf, but basically clean. The place did hold a somewhat stale odor of people who spent too much time in bed.

Ms. Ria had greeted him and Fat Patty wearing a robe, the flaps unbelted but overlapping. As soon as she sat, she let the sides fall open, exposing huge silicon jobs under a flimsy white tank top. Her ass was barely covered by a pair of red lace panties.

Said Simple Simon to the pieman, let me taste your wares.

The way Ria glanced at him, Jensen knew she was sizing him up as a possible trick. She looked familiar. Could be he had slept with her before.

He turned to Patricia Deluca, hoping his partner would wrap it up before daylight. They had already asked her the routine questions—who, what, where. Ria spoke in one-word answers. Even that seemed to tax her brain. She did let them rifle through Brittany's belongings. There wasn't much to sift through. A closet of hooker clothes and shoes, a bathroom holding pills, dope, and lots of condoms. No needles but several crack pipes. Jensen wanted to go home, but Fat Patty insisted on a few more questions. Deluca was new on the job . . . trying real hard. Jensen liked her. Funny, because he had never just "liked" any woman before.

Back to the living room. This time, Ria had elected to forgo the robe altogether. Patricia ignored the woman's brazen dress and said, "I just want to nail down what you told me, so stay with us a few moments longer."

"If it's only a few moments. I'm real tired."

"I appreciate your time. If you could just hang in there—"

"Do I have a choice?"

Patricia flipped through her notes, studying Ria's petulant face—round saucer blue eyes leaking mascara-stained tears. She had dyed her hair platinum, giving it little contrast to her ghostly complexion—not unusual at four in the morning. Her cheeks held slight pitting from teenage acne . . . a wasted-away body with very augmented breasts.

Ria made Patty and her extra poundage feel healthy in comparison. Deluca smoothed out her draping black suit. Half-sizes seemed to be designed by Omar the Tentmaker. As if fat women didn't have figures. Well, *she* had a figure. It was just a large one.

"You stated that the last time you saw Brittany was around eleven in the morning?"

Ria lit another cigarette, talked in a whisper. "More like in the afternoon . . . around twelve." Eyes to Jensen, eyes back to Deluca. "She was up before me. That I remember."

"And she was where?" Jensen asked. "When you got up?"

Her knees now totally apart. "I told you . . . just sitting at the table, drinking a cup of coffee."

Showing Jensen bush. He noticed a little mole on her thigh. A sense of déjà vu. He was really beginning to think that he had slept with her. "Drinking a cup of coffee."

"That's right."

"Maybe smoking as well?"

Ria paused, nodded.

"Was she smoking crack or tobacco?" Patricia asked.

Ria's eyes did another dance. She stubbed out her smoke. "You expect me to answer it?"

"We're from Homicide, ma'am, not Vice."

"You're cops," Ria answered. "That's enough for me."

Patricia said, "After she was done smoking, Ria, what did she do?"

A shrug. "Said she'd see me 'round. Then she got up and left. End of story."

"Did she tell you where she was headed, what her plans were for the day?"

Ria shook her head no.

Jensen said, "You said she serviced the hotels."

"That's what she told me." She shrugged. Thin shoulders attached to balloon breasts. Patricia wondered if they hurt her back. Ria added, "Hotels, motels . . . wherever there was business."

"Did she work with a pimp?" Jensen asked.

A sigh. "You know, I didn't know that much about her. We'd only been sharing this dump for a couple of months. I was gettin' a little tight on cash, so I figured I take on someone to help me out. She was the first to answer the ad."

"You two get along?"

"Sure. Why not? She did her thing, I did mine."

"So you don't know if she worked with a pimp?" Patricia continued to probe.

"Probably she knew a couple of guys who'd throw some business her way."

"Bellmen? Dealers? Pit bosses? Higher-ups?"

"In the beginning, she claimed she did lots of high rollers." Scratching her pebbly cheek. "Probably she did. I saw old pictures of her. She was cute."

Old—as in two years ago. Would they ever learn?

Patricia paused.

At least *her* big boobs were her own. Guys loved her boobs. As heavy as she was, she had no trouble getting guys. She said, "Did she have regulars?"

Ria gave a quick glance to Jensen. "I guess."

Patricia caught it. She wondered if Ria knew that Jensen had slept with Brittany. Then she wondered if Ria and *Jensen* had ever slept together.

The guy went through hookers like she went through diets. "Why'd she move in with you?"

" 'Cause she was broke and had nowhere to go. Her boyfriend had kicked her out."

"Boyfriend?"

"Ex-boyfriend, I mean. Didn't talk too much about him 'cept to say he had a bad temper and used to beat her. His name was Trent. He's a dealer."

Patricia asked, "Does Trent the Dealer have a last name?"

"I'm sure, but I don't know it."

"Was he her pimp?"

"Don't know."

"What hotels did she work out of?"

Ria gave some names.

"Good places," Jensen remarked.

"If you can believe her."

"She have a truth problem?"

"I dunno. Maybe at first she did work the high-end jobs. But she got into bad habits. You know, the nice places . . . they don't like bad girls with bad habits."

Jensen held up a small plastic sandwich bag. Hidden in the corner were a couple of brown crystals. He had found the shit in Brittany's bedroom. "She was running a little low on her supply. Who'd she go to for a fill-up?"

She waved a hand, spread her legs farther. "It's easy to buy in this city."

Patricia spoke slowly. "Where in specific did she buy?"

Ria spoke with disdain. "If you don't know, you ain't much of a detective."

"Could you narrow it down to a couple of places?"

She shrugged. "Sorry."

He traded looks with Deluca. Patricia said, "I think we're just about done."

Ria stood up. "I hope so. It's four in the morning. Night all." She walked to her bedroom, stopped at the door, turned. "Push the button to lock the door and let yourself out." A pause. Eyes on Jensen. "Unless you want to stick around . . ." A big smile. "In case something suddenly pops up."

Jensen returned her smile with a slow, sexy one of his own. "No, I think Detective Deluca and I have finished with our questions. Thank you for your time, ma'am."

Ria threw him back a burned look, answered, "*De nada,* Detective Jensen. That's Spanish. It means thanks for nothing."

"She had an ex-boyfriend." Patricia into her portable cell phone. "A dealer. Ria said he used to beat her."

Over the line, Poe answered, "His name is Trent Minors, currently a blackjack dealer at Shakespeare's. I have his address. I'm going there now."

"She ended up a mess, sir. I mean even before she died. A washed-out, dead-broke crack addict. Her roommate, too. Also a user. Both of them so young. It's so sad."

On the wire, Jensen said, "Sad but true."

Poe said, "I don't think I'm going to make it back to the Bureau right away. You two finish up your paperwork, then go home. I'll run what we have by Weinberg. Let's all try to meet with the loo sometime in the late morning."

"Where?" Patricia asked.

"How 'bout Myra's?" Jensen suggested.

"Okay. Myra's at ten." Poe checked his watch. "That should give you two about five hours of shut-eye."

"Sounds good," Patricia said.

"Fine with me," Jensen added.

Poe cut the mike, drove to Minors's address. The neighborhood was a mixture of small one-story houses and low-rise apartments. To Poe, even in the dark, it looked more than familiar. He had been here before, recognizing landmarks down to the apartment with the wrought-iron horsehead fence.

Then he realized he was about five minutes from Honey's. He had entered the area from the north instead of the south. He thought a moment about Ruki's keeping him at arm's length.

He depressed the accelerator, did a couple of screeching right turns, then parked in front of Honey's building.

Well, what does Ruki expect of me?

Nothing. That's the problem.

The call girl wasn't pleased to be awakened. Her hair was messy, eyes still heavy from sleep. She wore a bulky terry robe and had bunny slippers on her feet.

Her greeting to him: "Go away."

Poe put his foot in the door before she could close it. "Please?"

"Why don't you go bother Rukmani?"

"I would except she's working."

"So? One of the slabs is bound to be empty."

Poe kneed his way inside. "You are one sick woman."

A brush of pecan hair from midnight-blue eyes. "You know what time it is?"

"Four-fifteen."

"Big night, Rom?"

Hands in pockets, Poe bounced on his feet, stared at the walls decorated with hundred-year-old Audubon prints. "Professionally, yes."

Honey shut the door. "Professionally as in playing? Or professionally as in cop?"

"Unfortunately the latter." He turned the security lock. "You should always use your deadbolt, Honey. It's there for a reason."

"You look upset." She tightened her robe over ample breasts. The real labonza. Made her very popular. "Bad?"

"Girl named Brittany Newel. A former dancer at Havana. When she died, she was turning tricks for crack. Who knows? Maybe she was a runner as well. I'm about to visit her boyfriend. A dealer at Shakespeare's. His name is Trent Minors."

Honey shrugged.

Poe took out the stolen photo of Newel. "Know the girl, by any chance?"

Honey stared at the picture, but shook her head. "Nope."

A stretch of silence.

Honey sighed. "All right. Go sit on the couch."

Poe obeyed without question. She stood before him, then dropped to her knees and spread his legs. Unzipped his pants and went to work. Five minutes later, she was making coffee in the kitchen. She felt Poe encircle her waist from behind, kiss her neck.

"Thank you," he said.

"Pleasure's mine," she answered. "You're very good, you know."

"Good?" Poe was puzzled. "You mean fast?"

She laughed out loud, broke contact. Turned to face him, holding a coffee urn. "Am I making this for nothing?"

"Probably." Poe rubbed his eyes. "I've got to go back to work."

"Poor Romulus."

Poe took out his wallet. Honey put her hand over the billfold. "It's on me."

"No, no, no." Rom pulled out a hundred-dollar bill. "I pride myself on paying my bills."

Honey snatched the Franklin. "Far be it from me to deny a man his dignity."

Poe took out Brittany's picture, showed it to Honey again. "Look at it, Honey. Doesn't look a little familiar?"

Honey blew out air. "Rom, she's a face in the crowd."

"She danced at Havana—"

"You already said that." Irked, she pushed the picture aside. "I *don't* know her."

"Don't get peeved. I'm just doing my job." Poe paused. "You know how it is. A young girl working strange men. I wouldn't want anyone else to get hurt."

He looked at her pointedly. She matched his stare. "I know what I'm doing."

"You're a very savvy woman. Just take care."

"Always." She softened, kissed his nose. "Good luck and good night."

He shut the door softly behind him. A moment later, he heard the loud click of the deadbolt. Thinking of Brittany's mutilated face . . . good that Honey had taken him seriously.

FIVE

It was a typical minimum-wage apartment, but it was neat and clean and had tasteful repros on the wall—cubic forms and sketches. Poe's eyes jumped from the walls to Minors nervously flattening the carpet. The blackjack dealer had slipped on a gray sweatshirt and jeans, but hadn't quite gotten around to shoes. He had hairy feet. His face was long, with even features except for the mouth. Thin, tight lips gave him an unforgiving expression. To stop him from pacing, Poe asked for coffee. Minors brewed up a batch as bitter as his mood.

Angrily, he said, "I can't believe that Brittany sank *that* low." A pause. "Not that I'm not saying it was her fault that she got murdered."

"That's good."

The dealer reddened, looked down. "You're sure? That it's actually ... her?"

Poe sipped his wretched java, didn't respond right away. He drummed his fingers against the cup. Actually that was a good question. Newel had been found nude, without a purse, and half her face had been mangled. But the other half was identifiable as the woman in Havana's posed portfolio photographs.

Poe said, "We've had some preliminary identification—"

"So you're not sure?"

"We're proceeding as if it is Brittany Newel." Poe put down his cup. "You seem very angry at her."

Minors's face tightened, frowning lips turning into lines. "Why do you say that? I haven't seen her in months."

Poe took out a notebook. "I'm angry at people I haven't seen in years. Was the breakup amicable?"

"I was happy about it."

"Why'd you two break up?"

"She was out of control."

"Drugs?"

"What else?"

"How long had she been blowing crystal?"

"Long enough for me to say good-bye."

"When you two met, was she using?"

Minors sank down on a chair, drooped like a water-starved plant. "Nothing heavy."

"Pot?"

"Occasionally."

"Why'd she turn to a heavier case load?"

"Who knows?" Minors muttered. "It's this damn city. Takes over your life."

Poe said, "She was turning tricks."

Minors muttered, "Case in point."

"Is that why you beat her up?"

Minors blushed brightly. "I didn't *beat* her up—"

"You smacked her around, Trent. Save us both some energy and don't play Mr. Who Me?, all right?"

"So I got pissed a couple times—"

"A couple of times?" With dubious eyes, Poe gave him a look. "Who was really out of control?"

Minors blurted, "I didn't give a flying fuck about her *whoring! Okay?*"

Poe licked his lips, tapped his pen against his notebook. "Why not?"

Quietly, Minors said, " 'Cause we had this understanding."

"What kind of understanding?"

The dealer got anxious. "Just that we didn't butt into each other's business."

"Each other's business," Poe repeated. "Do you mean personal or professional business?"

"Both."

"So her whoring was okay because it brought in money?"

"It was *her* thing, Sergeant!" Minors exploded. "Her business, her money. *I* didn't have a thing to do with it. I wasn't her pimp, *okay*?"

"But you knew about it."

Minors was quiet.

"If you had this understanding about her whoring, Trent, why did you toss her?"

"Who told you I hit her?"

Poe ignored his question. "Did you beat her because you thought she was holding money back?"

"I *told* you I wasn't her pimp!"

"Then who was?"

A heavy sigh. Minors said, "She told me she was set up by hotels."

"Havana?"

"All of them." He swallowed hard. "She got around."

"And you didn't care?"

"I didn't *say* that," Minors whined. "I just said I knew about it and tried not to interfere."

Poe said, "Can we go back to my original question? If you *knew* about it, had this understanding . . . why did you beat her?"

Minors said nothing, leaving Poe to wonder what information he was sitting on.

"Did she take up with someone else, Trent?" Poe asked.

Minors stiffened. "Hey! I kicked *her* out. Not the other way around."

"After you found out she was shagging . . . who?"

Minors bolted upward. "I don't have to talk to you—"

"Sit down!" Poe commanded. He put the mug on the coffee table. "Stop acting so . . . emotional."

A long silence. Then the dealer sat down.

Poe stated, "Brittany had gotten involved with someone. Tell me who it was, and then I don't drag you downtown. You make my life easy, I don't have to say it came from you."

Minors cleared his throat. "She took up with the boss."

Poe paused. Did he mean Havana's pit boss? "Are you talking about Pete Delatorre?"

"Bigger than Havana." Minors hitchhiked his thumb in an upward motion. "And higher up."

"A casino manager—"

"Higher still."

Poe tried to keep cool. "This isn't twenty questions, Trent. Give me a name."

"How about Parker Lewiston?"

Poe opened his mouth and closed it. Lewiston owned half of downtown Vegas. Generally his taste in women ran a little older—mid-twenties and a hell of a lot more classy than Brittany Newel. Honey had been one of Parker's ladies. Before he had put Honey out to pasture, he had fixed her up. The papers to a condo plus a yearly stipend. So what had happened with Brittany? And why would Parkerboy be attracted to a cheap whore like her in the first place?

A pause.

Of course, to paraphrase Virginia Hill's statement to the HUAC, Newel, in her prime, could have been the best cocksucker in America.

"Hard to believe, huh?" Minors had turned acerbic. "Brittany with *Parkerboy*."

"Lewiston takes care of his women, Trent."

"I told you. Brittany was out of control!"

But Parkerboy never allowed his women to get out of control. If they used, he provided for them . . . kept them happy and content. Poe was suspicious.

Minors was saying, ". . . threw it in my face constantly." He turned his voice high-pitched and shrewish. Imitated, " 'You keep whopping me and I'm gonna tell Parker on you.' "

"But she never did. Because if she had, you wouldn't be working here . . . in this city." Poe waited a beat. "She was using big-time when she died. Who'd she get her stuff from?"

Minors shrugged. "Maybe Lewiston."

"Not if he dropped her."

"Then I don't know."

"Who'd she get her stuff from when you knew her?"

"Lewiston."

"She told you that?"

"Yeah." Angrily, he said, "Parkerboy made her what she is today."

"A corpse?"

Minors turned crimson, stammered, "No, no, I'm not saying . . . I'm not implying Mr. Lewiston had anything to do—"

"Stop sweating, Trent. He ain't in the room."

Minors looked over his shoulder. "All I meant was . . . well, she wasn't using heavy until she hooked up with him. He turned her into a crack whore.''

Poe noticed that Minors had dropped his voice a notch.

As if the walls had ears.

And maybe they did.

She had wanted to pretend she was sleeping, but Steve had caught sight of her open eyes.

"You still up, baby?'' he cooed.

She said nothing when Steve sat down on the edge of the bed and loosened his tie. Out of her corner vision, she saw him lower his hand, felt him stroke her shoulder. An instant wave of revulsion pushed through her body. But this time she was determined not to withdraw from his touch.

Make him think you're getting better.

Jensen continued to caress his wife. "I didn't wake you, did I?''

She shook her head no.

"Another rough night, honey?''

They're all rough.

"I'm fine.''

Her voice was a hush.

Jensen checked his watch—five in the morning. Reluctantly, he stopped petting her. Stood and took off his shirt. "Nasty night out. We found someone in the desert. And lots of paperwork. That's what took me so long.''

She nodded.

"It was . . . hard. This one in particular. Not that you have to worry about it. Some hooker who went with the wrong guy . . . obviously.''

He realized he was gripping his shirt, nails digging into fabric made wet by his sweaty palms. He bit back panic and tried to smile.

"Forget I said anything, Alison. I'm . . . running off at the mouth. I'm stupid sometimes.''

No response.

She knew he was aching to talk, to find an outlet for his troubled soul. Shouldering everything for so long. And still blaming himself for her illness. Silly. Because she had been decompensated long before he had started cheating.

But back then, she had hid it better. Still, she was certain that he had his suspicions.

She had been twenty when they had married; he had been thirty-two. Thinking about their wedding pictures. They had made such a handsome couple. When she combed her hair, she supposed they still looked good together.

Jensen drew back the covers of the bed. "You're still wearing your bathrobe, honey."

"Too lazy to change," she whispered.

"That can't be comfortable—"

"I'm fine—"

"It's so bulky, Alison," Jensen said. "Let me get you your silky nightgown. The one you say is so soft against your skin. Now, do you want the purple or the pink?"

"Pink's fine."

"Hey, it's fine with me, too." A weak smile. "You look *great* in pink, hon."

She swung her legs over the mattress, about to get herself upright. Steve was right there with a chivalrous arm. "Let me help you."

This time she shook him off. She straightened and looked him in the eye. "I'm not an invalid."

His face was wounded. "Of course not, Alison. I didn't mean—"

"Forget it."

Her voice sounded harsher than she meant.

"I'm sorry, Alison. You know me." Another weak smile. "I just love to baby you."

She felt moisture in her eyes, but couldn't let him see. To distract him, she let her robe slip to her feet, boldly allowing him full view of her fine form.

He gasped, a sharp intake of breath piercing his lungs. Whispering, "God, you're beautiful."

She looked away, but then returned her eyes to his face.

Eye contact. Tentatively, Steve moved toward her.

"Just . . . astonishingly . . . gorgeous."

Another step.

And she still didn't move away.

"Beauty . . . personified."

Now he was close enough to touch her. But he didn't dare. Both of them were waiting.

Finally, he said, "Can I kiss you, baby?"

She nodded.

Could it *actually* be?

He kissed her.

And she didn't stiffen.

"I love you," he whispered.

She didn't answer.

"Love you very much." Slowly, he encircled her body with his arms, drew her to his bare chest. "Love you . . . *oh* so much."

Still there. In his arms.

Carefully, he drew her down onto the bed.

This time, she'd let it happen. Because with the corpse in the desert . . . he was really hurting. And after all, she knew about that, didn't she?

As always, she climaxed in about five minutes. He came moments afterward, swooning with delight and words of love. How beautiful she was, how *responsive.*

Nice to be responsive, she thought. But having an orgasm was never the point of the whole thing. Just the product.

You see, now she was filled up with his sperm.

A great excuse to get up and go wash.

S I X

) "According to the computer, Newel's mother lives in Ohio."
Mick Weinberg slugged down black coffee. "We called the number—it was disconnected. So much for our hookup to Washington's Find a Person Search database."

Squinting behind his glasses. The lieutenant needed bifocals, but had been too busy to make the appointment. He lowered his specs, looked across the table at three of his homicide detectives. A good bunch . . . a tired bunch.

Weinberg rolled up the sleeves of his white shirt, loosened his tie. Stuffy without the fan. Moisture had formed in the pits of his muscled arms and on the top of his bald head. He wondered when Myra intended to turn it on.

He went on, "Nothing comes up by way of a father. So that means someone here who knew Brittany is going to have to make a formal ID. The ex-boyfriend's our best bet. Rom, you go call—Rom, you with us?"

Poe yanked open his eyes. "I'm here."

The lieutenant pushed Poe's coffee cup toward his sergeant. "Drink."

Poe picked up his mug, sipped, then drummed his fingers on the tabletop. "Is there any milk?"

Weinberg shouted, his voice carrying easily in the empty restaurant,

"Myra, could we get some Mocha Mix? Also maybe a little food? These good public servants need some nutrition."

The phantom voice responded, "The steamer's still heating up."

"What about the griddle?" Weinberg called out.

Myra answered, "If you beg, I suppose I can whip up some deli omelets."

Weinberg faced his crew. "Deli omelets okay?"

"Sounds great." Jensen suddenly realized he was famished.

Patricia answered, "I'll eat anything."

Someone started pulling on the locked glass door. Weinberg turned around, yelled, "We're closed!" Gesticulations. "We open at eleven." Flashing ten splayed fingers, then the index digit. "Eleven!" Frowned. To himself, the loo muttered, "Can't they read the damn sign?"

Poe continued to swallow the sour brew. "Were you talking to me, Lieutenant?"

"I just assigned you Brittany's ex-boyfriend, Trent Minors. Take him down to the morgue for a positive ID."

"Do you want Brittany ID'd in her current condition?"

"What condition, Poe? She's dead."

"Lieutenant, she's monstrous. Half of her has been flayed. Her left eyeball is miss—"

Abruptly, he stopped talking.

"What?" Weinberg asked.

Poe blinked. "Nothing."

"Don't give me that."

"A passing thought."

"So pass it by me, Poe."

"A flash of déjà vu." Poe hesitated. "When I was a kid, there was this case—a grotesque murder—maybe even more than one, I don't remember too well. Judging by today's standards—with guys like Jeffrey Dahmer and John Wayne Gacy—it doesn't seem extraordinary. But as a kid, I . . . we were all terrorized. Thought this guy was the bogeyman incarnate. That's what we called him. The Bogeyman. For a while, the whole thing terrorized the town."

"Which town?" Patricia asked.

"Here. Vegas."

Weinberg said, "I don't remember anything like this."

"Probably before your time, sir. Roughly twenty-five years ago."

"A good ten years before."

Poe said, "Even then I doubt if it infiltrated into the Strip. If the powers that were kept atomic testing under wraps, I don't imagine a couple of murders would be a problem. But back then, in the 'burbs . . ." He raised his brow. "It freaked us out."

"Do you even remember the specifics?" Jensen remarked.

Poe suddenly felt a chill. Things that happened in childhood . . . so much more intense. "There were rumors. Probably apocryphal, but they said that the killer had desecrated the corpses. He had scooped out the eyeballs—"

"Omelets, anyone?" Myra chirped. In the middle of the table, she plunked down a platter of scrambled eggs filled with pastrami, salami, and smoked turkey. Big chunks of flesh-colored meat gelatinously wrapped in quivering ovum.

Jensen said, "Ever notice how visceral-looking eggs are?"

The table groaned.

Unceremoniously, Myra dropped four plates and silverware onto the table along with a carton of Mocha Mix. She put graceful, blue-veined hands on her hips. She had short nails . . . immaculately clean. She was in her mid-fifties, hazel eyes with short gray hair cut like Prince Valiant's. A round, open face which, at the moment, spelled annoyance. She wore a white shirt, gray skirt, and white chef's apron. Tennis shoes covered her feet. "You have complaints, take it elsewhere."

"Looks good to me." Jensen picked up a spoon and a plate, then heaped eggs on his dish. "Looks wonderful, in fact. Thanks, Myra. I'm starved."

The woman smiled warmly. "More coffee, Steve? Orange juice?"

"Both would hit the spot, thank you."

Weinberg passed out the remaining dishes. "Help yourselves."

Patricia eyed the eggs. Now if she was going to eat toast, she'd better give herself a small portion of omelet. A pause. Then again, she hadn't eaten since dinnertime last night. And it was half past ten. Still, all that salami and pastrami. All that *fat*! Wherever she looked . . . subversion.

Poe poured Mocha Mix into his coffee. "You know, you're spoiling us, Myra."

"She spoils everyone." The lieutenant polished off his coffee. "We have so many people running in and out of our condo, I'm thinking about selling time shares."

"Everyone loves Vegas," Myra said.

"Everyone loves a freebie," Patricia said.

"You got that right, Deluca. We keep getting all these out-of-the-blue relatives popping in. People she's never *heard* of, let alone met." Weinberg looked at his wife. "But she lets them stay anyway."

"Just in case," Myra answered.

"In case of *what*?" Jensen asked.

Myra stared at him, shrugged.

"As if that explains it," Weinberg groused. "Are you going to turn on the fan, Myra?"

"Yeah, it is kind of stuffy, isn't it." She spooned eggs onto her husband's plate. "Eat before they get cold, Mick. I'll get the toast." Before Myra left, she tapped his head.

From his pants pocket, Weinberg pulled out a yarmulke. He placed it over his bald pate. To Poe, he said, "So what made you think of this twenty-five-year-old case? The scooped-out eye?"

"Probably."

"Was it true?" Patricia asked.

"Beats me." Poe shifted the conversation. "Loo, I think Trent Minors deals the noon-to-midnight shift. I'll try to catch him before he goes to work."

"Good idea. I also want one of you to go back and comb the scene of the crime now that we have some visibility. I got a uniform out there guarding the place. The sooner the better."

Jensen asked, "What should we be looking for?"

Weinberg chomped at a piece of pastrami gristle. "She was found nude from the waist up. Maybe some kind of top . . . shoes . . . maybe a purse." He washed down his breakfast with a full cup of water. "Some storm last night. The wind could have blown items all over the effing place."

"*If* the killer dumped her belongings along with the body," Poe said.

Patricia said, "Think the killer would want to keep a trophy, Loo?"

"Sure. But how likely would it be that he'd keep everything? We found her pretty bare-bones, no bad pun intended."

Poe speared a piece of smoked turkey, chewed it thoughtfully. "Patricia, you want to go out?"

"I'll go out."

"And me?" Jensen asked.

Poe said, "We still don't have any idea about Brittany's final hours. Someone should start checking out the bars—"

"Wouldn't that be better done at night, Sergeant?"

Poe nodded. "You can do that as well. But based on how low Brittany had fallen, she could have been a day-tripper, too. Someone should check out the naked city."

Jensen said, "I'll do it."

"I thought you had tickets to the fabulous Oldies show at the MGM," Patricia said.

"I . . . gave them away." Jensen sighed. "Alison hasn't been feeling well."

No one spoke for a moment.

Poe broke the tension. "How about this? After you two finish up with the crime scene, Patricia can comb the bars and Steve will work the bellmen. I think they'd open up easier man to man."

Besides, Stevie had lots of personal connections.

"Fine," Jensen answered.

Weinberg said, "What're you doing after the ID, Rom?"

"Figured I'd talk to Dr. Kalil. Find out how Newel died. See if she was skinned alive."

"Good God, is that level of detail truly necessary? I know, I know." Patricia helped herself to another serving of omelet. "Yes, of course it is. Find out if the guy is a sadistic killer or just a closet pathologist. Anyone notice if the body had stab wounds or bullet holes?"

"It was dark, Deluca," Jensen answered.

And old Steve had been as sick as a dog.

Poe said, "I couldn't tell, either. I'll ask Rukmani about it. It would be nice to know if we should be looking for shell casings or a discarded knife."

"Could you tell if the murder occurred at the body drop?" Weinberg asked.

"Didn't see a big pool of blood." Jensen paused. "For whatever that's worth. It was real windy last night."

"The desert sand is a natural litterbox," Poe said. "Blood could have been soaked up by the surface grit and blown away."

"And just as easily," Weinberg said, "if there was enough blood, it could have seeped down a couple of inches and spread out in the under-lying clay bed. And there it may lie still."

"So I'll root through the surface sand," Patricia said.

Again, Poe drummed the tabletop with his fingers. He said, "Aren't we forgetting about someone?"

"Lewiston," Patricia answered.

"What do you want to do about him, Loo?"

"Premature to question him."

"He fucked her, sir."

"Rom, she was a hooker. He is an eccentric billionaire who has probably fucked three quarters of the girls in this city. When you figure how much fucking was going on, their lives were bound to intersect. It doesn't mean anything."

"He's a link." Poe paused. "I could go to him with the angle that I'm asking for his help."

"He isn't going to swallow that horseshit. Parkerboy won't give us squat without proper papers."

"Loo, if Brittany's sugar daddy had been Joe Blow—"

"Who says Lewiston was Brittany's sugar daddy? The girl was a whore. They're notorious liars. You're basing all of this on the word of one disgruntled boyfriend."

"So let me ask Lewiston about it. Let him deny it."

No one spoke.

Weinberg relented. "All right. *After* you're done with the ID, and *after* you've finished with Dr. Kalil *and* the crime scene, then you can go attempt contact. But don't be disappointed if you come back empty-handed."

Jensen smirked. "You just want an excuse to go to the Laredo. No-limit tables. One-deck shoes."

Poe returned the evil grin with one of his own. But the accusation was true. Steve knew his number. Equally true, Poe knew Jensen's quirks . . . down to the eye color of his whores.

Too bad neither really knew Alison.

SEVEN

"If you're asking me about a smoking gun, I'm going to tell you no, nothing yet. These things take time, Romulus."

Rukmani was talking through a white paper mouth and nose mask. Head down, she was peering into a sea of tissue and viscera, probing at something red and squishy with a metal instrument. An hour ago, Trent Minors had been vomiting over Brittany's face. Now the young girl had been literally reduced to flesh and bones.

Again, Rukmani spoke . . . more like muttered. Poe could barely understand her. "Can you take a break?"

"A break?"

"Yes. Like a coffee break. Or a tea break?"

She looked up, covered the dissected body with a tarp. "Is the smell bothering you?"

"A little." Poe snapped his fingers as his eyes swept across the steel room of death. They eventually settled upon Rukmani, dressed in surgical blues. Wrapped up like an anoxic mummy. He said, "It's hard to talk in here."

"C'mon." She untied her mask, snapped off her gloves. "But only for five minutes. I don't like to leave my bodies unattended."

"Thanks." He kissed her cheek. She stank of formaldehyde.

Together they boarded a two-person staff-only elevator.

Staff only.

As if a morgue would be teeming with visitors.

They took the lift to the third floor. Her office was immediately to the right. About the size of a coffin, but it had a ceiling and a lockable door, and it was all her own. A standard-issue desk and a couple of chairs. A wall of bookshelves held medical tomes and pictures of her two grown children—twenty-five-year-old Shoba, a sophomore at Harvard Medical School, and twenty-seven-year-old Michael, a resident in radiology at Barnes Hospital in St. Louis.

Married in the old country, Rukmani had given birth to her son two weeks past her sixteenth birthday. The untimely death of her much older mercantile husband, a hidden cache of rainy-day money, and a couple of American relatives had given her a new life in the States. In the States, she wasn't judged by her caste or her in-laws. In the States, she wasn't forced to avoid the sun to keep her Indian complexion as Anglo-light as possible. Probably the reason why she had moved to Vegas. At the moment, Ruki was nutmeg-brown.

"Sit." All business. She said, "What specifically do you want to know?"

"Bullet holes?"

"Not yet."

"Stab wounds?"

"None so far."

Poe felt ill. "She died while this monster was gouging out her eyeball?"

"Not necessarily."

Poe drummed on her desktop, waited.

Rukmani said, "There are other ways to murder besides stabbing and shooting." She made an imaginary needle with her finger and stuck it in the crook of her arm.

Poe said, "He OD'd her first?"

"Or at least sedated her. That's my guess."

"You found something in her veins."

"Bloodwork hasn't come back yet." Rukmani pushed her glasses back on her nose, then put her hands over his to quiet his fidgeting. "You look tired. Did you sleep at all?"

"An hour at my desk this morning. What about you?"

"About four hours." A pause. "Come to my place tonight. I'll cook you dinner. If your face drops in the mulligatawny, I won't say a word."

"Sounds wonderful, but I'm probably going to pull another all-nighter."

"Romulus, you can't work effectively on an hour's sleep."

She was right. He said, "Nothing happens in this town before dark. I'll grab a couple of hours of sleep before I go out again."

Rukmani looked grave. "Why don't you live in a normal house?"

"I like where I live. It's very quiet."

"It doesn't have running water or electricity."

"Modern conveniences are highly overrated."

"At least get a box spring for the mattress."

"I couldn't get it through the doorframe."

"So get a bigger door, for godsakes."

"Why are you pissed at me? You know I'd love to come for dinner, spend the night with you engaged in wild, passionate lovemaking. Do you think I'm working by choice? I'm paid to do a job. Just like you."

"There's work," Rukmani said, "and there's work-obsessed."

"Ain't that the pot calling the kettle black?"

This time, Rukmani remained quiet.

Poe thought: *Maybe this is why she's so standoffish. She doesn't like my house. Or my hours. Still, she keeps the same hours.* He steered the conversation back toward business. "Why do you think she was sedated while he was . . . you know . . . flaying her?"

"The evenness of some of the gouge marks. Almost ruler-perfect parallel lines. If she had been awake, she would have been thrashing about, and the lines would have been squiggly."

"What about if he bound her?"

"Even so, she could have squirmed unless he had her head in a vise. Even with millimeters' worth of motion, there would have been waves or chinks in the lines. Some of the rakes were almost . . . surgical in their precision."

"Someone from the medical profession?"

"Possibly. Or someone who's very exacting."

Poe made a sour face. "So she was either sedated or dead when he . . . attacked her."

"There was evidence of fresh bleeding into the depressions. I'd say she was sedated. Very heavily sedated. Alive but unconscious. She probably never felt a thing." She gave him a weak smile. "Small comfort."

He thought about her words. "That could say something about the killer."

"Like what?"

"He's a control freak. Wants her completely defenseless so he can do his thing. Doesn't want to leave anything up to chance."

"Or maybe he has sensitive ears and doesn't like screaming."

Poe nodded. "You may have something there."

"Sensitive ears?"

"He doesn't like to hear screaming because he doesn't do torture for torture's sake."

"Just enjoys raking human flesh?" Rukmani shook her head. "I suppose a boy needs a hobby."

Poe was talking as much to himself as to Rukmani. "He likes killing. He likes . . . dressing his victim in a certain fashion. But like a hunter with his prey. Hunters don't get their kicks out of torturing animals. They like clean, kill shots. One big bam and the animal keels over. The thrill is the hunt."

"And the head on the wall afterward," Rukmani stated. "Something they can brag about. Maybe that's what she was. A trophy kill."

"She wasn't dressed or displayed like a trophy kill." Poe paused. "Of course, I got to her after she'd been in a windstorm. Who knows what she looked like before?"

Rukmani said, "I should be getting back."

Poe said, "Do you have a fix as to what kind of instrument made the gouges?"

"I was hoping you wouldn't ask me that."

"Go on."

"I've found flakes of metal lodged where it touched bone . . . consistent with a rake or some kind of tool. But I've also found bits of tooth enamel."

"Consistent with biting."

"No bite marks, Rom. More like . . . methodical tearing at the victim with the teeth." She looked away. "There was something very animalistic about this death. Like he was . . . eating her—"

"Oh Christ!"

"—or more like grazing."

"This is truly nauseating."

Rukmani scratched at her hair tucked under a scrub cap. "This has not been an easy autopsy. It's going to take a while before I come to anything definitive.'' She stood. ''I've really got to go.''

Poe got up as well. ''I can't entice you with a quick lunch at my place?''

''Lunch?''

''Well, lunch and munch.''

Rukmani laughed, hit his shoulder. ''I'd love to, but I've got this corpse—''

''Aha! Okay for you to refuse me, but—''

''Rom, you leave a body exposed for more than a short period of time, it screws up every—''

''When it's *your* ox that's being gored—'' Poe stopped talking. ''Why did I say that?''

Rukmani smiled with fatigue. ''My place, tomorrow night?''

''It's a deal.''

''We are really too busy. We never see each other.''

''Guess that makes us a true ideal American couple.''

''If we're going to lapse into mindless treadmilling and burnout, we might as well get married.''

''Name a date.''

She waved him off, kissed his cheek. ''Mind if I don't walk you out? Brittany Newel is calling my name.''

Poe snapped his fingers. ''You actually think of her as Brittany Newel?''

''You bet I do. She had a name in life. I'll be damned if I'll take it away in death.''

Day, night, it didn't matter, the bars in Vegas looked the same—dimly lit, smoky atmosphere, lots of tabletop slots and poker machines. The saloon at Casablanca sat in the center of the casino, a giant disk with tables and chairs rotating a full circle every hour. Usually lounges-in-the-round were reserved for places with a view. But the only vistas here were the gaming pits and rows of slots. Patricia knew that was the point. To entice the drinkers to leave and gamble.

It had been one hell of an afternoon. Productive, though. *She* had been the first to find evidence—a spike-heeled shoe. More important, she had found the purse—an ecru macramé thing about fifty yards from where Brittany had been dropped. Blended in perfectly with the sandy layer of Las Vegas desert. It contained her driver's license, two maxed-out credit cards, three hundred bucks, and several plastic cellophane packets of rock crystal cocaine.

Superficially, it appeared that neither robbery nor drugs had been a motive. But she knew that the whole thing could have been a setup to deflect Homicide.

Still, she had been proud of herself. Weinberg had congratulated her, slapped her back, then given her a list of bars to comb. Twenty of them.

And here she was, feeling as gritty as unwashed spinach, as dirty as a desert rat. She sat at the countertop along with a couple of pickled stragglers waiting for fresh crowds of gamblers to come and liven the evening, her eyes observing the natural ebb and flow of the casino. Cocktail waitresses with big bonkers, wearing gauzy stuff, their flat stomachs with jewels in the navels. They walked two and fro—from casino to bar, from bar to casino.

The bartender approached her. Aladdin he wasn't. Then again, she was no Jasmine. He was Samoan or Tongan or something that screamed Pacific Islander—an extra-extra-large with frizzy black hair. He wore black harem pants and a purple satin vest over a white see-through shirt. Sandals on his feet. His name tag said Nate.

Wiping the countertop, smiling with white teeth. " 'Lo.''

"Club soda," Patricia answered.

It was now six-thirty. Two hours of scouring the bars for Brittany's last stand had produced sore feet and a half-dozen hits—servers who somewhat recognized Newel's face. Unfortunately, no one remembered seeing her yesterday.

Casablanca was bar number twelve on the loo's hit list. She had consumed twenty—count 'em—twenty club sodas, which necessitated about a dozen trips to the bathroom. How she suffered for her art.

Patricia took out her badge, showed it to Nate, who looked at it without flinching. Didn't even back away. She was encouraged. Maybe he'd talk without a cattle prod.

"You want a twist with that, Officer?"

"Detective. Homicide."

His eyes blinked. "Would you like a twist, Detective?"

"Lime."

"You got it."

His eyes yo-yoed up and down over her girth, then jumped to her left hand. Patricia smiled to herself. Two humping rhinos.

Not that she was *that* bad.

Not like after she had left the service—honorable discharge, of course. She had thought she had it together . . . everything under control. But putting on those civvies, walking out of the base, feeling so dirty and violated. Then seeing him with that evil smile, giving her his famous little wave.

She had gone back to her apartment and had thrown up.

She hadn't ever been a thin girl. But there was chunky and there was obese, and she had crossed over to the latter. Within two years, she had ballooned to 250 pounds. She had never really figured out why she had suddenly reversed her self-destructive gorging. Maybe she had been sick and tired of letting Homer get the last laugh.

She had starved herself in order to pass the department physical, surviving on air and a can-do spirit. But as soon as she made detective, she had started eating again. Stuffing her face until she had been sure that no superior could possibly be interested in her.

And no one had been. Never even a hint of sexual impropriety.

Perversely enough, the guys had been nice. Supportive. Helpful. Even a pussy hound like Steve was always available to answer questions. Slowly, the pounds started melting. She plateaued at 175. Not bad for someone who was five-eight and big-boned.

Then this whole army sexual harassment thing hit. And Homer had called her—all sweetness and light. Eating to calm her nerves, she gathered her strength, called him, then told him off in explicit terms. It felt good! Unfortunately, she was suddenly back over 200. After a steady diet she was down to 185—holding steady.

Nate placed the club soda in front of her, along with a bowl of peanuts and a bowl of chips. Patricia pushed the bowls aside, took out a picture of Brittany Newel, laid it on the countertop.

Nate turned it around, studied it. "Yeah, I've seen her before."

Surprised by his honesty, she took out her notebook. "When?"

Nate shrugged. "Don't remember. Maybe a week ago. Maybe two weeks ago."

"Yesterday?"

Nate actually appeared to be thinking. "This is weird."

"Go on."

"I don't work nights here. I work at Barry's . . . a little nothing place, but you wouldn't believe the tips."

Patricia nodded as she wrote.

"It's a workingman's bar. Not like this." He screwed up his face in concentration. "I'm not sure. But she might have been *there* last night."

Patricia almost choked on an ice cube. "I see." *Calm, girl.* "About what time did you see her?"

"I'm not even sure if it *was* last night. I see a lot of people. I don't trust my memory." Nate paused. "You know, I'll be at the counter there at ten tonight. Why don't you come down and I'll introduce you around."

He gave her the address. She thanked him, said she'd be there at ten.

Suddenly sweating bullets. Moist armpits. Good thing her deodorant was holding. She wiped her face with a napkin. Sand and dirt blacked the pristine white paper. She knew she was filthy. She was embarrassed.

"I need a shower."

He cleared his throat. "You live far from here?"

She eyed him. "Why?"

"Dinner at eight?" He smiled boyishly. "I know a *great* Italian buffet, better than *anything* you can get on the Strip."

In other words, she looked like a woman who'd eat.

Patricia said, "How about tomorrow?" *By then I will have run you through NCIC.* "I still have work to do tonight."

Nate smiled wattage. "Tomorrow would be great!"

She took a final swig of her club soda. "Thanks for your help, Nate. Do you have a last name?"

"Oh sure. Malealani." He spelled it.

"And where do you live?"

He gave her his address, along with his phone number. Shyly, he said, "I gave you mine. Can I have yours?"

"In due time. I'll see you tonight at Barry's."

"Yeah! Great!"

The guy looked downright goofy. Of course, the costume didn't help. She stifled a smile.

He seemed rather innocent . . . dare she say it, unspoiled. Now, it could be an act. Yet he projected the genuine article. But that was Vegas—a mixture of predator and prey. And even she, as cynical as she was, had trouble telling the teams without a score card.

EIGHT

Exercise. Exorcise.

Stomping furiously on the treadmill, sweat dripping down—*pouring* down—as if her entire face were crying. Her wet palms were barely able to hold on to the handgrips. In a minute, they'd slip off and she'd go flying into space. Off the belt and into a wall like some Hollywood slapstick stunt. So as long as she could, she pumped her legs, running aslant on the instrument's full tilt. She felt it in every vertebra of her backbone.

To keep her mind off the pain, Alison thought of her research. The green book. All the answers were there if she'd just take the time to look in it. If she could only get off this blasted treadmill and *concentrate* on her research.

It drove her crazy. To *have* to run. But she did it because she was too afraid not to do it. If she stopped, terrible things might happen. The nasty voices could come back. The horrid visions might return—flashing images of blood and guts and sticky stuff. They never came when she was busy. Why leave anything to chance?

Running.

Running to nowhere.

An adequate assessment of her life.

To run, run, run without any fun, fun, fun.

But she stopped short of bludgeoning herself. She had come so far. It used to be that the fear kept her in bed almost twenty-four hours a day. Steve had to carpool, Steve had to cook meals, Steve had to shop and go to parents' conferences and do everything.

Now she could function. She could shop and pick up the kids from school . . . smile at the teachers and say hello. Often they'd smile back and say hello, too. And when she left the house, she made sure she was well groomed and presentable.

At times, she was oh so normal. A normal woman doing normal things. But then there were the other times. . . .

So that's why she ran.

If Mama had run, she might still be around today. But Mama hadn't run and that had been the problem.

The steady whir of the machine's motor buzzed through Alison's head. Her leg muscles contracting and expanding, the exertion building up her lungs and heart and stamina. The exercise was making her *strong*.

If only Mama had run.

But of course, in her own way, Mama had run. But not in a healthy way. Her strange forays during the night. Two, three o'clock in the morning, she'd be gone. Her disappearances had terrified Alison as a child. Papa had been no help at all, as he had been frantic with worry. Sometimes Mama had stayed away for days in a row. And when she returned . . . the way she had looked. There had been times when Alison had wished that Mama hadn't come back—this stranger so silent and sullen, her eyes feral and always bloodshot.

Drinking maybe.

Because her breath had turned fetid. As if she had lived on carrion.

The ensuing arguments. Papa asking her where she had been. Mama saying she didn't remember. Papa accusing her of lying. Mama going hysterical. Papa begging her to see a psychiatrist. Mama stalking out of the house.

The scene repeated over and over until finally it became moot.

Mama's nightime escapades. When she was ten, Alison had asked one of her own psychiatrists about them. Dr. Jones had called them fugue states. Alison looked up the word *fugue* in her junior dictionary.

A musical form or composition in which a theme is taken up and developed by the various instruments or voices in succession according to the strict laws of counterpoint.

Had Mama been playing music all this time?

The idea puzzled Alison for years. Until she was older and looked the word up in an unabridged dictionary. There were two meanings, the second one stating:

> *A state of psychological amnesia during which a patient seems to behave in a conscious and rational way, although upon returning to a normal consciousness, the patient cannot remember the period of time nor what was done during it. A temporary flight from reality.*

A temporary flight from reality.

Not so temporary in Mama's case.

When Alison didn't answer the doorbell, Poe took out his picks. A minute later, he was inside the house. She was exercising on the treadmill, her face as red and wet as a rain-washed plum. Her long legs were cutting long strides to keep up with an unnaturally fast pace. Her fingers were so tightly wound around the handlebars that the knuckles had turned bloodless. Her breathing was fast and furious and much too shallow.

Poe went inside her hallway closet, pulled out an octagonal red stop sign mounted on a dowel handle. He took the sign, placed it in front of her face.

As if she were looking at air.

Even before Poe did it he'd known that this time, it wasn't going to work. She was running too fast . . . out of control. Time to take action. Slowly, he reduced the machine's rate until she was barely walking. He let her go for five minutes, then turned off the treadmill.

She stood in place, not uttering a sound.

''Look at me,'' Poe whispered.

Alison met his eyes. Then she dashed into her bedroom. He heard a sudden blast of water rushing through the pipes. He'd give her ten, maybe fifteen minutes tops.

While waiting he realized he was hungry. It was half past six and Poe had eaten his last meal, at Myra's, well over eight hours ago. He returned Alison's stop sign to its place in the closet, then went into the kitchen and opened the fridge, happy to see it well stocked. He made himself a meatball sandwich with dark mustard on thick sourdough, poured himself a glass of orange juice. He ate slowly, hoped that the water would stop. Of course, it didn't.

With reluctance, he got up from the table, went into the bedroom.
Their bedroom.

Into the bathroom.

He opened the shower door, reached inside. The water had turned cold and Alison was shivering. He turned off the taps, placed a bath towel around her shoulders, and led her back into her bedroom, placing her in front of her dresser mirror. Carelessly, she let the towel fall to the floor.

Poe took in her nakedness, tried not to react. He held out her robe, then averted his eyes.

After a moment, she accepted it, slipped it on. Observing herself in her looking glass. She picked up a brush and began ripping into her hair. "I look like shit."

"You look gorgeous."

"I can't figure it out. No matter how long I run on that damn thing, I still have these big, fat thighs!" She pounded her flesh for emphasis. "Like saddlebags."

"You're as thin as a cat's tail. Shame on you for buying into that anorexia shit."

"Don't yell at me."

"You're overdoing it. It's not healthy."

"Can you kindly leave so I can get dressed?"

Poe paused. "All right, I'll leave. But if I hear the water running—"

"Stop it!" She threw her towel at him. But she was smiling now. And a beautiful smile at that. "Go make yourself useful."

"By doing . . ."

"Make some coffee."

"Where's your family?"

"Steve took the boys out for dinner."

"When did they leave?"

Alison gave him a slow, seductive look. "You're allowed to be here even if he isn't. I'm not chattel."

Poe wasn't too sure about that. "I'll make some coffee."

She joined him just as the pot had finished brewing. Dressed in a loose black tunic over black leggings. Her face was awash in an after-exercise blush, her blond hair combed and pulled back in a ponytail, emphasizing perfect cheekbones. Two gold studs decorated her earlobes. Her lips were coated in something pink and wet.

He poured two mugs of coffee: they sat at the kitchen table. The house was ranch-style, a decent-sized thing on a generous lot which held a pool.

It had a formal living room and dining room off an entry hall. The back part of the home was made up of an enormous kitchen, a breakfast area, and a den—the true living room of the house. At the moment, it was a bit messy—a stack of old papers, a couple of discarded items of clothing, a dirty dish on the coffee table. But Poe had seen it worse. The bedrooms were on the left side of the house—three of them.

"Why are you here?" Alison asked.

"Just to say hello."

"Yeah, right." She sipped coffee. "You've got that look in your eyes. What do you want? Besides to sleep with me. The answer is no."

"Alison, when was the last time I asked you to sleep with me? Like twenty years ago?"

"Try six months ago."

"What are you talking about?"

"You kissed me, Rom."

"Alison, it was your birthday—"

"Not a chaste kiss. You gave me tongue."

"You gave *me* tongue."

"I don't want to talk about this, Rom. Just drop it!"

Poe didn't respond. Instead, he began drumming his fingers against the tabletop.

Alison put her hand over his to quiet his fidgeting. "Steve was really working last night, wasn't he?"

"Yes."

"A corpse in the desert."

Poe eyed her. "He told you?"

"Occasionally we do talk. He was very upset by it. Did he know the woman, Rom?"

Poe shook his head no.

Alison studied him, *scrutinized* him. "You've become very hard to read."

Poe said, "It was an awful case. She was . . . messed up."

"Stabbed?"

Poe didn't answer.

"Just spit it out, Rom. I won't melt. He slept with her, right?"

Poe said, "Alison, do you remember the Bogeyman case?"

Anger coursed through her heart. Fiercely, she glared at him. Poe paled at her fury. "Wha . . . wha . . . what'd I say?"

Knowing she was irrationally angry, Alison softened her expression. "You don't remember, do you?"

He thought: *Oh God, what nerve did I touch this time?*

The Bogeyman. He had been around ten. Which meant Alison had been seven, maybe eight—

Her *mother*!

Anything associated with her mother . . .

He said, "It was right around the time of your mother's death. I'm sorry, I didn't think—"

"It's not just mere association. Think harder."

Poe was confused, remained silent.

"How could you have *forgotten*?" she chided.

"I . . . I'm sorry, but—"

"My mother . . . her death. The cops had ruled it a suspicious suicide. They came to my house to ask me questions—"

"Oh, *Christ*!" Mentally, Poe kicked himself. "I don't *believe* . . ."

How could he be so stupid! He had *been* there. The knock on the door. Two men in suits, one dressed in a cowboy hat and string tie with a turquoise clasp. They came in without even asking permission. Descending on the two of them. Two little kids. They'd been playing Clue—game number twelve or something like that. Her father had asked Poe if he could watch Alison while he did some grocery shopping.

Grocery shopping that took six hours.

Man, her dad had disappeared for a *long* time.

The men had introduced themselves as detectives. Started asking questions even though her father wasn't home. Questions about her mother that made her cry. It had been only a month or so after the funeral.

Finally, Y had shown up. The Paiute Indian—an old friend of both his and Alison's mothers—had materialized like some kind of apparitional savior. Seeing the police questioning two frightened children, the old man went ballistic. Poe still recalled the veins throbbing in the Indian's red neck. Y had told the cops—in colorful terms—to leave. As far as Poe knew, the fuzz had never returned.

Eons ago. When Y had been strong and vital. . . . Poe said, "Jesus, Alison, I am *so* sorry."

"They thought Mama was one of the Bogeyman's, you know. That she might have been with him the night she . . . killed herself. Because . . . she had cut herself up pretty badly."

Tenderly she reached for his hand.

"You can't remember everything. I'm sorry. I'm emotional these days." A small squeeze. "Why did you ask me about it?"

"Doesn't matter."

"Does this case remind you of the Bogeyman?"

Poe cleared his throat. "Maybe. From my faded childhood memory, perhaps there are some similarities."

He waited a beat.

"Faded memory is right. How could I forget? The whole thing . . . it's so clear in my mind now. Y popped in during the interrogation. Booted them all out. He was the real hero of the story."

"Absolutely." She took her hand off Poe's. "How is the old man?"

"Same as always. Gambling away his Indian benefits. Both he and my mom . . ."

Alison said, "He was very close to my mother. I think they were lovers."

Poe nodded.

"The Bogeyman case had a very disturbing effect on my mother."

"Alison, we don't—" Poe stopped himself. If she wanted to talk, let her talk. "Go on."

She composed her thoughts. "During the murder—rather *murders,* I think there were two of them—she became unusually agitated. Of course, she was disturbed even before the Bogeyman. But if you're looking for an excuse as to what drove her over the top, I'd say the killings."

Poe heard the front door open.

Angrily, Alison whispered, "I wish he'd just *go away!*"

"I'd better go away." As Poe started to rise, Alison grabbed his wrist. "What are you afraid of?"

Poe looked at her, sat back down. "Nothing."

The boys—Harrison and Scott—came charging into the kitchen. Both her sons were redheads like Alison's father. She hugged them like a mama lion. "Hey, sluggers. How's it cooking?"

"Hey, Mom," Scotty answered. "We brought you back some orange chicken and fried rice."

"Sounds great!"

"I'm going up to my room," Harrison said. "Homework."

Scott put the take-out bag on the kitchen table. "I gotta work on my math folder. Then you have to sign it."

"Fine," Alison said.

"I mean, you don't have to read it or anything. Just sign it."

"I don't mind reading it."

"I kinda prefer if you don't read it."

"Whatever you want, Scotty."

The boy looked tenderly toward his mother. "Are you okay?"

Alison forced herself not to cry. "Great."

Still, Scotty was skeptical. He kissed his mother's cheek. "Take care. Bye."

Alison stood up and gave her husband a half smile. "Thanks for taking them out."

Jensen kissed her on the lips, throwing Poe daggers from the corners of his eyes. Easy to think the worst. But he knew Alison. Moreover, he knew Poe. Married women weren't his thing. "Am I interrupting anything?"

"Not at all," Alison chirped. "You want some coffee, Steve?"

Jensen forced himself to smile. "No, I'm fine." He saw Poe getting up, said, "Don't let me rush you."

Feeling as wanted as ice on jet wings, Poe said, "Gotta go. Certain people await me."

Jensen mouthed, "Lewiston?"

Poe nodded.

Jensen said, "I'll walk you out, Boss."

" 'Night, Alison." Pointedly, Poe kissed her cheek. Just to show him it was all very innocent.

" 'Night." She turned her back and busied herself at the counter.

As soon as they were out of her sight, Jensen grabbed Poe's arm, shoving him out of the house. He slammed the front door behind them, all pretense of calm dissipating like smoke. "What did you two talk about?"

"Get your goddamn hands off me!"

Jensen blushed, dropped Poe's arm. He said, "What did you two talk—"

"None of your business," Poe answered. "And don't you dare interrogate your wife to get answers—"

"I'm not interrogating her, I'm interrogating *you*." Jensen spun 360 degrees on his heels, faced Poe with rage. "You think it's jealousy, don't you? You think I'm this big, bad jealous schmuck who's—"

"Steve, I don't know what you're talking about."

"You don't *goddamn* get it, do you? Every time you *talk* to her and start reminiscing about the good ole days, it sets her back. *You* don't see it. Because to you, your little talks are nothing but great fun. And because when she talks to *you,* she puts on her normal act—''

''Steve—''

''—but get her a couple hours later, when you're long gone, out screwing your whores or girlfriend or playing your cards being Mr. Asshole Carefree Bachelor, then she's left alone. And when she's alone, she sinks, Rom. And guess who has to *deal* with her shit!''

No one spoke.

Jensen exhaled forcefully. ''Every time *you* come to visit, you put her back six months' worth of therapy.''

Again, there was silence.

Jensen said, ''In case you haven't noticed, she's very fragile and disturbed—''

''I'm well aware—''

''You aren't aware of anything except what she tells you. And that's always her own slant. Her own bizarre thoughts. I'm not saying she can't be helped. But you ain't the one to do it, all right?''

Poe stuck his hands in his pocket, eyes looking upward, into a black, starry sky. ''If I've been . . . causing problems between you and your wife, I apologize.''

''I don't need your apologies, Rom. I need you to *leave her alone.* Understand?''

''Clearly.''

Jensen suddenly wilted, exhausted and spent. ''Weinberg's looking at me strange. You didn't tell him about—''

''No.''

''She ask about the case at all?''

''Who? Alison?''

Jensen nodded.

''Yeah. She said you were very upset last night. She asked whether you had slept with the victim.''

''And you told her no?''

''I won't dignify that with an answer.''

Neither spoke for a moment.

Poe said, ''You find out anything?''

''About Brittany?'' Jensen shrugged. ''Nothing that points to a killer. Just bits and pieces.''

''We should meet, compare notes with Patricia.''

"Give me a time and place."

Poe started snapping his fingers, stopped himself. "Back at the Bureau in what . . . two hours. Let's call it for nine."

"I'll be there." Jensen rubbed his face, looked up. "I've got to . . . don't want to leave her alone." His jaw tightened. "Although I don't think she relishes my company."

"Steve, I—"

"Forget it."

Poe nodded. Jensen was right. Leave it unsaid.

The big man patted Poe's shoulder, turned, and walked back inside his house. Poe remained rooted, his eyes racing across an endless inky sky, the sounds of his snapping fingers echoing in the stillness of the night. Slowly, he forced himself to move. To go away.

He had a giant headache.

Probably too much caffeine.

Next time, he'd cool it with the coffee.

NINE

Taking a couple of practice swings, the iron whizzing through the air. "How's your game coming, son?"

Poe answered, "I don't play golf, Mr. Lewiston."

"Pity." Several more slices into the air. Then the moment of truth. Lewiston bunched up his body in concentration, his eyes focused on the tee. He took aim and swung. A clean shot, the ball rising, falling, rolling across the ground. It fell into a sunken cup around fifty yards away.

That's how big the office was.

Poe estimated that it took up over half the top floor of the Laredo. Floor number twenty-six. Twenty-five actually, because the elevator had gone from floor twelve to floor fourteen. Lewiston's domain kept going and going, with desks and chairs and couches and tables, all of the furniture resting on a carpet of natural sod. *Verdant*, clipped sod. The temperature inside his working quarters was a muggy seventy-four degrees.

Lewiston leaned against his iron, said, "You say you *don't* play golf?"

"Correct." Poe was seated in a leather club chair whose legs were buried in the grass. The apparatus had settled slightly to the left, throwing his perspective off-kilter.

"Have you ever tried the game?"

"A few times."

Lewiston straightened. Poe felt the heat of the casino owner's eyes, peering at him as if sighting prey. Steely blue things that were reptilian-cold. A chiseled face with a strop-sharpened-razor shave, his complexion so smooth as to appear wet. Short haircut, the color too iridescent to be called gray. It was more like silver. At sixty, Lewiston stood erect and tall—about Jensen's height. For the golfing demonstration, he had donned a pair of black silk-and-wool slacks and a white silk shirt with the sleeves rolled up to his elbows. His feet were housed in black croc boots. He wore a string tie held together by a jeweled pendant—aquamarine maybe. He had thrown the tie over his shoulder lest it interfere with his shot.

"Son, you've never tried the game until you've tried it with me. Why don't you join me on one of my courses this Saturday? Golfing always puts me in a social mood."

"My handicap would be too big, sir."

Besides, fraternizing with the big boys is a no-no, Parker. Sort of ruins the objectivity.

"You know how to aim a gun?" Lewiston asked.

"Of course."

"Shoot a target?"

"Yes."

"Then golf should be a snap."

"I think holing a fifty-yard chip takes a little more finesse than blasting a cardboard cutout."

"Well, it shouldn't take more finesse," Lewiston insisted. "Because shooting has a lot more ramifications than sinking a putt. You should work some finesse into your shooting, son."

Poe was not about to be undermined. "Maybe it has something to do with split-second decisions. Difficult to have finesse when you're looking down the barrel of a shotgun." He whispered, "Hand's shaking too hard."

Lewiston smiled with brown-stained teeth. "You should work on that, too. Never let them see you sweat."

"I'll keep that in mind next time I'm running down an armed bank robber. Better still, I'll call you. You can bring down your clubs and really show him who's boss."

"In a tight situation, a Magnum might be the preferred weapon. You can always borrow mine."

"I wouldn't mind, but the department may have other thoughts." Poe balled his hands into fists to keep himself from fidgeting. "Thank you for seeing me, Mr. Lewiston. I really do appreciate it. Especially because you are a hard man to reach."

Two hours of plodding through the channels had accomplished zilch. But twenty minutes at the blackjack tables had caught their attention. Place had a new pit boss. Shame on Parkerboy for not keeping his guys up to date.

Lewiston said, "My staff knows how I value my privacy." The eyes squinted into small knots. "You seem to be a persistent fellow. One might even call you a pest. . . . or a gnat . . . or something annoying."

Poe appeared thoughtful. "With all due respect, Mr. Lewiston, I don't agree. Like take tonight. Instead of getting all mean-mouthed and pushy when I kept being put on hold, I just left a couple of messages. Figured I'd wait you out. So I just plunked myself down at a table and bided my time."

Poe took out a thick wad of bills with Ben Franklin on top. Slowly, he flicked the stack with his thumb, thousands of dollars dancing past like an old cartoon motion book.

"That's all I was doing, sir. Just passing time."

Again the apple-rot smile. "How 'bout we call it a going-away present?" A wave of the hand. "As in you . . . going away."

Poe pocketed the cash and took out a notebook. "I'd like to ask a few questions about Brittany Newel, sir."

"Brittany Newel?" Lewiston seemed confused. "Is the name supposed to be familiar?"

"She claimed she was one of your girls."

"Claimed. As in the past tense. Is she denying it now?"

"She's not saying anything, sir. She's dead."

Lewiston shrugged. "It happens."

"Did you know her?" Poe asked.

"Not that I can recall."

Poe took out a picture, showed it to Lewiston. "How about this girl? Did you know her?"

Lewiston looked at the photograph. "She's a pretty little thing. Who is she?"

Is Parkerboy shittin' me or what?

Poe said, "She doesn't look familiar?"

Lewiston held a perfect poker face. "Son, she looks like a thousand other showgirls in this city."

Poe said, "This was Brittany Newel."

Lewiston took another look at the photograph. "Shame. Don't think she ever worked here."

"Her employment tax records said she did."

Without missing a beat, Lewiston picked up the phone's intercom. "Lois, can you get hold of personnel. Find out if a young thing named Bethany—"

"Brittany."

Lewiston turned to Poe. "Spell the name for me, son."

Poe complied.

"All right, dear," Lewiston said into the phone. "Thank you, dear." Turning to Poe. "It's going to take time. Check in with me tomorrow afternoon."

After you've raped the files. Luckily Poe had been there first. He said, "Thank you, Mr. Lewiston."

The casino owner gave out a chuckle. "You're obviously a bettin' man, son. You've done well at my tables. I'll give you another hour and we'll give you double odds. How's that for being daring?"

Most of the games in Vegas were clean, because house odds usually worked magic without cheating. Still, there were thousands of ways to rig a game. Especially since casinos had dozens of cameras, giving them eyes to everyone's cards. Lewiston seemed out for revenge.

Poe wasn't about to play dupe. He rose from his slanted chair, extended his hand. "Some other time. No hard feelings?"

"Never." Lewiston took the proffered fingers, crushed them in his grip. "Not at all."

Poe counted to three, then pulled back his hand, smiling all the way. *Asshole!* His bones felt as if they had been put through a winepress. Yet he wasn't bothered too much. At least now his fingers were too sore to snap.

Lewiston said, "Now if you're not going to join me for golf on Saturday, you'd just better be running along." A slow grin. "Don't make me call my lawyer. City Hall wouldn't like it."

"Not necessary." Again, Poe pulled out his cash. "Can I get a cashier's check for this?"

"Downstairs." Lewiston intercommed his secretary. "Lois, can you show Detective Poe out, please?"

"Sergeant."

But Lewiston had picked up his iron and was whipping at the wind. Pretending not to hear.

Because of space problems, Homicide had moved away from the City Hall complex into its own building, mistitled an "executive park." Completely unprepossessing, the structure was an unmarked one-story stucco thing with a tile roof and a double-mirrored door, better suited to hold an insurance agency or an escrow company. There was a small parking lot in front, another paved area in the rear which fronted an architecturally similar low-slung box.

Still, the move was celebrated by Homicide; the detectives loved their new surroundings. Their own place, putting miles of distance between them and the other departments as well as the scrutinizing eye of the brass. It was a quiet sanctuary, somewhere to think and work. Standing behind the Bureau lay the Crime Scene Analysis building. Just a short walk from the desk to the lab, making it easy to check up on physical evidence. With the two places in such close proximity, things rarely got lost.

Sitting at his desk, Jensen took a break from his notes and leaned back in his chair. It was ten to nine. Meaning the others should be here soon. Deluca and Poe were notoriously punctual. Taking a deep breath, letting it out slowly. He got up, walked to the coffee station, and started a pot of decaf.

More than mistresses, more than alcohol or a night out with the guys, being in *this* squad room, alone at night . . . that gave Jensen peace. The workspace was designed as one large, rectangular room. Completely open. No cubicles to block sound waves. Everyone could hear cases being discussed. Important details were often picked up in casual conversation. The walls were painted pastel blue, the floor was done in wall-to-wall deep blue carpet. Square panels of fluorescent light checkerboarded the ceiling. Currently, there were fifteen workstations lining the walls, each detective having his/her own desk, chair, computer, printer, phone, and java mug.

What more could anyone need?

A fridge and Mr. Coffee machine in one corner, a gun vault in the other. The unit's vulture mascot was perched above the entrance door. During the day, the back windows gave a view of a parking lot. The appearance was definitely more like an office than a homicide bureau, but that was fine with Jensen.

He often watched the boob tube. One thing he could never figure out was how big-city TV cops worked in such chaos, trying to write reports with felons cursing, people shouting, women having babies. He guessed it made for good drama, though no one could think amid all that pandemonium. Here everything was low-key . . . quiet . . . like a small-town sheriff's office. Which was fitting, because Vegas had originally been built as a Western saloon town. Now, with a population of over a million, Las Vegas owned big city problems. Plus it had to cope with an enormous transient population. Outsiders often took their problems to the gambling mecca. And when things turned to shit, guess who cleaned up the mess?

Deluca walked through the door, threw her purse on her desk, and sat down. She ran stubby fingers through her freshly washed hair. Her face was flushed and open. "I got a lead."

Jensen straightened in his chair, took in a whiff of air. "Are you wearing perfume?"

"Just a splash." Patricia paused. "Did I overdo it?"

"No. Actually, it smells nice. What's the occasion?"

"It has to do with my lead." Patricia pulled out her notes. "I was questioning this bartender who kinda took a shine to me. His name is Nate—"

"Who's Nate?" Poe asked, walking through the door.

"A bartender who has the hots for Patty."

"That's Fat Patty to you, bub." Patricia winked at a blushing Jensen. "I know what you guys call me behind my back." She turned to Poe. "I got a lead. A bartender who might have seen Brittany at Barry's Place last night."

She gave them the address.

Poe took out his notebook, wrote it down. Jensen said, "Never heard of the place."

"It's a native bar," Patricia said.

"Native as in Native American?" Jensen asked.

"No, native as in native Las Vegan. Look at the address. Right in the heart of blue-collarville."

Poe said, "Betcha Y would know the place."

"I wouldn't doubt it," Jensen said. "Guy knows every bar in the city. How old is he, anyway? About eighty?"

"More like sixty-five, seventy," Poe said. "His face is just weathered."

"He looks like cured jerky," Jensen remarked. "Is he related to you? Or don't you readily admit to having Digger blood?"

"Of course I admit it. I'm proud of it." Notebook still in hand, Poe plunked himself down, propped his feet on his desktop. "How'd you hook up with this bartender, Patricia? What's his name, by the way?"

"Nathan Malealani."

"Hawaiian?" Jensen asked.

"More like Samoan. By day, he tends the Oasis in Casablanca. The bar was on Weinberg's hit list. Guess I got lucky."

"Sounds like you made your own luck." Poe turned to Jensen. "You find out anything we should know about?"

"Nothing radical." Jensen picked up a list from his desk. "I got two, three . . . four bellmen who threw Newel some action. No one used her as a regular—too unreliable because of her chemical problem."

"What was the split?" Poe asked.

"Fifty-fifty at first," Jensen said. "When Brittany started losing her looks, it dropped to forty-sixty. Mostly she made calls to them on the weekends when things got busy."

"Did she make enough money to carry her through the week?" Patricia asked.

"Depends on how much she made on weekends. Or maybe she simply hit Lewiston up for a loan."

Poe stuck a wad of gum in his mouth. "He denied knowing her."

The room went silent. Jensen broke it. "You actually *talked* to Par-kerboy."

"After two hours of getting the runaround, I became bored, started wandering through the casino. Lo and behold, Laredo done got itself a new pit boss."

Patricia smiled. "You did well, sir?"

"Yes, ma'am!" Poe yanked his feet off the desk, stood up, and clapped his hands in glee. "Double-shoe decks. I fleeced the SOB. Serves Par-kerboy right for keeping an officer of the law waiting."

Jensen said, "Dealers there don't believe in shuffling the cards?"

Poe laughed. "I had some lucky breaks. About an hour later, I get the familiar tap on the shoulder. I turn and smile and show Mr. Gil Lawson—probably né Guido Lombardi—my badge."

"Way to go, Poe," Jensen said.

Poe said, "Now the guy is stuck. He wants to kick me out, but I'm a cop. Doesn't know what the hell to do. So I figure I'd help him out. I'd leave the table without making a scene *if* I could have a word with the boss. Ten minutes later, I get a call. How's that for results?'' He laughed, shook his head. ''Guy's a golf fanatic. His entire office is carpeted in sod so he can take practice shots.''

''Aw, c'mon,'' Patricia said.

''I kid you not.''

Jensen said, ''Doesn't he own his own private course? The one off Sahara next to the Rancho Fiesta development. I played there once for some police benefit. It's a good course.''

Patricia said, ''He owns his own golf course?''

''Why not?'' Jensen said. ''Wynn owns the course at UNLV.''

''Yeah, but that one is open to the public, isn't it?'' Patricia said.

Poe shrugged. ''Anyway, the upshot is that Lewiston denied knowing Brittany. And I'm wondering why.''

''Maybe he didn't know her.''

''I don't think so,'' Poe said. ''He used the words 'I don't *recall*' knowing her. Like Reagan not recalling arm sales.''

''Maybe Reagan didn't,'' Patricia said. ''He *was* diagnosed with Alzheimer's.''

Poe said, ''Everyone knows Lewiston's a major lech, that he's done tons of girls. Why would he be squirrelly knowing Brittany?''

''It doesn't mean he's involved,'' Jensen said. ''Maybe he didn't want to get his hands sullied. You know, he starts saying, 'Yeah, I know her.' Then you start asking more questions. Easier to cut you off from the start.''

Poe answered, ''More like he's hiding something. I'd love to find out where he was last night.''

Jensen smiled. ''Why don't you question the hired help?''

Poe laughed. ''Great idea, Steve. Is this before or after I get the shit beat out of me?''

''C'mon,'' Patricia said. ''Bugsy's dead and gone—''

Jensen interrupted, ''But the image lives on.''

''They wouldn't do that to a *cop*,'' Patricia insisted.

''Probably not.'' But Poe wasn't too sure what would happen if he started stomping on toes. ''So what do we have? We have a girl shredded to death by some sadistic control freak who shot her up with dope beforehand—''

''How do you know that?'' Jensen asked.

''Rukmani's educated guess.''

"What else did she say?" Patricia asked.

Poe paused, flipped through his notes. "No stab wounds, no gunshot wounds, bits of metal found in a few tissue samples consistent with a metal implement, bits of enamel found that were consistent with tooth enamel. But no distinct bite marks. More like teeth tearing at the flesh."

He closed his notebook, looked up.

"Dr. Kalil thinks all this was done while Brittany was still breathing. Possibly unconscious, but alive. We've *got* to nail this monster."

Poe started snapping his fingers and winced. His hand was still sore from Lewiston's crushing grip.

"Okay, so we know that Brittany bar-hopped. Patricia's going to check out Barry's Place . . . maybe she was there last night. Maybe she left there with someone in tow. She also hooked." To Jensen, Poe said, "Any of your bellmen set her up with someone last night?"

"If they did, they didn't admit it to me."

Poe said, "Go back and lean on them."

"I'll do it, Rom. But I think Newel's call girl days for the big hotels were long past. If she hooked at all, I betcha it was for pushers in exchange for drugs."

"Since Patty and you are tied up, I suppose that leaves me to check out Naked City." Poe raised his brows. "With Brittany's arrest record, I'm sure she was an honorary citizen."

TEN

Nate hadn't been kidding when he said it was a workingman's bar. No pretense of attracting the tourist trade. The place was dark, smoky, and smelled ripe. Roomy, though. A horseshoe-shaped wood-laminate counter with red Naugahyde stools, plus about twenty tables and scattered chairs. A separate area for playing pool. Occupancy ran about a third full, but the night was young. Most of the drinkers were men, but there were some big-haired forty-plus women. To pass the time, they schmoozed or played the countertop slots and poker machines. A live poker game was going down in one of the corners.

Taking a moment to adjust her eyes, Patricia chose a seat at the far end of the counter. Six stools away sat two women in tight jeans and plaid shirts, drinking beer and flirting with the hired help.

Strangely, she felt at home. The place seemed friendly and everyone was behaving himself. And if anyone acted up, Patricia was sure that Nathan Malealani and his coworker—a man resembling a sumo wrestler—could take care of any situation. Nate had wetted and combed his unruly Brillo locks, had donned a shocking-pink Hawaiian shirt printed with palm trees and woody station wagons. Their eyes met; he waved her over, his bright smile luminescent across the room. Without thinking about it, Patricia found herself smiling back. She sat in front of him, then absently dropped three quarters into one of the slots. Pressed the button that said "play three." The barrels stopped at three cherries, her profits announced with dings and dongs.

Malealani said, "A good start."

"If I stop now, I'll stop a winner."

The bartender said, "That's the key . . . knowing when to stop." He pushed a button, removing the winning receipt from the machine. "I'll keep this for you."

"Thanks." Patricia studied the bartender with a cop's eyes. His name hadn't turned up a yellow sheet anywhere in the West, so she hadn't bothered with NCIC. That could be a mistake. But she knew she hadn't pursued it because she hadn't wanted to look too hard.

"I like the shirt."

His smile widened. "Thanks. It's one of my favorites."

Favorites? How many does he have? "Shows individuality."

"That's me. Can I get you a beer? Or is it still club soda with a lime twist?"

"I'm still working, so it's still water."

Malealani's smile dimmed at the mention of the word "work." Surely he didn't think she was here on a *social* visit.

Then again, she was wearing perfume.

He poured out a tumbler of club soda, his manner more reserved. "Guy working the bar with me?" He cocked his head to the right. "His name is Raymond Takahashi. We call him Big Ray."

"Makes sense. He's a big guy."

"Six-six. Mr. Bennington likes us big. You know, it's a psychological edge when things get hairy. Anyway, I think you should talk to Ray. I think he served the girl you're looking for."

Patricia sipped her water. "Did you ask him about her?"

"No. I didn't want it to come out wrong, so I didn't say anything. Besides, you know how it is. You mention cops, some people get nervous. I didn't want him to rabbit before you had a chance to talk."

"Smart thinking."

"Just common sense. Should I bring him over now?"

"That would be great." Patricia smiled. "Hey, thanks for your help. I appreciate it."

Malealani ran his fingers over the countertop. "Are we on for tomorrow night?"

Patricia shrugged. "How could I go wrong with an Italian buffet?"

The bartender tried to hide his glee. "Or if there's something else—"

"Italian sounds fine, Nathan."

Two girls roosted next to Patricia's right. She moved three stools over. "Better if people don't hear us."

Malealani said, "It's past ten. Gonna start to get crowded. I guess I should let you do your thing."

But he paused.

Not wanting to let her go.

She said, "I don't think I ever told you my name."

"It's on your card."

"Still, that's no introduction." She stuck out her hand. "Patricia Deluca. Most people call me Fat Patty."

Nate laughed. "How 'bout just Patty?"

"That's fine, too. I really should talk to your friend."

Malealani called out, "Hey, Big Ray." Beckoned him with a finger. "Want you to meet someone."

Big Ray stopped wiping the counter, froze, turned, stared, then lumbered forward. Not an ounce of fluidity in the man. Each physical action was done in a separate, robotic movement.

Like Nate, Big Ray was Melanesian. He wore an untucked blue rayon shirt over a pair of jeans. He looked like he was ready to bowl. He eyed Patricia, licked his lips. He nodded.

Malealani said, "This is Detective Deluca. She's looking for someone."

Patricia offered a handshake. "How's it going, Big Ray?"

Ray took it, his face as animated as a tile of slate.

"Who are you looking for?"

To Patricia, Malealani said, "You have the picture, don't you?"

Yes, Nate, I have the picture. She took out the photograph, showed it to Big Ray. "I'm with Homicide. This woman was found dead last night. Nate said you might have served her."

Big Ray said, "Yeah, I did."

Patricia almost fell off the stool. In the back of her cynical mind, she had suspected that Nate had been jiving her. But things were falling into place.

First the three cherries.

Now this.

Too much good luck. So when was it going to crash?

She took out her notebook. "You're sure it was this woman?"

Without hesitation, Big Ray said he was sure. "She didn't look this good. But the face was the same."

"What did she look like?" Patricia asked.

"I dunno. Just not good. Young but old." He looked around the room. "Belonged to the kind of women you'd find here. Like they've lived their lives in a trash compactor."

"Was she with anyone?"

"Came in alone. But she hooked up with someone pretty quick."

Malealani asked, "Who?"

"The young guy," Ray answered.

"The young guy?"

"Yeah, the young guy. He was short."

"Short?"

"Yeah, he was pretty short."

Patricia stopped writing, looked up. "Like how short?"

Big Ray marked off an area on his chest with the side of his hand. "Came up to about here."

Eyeballing it, maybe around five-eight or -nine. Patricia said, "What did he look like?"

Big Ray said, "Besides being short?"

"Yes."

Malealani said, "I don't remember no short guy."

Shut up, Nathan! Patricia said, "What did he—"

"He drank Dewar's straight up," Big Ray said. "You don't 'member him?"

Malealani scrunched up his eyes. "That guy?"

"Yeah, him."

Patricia said, "You remember him, Nate?"

"Sorta." To Big Ray, Nate said, "So he's the guy who was with the girl?"

"Yeah."

"When was this?"

"Right after she came in. Like around ten-thirty."

Patricia asked, "Did they leave together?"

"Well, I don't 'member if they walked out together. But both left 'round the same time."

"And when was that?"

"I dunno exactly. Around eleven-thirty, maybe midnight."

The body had been called in at 1:22 A.M. A small window of time to do the deed. The killer had worked quickly, raking and scooping. . . .

From the far end of the bar, someone shouted, "Can I get a beer around here?"

Malealani was already walking away, "I'll get it."

Patricia glanced around. The place was filling up.

Put some lead in it, girl.

"So they both left around midnight?"

"Yeah."

"What else can you tell me about the short guy?"

"He was skinny."

"Short and skinny."

"That about sums it up."

More people were coming in. Patricia figured she had maybe five minutes more. "How about his hair, Big Ray? Was it blond, brunette, bald—"

"Not bald." Big Ray was perplexed. "I can't remember the color."

"Well, was it straight or curly, wavy, thin, thick—"

"I can't remember his hair, neither."

Patricia's brain was racing. "Ray, by any chance was Mr. Short Thin Guy wearing a hat?"

Big Ray raised one eyebrow. First sign of life he'd shown. "Yes. That's it. He was wearing a hat. A black hat. Like Charlie Chaplin." A pause. "He had a ponytail. I don't remember the color. Just the ponytail."

Patricia wrote quickly. Malealani returned. Big Ray said to him, "The Dewar's guy was wearing a ponytail." To Patricia he said, "He was clean-shaven. 'Cept he had like . . . this peach fuzz all over his face. Like guys get before the beard comes in. A peach-fuzz mustache, too."

"Peach fuzz . . . so he was young?"

"Thirty. I checked his ID."

Patricia felt her heart race. "You checked his *ID*?"

Big Ray nodded.

"Do you . . . happen to recall a *name*?"

Ray didn't even ponder the question. "Not a clue. Just looked at his birthday. That I 'member." He gave the date.

"You remember anything else about his features? His eyes, for instance?"

Deadpan, Big Ray said, "Yeah, he had eyes."

Then the men laughed.

"Very funny." But she was smiling. To show she was a good ole gal. Just keep 'em talking. "You notice the color?"

"They weren't bright blue or green or anything." A beat. "Maybe like light brown, but I'm not positive. I don't stare at people unless they give me problems."

"How about his mouth—thin lips, thick lips—"

"Thick lips."

"And the mouth itself. Was it wide, narrow—"

"Just a mouth."

"With thick lips."

"Yes, ma'am."

"And his face? Was it long or short?"

"Longer than shorter." Big Ray looked around. "Uh, things are gettin' a little busy."

"I know. Can you give me another minute?"

"As long as you make it a fast one."

Patricia organized her thoughts. No name, but a birth date. A short and skinny man with a hat and ponytail. A peach-fuzzed Dewar's drinker with brownish eyes and thick lips. Not a photographic description, but it could have been worse.

"Big Ray, if you have about an hour tomorrow, I'd like you to talk to a police artist. Between the two of you, maybe we could draw up this guy."

The Melanesian shrugged. "All right."

A loud crash. The sounds of shattering glass. Someone yelling, "Yeah, well, chuck you, Farley!"

Big Ray peered over Patricia's head, shouted, "What's going on over there?"

Malealani was already at the scene. Big fat guy, but fleet-footed. His big, booming voice rang out, "Too much to drink, pal?"

"Fuck you—"

"Let me help you to the bathroom."

"I said—"

"Better yet, let me help you through the back door."

"Get your fuckin'—"

"Yeah, yeah!" Malealani started dragging some loudmouthed jerk in a red shirt across the floor. Opened the back door and away he flew.

Big Ray laughed. "They never learn." To Patricia, he said, "I gotta go mind shop."

He turned and lumbered away. Malealani came back a moment later, wiped his hands on his pants. "You want a refresher on that club soda, Patty?"

"No, I'm okay." Patricia slipped her notebook into her purse. "Actually, I think I'd better head back to the station. Write all this up before I forget."

"So I'll pick you up tomorrow at seven. I hope that's not *too* early. We gotta fit dinner in between my gigs." He waited a beat. "I'm off on Sunday. We can have a longer dinner then. There's this great Thai place about an hour out of the city. You never tasted anything so good."

Patricia said, "Uh, let's see how tomorrow goes."

Malealani scratched his head. "I'm being pushy. Sorry. Don't mean anything by it. I just get so tired of desperate people. Especially women. So many desperate women in this city. I guess you see that in your work as much as I do." He licked his lips. "All I'm saying is you really seem to have your act together."

Patricia wanted to scream, *Who? Me?* Instead, she chuckled, politely thanking him.

Maintain the image, maintain the pretext.

Because that's what Vegas was all about.

ELEVEN

Looking more like a radio tower than a casino, the Needle in the Sky was started in the late eighties, completed in the nineties. It was the tallest building in Las Vegas, but it was lonely at the top. In the middle of nowhere, it sat in an isolated pocket between the glamour of the Strip and the light fantastic of downtown renovation. What could be said about it? The view was panoramic and the Sunday brunch couldn't be beat. The interior sang paeans to the god of gaming future. But outside were the trenches. Behind the Needle sat a vacant lot of partial construction and piles of rubble. Dubbed Naked City by the locals, it had the dubious honor of hosting L.V.'s leanest and meanest.

Cab drivers were wary of people headed there at night. Knowing that, Poe always tipped big. He had left his own car in the Bureau's lot. No way he was going to drive his baby, park it on the street, leaving it prey for any jive turkey car thief desperate for a fix.

Poe detested the place, carrying a weapon and knowing there was a chance that he'd have to use it. Shoot-'em-ups were for the uniforms, for SWAT or special teams. Not for gumshoe homicide detectives trying to trace a hooker's last steps. Still, he'd cleaned the gun this afternoon. Sucker that he was, why hadn't he given Steve this assignment?

The taxi let him off in front of the Needle, picked up another fare, then got the hell out.

Poe started walking. Turned up the collar on his coat and stuck his hands in his pocket, feeling the bulge of his holster through the coat material. Wearing his gun on his belt because it made for easier access than his shoulder harness. Past the Union 76 sign, past the block-long General Store and Toon Town toy store. Into the bowels of the bleak.

A weeknight, but there was still some action. So many crack runners the dealers could have hosted a marathon. At the bottom rung of the ladder, the runners took all the chances, walked away with nothing. They ferried dope from the dealers to buyers in their cars, breaking off bits of the buyer's rock to feed their habits. The girls had it better than the boys. On slow nights, the girls could hook for extra cash. The boys had to resort to petty thievery.

If he squinted, Poe could make them out, scurrying and scattering like roaches in a Manhattan tenement. He found a dark vantage point, looked and waited. A Honda Accord with darkened windows slowed, pulled curbside.

Immediately, they came to service it. The winner was a green-haired girl in short shorts, fishnets, and leather brassiere. She came over to the open window, nodded. Glancing over her shoulders, feral eyes in the moonlight. Reaching into her black bra, she pulled out what Poe assumed to be a rock crystal of cocaine.

And that was it.

Transaction finished: the car went on its way. She darted back, her loose breasts flapping like water balloons. Disappearing under a pile of construction.

Another car.

Another transaction.

The scene was repeated over and over.

Sometimes the cops roared in and swept the place. More often, they let them be. Besides, more than one detective had a stoolie who worked the area.

No one daring to make eye contact, Poe knew he'd have to take action. Go out and turn over a rock. He spied a young white girl taking orders from an older black man. Poe could barely make out his features before he withdrew into the shadows. Poe made his move, pulling out a fifty, showing it to the girl.

She stepped forward a few feet, then stopped. Over here, buyers came by way of cars; no one was used to walk-ins. But Poe was patient, knew that eventually the fifty would prove to be the needed lure to catch the young girl.

Really young.

Behind a mask of makeup was a child of maybe fifteen. One of her eyes was swollen, and she had cigarette-burn marks on her arms and legs. Painfully thin, with pink hair and red lips that were cracked at the corners. She wore a torn black halter and a miniskirt with no underwear. She had to be freezing. It broke Poe's heart. He actually debated running her in, just to get her off the streets for a night. But without her hourly fix, she'd turn monstrous. LVMPD wasn't set up to do detox.

Poe waved the fifty in the air.

Still, she was hesitant.

Then he spoke. "More where this came from. And you can keep the shit. All I want is informa—"

She darted away.

Smooth one, Poe.

God, how he hated this place.

A moment later, the girl returned with her dealer. Around thirty, with a thin face and a goatee. He wore jeans and a leather bomber jacket. His fingers were encased in leather gloves with the fingertips cut off. Beckoned Poe onto his turf with a bent index digit.

Heart beating, Poe came forward, stopped short of being nose to nose. The dealer had a good four inches of height on him. He also pointed a snub-nose Special in Poe's face. His voice was surprisingly high. "You be a cop?"

Poe nodded.

"Lemme see some ID."

"Put away your piece. Then I'll show you ID."

"Why would I be doing that?"

"Because I reach into my pocket, you shoot, saying it was self-defense. C'mon, sport. I'm obviously not from Narc."

"Whatchu want?"

"Information about a girl."

"How much you be payin' for it?"

"Depends on what you tell me."

Slowly, the dealer lowered his pistol. "Talk."

"I got a picture in my pocket," Poe said. "I'm gonna show it to you." He brought out Brittany's photo. "She ever work for you?"

The dealer looked at the photograph. His face soured. "That be Brittany."

Poe rocked on his feet, restraining himself from snapping his fingers. "Yes. She was one of yours, then?"

The dealer smiled a mouth of ivories. "She didn't be no runner, but she be my bitch for a month. A good ho. Do anything I tole her to do. Got lots of money from her legs. But I see her again, I cut a smile in her throat. The bitch stole from me."

"Ah," Poe said. "So she hasn't been around lately."

The dealer shook his head. "She come in here again, she don't leave breathin'. No patience for that kinda shit. You see the bitch and she axes for me, you tell her what I said."

Poe said, "She isn't going to be asking for anyone. She's dead."

The dealer didn't blink. "Don't surprise me. You be stealin' from people, they got a right to take action."

Did you *take action, buddy?*

Poe held out the fifty. The dealer snapped it into his fingertips. Then he pointed to the teenager with the cracked lips and bruised eye. "I let you poke her for only twenty bucks. But you be wanting some crack . . . that be standard price."

The thought of sex with that child made Poe's stomach turn. "Thanks, but I'll pass."

Without a further word, the dealer disappeared.

Poe's eyes hunted around. It took him a moment to find the waifish pink-haired girl. She was hiding behind a pile of broken concrete. A flick of fire from a match illuminated her ravaged face. She brought the match into the wire-mesh bowl of her crack pipe. Sucked on the bit and inhaled deeply. Throwing back her head. Then it dropped forward, her chin plowing into her chest. Slowly, she found the strength to bring her head up as it lolled from side to side. She wiped her nose, her eyes gazing out to nowhere. Viewing a world out of focus.

From dealer to buyer, from buyer to dealer. Nicking off bits of crack to stave off the dragon. Her life disintegrating into the netherworld.

Hell had nothing over Naked City.

As the hour approached midnight, the urge got stronger. Not as strong as last night, but Alison knew she was powerless. It was better to prepare for it than to be caught off-guard. Last night had been bad because the urge had caught her off-guard. *And* she had tried to resist.

Never resist.

Never, ever resist.

Had her mother resisted? Is that what had driven her over that edge?

Or maybe the urges had driven her to take off on those long disappearances—the fugue states which were anything but musical. Had she felt the urge as strongly as Alison? Had the urge compelled her to run, to leave her earthly body and ascend to a higher place?

Well, if that had been the case—and often Alison had figured that so—well, then Alison did have pity on her mother. But Alison could afford pity, because she was a lot stronger.

To wit: her body. Just look at her body.

Because the sensations had started.

Once they started, she knew she had very little time left.

The boys had been asleep for over two hours. Steve was away. The opportunity was perfect.

No excuse for not listening to the urge.

Breathing hard as she felt her forearms and biceps widening . . . hardening. Her thighs and calves . . . a metamorphosis into something steely and superhuman.

At these moments, she knew she defied logic.

That or she was just plain crazy.

She really didn't know anymore. Nor did she care.

The *urge*.

Her body demanding compliance.

Throwing off her nightgown . . . standing naked and strong.

She dashed out the back door into the cold, clear, windless night, beating her bare breast. Her skin had turned icy, was studded with goose bumps. Her face had become something strange and foreign.

Running into the garage, lifting up the heavy trunk and twirling it about. Singing songs to God and the moon. Such wonderful newfound power.

She set the case down onto the floor, then began to root through it. Steve's old clothes. Never did get around to taking them to the Cancer Society. Tossing and throwing the vestments into the air, the cloth billowing down like sails in the wind.

So what would it be tonight?

Which shirt?

Which pair of pants?

Which pair of shoes? (That was easy. Steve's shoes still didn't fit her feet.) She'd have to settle for her own shoes.

Dressing quickly.

She observed her visage in a cracked mirror.

Veddy, veddy good. Urbane and suave.

The height of sophistication.

Now all she needed was a hat.

TWELVE

The compulsion to play was overwhelming. But Poe was known at the Needle, so he had to settle for a beer and a smoke at the bar.

Something to unwind.

His head hurt, he was tired, and he was dog-lonely. A quickie wasn't going to cut it. He needed companionship, needed to hear the music of feminine speech. He cursed himself for not making arrangements to meet Rukmani, but took solace in being noble. She needed her sleep.

Sipping suds, glancing at the pit, feeling very antsy. He rocked on the barstool, tapped his toes without rhythm along the foot railing. Scanning the crowds, he blinked, picked up his beer, and moved a dozen seats down.

Y glanced up, returned his eyes to his poker machine. A cigarette dangled from his mouth, a long tip of ashes just waiting to be flicked into a tray. Poe removed the smoke from the old man's mouth, dumped the discharge in a glass bowl, then placed it back between Y's lips.

The old man's brown face was creased with concentration. As usual, he wore a sand-colored leather shirt, a string tie with a turquoise pendant, and jeans. On his feet were Nike running shoes. His black hair was pulled back into a braid. With a touch of his hand, he discarded the eight of hearts. The machine replaced it with a two of diamonds. Again he crapped out.

Poe said, "Why'd you go for the three of a kind instead of the straight?"

"Odds are better."

"The idea is to beat the odds."

Y dropped another quarter into the machine. "The idea is to lose all my money, then pass out from too much alcohol."

"Ah . . ." Poe licked foam off his lips, stubbed out his cigarette. "To aid you with your goal, I'll buy you a beer."

Y didn't answer, steeped in indecision. He regarded the cards dealt to him on the monitor. Maybe Poe was right. Try to beat the odds. He'd try for the full house.

Poe frowned. "Go for the flush."

"Stop kibbitzing."

"I'm offering you sage advice."

Again, Y crapped out. He was about to drop in another quarter. Poe put his hand over the slot. The old man looked up. "What?"

"As long as I found you—"

"Found me? I was never lost."

"Can I ask you a question?"

"I can hear and play at the same time."

"What do you remember about the Bogeyman case?"

"Move your hand."

Poe took his hand away. Y dropped two bits into the machine. He said, "What specifically?"

"Everything."

Y tried for a flush. He wound up with a pair of aces. Still, it beat the machine's queen high. He said, "Everything's a tall order."

Poe sipped his beer. "How about this for starters. I remember rumors that the guy had taken trophies from his victim—"

"Victims. There were two of them."

Poe said, "Yeah, that was question number two. Why do I only remember one victim?"

"Because you were a kid and the second one wasn't publicized. A drifter girl. No roots here. The police were able to keep it quiet. They *needed* to keep it quiet. 'Cause the first one caused such a storm."

"Tell me about her . . . the first one."

"A local high school teacher with local ties. The papers got wind of it, turned it into a circus. The shit really hit the fan."

"How'd they tie the first and second victim to the same murderer?"

"How should I know? Do your homework. Go back and look in the police archives."

Y fished out another quarter. Poe put his hand around Y's bony fingers. "Could you stop one second?"

Y grunted, waited.

Poe said, "Do you recall something about . . . well, body parts?"

"You mean the eyes?"

"So the Bogeyman *had* removed her eyes."

Y didn't talk.

Poe said, "Yes? No?"

"You didn't ask me a question."

"Do you remember something about the Bogeyman removing the victim . . . victims' eyes?"

"There was talk."

"Do you know if it was true?"

Y stared at the younger man. "Why are you asking about the Bogeyman?"

"Similarities between it and this case I'm working on."

"So go back and check the records."

Poe nodded. "Did the Bogeyman ever have a name?"

"As far as I know, he was never caught."

"Did he have anything to do with the murder of Alison's mother?"

Y's eyes locked with Poe's. "Where'd you hear that?"

"Alison told me. She said that the police suspected her mother was the Bogeyman's victim. Because she was sliced up pretty bad."

Y continued to stare, his eyes cold and unforgiving. But Poe was not to be deterred. "You were close to the family. I thought you might know some inside information."

Y stubbed out his cold cigarette, lit another one. "You thought wrong, Sergeant."

"My mistake." Poe returned his glare with one of his own. "I'm just doing my job, old man."

"You're opening up wounds."

"Whose? Alison's or yours?" Poe leaned close to the old man. "Y, we both know the Bogeyman disappeared after Alison's mother committed suicide. Last night Alison told me that the suicide was suspect. It got me thinking. Especially after witnessing what I saw last night. You should see what this monster did to this poor girl. I want to find him.''

Y remained sour. "So why ask about the Bogeyman? You think he's returned after a twenty-five-year hiatus?"

Poe threw his head back. "Maybe."

Y inhaled his smoke, passed it to Poe. "So check the old records. Anything I'd remember is tainted with senility."

Poe took a drag on the cigarette, gave it back to Y. "I don't know about that. You're a sharp old coot." He snapped his fingers, then stopped. Studied the old man. "Are we related, Y?"

"Call me Dad."

"I'm serious."

"All Paiutes are spiritually related."

"I'm not going to get a straight answer out of you, am I?"

Y didn't respond.

"I've been thinking about doing a family tree," Poe said. "I don't think I'm going to find the Shoshones or the Southern Paiutes in the Mormon archives. Figured you're my best bet."

"You may be surprised. Mormons invaded our piece of the rock, lived on these fertile grounds at the same time we did. They taught us civilization. Meanwhile, the *marukats* reduced our thousand-year-old culture to a gift shop on Main Street."

"But you're not bitter, are you?"

The old man dropped another quarter into the machine. "Mormons and Paiutes had one thing in common."

"What?"

"Polygamy."

Poe smiled. "Guess pussy's the great equalizer."

Y managed to crack a begrudging smile. Then he turned serious. "You shouldn't be talking to Alison about her mother. She's delicate. Talking about the past sets her back."

Poe sighed. "Steve already lectured me."

"He's right."

"Are you staying here all night, Chief?"

"It's warmer than the streets."

"Want to crash at my place?"

Y considered the option. "But I haven't lost all my money yet."

"The machine'll still be here in the morning." Poe stood. "C'mon. We'll take a cab to my car." Y grumped as Poe helped him to his feet.

"Where do you get all your chump money, old man? I've never seen you do a day's work."

"Uncle Sam."

"That's right. You're a vet."

"I'm a Korean vet. Then I went and signed up for Nam. Which made me a Nam vet. I was a real warrior in my past."

"You're a real warrior now as far as I'm concerned."

"Then I get money for being an Indian or Native American or whatever shit they want to call us. Compensation for living in the wrong place at the wrong time." Y staggered and tripped, but regained his footing. "Yeah, I am a vet of foreign and *domestic* wars. Old Uncle Sam got his money's worth outta me. And now I'm gettin' my money's worth outta him. Do I have to sleep on the floor?"

"You can have the bed."

"Such genuine Christian charity."

"Call me Saint Romulus."

The phone was ringing as Poe crossed the threshold of his single-room clay house. Still cradling the old man, Poe turned on a battery-operated lamp, then picked up the receiver, tucked it under his chin while spitting out the grit of sand. "Yo?"

"Detective Sergeant Poe?"

An unfamiliar voice who knew his title. Not a good sign at one in the morning.

Poe closed the door with his foot. "This is he."

"Sergeant, this is Sergeant Willis Hollister up here in Reno."

"Oh boy." Y was getting leaden, his deep snoring interfering with Poe's hearing. "Could you please hold on a second?"

"No prob."

Poe settled Y onto the couch. He'd open it into the bed as soon as he'd dealt with this latest crisis. Because a call from Reno police always meant problems.

Into the phone, Poe said, "Is it my mother?"

"Yeah, that's exactly what it is."

"Where is she?"

"Unfortunately . . . at the moment, she's in jail."

"Oh my God."

"We tried to . . . avoid this inconvenience. In the past, your brother has always been cooperative in these kinds of situations. But we're unable to locate him at the moment."

Poe checked his watch. Sometimes when his brother had big assignments, he worked late. "Look, I'm going to make some calls. If you could stall the arraignment, I'm sure I can find someone to take her off your hands. Why clog up the courts—"

"It's gotta be soon, Sergeant. She's takin' up space and I gotta clear her from the books one way or the other."

"Give me your number, Sergeant Hollister. I can call back within fifteen minutes. Would that be okay?"

"I can give you fifteen minutes."

"Thanks. And if you're ever down this way—"

"When I go on vacation, I go fishing."

Hollister cut the line.

Frantically, Poe started dialing. His brother wasn't at work, he wasn't at home.

Shit, shit, shit!

Again, he checked his watch. Too late to catch a plane to Reno. And he really didn't feel like driving north. Even speeding it still meant hours of monotonous driving on winding roads. All this on little sleep.

He thought about Aunt Shirley, wondered if it would make matters worse. But with his brother absent, what choice did he have? He dialed her number. Luckily she picked up. Equally fortunate, she sounded reasonably sober.

"It's Romulus, Aunt Shir—"

"Romulus! How nice of you to call."

"Thank you very much." A beat. "I kind of need your help."

"Oh, what can I do for such a nice boy?"

"It's Mom."

"Now what has that woman gone and done this time?"

Nothing you haven't done yourself. Poe said, "I think she drank a little too much. I think that's the problem."

"So . . ."

Y snorted, rolled over, and tucked himself into the crevices of the sofa. Poe sniffed and winced. The old man was sweating alcohol.

He said, "Uh, Mom's at the police station. I was wondering if maybe you could get yourself a cab and pick her up. I'd pay for it, of course."

Shirley tsked and tsked. Then she hemmed and hawed, whiffled and waffled.

Poe added, "And of course, I'd compensate you for your time."

"Oh, Romulus. How *kind* of you. But you know I don't expect anything for helping out my own sister."

"Of course. Just a little something. I insist."

"Well, if you insist." A pause. "Where is your brother?"

An excellent *question.*

"He must be working on something very important. Uh, could you call the cab now, Aunt Shirley? Better yet, I'll do it for you."

"Oh, that would be sweet."

"My pleasure. Just . . . you know . . . you might have to pay something in cash for her release and sign some papers."

"Dear, I know the drill."

Despite his fatigue, Poe smiled. "Thank you, Aunt Shirley."

"You know, Romulus, I've been thinking about coming down and paying you a visit. My arthritis is acting up . . ."

Groan.

But Poe said, "Aunt Shirley, you're welcome anytime." His head was throbbing—jackhammers in his brain. "I'm going to call you that cab now. Good-bye, and thank you."

"Good-bye, Romulus. And tell the taxicab to give me a minute to get dressed."

"Sure." He hung up.

That was rich. One drunk looking after another. Still, what was the *worst*-case scenario? The two ladies would get pickled together, go out, cause a scene, and then both get arrested.

By then maybe it would be morning.

The howling of the coyotes aroused him. A commonplace sound but particularly fierce tonight. According to native legends, coyotes meant death. But coyotes had also honored man by stealing fire for him. So which kind of coyote was out tonight? Poe opened an eye, realized he was sleeping on the floor. He repositioned himself, his back aching, his head pounding. He glanced up.

From his perspective, it appeared that Y was gone.

Slowly standing erect, Poe rubbed his face, yawned, blinked several times. Moonlight streamed in from his bare windows, the rays sparkling with dust brought in by last night's wind.

Indeed the bed was unoccupied.

Poe picked up his pants, checked his wallet. Being a hopeless compulsive, he made it a habit to start each day with five twenties in his main billfold with a single hundred-dollar bill tucked into a credit card slot for whores or emergencies. He diligently stocked his wallet every night before he went to bed.

Sure enough, two twenties were missing. Shrugging it off, Poe went to his hidden cache of money, refilled his wallet. He plopped down into the fold-out bed, then bolted up.

The sheet and cover were drenched with the stink of sweat and booze. He stripped them off the couch, placed them in his overflowing perforated bag. No getting around it. Tomorrow morning, he'd be at the Laundromat, drinking his coffee while soaping his clothes.

He picked up his sleeping bag from the floor. Sinking onto the bare mattress, covering his head with his bag, shuddering as the coyotes sang their dirges. The Mojave Desert hosted many wildlife preserves. Often Poe had espied bobcats, wild horses, mule deer, and errant bighorn sheep. And wherever there were free-ranging animals, there were coyote. Judging from the feral whooping, whatever the scavengers had caught was cause for celebration.

A big haul: Poe hoped it wasn't a human one.

THIRTEEN

He arose just before dawn, stiff and cold. Poe put on a pair of slippers, turned on a battery flashlight, and carried it and a bottle of chemical solvent with him to the outhouse. Returning to his compound—an architectural composite of clay beehive and old shanty town—he swept the dirt floor, made the bed up with fresh sheets, then folded the ensemble back into couch form. He donned baggy sweats and took off for his morning run.

The sun had yet to break through a barrier of gray clouds, but the sky was endless. Not a hint of civilization as Poe jogged upon the desert floor, hugging the foothills of the Western mountain ranges. At these times, he realized why he put up with bare bones, trading in plumbing—even more desirable than electricity—for an outhouse. Yet, here he was at peace with nature as he raced in air filled with nothingness.

Arriving home sweaty and awake, he turned on a battery-operated TV, watching a staticky screen the size of a postage stamp. No new murders in Clark County, which was always a positive. In a backpack, he neatly packed his gun, a lunch of raw fruits and vegetables, and cold cuts kept fresh in a picnic cooler. He loaded the backpack and his laundry bag into his car. He planned on showering at the department's gym.

Once on the road, he dialed his brother's house in Reno on his cell phone. No answer.

Strange.

The next logical step would be to call up Aunt Shirley. But the day was too nice to be wrecked. If it was bad news, it'd keep. Instead, he punched in Rukmani's number. She picked up after the third ring; her voice was groggy. '' 'Lo.''

Poe said, ''Are we on for tonight?''

''Yes.'' Sounding furtive. ''I'll talk to you later.''

''Want to meet for breakfast?''

''Hold on.''

She sent him into an electronic void, clicked back on a moment later. She whispered, ''It'll take me about a half hour. I gotta clear house first.''

Oh. That!

From the beginning, Poe had known he wasn't the *only* one, just the *favorite* one. His own fault. She had extended an offer last night. And he had refused. Well, work had refused for him.

He said, ''I'll be at Beeny Boy's.''

''You're doing your laundry?''

''What else?''

''I'll see you in about thirty minutes.''

''I think it's fair to warn you that I haven't showered yet.''

She laughed. ''Romulus, I'm sure compared to the folks I work on, you'll smell like French perfume.''

Weinberg dug into his pastrami omelet, shoveled a forkful into his mouth. He studied the composite drawing made by the police artist. ''Mr. Bland White Guy.''

Patricia said, ''Young-looking, too. But Big Ray said his ID put him at thirty.''

''I've seen faces like this before,'' Jensen said. ''Guys with not much facial hair and kind of nondescript features. They age like old women. And they're hard to pick out in a crowd.''

Patricia said, ''At least we've got *something* to work with.''

''That's true.'' Weinberg put down the drawing. ''You did good, Deluca.'' He picked up a saltshaker, began to rain sodium onto his fat-laden omelet.

Jensen stared in wonderment. ''How do you eat like that and not come down with a coronary?''

''My cholesterol is one-seventy. Read it and weep, Jensen.''

Poe knocked on the doors of the locked restaurant. Myra scurried over, let him in. "You're a little late for eggs, but I can put some rye in the toaster."

"Thanks, but I had breakfast."

"Coffee?"

"You bet." Poe sat with the others, lifted the composite off the table. "Good going, Deluca."

She said, "I'm a credit to my profession."

Poe pondered the sketch. "Guy looks familiar, but I can't place him."

Jensen said, "My first impression, too. But the harder I tried to finger him, the more he slipped away."

"He's got a common face," Patricia said. "Not a bad-looking guy."

Jensen said, "He looks . . . I don't know . . . wimpy."

"I wouldn't call him *wimpy*—"

"Ordinary." Poe ran his finger through wet black hair. "It'll make him hard to find."

Jensen added, "Why the hat?"

"What do you mean?" Poe said.

"No one these days wears a felt hat except as part of a costume. I did that once for a Halloween party. Only time I ever remember wearing a hat."

Poe put the picture down. "But what if you were interested in either hiding or changing your appearance."

Weinberg raised his eyebrow, readjusted his yarmulke on his bald head. "I like that, Poe. Our man doffs the hat, it throws off our entire perception." Again, the lieutenant considered the face. "Know what I'm going to do? I'm going to have Mel redraw the guy without the hat. Also, I'll have him draw our guy with a mustache, figuring that he likes disguises."

The loo polished off his breakfast.

"Next step is legwork. Start showing the picture around the bars to see if we get any bites. Who's doing what today?"

"I've got a court case at twelve," Poe said. "After that, I'm back at the Laredo to see if Lewiston's secretary found the file on Brittany Newel."

Jensen said, "Parkerboy ain't gonna give you anything."

"Steve, he's got to give me something. Her employment taxes show that she worked for him. He can't explain them away."

"It still doesn't prove he knew her personally," Weinberg said.

"But it does prove she worked for him, even for a short period," Poe said. "After the Laredo, I'm free, Loo."

"So this is what we'll do," Weinberg said. "Patricia, you take the casino bars. Jensen, you take it to the bellboys and any other pimps." The lieutenant's eyes zeroed in on Poe. "What the hell got into you last night?"

"Pardon?"

"You going to Naked City without proper backup. That's not the way we operate around here."

"It worked out all right."

"Don't do it again." A beat. "You learn anything?"

"I located a pimp that Brittany once worked for. She stole from him. He said if he ever saw her again, he'd slit her throat."

Weinberg sat back in his chair. "He resemble our friend?"

"Not in the least. For starters, he was black."

"He could have hired out."

Poe shrugged. "I doubt if he thought she'd be worth the effort. Guy must have a stable of a dozen female flaggers."

Jensen said, "How much did Newel steal from him?"

"He didn't say. I don't even know if she took cash or rock. Just that she took something."

Myra came over with a pot of coffee, poured a cup for Poe. "Mickey, did you remember to order the extra chairs?"

"R and R Rentals," the lieutenant answered. "They assured me they'd be here by four."

"What a doll!" Myra said. "I've got a hundred and fifty people coming in tonight. Sam Silverman's eightieth birthday. For the last forty-five years, Sam's been celebrating his birthday in Vegas. Last year, his son turned very religious and started keeping kosher. Sam was distraught, thinking that his son wouldn't eat at his party. Then he discovered my place."

Her voice dropped to a whisper.

"He's paying me double what he paid the *trayf* place who hosted his party last year, that's how happy Sam Silverman was. Thank God for the Jewish born-agains. They pay the rent. How about some refills?"

Patricia put out her cup. She just loved coffee. It not only hyped her up, but had zero calories. "Thanks, Myra."

To Weinberg, Poe said, "You know, I'm going to be downtown anyway for court. Why don't I stop by Freemont and scan some mug books? See if I can't find a candidate that matches our composite. Also I could run the Newel case through the Crime Analysis hookup down there. See if it gives me any other recent cases.''

"Like what?'' Weinberg asked. "We haven't had a desert dump in over a year.''

Poe's brain worked frantically. "How about last February? The Filipina women we found in the plastic bags?''

Jensen said, "They were left in a truck-size communal waste container, buried under three feet of garbage. Rotting but otherwise intact.''

"Except for the gunshot wounds in their heads,'' Patricia added.

Jensen said, "Newel wasn't shot, she was ripped apart like an animal. She was also found in the open desert. I don't see any connection, Poe.''

"They were both body dumps.''

"All bodies gotta be dumped somewhere.''

"It's worth a shot,'' Poe insisted.

Weinberg said, "I haven't heard of any recent similiar case. But sure, try it out, Poe. As long as you don't waste time digging up bones that don't mean anything.''

Poe agreed.

A couple of hours in Records was all that he needed.

The Downtown Metro building wouldn't be winning any architectural awards, but Poe gave it an A for effort. It was an eight-story thing, shaped like a cylinder missing a wedge with its center hollowed out for a court-yard. The courtyard was floored with pavers and decorated with oversized concrete planters designed not only for interest, but also to prevent way-ward cars from smashing into the structure. The streetside perimeter wall was made from stone and adorned with a cryptic primitive mural of tile in primary colors. The courtyard exterior wall was a continuous sweep of glass windows and concrete balconies.

Police records were stored on the first floor next to the Traffic Division. Thousands upon thousands of case files arranged according to number. To look up the case required a trip to the card catalog, then an exhaustive search through shelves of folders. Poe knew right away that he'd hit blanks. The files started in the mid-1990s.

Which necessitated a trip to IAD. Like Homicide, IAD had its own separate building, which housed past files stored on microfiche. In the meantime, Poe did what he could at Metro.

Ambling up the stairs to the second floor. Most of Metro's detectives were housed here. Each detail had its own squad room. Ten detective quarters surrounded the interview rooms, which, like islands, sat in the middle of the floor. Spotting an empty Crime Analysis hookup in Fugitive turf, Poe pulled up a chair and entered the particulars of the Brittany Newel case.

Waited as the cursor blinked.

Over the next hour, the computer spit back twenty similars which had taken place in the last two years.

Serial killers who took body parts as trophies—lots of scalping.

Serial killers who gouged and mutilated.

Serial killers who cannibalized their victims.

Grisly stuff, but none screamed Newel's MO.

When the clock struck three, Poe had had enough. He logged off the computer, then took out the composite and scanned the recent mug books. Finding nothing applicable, he gave up, left Metro, and headed to Internal Affairs Division, arriving at the building five minutes later.

Clearing the reception room at IAD, he made his way to the bowels of Records, where he was blocked by the file clerk. A very efficient young lady who wore her hair in a bun. Her name plate read Madison.

"You haven't filled out the papers correctly."

Poe politely explained that he was not sure what case he was looking for, only that he'd know it when he saw it.

"Detective, you know and I know that you can't go browsing through files without authorization. It's a violation of civil rights—"

"A dead person has no civil rights." Poe kept his temper in check. "It's a twenty-five-year-old case. She isn't going to come back to sue."

The clerk frowned. "Do you at least have a year for the case?"

Poe rubbed his face. "Nineteen seventy-two or -three."

"I said a year. In the *singular*."

"I gave you a two-for-one. C'mon. Give me a break!"

Madison rolled her eyes—an old schoolmarm who didn't believe his excuse for not having his homework. "How long are you going to be?"

"Maybe an hour."

Madison motioned him inside the crypt.

Within fifteen minutes, Poe was alone with the films, cases flipping by with a flick of the wrist. He felt his heartbeat, heard his steady breathing; he was the only one in the room.

There was no Bogeyman case file: that was the sensationalized name invented by the media. He found only one twenty-five-year-old unsolved murder case that had all the elements.

Her name had been Janet Doward.

Y had told him she had been a schoolteacher. In fact, she had been a teacher's aide, only nineteen at the time of her demise. She had found her grave in a desert stretch off Spring Mountain Road . . . about a quarter-mile away from where Treasure Island now stood.

So close to the Strip. But back then there had been loads of empty lots and parcels. So much empty space. It was the Las Vegas Poe had loved, had tried to reinvent with his own measly piece of homestead perched in the middle of nowhere.

Reported missing. There had been search parties. A week later, the partially decomposed body had been discovered. Confirmation had been made by dental records.

The police crime photos.

Enough to make a vegetarian out of the most dedicated of carnivores. Between the deep slashes and the blowflies, there hadn't been much flesh left to work on. What wasn't rotting had been baked into sun-dried tomato texture, on its way toward mummification.

Autopsy indicated that she had been hacked by something with a serrated edge. The skin had been ripped and torn. Doward's eyes had remained with the body, but had been pulled from their sockets. Poe stared at the black spaces heavily infested with white maggots.

Taking notes as he bounced in his chair, his legs shaking, his foot tapping loudly. He tried to steady his limbs, but was unable to stop the palsied activity.

He read on.

The corpse had been damaged by animal scavenging. Bite marks in the buttocks and thighs.

He looked away, covered his face. He forced himself to take a deep breath, then let it out slowly. A few more breaths.

Stop tapping your foot, Rom.

His fingertips making contact with one another.

And don't snap!

He had seen dozens of dead bodies. Why was this murder affecting him so much?

Think about the case.

Similarities:

    1. Desert dump.

    2. Torn flesh.

3. Eye involvement.

4. Possibly both were victims of scavenging activity.

Differences:

1. No knife marks on Brittany.

2. No bite marks on Brittany.

Body fluid analysis:

Stagnant blood taken from the aorta and saphenous vein.

BAL 0.005.

Oral swab.

Nasal swab.

Vaginal swab.

Anal swab.

Some evidence of sexual activity. How long ago was anyone's guess. Results likely tainted because of the advanced state of decomposition.

Fingernail and toenail swab: microscopic findings of hair, blood, skin, and dirt.

He rubbed his eyes, took more notes. Poring over the minutiae. When he checked his watch, he found he had been sitting at the machine for over an hour. Madison was bound to be checking up any moment. Time pressing him, he forced himself to move on to the Bogeyman's other victim. Y had said she had been a runaway.

Poe began searching the files, flipped and searched and flipped and searched.

Cases passing by as quickly as the seconds.

But nothing about a murdered runaway in the same time frame.

Blinking hard, Poe turned the wheel backward. How could he have missed it? Another file had to be in there somewhere. Y had said that there had been two victims.

He scanned as quickly as he could.

The only reference he found was something that had occurred a full year *after* Janet Doward's murder—a year and a month, to be exact.

A Jane Doe around sixteen years old. A desert dump. A couple of postmortem snapshots. Her throat had been slit. And her eyes had been gouged.

Footsteps. Madison was on the warpath.

Poe quickly scribbled down the evidence.

Similarities:

1. Both desert dumps.

2. Both eye involvements.

Differences:

1. No signs of scavenging.
2. No bite marks.
3. Slit throat (Brittany's throat not slit).
4. More than a year apart.

Body fluids:

BAL .12—she was probably drunk.

Oral swab, nasal swab.

Vaginal and anal swab: positive for semen.

Fingernail and toenail swab: hair, blood, skin, grass, sand, and dirt.

He heard Madison calling his name.

"Coming!" Poe gathered up his notes. He could reconcile the forensic differences, because there were still lots of similarities. What he couldn't reconcile was the passage of time between the two dates.

But Y had said that there had been two victims.

Poe paused.

Unless Y was lying.

Always a distinct possibility.

FOURTEEN

Shutting the door to his house, Poe jumped when he saw the giant on his couch, the cushion flattened under his weight. A carpet bag was at his side.

The big man stood.

Four feet worth of legs made of thick and heavy bone. Apelike arms emanating from a dense torso. Baseball-mitt hands attached to ham-hock forearms. A muscular bull neck. The prognathous jaw jutted out from the face, slightly agape and askew like a door dangling on one of its hinges. Deep-set, angry black eyes made piggishly small by an oversized, protruding forehead. Thick, straight black hair combed off the brow. He wore his usual black suit over a white shirt. No tie. His shoes were as big as rowboats. He licked his rubbery lips.

"Hello, Rom."

The voice was nasal and deep and flooded with fury. Poe's speech faltered. He started snapping his fingers, then choked out, "I've been calling your number all night."

"I don't doubt it. You're snapping."

Immediately Poe stuck his hands in his pockets. "Something to drink, Remus? A beer maybe?"

"I'm fine."

"Take one anyway." Poe pointed to the couch. "Have a seat."

Remus sat.

Poe closed his eyes, opened them. Went to his picnic cooler and no-ticed his hands were shaking. He took a deep breath. Remus always had that initial effect on him. Because of his girth and elephantine features, Remus had that initial effect on everyone.

Remus.

His brother.

His twin.

His *identical* twin, up until the age of ten. Poe supposed they were still identical genetically, because they were hatched from the same egg. But the word *identical* was hardly applicable anymore.

They had been tiny boys. Tiny, tiny boys, Poe being about an inch taller than his brother, but still not tall enough to make a percentage scale. Their mother had taken them from expert to expert, and all of them had suggested growth hormones. But Mom had been reluctant. The doctors had tried to reason with her. The boys were trailing in growth, and their bone plates were beginning to close, indicating that their final height wasn't far off. If the doctors didn't intervene soon, all would be lost.

Even after Mom agreed, she had remained cautious.

Do it one at a time.

They had started with Remus, because he had been the smaller of the two. Treatments began. Immediately they had sent the child's pituitary into overdrive. Remus grew at an alarming rate. His bones seemed to elongate overnight, causing him months of severe skeletal aches and blinding headaches. After six months, they stopped the shots.

But Remus had fooled them all and kept growing. At eleven, he had become an acromegalic giant.

The disparity in their heights had given both brothers long hours of sleeplessness and nightmares. As midgets, they had been objects of de-rision. With Remus's newfound stature, they had graduated to pariahs. No one had dared to taunt them, as Remus had finished off many a bigmouth with one well-placed punch. But no one had dared to converse with them, either.

Being anxious, compulsive, and wee-bit, Poe had found solace in a multitude of tics. He began to drum his fingers endlessly; he developed a stutter. Drawn together by their freakishness, the brothers became close. Slowly, they developed a cast of misfit friends, somehow plodding through the agonizing teen years.

Rom had found himself in an odd position, secretly envying his gigantic brother. Yes, Remus was ugly and weird, but at least he was *tall.* Relentlessly, he begged his mother for hormone treatments.

His biggest ally turned out to be his brother.

They goofed with me, Remus had bellowed to his mother. *They'll get it right with Rom. You can't let him stay like that. He's worse than I am.*

Shell-shocked, his mother broke down and began an arduous search for a doctor whom she could trust. In the meantime, Poe's plates were inching toward the finish line. Finally, Mom found someone acceptable as Poe's paltry height nosed upward at a terrifyingly slow rate.

At seventeen, Rom had reached his adult height. Fitted for his high school cap and gown, he had measured out at five-seven and a quarter, grateful for every millimeter. He had his brother to thank.

Steadying his hands, Poe carried over a couple of glasses of beer. "It must be serious."

Remus downed the suds in a single gulp. "I need you to take Mom."

Calm. Poe said, "For how long?"

"Forever."

Dread shot through Poe's veins. "You can't be serious—"

"I'm very serious."

Poe started to pace. "Remus, *look* at this place. I can't put up a dog, let alone a person. I've got no plumbing, I've got no electricity—"

"So move into a normal apart—"

"Remus—"

"Rom, being a hermit doesn't relieve you of your responsibilities, any more than being a freak relieved me of mine!"

Poe said nothing, his mind a scrambled mess.

Remus said, "I've had her for the past fifteen years. Now it's your turn. Even geeks have a life."

Poe tried to talk, but words lodged in his throat. His heart hammered like a steam drill. *Try empathy. Calm him down.* "I can see that you're . . . stressed. And I know you've done all the work. So . . . you have a right to make some demands."

Remus waited. Poe's brain was racing. "I know you don't want to hear this, but—"

"Then don't say it."

"Remus, Mom is really too much for either of us. There are lots of nice communities—"

"No."

"—who specialize—"

"Out of the question."

"She'd make lots of friends—"

Remus bellowed, "You will *not* put her in a home."

"Rem—"

"Farm her out like some broken animal."

"Can you just hear me out?"

"I don't want to hear you out!" Remus pointed an irate finger in his brother's chest. "This is the situation. She is your mother. She is my mother. You left fifteen years ago without a thought to *me* or *her*. Without complaint, I've shouldered the responsibility. Well, now I've got plans, Rom. Big plans. So guess what?"

Poe bounced on his feet, suddenly curious. "What kind of plans?"

"Stop changing the subject."

"Excuse me, bud. You barge in and expect me to make major life decisions in five minutes—"

"That's exactly what you did to me when you packed your bags and left fifteen years ago."

"I've filled in whenever you needed. I've taken her for weekends, I've taken her on vacations—"

"You want a medal, Rom?"

"No, but a little consideration might be nice. Give me a moment to digest what you're asking me."

"Bro, you can have a whole three weeks. Because that's when I'm moving her down."

Poe was shouting. "Remus, you can't spring this on me!"

Remus picked up his carpet bag and headed for the door. "I'll see you later."

Poe blocked the doorway—a showy gesture, but a futile one. If he wanted, Remus could swat him away like a gnat. Instead, the giant waited.

Poe said, "Don't leave. This isn't . . . can we talk about this rationally?"

Remus didn't move.

Remember the police training, Detective. Domestic disturbances? Diffuse! Placate!

Poe spoke quickly. "I can hear the desperation in your voice. Bring her down."

Remus's massive jaw fell open. He snapped it shut. "You're serious?"

"Yes. But if she is under my care, I'm going to do it my way."

"Meaning?"

Poe started snapping. "I can't live with her, Remus. I know you have, and I admire your filial devotion, but I'm not that noble. I cannot live with Mom—"

"That's unacceptable."

"I'll set her up in a nearby apartment."

"She needs *care*."

"I'll hire a nurse."

"Putting her out to pasture," Remus spat out.

"I promise I'll visit her every day."

"You're full of shit, Rom."

Poe rubbed his face. "You've got to compromise, bro."

The minutes passed.

Finally, Remus said, "Okay, here's the deal. You say you can't live with her. Believe it or not, I understand." A pause. "She's getting worse, Rom. Sneaking out at all hours of the night. It's bad. She needs constant watching. So you'll need to hire someone who can deal with that."

"I'll start looking right away."

Silence.

Poe asked, "Where is she now?"

"I've got someone guarding both her *and* Aunt Shirley."

Poe started panicking. "I don't have to deal with Shirley, do I?"

"No, I'll keep an eye on Shirley. She's not as bad as Mom . . . yet."

Poe felt suddenly ashamed. "Remus, I appreciate what you've done all these years. I know it's been hell."

Remus looked away. He said, "Okay. Set her up in an apartment. But here are *my* conditions. Are you listening?"

"Go on."

Remus got up, started pacing. "Every morning, go have coffee with her. Make her eggs and cereal. And don't leave until she finishes eating. Also, you're going to have to routinely check the apartment for booze and cigarettes. She sneaks in contraband. And it's not enough to tell the help about it. She bribes them not to tell."

"She has free cash to bribe help?"

"Yeah, she gets a small stipend from some government agency."

"Welfare?"

"No, I don't think so." Remus stopped walking. "Probably has something to do with her Native-American background, living here in the sixties. It's not much, but it's enough cash to buy cheap booze. Just take the bottles away. I don't care what you do with it as long as she doesn't have it.''

''All right. What else?''

''You've got to eat dinner with her. I'm not saying you have to *eat* with her, but you make sure she eats. She forgets to eat, Rom. If she doesn't eat, she gets sick the next day.''

''What about lunch?'' Poe asked.

''Make her a tuna sandwich and put it in the refrigerator. Tell the nurse to watch Mom eat it. After she eats lunch, she usually watches her soaps. Then she takes a nap. When she wakes up, the nurse usually bathes her. After her bath, she likes to take a walk. When she's finished with her walk, it's close to dinnertime. I usually try to be home by then . . . watch her eat. I go back to the office around seven . . . eight. By then, she's pretty tired. She's been very tired lately.''

Poe felt a crashing headache. ''Why's that?''

''Who knows? She's not a well woman.''

''She's never had a surfeit of energy.'' Poe blinked several times. ''Anything more?''

''That's it.'' Remus paused. ''If you can do that . . . for let's say . . . a year. Take her for a year. Then I'll come back and take her off your hands.''

A year?

Shut up, Poe. At least it's time-limited.

Instead, he blurted out, ''From 'taking her forever' to 'taking her for a year'?''

''Are you complaining?''

''Of course not.'' Poe realized they were both still standing. ''C'mon, bro. Sit down.''

Remus went back to the couch, rubbed his eyes. ''I'll have another beer if you've got it.''

''You bet. Are you going to spend the night here?''

''I've been comped at Buckingham Palace.''

Poe's eyebrows rose as he went to his cooler. ''What's the occasion? Doing some work for the Sultan?''

''As a matter of fact, I am.''

Poe stopped in his tracks. *''What?''*

''Sit down first.''

Poe brought over the beers and sat. ''Go on.''

Remus said, "You know he's just completed a new casino—Palace North—in Tahoe."

"Yes."

"His highness has a home on the Nevada side. Now he wants a home on the California side. Something very private and hidden. He talked to some of us local guys up in Reno. He talked to me. Next thing I knew, he handed me a check—a quarter million advance for the plans."

Poe spit out his beer.

Remus said, "For my architectural fee, he agreed to ten percent of the building cost."

Poe stuttered, "Wh . . . wh . . ." He coughed, then swallowed. "What's the proposed cost?"

Remus stifled a smile. "Around fifteen, twenty mil—"

"Holy fucking *cow*!"

"The Sultan is a perfectionist," Remus said gravely. "I'm on call twenty-four hours a day."

"Hence the reason you're here," Poe said. "When did all this happen?"

"About four, five months ago."

"And you didn't say a thing to me." Poe broke into a grin. "You son of a bitch!"

Slowly, Remus smiled back. "The Sultan's a very short man, Romulus. I think he hired me because this way he can push around a very tall man."

Poe slapped his brother's steel-plated back. "Man, that is just terrific, Remus. I am so *proud* of you!"

"It's not a done deal yet."

"Hey, if he fired you tomorrow, you'd still walk away with a quarter million dollars." Poe beamed like a new father. "You want to go out for dinner, or— Shit, I promised Rukmani I'd take her out. You can come with us if you want. Maybe we can take in Richard Jenni. I know you like him, and he's in town."

"Thanks, but I've got a business meeting tonight." Remus took out a handkerchief, wiped his sweaty brow. "Tomorrow I have meetings all morning. I'm out on a one-fifteen plane. We could meet for lunch around eleven if you want."

"Name it and claim it."

"Anywhere as long as it's *not* on the Strip."

The only place Poe could come up with was Myra's.

Remus stood. "I'll call you in a couple of weeks . . . so we can arrange the move." A beat. "You're not going to change your mind on me?"

"No."

"No sudden vacations?"

Poe said, "I said I'll do it, I'll do it."

Remus shook his brother's hand, held it longer than necessary. "I'll see you tomorrow at eleven."

"I'll be there."

The two men paused, then hugged good-bye.

The winds had kicked up, howling and ululating like caged demons, smashing sand and grit against the windows. They woke Poe from a dead sleep, sending an icy chill through his veins. He tried not to fidget, not to toss. His eyes skittered about the dark room like crap dice across the felt, landing on Rukmani. She was out to the world, curled up under her blanket in silent sleep.

Taking carefully measured steps, Poe nudged out of bed, slipped on his pants and shirt. Tiptoeing into the kitchen, he opened her fridge, poured himself a glass of orange juice, envying her appliances. He shivered as he drank, his mind still buzzing from his earlier encounter with his brother.

As if he didn't have enough on his mind without Mom. Ah well, he'd hire good help. Money wasn't a big problem. And if he ran short, Remus would kick in whatever was required.

It wouldn't hurt him to extend himself a bit. She was his mother, she hadn't had an easy life. Secretly, Poe was hoping that the indentured servitude might help assuage deep-harbored guilt for dumping her on Remus all these years.

Then again, what kind of life did his brother have? He never dated, never had any outside hobbies, never even seemed to want to acquire any. For him, it had always been work and Mother. Poe had always felt that Remus had used Mom to rationalize his isolation. Maybe being away from her, Remus would develop himself, even make a couple of friends. Poe hoped so. He liked his brother. Residing alone was fine, even desirable. But living alone was a curse.

The wind slapped against the window, making him jump. He wondered how Rukmani slept through it, though she had to be used to the noise by now. The luck of the draw, just the way her apartment was situated. Never a good thing to live downwind from the desert.

FIFTEEN

The giant said he'd take a cup of coffee while he waited. He kept checking his watch every thirty seconds. Myra brought back a fresh pot, asked him how he was enjoying his stay. He said he'd been brought up in this town, that he had never liked it much. He was here on business. At the moment, he was waiting for his brother.

When an out-of-breath Poe sat down at the table, Myra almost overfilled the giant's cup.

"Sorry I'm late." Poe was panting. "My car wouldn't start. I called the hotel, but you had left."

Giant's facial reactions were slow. But Myra thought that he looked appeased. She asked, "Where is it now, Rom?"

"At the Bureau." Poe took a sip from Giant's coffee cup. "Myra, this is my twin brother, Remus."

His *twin* brother? Rom was on the smallish side; Giant probably cleared a seven-foot marker. Why was Poe pulling her leg? She said, "Nice to meet you."

"Likewise."

Poe said, "This woman makes the best food in town."

Myra smiled, desperately trying to note a family resemblance. "What can I get you, Romu—Romulus, Remus." She laughed. "That's kind of cute."

No one spoke.

Myra blushed. "I guess you got a lot of that as kids. I'm sorry. I didn't mean—"

"It's nothing," Poe said quickly. "It was during my mother's Roman mythology stage. I think at that time she had changed her name to Vesta. How was the party last night?"

Myra brightened. "It went off without a hitch."

"That's great."

"What can I get you, boys?"

Remus brayed laughter. "A long time since I've been called a boy."

Poe smiled, "How about a corned beef sandwich?"

"And for you, Mr. Remus Poe?" Myra said.

"Turkey on rye. Mustard, no mayo." Again, Remus smiled. "Nice place you have here."

Myra blushed again, touched the giant's shoulder. "Thank you. I'll be right back."

When she was gone, Remus said, "That's your boss's wife?"

Poe nodded.

"She seems nice."

"She's lovely. The loo is a lucky man. You've met Weinberg, haven't you?"

"Maybe around ten years ago."

Poe said, "Sorry about being late. How much time do you have left?"

"Actually, I'm okay. I'm taking a later flight out, because I've left some unfinished business. So we're fine." Remus watched his brother drink up his coffee. His hands were shaking. "This whole thing with Mother, Rom. Is it coming at a bad time for you?"

Poe looked up, surprised by his brother's acuity. "No, it's fine."

"What are you working on these days?"

Poe pointed a finger at his chest. "Me?"

"Who else would I be talking to?"

"Murder. What else?" Poe put down the cup, called out to Myra, "Another coffee when you get a chance." He rubbed his arms. "Man, some storm last night."

"The wind howled bloody murder up on the top floors." Remus frowned. "I hate this town. Why you moved back still mystifies me. Especially after what it did to us."

"Reno wasn't for me."

"You didn't give it a fair shake."

"That's true."

Remus thought: *You did it for Alison, and she dumped you anyway.*

Poe continued, "No, Las Vegas wasn't great to either of us. But I've come to terms with it."

Myra brought the coffee and sandwiches. "Anything else?"

"No, thanks," Poe said.

Myra smiled, poured the coffee, and left. Remus finished off half his sandwich in three bites. "What's bothering you, Rom? Is it Mom?"

"It has nothing to do with Mom."

Well, maybe a little.

Remus said, "Then what is it?"

Useless to lie to him. Remus could X-ray his soul. Poe said, "Do you remember the Bogeyman? It was a murder case that happened when we were around ten."

"Of course I remember it," Remus said. "Why?"

Poe noticed his brother had paled. X-raying souls ran both ways. He said, "It's very similar to a case I'm working on. Why are you reacting so strongly?"

"I'm not."

"Yes, you are."

Remus finished his sandwich, drank coffee, then put down the cup. "What do *you* remember about the case?"

"Just that it scared the shit out of me."

"Anything else?"

"I recall something about the murderer taking out the eyes of his victim. Yesterday I went over old records, found what I thought was the actual Bogeyman case. Or rather, *one* of his cases. You know, I spoke to Y about it. He told me there were *two* cases. But I couldn't find a matched set in the same time frame. All I could find were two desert dumps a year apart. Either I missed something in the files or Y was lying to me. And if he was, why would he do that?"

"Y was right. There were two women, Romulus. Both were murdered around the same time. Whether by the same man or not . . . who knows?"

Poe stared at his brother. "You actually *remember* that?"

"Distinctly."

"I'm impressed."

"You shouldn't be. The Bogeyman case made a big impact on me. It happened right around the time I was finishing with my shots. Maybe they had even taken me off treatment. But I was still in a lot of pain and

I was still missing a lot of school. To take my mind off the boredom and agony, I read everything I could get my hands on, including the local throwaway papers, which carried the police blotters. Crime interested me. I think it gave me perspective. That there were actually people worse off than I was.''

Poe said, ''I can't believe you remember that far back. And so *clearly.*''

''It's not remarkable.'' Remus picked up his half of his brother's corned beef sandwich. He took a big bite. ''Not remarkable at all, considering at one point the police thought I was the Bogeyman.''

''Wh . . . ?'' Poe's hands started to shake . . . remembering words from ghosts past. Kids taunting in singsong voices: *Your brother is the* Bogeyman! *Your brother is the* Bogeyman! Poe's mind . . . one gigantic mass of repressed brain cells. He choked out, ''Wh . . . what are you talking about?''

The big man looked down. ''Police had sent a couple of detectives over to our house to talk to me. Apparently, some of our classmates had reported me to them. They said I had changed into some kind of a monster . . . which I suppose was true.''

Poe flushed with rage. ''They were all *assholes!*''

''I suppose I had been acting *scary* lately. I did break more than a few bones.''

''The fights were always provoked.''

''The police didn't see it that way. They came over, started questioning Mom and me. Grilling us, actually. She tried to explain that hormones had been doing stuff to my system. But that only added to their suspicions. That the chemicals must have been driving me to do these . . . acts of terror. Because what the police saw was this grotesque, hulking kid with lots of unexplained absences—''

''Questioning a child like that is grotesque.'' Poe thought of the police, how they had barged in on Alison and him. *She should have sued.* Out loud, he said, ''We should have sued.''

''Funny you should mention that. They wanted us to come to the station house. At that point, Mom said she was calling her lawyer.''

''What lawyer? Mom didn't have a lawyer.''

''Maybe she said *a* lawyer instead of *her* lawyer. Anyway, she *did* threaten to sue them.'' Remus actually smiled. ''Rom, she was marvelous. She started spouting off legal cases like Clarence Darrow—instance after instance in which people had sued the government and had received millions in damages.''

''*Mom?* Where'd she come up with the knowledge?''

''Beats me.'' Again, Remus laughed. It came out as ox bellows. ''I think she made it up as she went along. But it worked. She scared them off and they never bothered me again.'' A beat. ''Of course, it helped that the murders suddenly stopped.''

''I never knew.''

''We didn't tell you. You had your own problems. Besides, both of us were too ashamed.'' Remus finished his brother's sandwich. ''I've eaten your lunch.''

Poe signaled for two more sandwiches.

Remus said, ''Getting back to the original question . . . the two cases. I don't remember too much about either murder. I do recall something about the eyes.''

''So I wasn't crazy. You do remember that.''

''Yes, I do.''

Poe sighed. ''Like I said, I only found the one murder file on microfiche in that year. Janet Doward. The only other file I found which halfway matches Doward was dated a full year later.''

''Files can be conveniently misplaced, dates can be changed.''

''Remus, the victim was a runaway without connections. A nobody. Why would anyone bother to misplace or misdate her file?''

''Could be her killer was a somebody.''

''Rom, tele—''

Poe screeched, jumped up. Myra had been standing behind him. She was holding a cordless phone. ''Sorry. I didn't mean to sneak up on you.''

Poe smiled weakly. ''I startle when I'm concentrating.''

''Mickey's on-line for you.'' She handed him the phone. ''Just push the red button.''

Poe punched the talk dot. The receiver immediately filled with static. He shouted, ''Yes, Loo.''

''Myra says your brother's in town,'' Weinberg yelled.

''Yes, sir.''

''How long is he staying?''

''He's leaving this afternoon.''

Weinberg said, ''Then it's too bad I've got to interrupt you. Another dump right off Red Rock.''

"Christ!"

"Not like the first. A clean kill. Still, you'd better come down." Weinberg gave him directions.

Poe said, "I'm on my way."

"Say hi to your brother for me." Weinberg cut the line.

Remus said, "Bad news?"

Poe said, "Bad for me, worse for the victim."

Remus sighed a gust of wind. "Rom, if Mom is too much—"

"Actually, at this point, I think Mom will be a nice diversion." Poe stood. "I've got to go."

"How are you going?" Remus asked. "I thought you didn't have a car."

"Oh *shit!*"

Remus gave him the keys to his rental. "I'll grab a cab. Just take it back for me."

Poe hefted the keys. "Thanks. Really. Thanks a lot."

"Take care of yourself, Rom." Remus stood, grabbed his brother, enveloping him in a bear hug that nearly broke Poe's ribs. For the sake of fraternal love, Poe put up with being squashed. In some primordial way, it felt comforting.

The area had been roped off, a yellow ribbon waving in the leftover breeze. The meat wagon was there; so were the techs. Everyone wearing sunglasses, the campsite looked like a cataract convention. Sand stirred about the desert floor, swirling like a scarf. Poe kept his brother's rental roadside, parked and walked a hundred feet, over to the center of action.

When he saw the pink hair, he felt his stomach bolt.

She had been tossed carelessly—a marionette with broken strings, whitish pipestem limbs. So frail . . . just as he had remembered her. It broke his heart. She wore an iridescent green miniskirt. She was nude from the waist up.

No rake marks.

She was covered with sand—in her face, eyes, nose, and ears. A vivid knife swipe ran across the girl's windpipe. He felt his breath quicken. "I just saw her a couple of nights ago at Naked City. She was a flagger for Brittany Newel's pimp."

"Christ!" Jensen said. "You're sure it's the same—"

"Positive. Same face, same dress . . . and that hair. . . ."

Secretly, Jensen was relieved. *Poe* was connected to *this* one. Plus, he was sure he hadn't slept with her.

Weinberg said, "Do you remember the pimp, Rom?"

"Absolutely."

"Well enough for a composite?"

"Yes."

The lieutenant said, "This certainly sheds a different light on everything—a common link between this murder and Brittany Newel. Did Newel have any African-American evidence transfer on her, Poe?"

"None that I can recall. I'll check."

Weinberg wiped grit from his eyes, stuck his hands in his pockets. "Okay. This is what we'll do. Deluca and Jensen will finish up here. Keep an eye out for the examiner while you comb the area for evidence."

The two detectives nodded in unison.

"Rom, you get yourself some backup and go to Naked City," Weinberg went on. "See if you can find the pimp. If he's not there, find out where he went. If you have to, use some spinach to get the residents gabby."

"Fine."

"If you can't find the pimp, go downtown and talk to Mel. If you can't find Mel, Cindy can help you out using the computer's Draw-a-Face."

"I'll also look through the mug books," Poe said. "Find out if he's been bad before . . . well, we know he's been bad. See if he was ever arrested locally."

Patricia hadn't taken her eyes off the body. She couldn't believe how happy she had been with Nate. Now the glow of yesterday's evening had turned arid as the sand in her shoes. "She was *so* young."

"A child." Poe swallowed. "I almost ran her in. I . . . should have."

Weinberg said, "The murder happened last night, Poe, not two nights ago when you saw her. And even if you had arrested her, she would have been out within hours. Open prey. Which was obviously the case."

Poe nodded solemnly.

Weinberg had spoken the truth. The loo was also trying to make him feel better. Still, his words rang hollow.

SIXTEEN

"That's him!" Poe jabbed his finger at a mug shot. "Or technically, that's *he*."

"You're sure?" Patricia said.

"Positive. Just give him a goatee." Poe picked up a pencil, drew fine lines around the chin. He regarded his handiwork. "That's my guy." He read: "Ali Abdul Williams. Booked for aggravated assault a year and a half ago in June."

He shut the mug book with a thump.

"Okay, let's run him through the network. See if he has a local address, a local phone number, any local relatives. Find out who his associates are. I'll talk to Weinberg about getting a warrant for his arrest and a search warrant for his apartment."

"Will do."

"For sake of closure, we should find out if he did time. And if he did, who his parole officer is. If he's still on parole, we can arrest him for parole violation."

A pause.

"I was *that* close, Patricia." Poe measured off a small distance between his thumb and index finger. "Pisses me off." He exhaled. "Even if Williams didn't do Brittany, I should have nabbed him while I had the chance. Locked him up before he did the kid Jane Doe. Do we have a name for her yet?''

Patricia shook her head no. ''Sir, you can't arrest someone proactively—''

''Due process sucks!''

Patricia said, ''This pimp Williams . . . he knew you were a cop, right?''

''Yeah, I told him I was a cop.''

''And then—after you told him you were a cop—he says to you that he'll slice Brittany Newel's throat if he ever sees her again. Correct?''

''Go on.''

''Then Williams offers you the kid Jane Doe.'' She tried to organize her ideas. ''Like he made *sure* that you *saw* her.''

''More like he was trying to get some money out of me.''

Patricia continued her train of thought. ''Next thing, Kid Jane Doe shows up dead, murdered, with her throat cut. Leaving us to think that Williams did it. Now is the guy *that* stupid or are we missing something?''

Poe clasped his hands tightly so he wouldn't snap. ''Most criminals are very stupid.''

Patricia was silent.

Poe said, ''Are the two murders related? I don't know. What do we know?'' He ticked off his fingers. ''Both were desert dumps, left in the same vicinity. Both were associated with Ali Abdul Williams—''

''But they died in very different ways.''

''Meaning?''

''I'm thinking that maybe someone is trying to link the two murders to throw us off track. We're out looking for Williams, but meanwhile the *real* murderer is getting away.''

Poe wrinkled his nose.

''I'm just throwing out ideas.''

Poe paused. ''I see your point. But you're getting ahead of yourself. First, let's find Williams. Then when we find him, we can ask him these questions ourselves. By the way, where's Jensen?''

''Alison wasn't feeling well. He knocked off early to be with her. You want me to page him?''

''No, it's not an emergency.'' Poe took out his notebook. ''Okay. You run Williams through the network, I'll go back and look over Newel's file. See if some prints or latents were lifted from the scene. Now that we have a suspect, we can run the prints through the computer to see if they match up with Williams. Sure be nice to get a positive. It would buttress our case when we question him.''

''If we find him.''

''We'll find him. They never run very far.''

''Unless he's dead,'' Patricia said. ''Although I suppose even then he's likely to surface. Just not in a usable form.''

Rukmani spoke from behind a surgical mask, looked down at the dissected young body lying on the cold metal slab. ''From her teeth and bones, I'd say she was around fourteen. Her twelve-year molars are erupted, but the crown hasn't nearly cleared the surrounding gingiva . . . even on the mesial side. Here, take a look.''

Poe held out his hand. ''I believe you.''

''You're suddenly so squeamish.''

''No, I'm not squeamish. Nor am I ghoulish.''

Rukmani smiled beneath her mask. ''I took some radiographs of her maxillary teeth *in situ*. Her wisdom teeth aren't fully formed . . . no signs of root formation, which is consistent with a person under sixteen. I'll shoot the mandible once I've disarticulated it from the body.''

Poe raked his hair with gloved hands. ''How long had she been lying out there?''

''She was past rigor . . . lividity had set in. At least twenty-four hours, but probably not longer than forty-eight. I found some eggs but no maggots.''

''But she could have been murdered as far back as two nights ago?''

''Possibly.''

Two nights ago. Right after he had visited Naked City. His heart sank. He should have run her in. Instead, he had played nursemaid to Y. What a weird night that had been. The piercing coyote howls that had awakened him. Y abuptly disappearing. Poe said, ''Was she raped?''

''She had sex before she was murdered. Consensual?'' She shrugged. ''Is prostitution ever consensual sex? She had her appendix taken out, by the way.''

''Is that significant?''

''Just that the surgery was done well. No back-door butcher job. At one point, someone cared.''

Rukmani draped a tarp over the body, dropped the mask from her face.

She adjusted her glasses, picked up a Styrofoam cup of coffee, and drank. The amphitheater lights gave her hair a polished sheen. "Have you had a chance to look at apartments for your mom?"

"I've got a couple of appointments tomorrow. How can you drink coffee in here?"

"Gotta keep the fluids up. What have you found?"

"I found a great place about two blocks away from you."

"How convenient."

"I'm telling you, Ruki, because if you think it might be a problem—"

"You mean I might take exception to your mother calling me up at all hours, talking about her lumbago? That's what she did the last time she was here. And we'd only known each other for a week."

"What is lumbago, anyway?"

"Rheumatoid arthritis." Rukmani wiped sweat from her forehead with her elbow. "She really does have it bad, poor thing. I like your mother, even though she calls me 'that sweet little Indian girl.' "

"My mother's American Indian. She's giving you a compliment." He paused. "I shouldn't be dragging you into my mess."

Rukmani would have tousled Poe's hair, but she was wearing gloves. "I know this isn't easy for you, Poe. Anything I can do to help."

Poe nodded. "Thanks."

She wrapped her face mask over her nose and mouth, then uncovered the body. Eyes directed downward, she said, "I had a chance to look at one of her fingernail scrapings. She fought like a tiger, Rom. I got some good skin samples. You should be looking for someone with lots of scratches."

Skin samples. Poe said, "Could you tell if the skin was black or white?"

"Caucasian."

Poe tried not to register disappointment. "Do you remember if there were scrapings under Brittany Newel's nails?"

"Yep, there were. But not like this one."

"What kind of skin?"

"Also Caucasian."

Poe snapped his fingers. Caucasian skin clouded Ali Abdul Williams as the murderer of either girl. But that didn't rule him out as an accomplice. He was a connection between the two girls and needed to be found. "Anything else?"

"If I were the betting type, I'd say the crime happened outdoors. Her nails were filled with dirt, sand, and grass."

"Grass?"

"Yeah, grass. The thin green stuff that's usually found in front of most suburban houses."

Poe said, "Not in Vegas. Out here it's sand, not sod."

Rukmani looked up. "What are you talking about? There's plenty of lawns out here. Conservation of water is a forbidden concept in these parts. Lord knows what's going to happen when the well runs dry."

"I'm not talking about little patches of lawn. More like the public places . . . empty lots. They're sand-filled."

"How about those posh developments—River Ridge, Pecos Canyon, Dorado Springs? They all have huge expanses of lawns with sprinkler systems to keep them going."

"I'm not saying that grass doesn't *exist*. Just that it's not natural vegetation in the desert."

"Well, that's certainly true." Rukmani returned her eyes to her work.

Poe blinked several times. His thoughts traveling to a certain high-powered office. "Did you find grass under Brittany Newel's fingernails?"

"No, I don't believe so. But I'll check it out for you. Why?"

"Just curious." Poe shrugged. "Is there any way to find out what type of grass was under her nails?"

"You mean like take the cuttings to a plant specialist?"

"Exactly."

"Yeah, I could order it. It'll cost."

"That's all right."

"Consider it done. Pass me the scalpel. I'm going to sever the ligaments that hold the mandible to the TMJ."

"I think it's time for my exit line."

"Make it a good one. How about reciting something from the farewell scene in *Casablanca*?"

"How about a late, late dinner? Cuban at Havana?"

"Great. That's even better than Bogie."

Jensen exploded as he gave a final shove deep inside Gretchen. Holding those bodacious ride-'em-cowboy hips, his hands squeezing her luscious, ripe ass. She gave out her little moan—a signal that she was waiting for him to withdraw. But damn if he didn't want to savor the moment. Finally, he pulled out and collapsed onto the bed.

"Wow!" Gretchen exclaimed. "That was just great!"

Jensen grunted.

She slapped his ass, got up, and headed for the bathroom, her surgically perfect tits holding a stiff posture as she walked. A moment later, Jensen heard the water running. He looked down at his body. His cock was still semierect. Give it a few minutes more and he'd be ready for round two. He wanted to tell Gretchen not to bother to douche, but why not screw a clean woman?

She returned a minute later, buried her hips under the sheets. Jensen looped his arm around her neck, brought her mouth to his, then inched those fantastic lips to his crotch. She gave him a long, lubricious suck, then lifted her head.

"Why do you stay with her, Stevie? We could be doing things like this every night."

Doesn't that sound like heaven? "She's a sick woman, baby. I just can't leave her. I'm not that type of guy." Again, he aimed her face at his groin. She began to mouth him deeply. He felt himself growing down the shaft of her throat.

Then she backed off. "She's manipulating you, you know. She doesn't fuck you, but then she gets all mad when you fuck me. If that isn't being a manipulative bitch, what is?"

He felt his pecker deflate. Why the hell did she always want to talk about *Alison?* "Baby, don't be concerned with my problems."

"Of course I'm concerned with your problems, Stevie. I love you."

He wanted to shout: *Don't say that!* Instead, to his horror, he heard himself say, "Well, I love you, too. But it's just not the right time—"

"It'll never be the right time."

Goddammit, Rom, where's your fucking page when I need it? "Baby, you have to be patient."

"Stevie, I've been patient." Gretchen was all pouty now. "It's been almost six months. I do have limits."

He really didn't feel like breaking in another woman. *Stall her, you asshole!* "Baby, I love you so much. I just need a little time—"

"Stevie, we had this same discussion a month ago."

"I need more time, Gretchen."

"How much more time?"

"Another month. That's all. Then I'll leave her, I swear. Please? Just give me a month to arrange something for my sons."

"Stevie, I love you, but I don't believe you. I think you're giving me the runaround."

And then his pager went off.

Thank you, God! He looked at the blessed box. "Dammit," he said, containing his joy. "It's the station house."

"Oh, drat!" Gretchen exclaimed. "That stupid thing is always going off at the wrong time!"

Excitedly, Jensen punched Rom's number into the hotel's telephone. The line connected. "Yo, Sergeant, it's Jensen."

Over the line, Poe said, "I heard you went home because Alison wasn't feeling well. I stopped by your house. But you weren't there. Did you go out for cigarettes?"

Sarcastic prick! Jensen said, "What can I do you for, Sergeant?"

Poe paused. Steve sounded so . . . *happy.* "I found the name of the kid Jane Doe's pimp. Ali Abdul Williams. Far as we can tell, he's rabbited. But I do have a search warrant for his apartment." He gave Steve the address.

Jensen said, "I'll be there in ten minutes."

"Man, you're an eager beaver." A beat. "Trouble in paradise?"

"Yes, sir, that is correct."

Poe smiled. "Then you owe me for this, don't you?"

"Indeed I do." Jensen cut the line.

Poe grinned. He liked having Stevie in his debt.

SEVENTEEN

Bad Guys 2, Poe 0.

Naked City had turned up zilch. Ali Abdul Williams was a tornado that had come and gone, leaving destruction in its wake. No one had admitted to even knowing him, let alone being a friend, associate, or relative. A.A. had stayed in a single-room bungalow sty in North Las Vegas, and Poe had given Jensen the dubious honor of searching it. The confiscation included several handguns, a sawed-off shotgun, several cellophane bags of rock crystal, and a stash of pot crawling with a plethora of insects thought to be exclusively indigenous to the Amazon. Poe had finally made it to dinner around ten-thirty, thanking God for the weekend.

Rukmani had offered plenty of sympathy as well as her bed for the night. But after sex, she moved away from him and drifted into her own world. Poe felt restless. Wiggling out of the soft sheets, he tiptoed away, left a note, and was out cruising the Strip at one in the morning. He still hadn't given back Remus's rental. The car lady over the phone had been a bit miffed, as the Volvo should have been returned six hours ago. But being as Poe was police, she had been cooperative if not friendly.

He pulled into valet parking at the MGM Grand, left the keys with the attendant. Walking into the lobby, straight into the Emerald City diorama. Scarecrow, Tin Man, Cowardly Lion, and Dorothy were happily romping

125

through a twinkly-lights field of narcotic-laced poppies, just minutes away from disaster. If that wasn't a metaphor for Vegas, what was?

He got away with a couple of hands of blackjack before being given the nod. Bad timing, because he was down a couple of grand. If Ms. Lady Luck was going to be fickle tonight, he might as well work.

He took out two pictures—the composite of Mr. Caucasian Ponytail and a full-faced mug shot of Mr. A. A. Williams minus his booking number. Poe started by showing the pictures around at the Sports Lounge, then went through the entire casino. Thirty minutes later, he proceeded on foot down Las Vegas Boulevard. Casino after casino, bar after bar. Asking the same question: Do you know or recognize either of these people? Most of the time he was met with shakes of the head. He did get "Maybe I did see him . . ." a few times. Taking down their names for future questions. Anything that might give him a break.

By the time he hit Caesars, he was awash in fatigue. The place was monstrously large; it was an aerobic exercise just to make it to the room elevators. He inched his way through the weekend throng, methodically working the bars as tuxedoed waitresses flitted through the pits carrying trays of complimentary drinks. Lights flashing, slots dinging and donging, smoke wafting through the area like mist. He felt a headache coming on.

Why didn't he just stay with Ruki? Why didn't she ever wake up when he left?

It was a little past four when Poe took a last look around. The floor space was so expansive he felt as if he were surveying land. Eyes sweeping past the barstools. He blinked, rubbed his aching forehead, then looked up. About one hundred feet away, he spotted a bowler hat sitting atop a ponytailed head. The figure was dressed in black and was moving toward the exit.

Poe's heart took off as he ran in long strides down the carpeted path through the casino, pushing zombied people moving slow in the wee hours of the morning. He spied Ponytail just as he was leaving through double glass doors. Poe bolted toward the exit, stepping outside into a cool, clear, neon-lit night.

A quick once-over.

A glimpse of the bowler hat under the Caesars marquee. Poe dashed down the elongated valet driveway, almost caught up with the figure. But his body must have given off some kind of extrasensory fight-or-flight vibration. Because as soon as Poe hit the public sidewalk, Ponytail started tearing down the near-empty street.

"Hey!" Poe shouted as he ran. *"Stop! Police!"*

His voice echoed in the nighttime air; he knew Ponytail had heard it. But the cry just made the fugitive pump his legs harder, leaping like a cougar, his steps lithe and coordinated. With each beat of the pavement, the son of a bitch increased his lead.

Goddamn this job, Poe muttered. Panting like a mutt, his chest stabbing pain as his legs stretched to the max. At full speed, trying to keep pace with the asshole. He thought about drawing his gun, then nixed the idea. He was running too fast, there were still people on the streets, and it was too dark to aim well.

"Stop! Police!" he screamed. *"Police!"*

But Ponytail kept going, dodging cross traffic as he sprinted toward the Mirage. Poe ran harder, kept on Bowler's ass, wondering how he managed to run so fast and still keep the hat on. The fugitive kept going and going, finally ducking into Treasure Island.

Yo ho ho, my fucking *ass!*

Once inside the casino, Poe knew he was screwed. He stopped, panting hard. Wiping sweat from his face. There was no sign of the hat. The place had people even at this hour. Treasure Island was always busy during weekdays, jammed on weekends. It was a manageable casino, friendly to families, and floored lots of cheap slots and low table minimums. The kick-off night of the weekend always packed them in.

Poe's eyes skated over the floor.

No hat. No ponytail. No nothing.

A half-hour search proved fruitless. Defeated and deflated, he finally called Weinberg from a pay phone, bringing him up to date.

Poe said, "As soon as he made it through the doors, I lost visual contact. He could still be in here. But by the time we clear everything through hotel security and get the men out here to search, he could be halfway to Reno or L.A. or deep into the Mojave. It's your call, sir."

"Well, this is just terrific," Weinberg grumped. "Now the sucker knows we're onto him."

Poe reddened as he felt blood throb in his head. He held his temper in check. "Loo, all I did was follow him—"

"You had to *identify* yourself as a cop, Poe?"

"Only after he bolted from me. That's standard operational procedure—"

"Poe, how'd you let him *slip*? You're the quickest runner on the entire force."

"The guy flew like wind." Poe became enraged. "Aw, *screw* it! You want me to say I fucked up? Fine. I fucked—"

"Poe—"

"What do you want me to *do, sir*?"

"First calm down."

"I'm *calm*. Now what?"

Weinberg paused. "Did you get a good look at his face?"

"No, Loo, I did *not* get a look at his face—good or otherwise. I did, however, get a very good look at the *hat*. It was a black bowler. He was very thin and agile. I chased Stan Laurel with a ponytail."

Weinberg chuckled. "At least we know this guy really exists."

"Isn't that comforting?"

"No need for sarcasm, Romulus."

"May I go home and collapse, sir?"

"Anytime now."

Poe was about to hang up. Then he said, "I can't believe the fucking hat stayed on during the entire chase. He must have applied Krazy Glue to his head."

Again, Weinberg laughed. "Go home and get some sleep."

"I think I'll go directly to the Bureau. Write up this miserable failure—"

"Don't whip yourself, Poe. We'll find him. See you on Monday."

Weinberg hung up. What Poe should have done next was grab a taxi back to the Grand and head out for the Bureau. Write up the chase before the scene faded from short-term memory. Instead, he headed for the Hi Ho Matey Bar. He requested a beer, lit a smoke, and glanced around the area.

Spotting the braid.

Poe waited until he had the glass in his hand. Then he took his brew and his smoke and sat down next to Y. As always, the old man was playing a poker machine. Tonight he wore a black suede shirt, black jeans, and a string tie held together with a malachite clip. A cigarette drooped from his lips. His usual plait was loosely tied and kept in place by a beaded thong.

Poe inhaled smoke, let it out slowly. "You disappeared on me a couple of nights ago."

Y dropped a dollar token in the machine. "Next time I'll write you a thank-you note."

Poe replaced Y's old cigarette with a fresh one. He put the smoke in his mouth. "Where'd you go?"

"Around."

"*Around?* My place is in the middle of nowhere."

"I'm Southern Paiute. All desert land is my home."

"Oh, stow it with that shaman crap. Your family wholesales cigarettes, ekes out a living by pocketing the difference between federal and tribal tax."

"That doesn't mean I don't know the old ways."

"The old ways?" Poe nodded. "I see. You must mean drinking yourself blind and living on welfare."

"Hostile tonight, Romulus?"

"I was concerned about you, Chief," Poe said. "You shouldn't be wandering off at night. There are animals out there—things like snakes, cougars . . . coyotes. Man, they were howling like the devil after you left. You could have gotten hurt."

Y lost the poker game. "You're giving me bad vibes."

"No, you're just playing poorly." Poe put a token in the machine. He wound up winning three to one. "See?"

Y moved one stool down, started playing another machine.

Poe said, "Buy you a drink?"

"Get away."

Poe was quiet. Y licked his parched lips. "Well, I suppose you could buy me something."

Poe ordered him a vodka straight up. Like drinking firewater. Y took it and drank it in several gulps. Not a word of thanks. Screw him! Poe smoked down his cigarette, crushed it, then got up to leave. Y held his arm.

"You ever look at the stars, Romulus?"

"No Indian mystic *moxoam-puts*—spirit-in-the-sky—shit, okay?"

Y smiled, his lined face cracking like parched leather. "Your mom taught you some words, Rom?"

"None of the good ones."

"Sit down."

Poe sat.

Y said, "As a kid, I knew the constellations like the back of my hand. Since the rivers were dried up . . . the land gone . . . on the reservation, there was nothing to do but drink. And when you're too young to drink, you wind up doing a lot of staring."

Y put another token in the machine.

"I know this sky like an old friend, Romulus. The Big Dipper always points me in the right direction. As far as snakes . . . I have my ways. If they bother me, they don't last long.''

"What ways, old man? Do you insult them to death?''

Y shook his head. "Ask your mother.'' He pounded his fist against the table. "Damn!'' He put another coin in the slot. "You ever kill rattlers, Romulus?''

"As a kid, all the time. In the summer we used to drive out to Sunrise Mountain and shoot the suckers as the sun went down, just when they started coming out . . . when things cooled off. We used to sell the skins at outrageous prices to naive tourists. Mom would often make stew out of the meat.''

"How is your mother?''

"Funny you should ask about her. She's coming out here to live for a while.''

Y stopped playing the machine. "Who's going to take care of her?''

Poe was offended. "*I* am. I'm setting her up. I've found her an apartment. Now all I have to do is locate a full-time nurse.''

"Ah.''

"What do you mean, *ah*? I'm going to take care of her. But she's not well. She needs constant care. That's all.''

Y started up the machine. "No, she is not well.''

Poe studied him. "I didn't mean she's going to die tomorrow. Why did *you* say she isn't well? Do you know something I don't?''

"No. I said she isn't well because you just said she isn't well. I'm trying to be agreeable.''

"Well, don't be,'' Poe said testily. "It doesn't suit you.'' Still, he was disconcerted. Even disregarding all that Indian hoo-ha, when Y made statements like that, it usually held ominous overtones. Poe said, "I'm going back to the Bureau.''

Y said nothing, continued to play.

"Would you like to see her when she gets into town?''

"Yeah, I like your mother.''

Poe examined Y's face. It revealed nothing. Without a word, he stood and walked away.

She came in at four-thirty, wearing a short red dress that hugged her body like a lover. Her hair was long and loose, her skin held a sweaty sheen. Not a drop of makeup except for a fresh application of lipstick. She was carrying a paper sack, tucked under her sleeveless arm. Jensen stopped pacing, too shocked for words.

"My dad still here, or did you send him home when you got in?" Alison asked.

Jensen couldn't answer. He didn't know whether he wanted to strangle her or make love to her. Instead, he suprised himself by acting the irate husband. "Where the *hell* have you been?"

She rolled her eyes and headed for the bedroom. Jensen followed, kept his voice down to a furious whisper. "I asked you a question!"

Alison shrugged. "I'll tell you if you tell me."

"I was *working*!" Spittle spewed from Jensen's mouth. "You don't believe me, ask your midget friend."

"Rom was here, Stephen, looking for you. Wondering where *you* were, since you told him you wanted to knock off early to be with *me*. He was rather stunned by your absence."

Jensen's brain started racing. That's right, Poe had said something about stopping by the house. Asshole was always . . . Alison was waiting for him to talk. *Think of something, you jerk!* But nothing came out.

Again, Alison rolled her eyes. "I was the one who gave him your hotel's phone number. So why don't you end this conversation before it blows up in your face."

Jensen felt his resolve weakening. He whined, "I *was* working!"

Alison threw the paper bag into the closet, tried to unzip her dress. "I'm sure you were working very hard. Help me with this thing. I think it's stuck."

Jensen went over, unzipped her dress. Quietly, he said, "Where'd you go?"

"Just out."

Just out.

Just like her mother.

God, don't even think about that.

He asked, "Anyplace in specific?"

Alison stepped away from her husband, stepped out of her dress. "I casino-hopped. I won four hundred and twenty bucks on slots. Must have been my night."

"Did you go out with . . . with anyone?"

"Nope, no one. Just by my lonesome."

Jensen didn't believe a word she said. Still, this time, she had been responsible enough to call her dad to watch the kids before she left. And even if she had fucked someone . . . no, he didn't want to think about that. Anxiety coursed through his body.

Where had Poe gone tonight? He'd said something about dinner with Rukmani. Probably at her place the entire evening. *Calm . . . calm. Don't press her. Don't press her.* At least she was acting normal . . . talking . . . interacting with him. Besides, she looked so damn good.

Jensen walked over, slipped his hands around her waist. "I'm not trying to micromanage your life, Alison. I was just worried about you. That's all."

She turned around, stroked his face. "Poor, poor Steve."

He brought her to his chest. "You know how much I love you. How much I care."

She answered him by stroking his crotch.

And damn if he didn't respond instantly. Within minutes, he was inside her. The excitement was overwhelming as he desperately tried to hold back long enough for her to climax. Goddamn perverse when fucking your own wife was more of a turn-on than fucking your mistress. He felt himself about to give way, willed himself to keep going.

Seconds later, she shuddered beneath him. He answered her call by erupting with volcanic action—a physical release of stress and androgens. She pushed him away and headed for the bathroom. He knew he should have followed her. But instead, he made the mistake of closing his eyes. The last thing he heard was the water running.

The bath was so hot that in a previous life it might have burned her flesh. But Alison had learned to tolerate things that would do in most mortals.

It was all happening so fast.

Faster than her research could explain it. Or maybe she just hadn't looked hard enough. Because she was sure it was all there. If she could only find the time. . . .

Is that how Mother had felt? Had it come upon her equally fast? Had she felt the same way? Stronger . . . smarter . . . more and more immortal?

Because she knew she really was becoming immortal. She'd realized that tonight when she outran Romulus.

Soaking in the searing water.

So he was onto her. Or rather onto her in disguise. She knew that had to happen *eventually*. But she didn't expect it to happen so fast.

Everything . . . so fast.

Which made it all the more exciting.

Outrunning Rom.

Her physical strength was now clear. That she could outrun Rom . . . or any man . . . well, that was no challenge. Yes, she could outrun Rom. But could she *outwit* him? Because mentally, she hadn't changed. She was still the same, and so was he.

Romulus.

He had been a tiny boy who had always been there to do her bidding. How he had adored her, mooning over her like a sick puppy. They had been each other's first. The physical relationship had lasted for six months. Then she reached high school, and somehow had made it into the in-crowd. There was no longer a place for him in her life except as a whipping boy. But he hadn't understood that. Because no matter how she had demeaned him, he had always come back.

Tears rolled down her cheek.

She knew it couldn't last forever. But did it have to end so fast?

She was losing her hold. He was drifting away, spending time with that so-called girlfriend of his. He even left the house *early* to go have dinner with her. Even though she offered him dinner at *her* house— alone—just the *two* of them. He'd always canceled his dates in the past. Why hadn't he canceled this one? Even after she had asked *twice*. And why that woman? She was too old for him. *Way* too old!

More tears.

He was getting back at her. *That* was it. He was getting back because he had always felt that Steve was too old.

Of course, that was it. This was all about *revenge*!

She wiped her face, but she couldn't stop crying.

The look in his eyes when they talked. Distant. Remote.

Maybe it was because Steve had told him off. But Rom had never let Steve interfere with their relationship in the past. It had to be *that woman*.

Everything . . . so fast.

Get a grip on it, Alison!

Squeezing her eyes shut. Picturing the octagonal stop sign.

Stop. *Stop!*

Slowly, she shut off her ocular water taps, her mind bent on *her* revenge as she soaped up her hair for the fifth time.

If she couldn't dangle him with love, she'd engage him in other ways.

A nice friendly game of cat and mouse.

Or more like hunter and prey.

EIGHTEEN

Walking into the squad room, Poe smiled when he saw a dozen long-stemmed blood-red roses sitting in a vase on Deluca's desk. He said, "Must have been a good weekend."

She didn't look up. Her face matched the color of the flowers. "It had its moments."

Poe hung up his jacket. It was half past seven. Both he and Patricia were early risers—the only occupants in the house. "How's old Nate doing? Spot any more bad guys for us?"

"Don't believe so."

Poe sat at his desk, turned on his computer and modem. "Let's see what mayhem happened over the weekend." He waited for the machine to go through its virus check. "Where'd you two go?"

Patricia said, "We ate our way across the state."

Poe smiled. "Seriously."

"I am serious. We ended up in Reno, took in a floor show there. Then Nate wanted to try out a Swedish buffet. We thought about skiing in the Sierra Nevadas, but I was afraid that in our white ski suits, we'd be mistaken for gigantic snowballs. Or polar bears."

Poe laughed. "You're awful."

"We did wind up doing some cross-country skiing. By the end, I lost my weight in water. Soaked clear to the bone with sweat." A sigh. "But man, was it beautiful in the mountains!"

"You should have picked up my mother as long as you were in Reno."

"Yeah, how's that going, sir?"

"I'm still interviewing nurses." Poe rubbed his forehead. "Ruki knows a lot of people. We'll find someone."

"Did she finish the autopsy on Kid Jane Doe?"

"I'm pretty sure she did, but I think she wants to go over her transcripts. We should get a preliminary soon. Maybe by the middle of the week." A beat. "She did tell me something important. There's a high degree of probability that Kid Jane Doe died of asphyxiation."

"Asphyxiation? Are you sure?"

"That's what she said. Something about the bluing of the alveolar cells, whatever that means."

"Did Kid Jane Doe drown?"

"No . . . no water in the lungs. And she did a test that ruled out carbon monoxide poisoning. Rukmani's certain that Jane Doe wasn't strangled manually or with an implement. Because even with the neck cut, she didn't see ligature marks, indentations, or depressions in the throat region, front or back. Ruki said *if* the kid was strangled, it was a soft strangulation—like a pillow over the face."

"Or a plastic bag over her head."

"What makes you say that?"

"Dealers have lots of plastic bags."

"Which brings up another touchy point. She found Caucasian skin cells under both Doe's and Newel's nails . . . sort of ruling out A. A. Williams as her sparring partner. Rukmani said that the kid fought back like a tiger."

He paused.

"Now the tiger part kind of negates a gentle strangulation. If she went down fighting like a demon, it doesn't seem logical that someone could do her in by gently placing something over her face."

Poe cleared his throat and tried to make sense out of the facts. "We know that Teen Doe was a hooker and Williams was her pimp, right?"

"Right."

"Say he gave her over to someone who wanted it rough. Say it got *too* rough. The kid protested, the john put a pillow over her head to quiet her down. Only problem was he did it for too long."

He stopped speaking. Patricia asked, "And then what?"

Poe scratched his head. "I don't know. Maybe Williams found the kid dead, got nervous, and split." A pause. "Then why slash her throat? Especially after Williams *told* me that he'd slit Newel if he ever saw her again. Like you said last week, he can't be that stupid. but it seems almost as if he wanted to set himself up."

"Or someone else is setting him up."

"Good point. I suppose we'll know more after the autopsy's complete. Rukmani's going over the slides again. She should get back the blood and gas reports sometime this week."

"Which will tell us if Kid Doe was drugged like Brittany Newel."

"Yeah, interesting to see if both were sedated. Because the two cases are alike, but not alike. As if someone is *trying* to be a serial killer, but doesn't quite have all the moves down yet." Poe snapped his fingers. "Do we have any leads on the identity of Kid Doe?"

"Not yet. I ran her through Youth Runaway Shelter and Juvenile Court Services Abuse and came up empty. I'll put in a call to National Child Services and the National Runaway Register. Fax them over some sanitized pictures of the girl, then input the information on her directly from my computer."

"Sounds like a good plan." Poe regarded the monitor. The screen saver on his machine was flashing images of western movie star he-men. At the moment, John Wayne was turning into Clint Eastwood. He punched in a code number and hooked into the LVMPD "Currents" file.

Pulling up the weekend activities.

A couple of gang-related shootings in the north end. No deaths. The wounded were at the University Medical Center.

Several car crashes on the highway, but only one was fatal. Saturday afternoon, three o'clock. Witnesses said a van had hit the center divider, flipped into the air, and bounced upside down several times on the roadway before alighting on the desert floor. By the time the medics arrived, they found a mangle of human flesh. Fatalities were a black male in his thirties and a white female appearing to be in her late teens. Poe brought up the highway patrol photographs taken at the scene onto his monitor.

He winced. The man had been decorticated, his skull sheared off by a piece of metal. His eyes were browless. Blood had poured out from the brainless head. His face was a bloody pulp, yet the goatee was still intact.

Poe's eyes widened. "Oh my God!"

"Excuse me?" Patricia said.

He jumped up from his chair, leaned closer to the monitor. "It's him! A. A. Williams—Jane Doe's pimp! Come take a look!"

Patricia got up, walked over to Poe's desk, stepping back when she saw what was on the screen. "What *are* you looking at?"

"A car accident out on Route Fifty." He pointed to the face. "The goatee. That's Williams's goatee! See it?"

"Yes, sir." In fact, all Patricia saw was something nauseating.

Poe said, "That's got to be Williams! Only one way to be certain. Find out where they took the bodies and check out the prints." He pounded the table. "Dammit! He was here all this time and we let him get away." *Just like Mr. Ponytail.* He began to pace. "Damn these weekends! Too many people clogging up our walkways! Can't find a goddamn thing, let alone a person!"

"You want some coffee, sir?" Patricia offered. "Maybe some *decaf*?"

Jensen walked through the door.

Poe said, "Hey, Stevie. C'mere and take a look at this."

Jensen's voice was steely. "Why'd you come to my house, Poe?"

Poe stopped pacing, feeling hairs spring up at the base of his neck. "What are you talking about?"

"Friday. Why'd you come to my house?"

Poe glared at him. "To look for you."

"Ever hear of a phone?"

Patricia said, "I . . . need to go to the bathroom." She fled.

Poe waited a beat, then said, "Patricia said you had knocked off early. I called, Jensen, but no one answered. I got a little concerned, so I stopped by—"

"My family is none of your goddamn business—"

"Jensen, I came looking for you. You weren't home, I left—"

"After carrying on a nice little conversation with my wife."

"It was hello and good-bye."

"Bullshit!" Jensen advanced on Poe, poked him in the chest. "Alison told me she gave you my hotel's number. Now just what were you two talking about? What a terrible bastard I am?" Another poke. "How she deserves better?" A third one. "What, Poe? What little morsels did you put in her mind? Tell me *what*!"

Poe swatted his hand away. "She was shittin' you, Jensen. She didn't give me anyone's number and I didn't call any hotel. I had *no* idea where you were. I *paged* you, you idiot. *You* called *me* back."

Jensen's mouth fell open as his brain kicked in.

Trouble in paradise?

Then you owe me for this, don't you?

Poe took a step backward, his hands trembling as he shook his own finger at the big man. "Jensen, we've got too much baggage between us to work together. Go find an assignment under Baylor or Marine Martin. As of this moment, you're *off* my cases."

Poe walked back to his desk, sank into his chair. Eight o'clock in the morning and his head felt like a drumskin.

Jensen stumbled over his words, his head sagging in hangdog style. Alison had been so damn convincing. And like a fool, he had believed her lies. Would he ever learn?

"It's just . . . she's been acting crazy, Poe. Like her mother. She was out until four-thirty in the morn—"

"Jensen, I don't give a rat's ass about your prob—" Poe stopped talking, spun his chair around, and turned to him. "You want to know the truth, Stevie? Yes, I have feelings for your wife. But of late, I find Alison a *royal* pain in the ass. You want to know what *really* happened Friday night? I went over to the house, looking for you. She said you weren't home, implying where you probably *were,* and I, like a moronic dumb shit, gave her all this sympathy that, in the end, just makes her despise me. I don't even know why I even play her game anymore. I'm not even getting laid."

"Neither am I . . . well, not quite—"

"Jensen, just do your job and leave me the fuck alone."

Steve licked his lips and said, "She said you offered to take her out to dinner."

"That's crap!" Poe said. "As a matter of fact, she invited *me* to dinner. Alone. In *your* house. Know what I said? I said, 'No thank you.' Then she got all teary-eyed. Frankly, I *didn't* care about her problems. I had a date with Ruki, and I'll be damned if I let her ruin this relationship. Far as I'm concerned, you can both go to hell!"

To the air, Poe shouted, "You can come out now, Patty. The war is over."

She shouted back, "I'm scared."

Poe said, "It's okay. Steve and I are speaking again." He beckoned him forward with a finger, waited for him to walk to the monitor. "Look at this."

Jensen grimaced, "What am I looking at?"

"A car accident. See this? It's a goatee. I think this bloody mess was at one time our psycho pimp, Ali Abdul Williams. Since you are now on my official shit list, *you* investigate the accident. Talk to the highway patrol and find out if the guy had ID on him. Find out who the girl was as well. Since the faces aren't in recognizable form, find out where the medics took the bodies and print the hands and feet of both victims. Any *questions,* Detective?''

Jensen took Poe's coffee cup, drank it down to the bottom. ''No hard feelings, Rom?''

Poe rolled his eyes. ''Get me some coffee!''

Jensen sighed. ''It's gonna be one of *those* weeks.'' He poured water into the machine.

''Stop feeling sorry for yourself,'' Poe said, ''At least your mother wasn't arrested.''

''I'll take an arrested mother over a crazy wife.'' Jensen felt clubbed and winded. ''God, Poe . . . we're a sorry lot.''

''Speak for yourself!''

Patricia looked out the rear window. ''Herrod and Marine Martin just pulled into the parking lot. We'd better look neat and efficient.''

''Fuck it,'' Poe said. ''I outrank both of them.''

Jensen said, ''Go easy on Herrod, Poe. He just became a grandfather.''

Poe paused. ''Isn't that a *good* thing?''

Jensen said, ''Not when you still think you're twenty.''

''He's major-league depressed,'' Patricia added.

Poe frowned. ''What's this world coming to when you're upset about becoming a grandparent?''

Patricia said, ''It's this city, sir. It does *strange* things to your head.''

Picking up his phone line, he said, ''Poe.''

''I got news.''

Jensen sounded excited. Poe told him to hold on while he got out his notebook. Then he said, ''Shoot.''

''I got prints from the bodies, ran them through the National Print Register. You ain't going to believe this. I actually got some positives.''

''Good going.''

''First, our skulless man is . . . or was . . . Williams.''

''And the girl?''

''Katerina Barns. Eighteen. She worked as a prostitute up in Elko for around three, four months, then disappeared. During the interim, she must have hooked up with Williams. Anyway, she was arrested in Vegas for crack possession a month ago. Spent a week in jail and then was released due to lack of space.''

Poe was writing furiously. ''You did good.''

''I ain't nearly done.'' Jensen was breathless. ''Get this, Rom. There was also another white teen female with them in the van. Highway patrol postulated that she was sitting in the back without a seat belt, was pitched from the van upon impact with the center divider, was thrown clear across the westbound highway, and landed about twenty feet off the right shoulder. Man, talk about bad luck. The van wound up landing on top of her, crushing her like an olive press—''

''Jesus.''

''Yeah, it was bad. But it gets worse. Now when is an accident not an accident?''

''Go on.''

''Nothing official yet, because the investigation isn't complete, but a little bird told me that the van had been monkeyed with.''

Poe sat up at his desk. ''Really!''

''Something about the bushings in the upper arm control. You know anything about cars?''

''Enough to know that the control arm has to do with the steering box.''

''They haven't even gone over the brakes yet. And that's not all. Are you ready for this?''

''I'm taking it all down.''

''Williams had money on him. Twenty grand in hundreds, Rom. Two neat little bundles of ten grand each, wrapped up with a hundreds band. Crisp, new bills—''

''Counterfeit?''

''No, the real thing. Just fresh from the bank.''

''Can we trace it?''

''Maybe.''

''Good job. Stick around, see if you can find out more about the car. I'll page if I need you. Keep in touch.''

''Will do.''

Poe hung up, collected his thoughts as he bounced his knee up and down.

Okay, what do we have, what do we have?

Basics: It appeared that A.A. had packed up and was heading west, probably to set up shop in L.A. He had two girls with him and a shitload of money.

Where'd he get the money?

That was easy. Crack dealers made thousands a day. Not hard to believe he could have collected twenty grand in a short time given that he was dealing plus he had at least three girls hooking for him.

The miracle was that he had actually kept some of the bread. Dealers were notorious squanderers, couldn't keep a dime to save their souls. That A.A. had actually amassed twenty gees in crisp one-hundred-dollar bills . . . that didn't sit well, especially since he lived in a pisshole of an apartment. The money smelled of payoff.

Combine a payoff with a car that had been worked over, one could draw an interesting conclusion: that Williams had known something bad. That he had been fleeing because something was rotten in the state of Nevada.

NINETEEN

After entering the data into the computer, Poe examined his notes.

The cases:

Brittany Newel—twenty-three-year-old desert drop, raked and gouged, with a missing eye. Heavily sedated when murdered. Former dancer who hooked for Williams, and, according to her ex-boyfriend, had a relationship with Parker Lewiston. A drug user. The scraping under her fingernails had shown white skin cells, dirt, and no grass.

Kid Jane Doe—a teenager, probably not more than fourteen, fifteen. Desert drop who died by asphyxiation, but also had her throat slashed. Hooked and flagged for Williams and addicted to crack. Her nail scraping showed white skin, dirt, sand, and grass. Her eyes had been intact when the body had been found.

Katerina Barns—the eighteen-year-old who died along with A. A. Williams in a suspicious car crash. She had worked as a hooker in Elko. She had also been one of Williams's girls. She also had an arrest record.

Lydia Townsend—the seventeen-year-old who was crushed by the van. Presumably she had also worked for Williams.

Patricia looked over Poe's shoulder to the monitor. "Too bad Williams got himself scalped. He was the common thread."

Poe rubbed his aching forehead. "The two desert drops had Caucasian skin under their nails."

"It could mean that they didn't scratch Williams when he killed them."

"I've got another postulation. Williams brokered the two girls out to a sadistic white john. First, he gave away Brittany. Sadistic White John killed her, but kept Williams quiet with twenty gees in crisp bills. The second time White John did his stuff, Williams got nervous. The john was out of control. Williams decided to take his crew and split. This agitated White John, because Williams knew too much. So White John booby-trapped his car."

"And your candidate for White John is Lewiston."

"Why not? He's got lots of grass in his office."

"Sir, Brittany Newel didn't have grass under her nails. Besides, tampering with a car is not a practical way to kill. Lewiston isn't a man who'd leave things up to chance."

She was right.

Patricia said, "But I like your theory, sir. It explains everything." She waited a beat. "Well, I've got a bit of news. A possible identification for Kid Jane Doe. She's a runaway from Nebraska. They're sending over dental records."

Poe nodded. "Are there parents?"

"There's a mother. She's a secretary for a major farming equipment manufacturer. She's worked there for thirty years. She was very broken up when I told her the news. She told me her daughter had been out of control. Then she started doing the mea culpas. It was hard to hear. Her grief sounded so genuine."

"I'm sure it was."

"Her daughter's name is or was Sarah Yarlborough."

Poe shook his head. "She didn't look like a Sarah to me. Maybe a Heather or an Amber . . . not a Sarah."

Marine Martin looked up, saw Poe conferring with Fat Patty. He stood up, brushed off his perfectly creased khaki pants and starched white shirt, then picked up a folder from his desk. He marched over to Poe. "For you. From Jensen."

Poe took the envelope from Martin. "How's it going?"

Stiffly, Martin answered, "Any break in the cases?"

"Nothing yet."

"Keep going. Perseverance. Name of the game."

Poe saluted. Martin marched back to his desk, which was buried under and pasted with Marine paraphernalia—badges, posters, slogans.

What this country needs is a few good men.

No, what this country needed was a lot fewer bad guys.

Poe broke open the seal on the envelope, flipped through the pages. Highway Patrol Accident Report. Preliminary finding on the van. *Way to go, Jensen.* To Patricia, he said, "Where is Stevie?"

"It's past five, sir. I believe he went home."

"Past five?" Poe looked at the wall clock. Where did the day go? Though he was glad it was gone. The week had been a scorcher. Hell had chosen to turn up the thermostat early this year. He said, "I've got to meet Rukmani." He stuffed the accident report in a briefcase. "I'm forgetting something."

"What?"

Poe looked at his monitor and remembered. No time. He turned off his computer. "Remind me to add Janet Doward's name to my list."

"Who's she?"

"Victim of a murder case that's been plaguing me for twenty-five years."

"What does she have to do with our murders?"

"Maybe something, probably nothing."

Walking out of the Hayward Convalescent Home, Rukmani wiped sweat from her forehead, smoothed out her pink-and-gold silk sari, then put on her sunglasses. The week had turned blisteringly hot—unusual for May, but not unheard-of. "So what did you think?"

Poe shrugged.

Rukmani remained positive. "I liked Karen. She was friendly, warm ... pretty, too. Not that your mother will care." She elbowed him playfully. "But why not have someone who's pleasant on the eyes?"

Poe didn't answer—quiet and sullen. She knew his recent cases weren't going well. Compulsive that he was, he kept going over details, concentrating on minutiae, hoping something might materialize. But sometimes it just ain't there.

She said, "You must have garnered some kind of an opinion."

Poe said, "She's a flake."

"A flake? Poe, she's been working as a geriatric nurse for over four years."

"She's too young."

"She's twenty-nine."

"She's had breast implants."

Rukmani stopped walking. "What does that have to do with anything?"

Poe brushed hair out of his eyes. He rolled up his sleeves, feeling limp from the sudden, oppressive heat. The sun was baking the sidewalk, turning the concrete into clay cookware. He could feel fire through his shoes. "Women with breast implants don't take their work seriously."

Rukmani took off her sunglasses, squinted at him. "What kind of cockamamie conclusion is that?"

"It's true." Poe started toward the car.

She slid her glasses back on, said, "What's the real problem, Rom? Afraid *you'll* get distracted?"

Poe picked up his pace.

Rukmani had to jog to keep up with him. "You're full of piss and vinegar today. Why don't you go out and get yourself a nice blow job?"

Poe stopped short in front of his newly repaired Honda, jamming the key into the lock and throwing open his door. He hunkered down into the driver's seat, unlocked the passenger door from the inside, then turned on the air conditioner full blast.

Rukmani slid in, turning the vent toward her face. "You've got a 'tude. Just take me home."

"I have every intention of doing just that."

"You know, Romulus, I'm happy to give you help. But you might try acting a tiny bit appreciative—"

"Why do you mention blow jobs every time I get upset? Like all of my problems could be solved by one good round of head."

"It's worked in the past." She exhaled. "It was meant tongue-in-cheek. Besides, this has nothing to do with blow jobs. It has everything to do with you taking responsibility for your mother. I know you haven't had it easy, Poe, but you're not the only Hardluck Harry around. It wouldn't hurt you to act decent—"

"You have complaints?"

"Maybe a gripe or two."

"Then here's what you do, Doctor. You write them all down and send them to me with a SASE. I'll get back to you."

Rukmani bit her lip, then said, "Are you trying to tell me something?"

Poe tapped the wheel and didn't answer.

Rukmani said, "Well, at least Alison'll be happy. She'll get her errand boy back!"

Poe jerked the car over curbside, shut the motor, and flipped Rukmani the keys. "You take the car. *I'll* walk."

Quickly, Rukmani grabbed his arm. "C'mon. I'm tense . . . so are you. This isn't right."

Poe hadn't moved. He was still halfway out of the car.

Rukmani tried to hide her trembling voice. "It's hot outside. Please."

Poe came back in, shut the door, eyes focused on the car's ceiling. Rukmani put the key in the ignition to turn on the air conditioner. Neither one spoke.

Finally, Poe said, "I'm tired, I'm grumpy, and I have a headache. Let's call it a day."

Rukmani nodded. "Fine."

He started the car. They rode in silence, which drove Rukmani crazy. She needed conversation. *Talk about work.* It was neutral ground. "Patricia called me. She said she found out Teen Jane Doe's identity."

"A possibility. Sarah Yarlborough—a fifteen-year-old runaway from Nebraska."

"A young life ended in such a cruel way! What a shame!"

"Somebody'll be sending you the dental records."

"Okay. That'll work."

More silence.

Rukmani tried once again. "I should be getting blood and gas reports back any day now. Sorry it's taking so long. But it has to be done right to be meaningful."

"Of course."

Again no one spoke. At that point, she gave up. Poe drove to her apartment, parked the car at the curb. To Rukmani's surprise, he got out and opened her door.

He said, "I'll walk you up."

Her first impulse was to say, "Not necessary." But she nodded instead. She fumbled for her key, then finally inserted it into the lock, looking plaintively into his eyes. "Come in, Rom. I'll make you some spicy Masala iced tea from Bengal."

Poe hesitated, then walked in, sinking into her pillowed couch. The room had been cooled by an air conditioner that droned more than it hummed. But her place was always full of light, pleasant and immaculately clean. She lived in a two-bedroom apartment filled with pastel colors—a pink-and-green-print couch, rose velvet chairs, ivory carpeting. The legs and frames of her coffee and end tables were dark mahogany intricately carved in the filigree patterns that typified Indian woodcarving. A carved ivory top was set into the coffee table, protected by panes of glass. The dining area was an open space off the living room and held a simple stone table with four chairs. The kitchen was diminutive but tidy, the cabinets finished in sparkling white lacquer. Poe stared at the pictures on her wall—multilimbed Indian gods and goddesses—as well as a couple of photographs of some rajah's palace. Several gilt animal/human statues had been placed between the medical tomes on her bookshelves.

Rukmani took off her glasses and said, "Tea'll just take a moment. Is it cool enough for you?"

"The temperature is fine. I'm not really thirsty right now. Have a seat."

Rukmani sat. "This sounds ominous."

"Not at all." Gently, he said, "It's been a hard week. I'm not making much headway on my cases, and my neurotic brother has been driving me crazy. I'm sorry if I've upset you."

"Likewise."

"In the future, however, I'd appreciate it if you didn't mention the words 'Alison' and 'errand boy' in the same sentence."

"That was nasty of me. I'm sorry." A beat. "I just wish she'd—"
Cut your losses, Ruki. "Never mind."

Poe tried to keep his voice even. "I know you think she's jerking my chain. And maybe you're right. But she's an old friend, Ruki. Her husband is a ninny without a clue. I can't desert her, because she has no one else. Her problems are usually cyclical. You'll see. She'll calm down."

"Yeah, when we stop seeing each other, I'm sure she'll be wonderful." Rukmani suddenly stood. "I'm getting tea for myself. Are you sure you don't want any?"

Slowly, Poe rose. Strolling over, slipping his arms around her waist. He pressed her back into his chest and said, "If Alison becomes a problem, she's history."

She turned to face him. "She already *is* a problem." A sigh. "Look, I understand the magnetic pull that the past can have. I'm not asking you to choose. Besides, your business is your business. If I don't want you meddling in my affairs, I shouldn't meddle in yours."

Poe dropped his hold on Rukmani. "I've got to go."

Again, Rukmani held his arm. "Why are you so pissed off? What do you *want* from me?"

"Ruki, it's one thing to look the other way and tolerate an occasional dalliance. But aren't you ever *bothered* by it?"

Rukmani stared at him. "Of course I'm bothered. I'm not a rock. I have feelings. But there's nothing I can do. So why sweat it?"

"It's *that* attitude that pisses me off. You're so casual about everything—life, death, sex, blow jobs. Like some Buddhist monk. It's all one grand illusion."

Her voice quivered. "So how should I act? Jealous? Snoopy? Distrusting? And what would you do if I started making demands? You'd be out the door in a minute."

"There's a big difference between raving jealousy and total apathy."

"On the contrary, it's a very fine line. You've got a fierce need for independence, Romulus. Look at how you live, where you live, the strange hours you keep, your longest relationship is with a woman who treats you like dirt. Which guarantees you complete failure with other women in the future. You don't want to be tied down to anyone or anything. Which really is the heart of this matter. Your mom is going to cramp your style. And you don't like your style cramped. Which is why I'm so damn *casual*. If I started getting pushy, you'd be long gone."

"What are you *talking* about? *I'm* the one who keeps telling you to name a date."

"In my book, that's *not* a serious marriage proposal." Rukmani imitated, " 'Give me a date.' That's nothing but a carefully constructed cop-out meant to make you feel righteous."

"So *what* do you want? For me to get down on my knees?"

"It would be a start!"

"God, you're . . . imposs—" He started to kneel.

Rukmani held him back. "The answer's yes."

Poe stared at her, not truly believing what had just transpired. "Okay. So . . . everything's settled."

"Guess so."

Neither spoke. Then Poe said, "My house is kind of small . . ."

Rukmani sighed. "You know, it doesn't have to be right away. I know what that rattrap means to you." She began to stir ice into a tall pitcher filled with tea. "It's okay, Rom. We'll work on compromising later. For the time being, you keep your place, I'll keep mine."

Poe laughed nervously. "You're just as scared as I am."

She poured the tea into tumblers, then rubbed her forehead. "To me, marriage is equivalent to slavery."

"So why would you want to do it again?"

She stared at her tea glass, her eyes red and moist. "I like you."

Poe held back a smile. "I like you, too."

She took a deep breath, let it out slowly. "My parents aren't going to be happy. Neither will my kids like it. You're not Indian. At least, not the right type of Indian."

"Since when has race become an issue in your life?"

"Old ways die hard." She sipped tea, handed him a glass. "Ah, perfect!" Abruptly, she studied him intently. "You're lighter than I am—which is actually a plus. But you've got a lot of yellow in your skin tones."

"Blame it on Mom."

"Even so, with a few strategic applications of makeup, you could pass. If I cut your hair, teach you a few customs and a few words of Hindi . . . call you Siddartha . . . just maybe we could pull this off. I'll tell them that you're very acculturated."

"You are kidding, aren't you?"

She stroked his face. "It's all physical, you know. I'm totally enthralled with you sexually."

"Me?"

"My first husband was an old, ugly man. Sex with him was not only painful, but torturous. Rom, I see you, I see God—or what God meant sex to be." She sighed. "I shouldn't be telling you this. It'll just swell your head."

Poe turned serious. "As long as we're playing true confessions, I suppose I should tell you." He looked in her eyes. "I can't have children, Rukmani. I'm sterile."

Stunned, Rukmani stared back and said nothing.

Poe looked away. "I had these hormone treatments when I was a teenager. It resulted in some kind of weird adverse cellular reaction that basically fried my gonads. I didn't even know about it until I found out that Remus was sterile. Even so, his treatments were a lot more aggressive. So it really came as a shock."

Rukmani took his hands. "I'm so sorry."

Poe attempted a smile. "I've made peace with it. But if it's important to you . . . having more kids . . ."

"It's not a problem."

Again, Poe smiled weakly. "Great."

Rukmani held his face. "We always used birth control. Why didn't you tell me?"

"I was embarrassed." He turned away. "I have a lot of . . . unusual habits. Flaws that are highly visible. Why add a hidden deficiency?"

Tears welled up in her eyes. "Rom, there is nothing deficient about you in any way, shape, or form."

Poe smiled, wiped her cheeks with his thumb, kissed her lips. "Is Hindi a hard language?"

Rukmani rocked her wrist back and forth.

Poe's beeper went off. He glanced at the number across the read-out. "Remus. What does he want this time?"

"Better than Alison."

"Moratorium on her, please?"

Rukmani gave him the peace sign. Poe punched up Remus's number on his cellular. "What's up?"

"Mom's missing!"

"What?"

"I've just finished up with the airlines. It took me over two hours just to convince them I was legitimate. It appears that she bought a ticket that should have put her into Las Vegas around eleven this morning. Are you at work?"

"No, I'm at Ruk—"

"Can you check your house for me?"

There was *booze* in his house! Poe said, "I'm on my way."

"Rom, I feel terrible about this. Do you want me to come down?"

"Premature. I'll take care of it." He put his hand over the receiver. To Ruki, he said, "My mother's missing. I've got to go home—"

"I'll come with you."

Remus said, "Rom, I swear I've never yelled at that woman in my life. But today . . . she just got to me. God, if anything happened—"

"Nothing's going to happen."

"She thinks I've kicked her out of the house. I tried to explain that the move was just temporary."

"I'm going home right now."

"Romulus, you can't put her in an apartment. She'll see it as another rejection. She's too unstable—"

"I'll take care of it, Remus."

"You'll call me?"

"Just as soon as I know something."

"I'm sorry to dump all this in your lap."

"She's my mother, too."

"You've been terrific," Remus said with gratitude. "I'll never forget this, Rom."

A real hero, Poe thought. "Go back to work, Remus. I'll call you as soon as I find her."

Rukmani handed him the keys to his car as she locked up her apartment. "Don't worry. We'll find her."

Poe rolled his eyes. "That's what I'm afraid of."

TWENTY

She burst into tears as soon as Poe opened the door. "It's so nice of you to do this for me!" Wailing as she ran to him, she threw her chicken-bone arms around his neck.

Poe hugged her back, wrinkled his nose at her breath. Scanning the room, he saw the carpetbag resting on his couch, a plastic bag overflowing with comestibles on the counter next to his hotplate. Abutting the plastic bag was his flask of Dalwhinne, the booze a third down. He mouthed to Rukmani to put it away.

Out loud, he said, "Great to see you, Mom."

"My beautiful son," she sobbed out.

"Love you, too," Poe said.

Once she had been substantial—a thick woman with pendulous breasts. Over the last ten years, she had turned delicate, around one hundred ten pounds if that. She had been five-five, but age seemed to have pared off an inch. Saucer brown eyes dripping big globules of tears. Her face was thin, cheekbones jutting out like shelves. Her lips were cracked, her complexion was dry. Her skin tone, normally a shade or two darker than his, appeared wan. The simple hour airline trip had tired her. Wiping her eyes, she pulled away, observed him at arm's length. "I think you grew."

"I don't think so."

"Yes, you did. I swear, Romulus, you get taller and taller every time I see you."

No, Ma. You just get shorter. "Really, I don't—"

"You're so beautiful." She turned to Rukmani. "Isn't he beautiful?"

"The best."

Mom smiled at Rukmani as if she finally realized who she was. "And how are you, dear?"

"I'm fine, Mrs. Poe. How are you?"

"Oh, please call me Emma."

Poe extricated himself from his mother's grip, picked up her shot glass, the bottom tinged amber. "Sit down, Ma. Can I get you a soda?"

"Oh, I'm fine. I made myself a little drink. I was thirsty. I hope you don't mind."

Poe smiled, feeling a yoke tighten around his neck. "Mom, you're a little bit early—"

"Actually, I've been waiting here at least four hours." To Rukmani, she said *sotto voce,* "That's why I got so thirsty."

Poe said, "I meant you weren't supposed to come down for a couple of weeks."

Emma stiffened. "I had a fight with your brother. He said terrible things to me."

"I'm sure he didn't mean any—"

"I think this big project went to his head. Mr. Bigshot. Working all the time. Think he cares a fig for me?"

Poe tapped his forehead, pulled out his cellular. "As a matter of fact, he cares very much." He called up Remus's exchange. A moment later he was connected to his brother. "She's here. She's safe."

"Thank God!" Remus bellowed. "Let me talk to her."

"Sure you want to?"

"Put her on, Rom."

Poe gave the phone to his mother. "It's your bigshot son."

"I don't want to talk to him."

"Ma, don't be difficult."

Emma remained as still as stone.

Poe said, "Mom, if you're going to act like a baby—"

She grabbed the phone. "What do you want?"

Poe wagged his finger. "Be nice."

They started to talk in earnest. While they conversed, Poe took the opportunity to rinse her dirty glass with distilled water. Emma had also downed a couple of bottles of his Dos Equis. No sign that she had eaten anything solid.

Rukmani spoke in soothing tones. "What can I do?"

"Shoot me."

"Rom—"

"Go through my cooler. Remove all the beer and take it home with you. I've also got some canned tuna and a half loaf of rye bread. If you don't mind, could you make her a sandwich?"

Rukmani made a face as she rooted through the cooler. She pulled out the tuna. "You've also got some sliced mozzarella. Could I make a cheese sandwich instead?" She put the fish can to her ear. "I hear my ancestors talking to me."

Poe chuckled. "What evil deeds did they do on earth to regress to the state of Starkist?"

Rukmani spoke in a clipped Indian accent. "It is not our place to explain how Siva selects his souls for metempsychosis."

Poe laughed. "Meta *what*?"

Emma spoke up. "Romulus?"

Poe turned to face her. "Yeah, Ma?"

"*He* wants to talk to you."

Poe walked over to her, retrieved his cellular. "Yo."

Remus bellowed, "I think I should come down."

Poe said, "As much as I'd like that, it's not necessary."

Remus was unconvinced. "You're sure you're up to this?"

"You've certainly had an attitude change in a week. One minute you're in dire straits, the next you're ready to reverse the edict. Relax. I'll call you when I need you."

Neither spoke. Finally, Remus said, "Could you call tomorrow? Just to give me a progress report?"

"Will do."

Remus said, "I think this is the most we've spoken to each other in fifteen years."

He was right about that. Poe said, "I've got to go. Take care." He hung up, slipped the phone into his pocket. Removing the carpetbag from the couch, he sat next to his mother. "Ruki's making you a delicious cheese sandwich. Isn't that nice of her?"

"Very nice."

"So you will eat it?"

Emma looked offended. ''Of course I'll eat it.'' She took her son's hand. ''So . . . this is nice.'' Abruptly, she bolted up and opened her carpetbag, dumping its contents onto the floor. ''I don't have much . . . it's a little dirty what I do have. I haven't done the laundry for a while.''

''I'll wash it for you.''

''Oh, here it is!'' Emma picked up a small brown case. ''I was so worried I left it home.'' She opened the box, showed her son a set of ivory tiles.

Poe smiled. ''You still play mahj? That's good.''

''Do you play?''

''Not anymore.''

''It's a wonderful game.''

''Yes, it is.''

''Oh, you are so wonderful!'' To Rukmani, Emma said, ''Isn't he wonderful?''

''A peach.''

Poe felt his head throb. He took his mother's hand and squeezed it. ''Ma, sit down.''

Emma sat.

Poe started out, ''Ma, I love you—''

''I know you do, sweetheart. We're going to have such fun together.''

Rukmani brought in the cheese sandwich, noticed the clothes. She gave Emma her snack, gathered the vestments in her arms, and threw them back in the old woman's carpetbag. ''I'll take care of this.''

Poe said, ''I can do it. I know you're busy.''

She waved him off. ''I've got my own laundry to do.'' She paused. ''As long as I'm doing hers, how about yourself? You've been sweating buckets these last twenty minutes.''

Poe studied her. ''Are you sure?''

Rukmani turned her hands into talking puppets. She spoke in kid voices.

''Are you a sucker?'' asked the left.

''Yes, I am a big sucker,'' answered the right.

''How big?''

She spread her arms apart. ''This biiig.'' In her own voice, she said, ''I'll take your dirty underwear now.''

Poe went over to his hamper, pulled out a pile, and stuffed it into her arms. ''Happy?''

''Ecstatic.'' Rukmani winked. ''I'd forgotten what it was to feel married.'' She smelled his clothing. ''Not too bad. Nice seeing you again, Emma.''

''Oh nice seeing you, too, dear.''

''How about if we all go out to dinner later tonight?'' Rukmani suggested. ''Rom's larder is a bit bare.''

Emma said, ''Why, what a lovely idea! Can we go to that place far up in the sky? It makes me feel like I'm flying.''

Rukmani said, ''She mean the Needle?''

''I think so,'' Poe answered.

''Needle it is,'' Rukmani said. ''I'll need your car, Rom.''

''Keys are on the counter.''

''I'll see you both in a couple of hours.''

''Thanks.'' Poe waited until he heard the car's engine fade to nothing. Then he turned to his mother. ''How are you doing?''

''Just fine.''

Poe exhaled. There was a long moment of silence. Finally Emma said, ''Spit it out, Romulus.''

''Mom, I got you a place of your own.''

Emma's eyes moistened.

Poe shook his leg as he continued to talk. ''A lovely one-bedroom apartment very close to Ruki's place—''

''But far from you?''

''Ten minutes by car. You need me, I'm there in a snap.''

''How about if I want to see you? I don't *drive,* Romulus.''

''I've hired someone just for that purpose,'' he lied. ''A wonderful woman who's also a nurse. So if you need anything, she's right there. And if you want to pop over to my place, she can take you—''

''I'm dying, Romulus. I have cancer.''

Poe nearly choked on his saliva. His head started to pound as furiously as his heart. He *couldn't* have heard right. But he knew his ears were fine. A play for pity? He didn't put it past her. Yet the way she looked, her physical deterioration. She was telling the truth.

If he had been a woman, he might have cried.

Alison couldn't get out of bed. Her latest forays had left her exhausted and drained. She had vomited at least four times, yet the nausea refused to abate.

God was punishing her for her evil, that she knew. But it really wasn't her fault. It was the forces driving her, the voices telling her what to do. And they were so insistent. When she did her research, the voice always went away. Because they didn't like it when Alison knew too much. If she could just get out of bed, she could do her research, and then the voices would fade.

So tired and weak . . .

Breathing was laborious. The air felt charred and burned with each inhalation. Sweat dripped from her body. Every inch of her was feverish. (Was she in hell or was it just Las Vegas heat?) Her limbs ached, her stomach groaned as waves of acid spewed up through her esophagus. She hadn't bathed or washed in twenty-four hours, and she felt as sullied as muck.

Steve would bring the kids home soon. She'd have to look presentable. Otherwise he'd think it had something to do with her illness rather than a simple virus. The virus ruse could only last so long. It wasn't a virus. It was the voices. But she couldn't let on.

All that eating and gorging. (What exactly had she eaten?) She was retching . . . coughing up wisps of fur like a cat with a hairball problem. She hated herself.

Maybe that's why Mother had done what she had done. Had she felt like Alison did now . . . despising every inch of her wretched body?

She checked the clock. Steve would be home soon.

A week ago, time raced like a firestorm. Now it dragged as if weighted with chains.

Slowly, she inched out of bed, crawling on all fours to the bathroom. Reaching up to run the water. Hot water. Anything to remove the stench and dirt and grime and filth.

Couldn't let the kids see her like this. Steve would protect her for only so long. Then he'd get angry.

She lay prostrate on the floor as the water ran. When the tub seemed as if it should be filled, she stretched her arm, groping for the taps. She felt the familiar grip and turned them off. Hoisting herself onto the ledge, she tumbled into the basin, her body still wrapped in a terry robe, hugging her like a needed second skin.

Soaking away the pain.

Why was this happening to her? Was there some genetic program she was missing? If she could just find the time and energy to do her research.

All her papers, clippings, files, the answers were there. She was positive. Because the green book had told her so. But the work needed organization, meticulous planning and filing, not loosely meshed thoughts of an insane woman.

Last week she had been on top of the world. Now she felt as lifeless as her yellow patch of lawn. Maybe it was the weather, the sudden heat that brought out the predators. She was acutely sensitive to changes in the atmosphere.

Soaking.

Had to take off the robe. Steve would know there was something wrong if she continued to bathe in her robe. She couldn't show him how much she needed the skin. Had to keep it a secret. All her life . . . a series of secrets. So many secrets . . . so *many* secrets.

TWENTY-ONE

Ruki was clearly sitting on something, waiting for the right moment. So wrapped up in her excitement she hadn't noticed his misery. Or maybe Poe hid it well. Mom certainly hadn't let on, leaving him to wonder about the gravity of her condition. But then every so often she'd stop eating, lift vacant eyes, and stare out the picture windows.

At the apex of the city, the Needle's view was a panorama of hotels bathed in a sea of coruscating lights. Beyond the glitter was a sprawl of low-rise housing bleeding into mile-long flats of pink clay. At this hour, the desert was a black hole of nothingness; the majestic purple mountains became looming shadows that reminded Poe of his insignificance.

He tried to pay attention to the conversation, but he had little to contribute. The women did most of the yakking, talking about food—growing food, buying food, preparing food, and cooking food. They swapped dozens of ethnic recipes. Ma had stopped cooking years ago, since before he left Reno. The last time he had seen her anywhere near a stove had been the day her apartment kitchen had almost blown up from a grease fire. Mom had been sacked out on the living-room couch.

But Poe could remember a time—the Sunday dinners with Grandma. His mother's family had moved to St. George, Utah, when she was twelve, but her Paiute heritage remained a staple in her life. Grandma's menus had always been simple but delicious. Roasted birds served with cakes made from ground pine nuts and white mesquite beans. A salad of Indian spinach, bitter greens, and mixed roasted seeds. Cholla fruit and berries sweetened with sugar. Poe had adored his grandmother's traditional cooking up until he had started school. Mingling with kids whose ideas of fancy cuisine had meant mustard with their salami sandwiches.

His first day of kindergarten . . . pulling his lunch out of his greasy brown paper sack. Licking his fingers as tots stared contemptuously at his food. They had never seen a whole roasted pigeon complete with head.

Eeeuuuu! That looks gross!

From that day on, he and Remus had opted for peanut butter sandwiches on white bread.

A hand on his shoulder. Poe looked up. Somehow, Patricia had materialized. She was with a date—some big Polynesian guy wearing harem pants, a white linen shirt, and a purple stone-studded vest. Aladdin on steroids.

Patricia was talking to him. ". . . is Nate Malealani."

"Ah," Poe said, shaking a very big hand. "Our eyewitness link to our mystery man."

"Find him yet, Sergeant?"

Found him and lost him. "Not yet," Poe said. "But we will."

Malealani felt as if everyone was staring at him. "Sorry about the dress. I just got off work at Casablanca."

Emma said, "I think you look cute!"

Poe smiled. "Detective, this is my mother, Emma Poe. Dr. Kalil, you know—"

"Rukmani, please." She smiled warmly. "Come join us. Eating is always more fun in groups."

Patricia and Nate looked at each other. He said, "We're not interrupting?"

"Not at all."

Chewing a morsel of Chinese chicken salad, Emma tried to master enthusiasm for her food. "Buffet's great here!"

"Probably the best in the city," Malealani said. "But if you really want some *great* eating, you gotta drive a little."

Emma wiped her face. "Where?"

"These little out-of-the-way places," Patricia answered. "Nate knows them all." She turned to her date. "Being as your time is more limited than mine, I suggest you brave the lines. I'll be with you in a minute."

He scowled. "I hate to go up alone in these duds. I feel like a freak."

"I'll be there in a minute." Patricia patted his weighty shoulder. "Go on. I know you're hungry." As soon as Nate left, Patricia rolled her eyes and added, "He's *always* hungry."

"Honeymoon's over?" Poe teased.

Patricia shrugged. "Actually, Nate's a good guy." Her eyes darted between Rukmani and Emma. Poe knew a hint when it bit him in the ass. He said, "Ma, why don't you go keep Nate company. Help him out with the buffet."

Again, Emma looked up, a forkful of moo goo gai pan halfway between her plate and her mouth. "The boy looks like he knows his way around food."

"Ma—"

"All right, all right." She peered at her son. "You're trying to get rid of me."

Poe smiled, said nothing.

She stood slowly, then walked reluctantly toward the groaning tables of food. Poe thought he detected a slight limp. His imagination?

To Rukmani, he said, "So what have you to tell us?"

Rukmani said, "It's that obvious?"

Patricia said, "You ain't much of a poker player, Dr. Kalil. What's up?"

"I got the bloods back on Sarah Yarlborough. Her body had been loaded with crack, but nothing else separated out on the gas chromatography chart. Unlike Newel, she hadn't been heavily sedated with barbiturates."

"In the killer's mind, crack could have taken the place of barbs," Poe told her. "Why ply her with drugs when she did the job herself?"

"A good point," Rukmani admitted. "Still, the deaths were significantly different. Brittany was drugged, then tortured to death. She probably died of voluminous shock and profuse bleeding, as she had very little liquid left in her body. Sarah, on the other hand, died of asphyxiation, with the throat cutting done postmortem. She was very well hydrated compared to Newel."

"The throat was cut after she died?" Patricia asked.

"Most definitely."

"How can you tell?"

"By blood loss," Rukmani said. "The jugular had been severed. If that had been done premortem, her heart would have still been beating, draining the body of fluid with each pulse. When the throat is cut after death, there is some direct vesicular drainage, but nowhere near the serum loss that one gets with a pumping heart.''

''So you *don't* think the deaths are related?'' Patricia asked.

''I'm not saying the same person couldn't have done both,'' Rukmani said. ''But the deaths are different forensically.'' She suddenly smiled. ''Look at your mother, Rom. She's holding court around the Szechuan veal.''

Poe regarded the buffet. Indeed, Mom seemed to be lecturing not only Nate, but a group of tall, towheaded tourists speaking some esoteric, Scandinavian-sounding language. As Mom pointed to different dishes, her mouth worked a mile a minute. Nate stood next to her, rocking on his feet, watching Emma explain the nuances of Las Vegas cuisine.

''Your boyfriend looks lost,'' Poe said.

''I'll go rescue him,'' Patricia said.

After she had left, Rukmani turned to Poe. ''Are you all right? You're snapping your fingers, albeit silently.''

Poe clasped his hands as he stole a glance his mother's way. She was filibustering around the pork spareribs. He whispered, ''Act casual, okay?''

Rukmani smiled with concern. ''What is it?''

''My mother has cancer. . . . *Casual,* Ruki.''

Quickly, she laughed to hide her shock. Under her breath, she muttered, ''Oh my God!''

''Also, I got a page from Steve about twenty minutes ago. Alison's been sick for the past couple of days. He's worried about her.''

''So tell him to call a *doctor.*''

Poe kept his patience. ''He had to go out tonight with the kids—an open house at their school. He didn't want to leave Alison unattended, but he had no choice. He asked me to stop by just for a short time. I think I should.''

Rukmani fought anger. ''Considering what you just told me about your mother, I think Alison should wait.''

''If Alison had called, I would have said no. But being as Steve called . . .'' Poe forced a smile. ''It must be bad.''

''Not as bad as your mother.'' Her voice rose. ''I think you've got your priorities mixed up, Sergeant.''

''Shhhh,'' Poe whispered. ''My mother is my first priority. But she's going to need a *lot* of my time. Alison I could probably polish off in an hour. If you wouldn't mind, I'd like to take the car. Could you take my mom back home in a cab? I'll be there as fast as I can. Then, with my mind clear, we can deal with the greater issue.''

Rukmani boiled with rage. But she knew better than to start up. No matter how many certificates and degrees she had amassed, she never quite felt peerage with men. Too many years of subservience at too young an age. She took a deep yoga breath, let it out in measured seconds. ''Do what you have to do. I'll take care of your mother.''

''Don't mention anything—''

''Rom, I'm not stupid.''

''I didn't mean to . . .'' Poe looked over his shoulder, at his mother, who was rapturing over the wontons. He met Rukmani's eyes. ''If you weren't in my life, I'd be going nuts. Your help is not only appreciated, but invaluable. Thank you.''

Rukmani nodded, continued to yoga-breathe. After a minute, she was able to shunt away the fury. She peered into Rom's eyes—incredibly stressed. Why hadn't she noticed it before? She was a doctor, for God's sake. He needed her professionally as well as emotionally.

''I'm very sorry,'' she said softly. ''What kind of cancer does she have?''

Poe sighed, then remembered to smile. ''Leukemia. Isn't that usually a kids' disease?''

''Yes, but adults get it as well. Do you know what kind?''

''She told me, but I wasn't processing the information too well.''

''Lymphocytic? Myelogenous?''

''You're looking a bit intense for lighthearted conversation, Ruki.'' She laughed. ''Better?''

''Much.'' Poe took her hand. ''I think she said something about lymph nodes. I have some of her medical records that she brought with her from Reno. She stole them from the offices, hid them in her mahjong set.''

''I can see that your mother's a fighter.''

''Absolutely.'' But Poe had seen despair in Emma's eyes. ''I skimmed some of the papers, but was lost. Doctors have their own jargon. They're back at the house.''

''Has she undergone any treatment?''

''Not yet.''

''Oh boy.'' Rukmani kissed his hand and grinned. ''The hordes are returning, piled platters of food in hand.''

Poe raised his wineglass. ''A toast to Emma. For a long, healthy life.''

Ruki clinked his glass. ''Amen, brother, amen.''

*   *   *

In the most cheerful voice she could muster, Alison called out, "I'm in the bedroom, guys."

Poe said, "It's me, Alison. Can I come in?"

She became cross. "You're already *in*."

"Can I come in the bedroom?"

Quickly, Alison pulled out a compact from her nightstand. She dabbed on blush, smoothing it over her pale cheeks with the tips of her fingers. A smattering of lipstick. Nothing else. That would be overdoing it. She brushed her silken hair, straightened her slinky robe, the hem falling a couple of inches above her ankles. After plumping up her pillows, she sat up straight.

"Come in."

Poe opened the door. "Steve asked me to check in on you. He said you weren't feeling well."

"Steve?" She made a face.

"He said you had a nasty case of the flu." He regarded her face. "You look pretty good, actually."

"Pretty good?"

"Very good," Poe amended. He sat down on the corner of her bed. "How do you feel?"

She sighed. "Comes and goes. I'll live. What's wrong with you?"

"Nothing."

Alison's eyes bored into his. "You're lying."

"Can I get you something to drink?"

She continued to study him. "You're acting distant."

"It's fatigue. Can I get you something to drink?"

"How about some wine?"

"How about some orange juice?"

She shrugged. "You're no fun."

"I know." Poe felt his patience ebb. "You've told me that many times in the past." He left the room, then returned a moment later holding a glass of juice. "Here. Drink."

Alison took the glass and sipped, eyeing him over the rim of the glass. "You're supposed to be cheering me up, not weighing me down."

Poe was quiet. Alison leaned over, patted his hand, then sat back up. "You're looking rather buff, Rommie. Have you been working out?"

"A weight here and there. Nothing that should make a difference. But thanks for the compliment."

She drank her juice and waited for him to carry his fair share of the conversation. When he didn't, she said, "You're acting very stiff. Is your girlfriend giving you problems?"

"Not at all." Poe paused. "My mother's in town."

"Aha!" Alison said triumphantly. "I knew it was something."

"She's going to be staying here for a while. Remus has a big project. I told him I'd take her off his hands."

"Do-gooders never prosper."

"You're right about that."

"Why don't you bring her by? She always liked me. I think she was always hoping that . . . you know . . . you and I would . . ."

Wasn't my fault that we didn't. Poe said, "Maybe after she gets settled into her apartment, I'll bring her by."

"I always thought your mother was real cute."

"Cute?"

"Well, maybe I mean . . . attentive."

"When she wasn't drunk, she was very attentive."

"You're so hard on people, Romulus. Why do you always look at life in a negative fashion? It's your downfall. No one wants to be around a sourpuss."

"I'm not being negative, I'm being truthful. I love my mother dearly, but she was a drunk. Still is, for that matter." He stood. "Can I get some juice? I'm very thirsty."

"Be my guest."

He left for her kitchen, poured himself a tall glass of OJ, then laced it with Stoly. He guzzled half the tumbler, then came back into the bedroom. "Much better."

"So . . . how is she?"

"Mom's been better, but she's still alive and kicking."

Alison licked her lips, hiked up her robe an inch or so. "I meant your doctor girlfriend."

"Rukmani's fine."

"Doesn't she have grown children?"

"Yes."

"Doesn't that bother you?"

"Why should it bother me? They don't live at home."

"I mean that she's so . . . she's Stephen's age, isn't she?"

"A little older, actually."

"And that doesn't bother you?"

"No."

"What happened to you?" Alison teased. "You used to be so picky."

"I'm still very picky. Why are you asking questions about Rukmani? You've never been interested in my girlfriends before."

Alison tensed. "I was just making conversation. Forgive me if I touched a nerve."

Poe laughed. "Like you'd care a heap even if you did. What else can I get you?"

"How about a good lay?"

"Alison—"

"You never deliver on the real important issues."

"*Au contraire,* I did deliver at one time. But that was then and this is now. What has gotten into you today? Virus must have gone to your head."

Alison folded her arms in front of her chest and sulked, waiting for him to initiate conversation. When he remained silent, she tried another tactic, trying to sound as casual as a summer's eve. "How's the case coming? The one that reminded you of the Bogeyman case."

"I have a few leads. We'll solve it. It'll just take time."

"Nice to have such confidence. They never solved the Bogeyman case, you know."

"I know. But I wasn't on the force back then."

Alison laughed—tinkly and light. When she smiled, she was so beautiful. Again, she kept her voice airy. "So what do you know about it?"

"My case or the Bogeyman case?"

"Both."

Poe regarded her. "A couple of weeks ago . . . when we talked. You told me you remembered the Bogeyman quite well."

"Yes."

"Do you know for certain how many victims he took down?"

"I told you I thought he had killed at least two. If my mom . . . well, then maybe it would have been three."

Poe scratched his head. "Interesting. I only found one case file in his time period that matched the Bogeyman's MO."

Abruptly, Alison turned pouty. Poe sighed. "What did I say this time?"

She shook her head.

He stood. "So don't tell me—"

"Did you look up my mother's file?"

"No." He regarded her. "I wouldn't invade your privacy."

"Just that I told you that she could have been his victim. I thought maybe—"

"You thought wrong."

Alison inspected him with hard eyes. "Considerate of you to be thinking about *me* instead of your *case*."

"That's me. Just one heck of a considerate guy." Poe checked his watch. "Steve should be coming home. I'd better go."

"Didn't he send you over here in the first place?"

"It doesn't mean he wants to see me when he gets home. Refresh your drink before I go?"

"Not unless you add vodka to mine like you did to yours."

"I can indulge." Poe smiled. "I'm not sick."

"Not yet."

"What is that supposed to mean?"

"Just that I hope my virus isn't contagious."

Without thinking, he leaned over and kissed her on the lips. "Hope not. Good night."

She didn't answer.

"I said good night, Gracie."

Alison turned away, refusing to acknowledge his departure.

He shrugged and walked out of the room, making a mental note to look up her mother's suicide file.

TWENTY-TWO

Poe watched as suds from his beer dripped over the rim of his glass and onto his fingers, thinking: *I don't want to go home. I really don't want to go home.*

Honey said, "I think you need a napkin." Tenderly, she wiped his hand, then kneeled before him, her long pink peignoir sweeping over the floor like a bridal train. She looked up with those oh-so-concerned eyes that could only belong to professional call girls delivering TLC at $250 an hour. She placed her hands on his knees, her nails long and red. "Tell me how I can make the boo-boo better."

"You just did." Poe was full of self-loathing. The pathetic call he had made to Rukmani: *It's taking a little longer than I expected.* A lame excuse, as if Rukmani hadn't seen through it. She had said nothing over the phone, but her former words kept chastising his war-weary brain. *This isn't about blow jobs, it's about responsibility.*

He said, "I think I'm getting married."

Honey broke into a bright smile. "That's wonderful." A pause. "Are you happy about it?"

"Very."

"Rukmani?"

"Yes."

"You two are a great couple."

"I think so."

Honey hedged. "Tolerant of each other's needs."

"Up to a point."

"Ah!" She paused. "So is this your finale?"

Poe sipped beer. "Maybe. Anyway, if you don't hear from me, at least you'll know it had nothing to do with you."

"I'm egotistical enough to assume it never has anything to do with me." She tapped his knees, then stood. "Rukmani's so . . . accomplished. Especially when you consider where she came from. I wish you two lots of happiness."

"Thank you."

"When's the big day?"

"I don't know."

She cocked her head in a coy manner. "Tentative, are we?"

"It's mostly for her. Her first marriage was more bondage than partnership. She's a little commitment-shy."

"And you?"

He smiled. "More like tentative." He thought a moment. "Honey, how long were you with Parker Lewiston?"

She was taken aback. "Where did that come from?"

"Just curious."

She wagged her finger at him. "A good woman never kisses and tells."

"I'm not asking you for details, just a time frame."

Honey chuckled. "We were together around two years."

"And he was good to you?"

"The best."

"Kinky?"

"Sergeant, I do believe that falls under kissing and telling."

Poe plowed on. "And his taste in women . . ."

"Was excellent."

"He didn't hide some nasty perversion in the closet?"

"Why are you so interested in Parker Lewiston?"

"Remember about two weeks ago, I showed you a picture of a murdered hooker?"

"How could I forget? You shoved it in my face."

"Supposedly she was one of Parker's."

"And?"

"He denied knowing her."

"So?"

Poe finished off his Dos Equis, then debated having another brew. Honey's was stocked better than most bars. "Just wondering why he'd lie like he did."

Honey poured herself a cup of coffee. "Could be a number of reasons. You could have gotten your information wrong. Or Parker might not have remembered such a cheap little slut."

"You just said his taste in women was excellent."

Honey frowned. "His taste in his real women."

"Ah!" Poe smiled. "I see."

But Honey was still pissed. "Perhaps Parker just didn't want to get involved in your sleazy little affairs, Rom."

"*My* sleazy little affairs?" Poe was incredulous. "You mean murder?"

Honey stiffened. "All the more reason for Parker to keep his mouth shut. He didn't get where he is today by making mistakes."

"Mistakes like wielding a knife."

"My, you're feisty today. I think you're going through Honey withdrawal."

Back off, Poe. "Probably."

She drank her coffee, then softened her tone. "If you want my opinion, I'd say that the little tart didn't seem like his type. He prefers women who are not only beautiful but sophisticated and clever. He enjoys talking. When we were together, I do believe I dispensed more advice to him than he did to me."

Don't flatter yourself, babe. You're nothing but a whore. And you, Poe, are nothing but a jerk!

He stood up. "Thanks, Honey. Thanks for everything."

She beamed. "Can I kiss you good-bye?"

"I'd be insulted if you didn't."

She gave him a long, passionate kiss.

It tasted like poison.

It was only a forty-five-minute diversion, but it felt like hours. He dragged his body into his house, where the lights were as dim as his spirits. A bespectacled Rukmani, garbed in a flowing purple dress, was seated in a chair, reading papers by his battery-operated lantern. A sweaty sheen covered her nutmeg skin. His house had no air-conditioning, only a moribund battery fan which kicked up a hot wind and blew it from one side to the other.

She looked up from the sheaves, wiped her face with a tissue. "She's sleeping. I opened the couch. I figured that was okay."

Poe stood at the doorway, perspiration dripping from his forehead, his eyes feeling like fire. He swabbed his face with his sleeve. "I went to Honey's."

"I figured as much. Come in, but leave the door open. The circulation feels good."

He walked inside and pulled up a stool next to Rukmani, pausing before he sat down. "I don't even know why I did it."

Rukmani shrugged. "Asserting your independence against me. Evading the crushing responsibility of caring for a sick parent. You're a horny guy. Take your pick."

He was silent.

Rukmani said, "Just don't lie to me, Romulus. You never lied before. Don't start now."

Poe looked at his lap. "I'm sorry."

"Life is short. People aren't perfect. Forget it."

He noticed the papers she was reading. "I see my mother must have told you about her condition."

"She knew you had told me something. So she filled in some details. The rest . . ." She held up a thick pile of records. "Working my way through the medical muck."

"Remus doesn't know. She doesn't want me to call him." Again, he wiped sweat from his face. "I have to, Ruki. I owe him that."

"I agree."

"I'm tired now. I figured I'd do it in the morning."

"Sounds logical."

He started to speak and realized there was a lump in his throat. He coughed in his fist, then said, "I don't want her to die."

Rukmani took off her glasses. "Let me tell you the situation from a medical standpoint. Because before I started certifying deaths, I did a lot of plain old microscopic pathology. So I know what I'm talking about."

"You always know what you're talking about. Go on."

"First off, I've been going over these diagnoses. She does have some form of lymphoma slash leukemia, but an unusual presentation. Not cut-and-dried, but what in life is? Anyway, without being able to examine the biopsies and peer at the cells, I'm forced to extrapolate. So none of this is carved in stone."

"I understand."

"The most accurate description seems to be chronic lymphocytic leukemia with a systemic profusion of moderately well differentiated cells. Which is actually very good."

"Really?"

"Really. The more differentiated the cells, the better. Rom, she's not saddled with a death sentence. We've got bona fide protocol and treatment which has proven highly successful."

She held up two fingers.

"Two things. First, I've got to run some extensive tests to figure out if she has more of a lymphoma or more of a leukemia. Treatment is a little different depending on which disease is the more pronounced. There seems to be lots of blurring. She has disseminated cancer cells indicative of leukemia as well as localized neoplasms in the organs of the immune system—which points to lymphoma."

"So that's weird?"

"It's not unheard-of for lymphomas to convert to leukemias and vice versa. The fine tuning can be taken care of by meticulous lab work and a personally designed protocol. The trick is . . ."

She sighed.

"The trick is to get her into a hospital. She doesn't want modern medicine. She wants an Indian faith healer."

"I know."

"She's been over this with you?"

"Yes. Truthfully, I was too stunned to argue. Not that it would have done any good."

"I'm all for holistic medicine. We Hindus believe in some way-out stuff. And I've seen mystics work miracles with my own eyes. But on a day-to-day basis, I'm real big on Western medicine—things like vaccinations and antibiotics. They've saved lots of lives, and I'm not one to argue with empiricism."

"You don't have to convince me." He licked his dry lips. His armpits were drenched in sweat. "Could you talk to her?"

"I'd be happy to, except I think I'd be viewed as the establishment. Should come from someone else. Does she have any relative that she looks up to?"

Poe thought for a moment. "There's Y."

Rukmani gave him a thumbs-up sign. "Brilliant. Do you think he'll be cooperative?"

"I think he'd help." He looked at his watch. Ten to eleven. It felt like midnight in hell. "It's not that late. I bet I can find him."

"Why don't you call it a night, guy? You look so tired."

"I'll be fine." He kissed her hand. "Again, I'm sorry."

She let out a small laugh. "I didn't realize you had such a capacity for guilt. If I were the type, I could really milk this." She kissed his hand back. "I do care, actually. Just not all that much. You're going to do it again. So will I. Fidelity will take time for both of us. Take me home now? I'd invite you for the night, but I fear you're already spent."

She was right about that. "I have to look for Y."

"How convenient." She stood up, stowing Emma Poe's medical records in a plastic bag. "I'll take these home if you don't mind."

"Thanks for everything."

"How's Alison, by the way?"

"As crazy as ever."

Rukmani waited a beat. "I know she's gorgeous, Romulus. But she's also manipulative and very disturbed. It can't be all physical. What do you *see* in her?"

Dashed hopes. "She's as close as I have to family here."

"She's dysfunctional, Poe."

"My entire family is dysfunctional." He looked at her. "And you're so normal all of a sudden?"

"Sure, I have problems. Who doesn't? But I am able to operate in a social context. And I do perform a useful service for society." She grinned. "And let me tell you something. I must do a bang-up job. Because my patients never complain."

TWENTY-THREE

The night had retained most of the desert heat, so Poe found it pleasurable to be anywhere air-conditioned. Each year he swore he'd buy a generator. But when push came to shove, he was either too busy or too tired to make the effort. He plodded through the Mojave's inferno summers, rationalizing that sweat was a good thing. It cleansed the body. Certainly he could use a good scrubbing now.

By the time he located Y, it was close to one in the morning. Wearing jeans and a red buckskin tank top, the old man was manning a poker machine at the Flamingo Hilton, his flabby arms feeding the insatiable money chute. His head was encircled with a beaded band. Poe had come prepared, presenting him with four rolls of quarters. Y glanced at the cylinders, pocketing them in one fluid motion.

Poe said, "How's your luck been holding?"

"Steady enough."

"Good for you."

"What do you want?"

"A favor."

Y waited a beat, then continued playing. The pause was Poe's indication that Y had heard him.

"It concerns my mother." He waited for Y to get his electronic poker cards. "She's sick, Y. She needs some tests, but doesn't want to go into

174

a hospital. Actually, she doesn't want any Western medicine. She wants an Indian shaman.''

"Shamans are Western medicine. We were in the West long before the *marukats* came and stole our land.''

Poe kept his patience. "I realize that. Nobody's claiming righteousness for what was done hundreds of years ago. I'm talking about a very sick woman who can be helped by modern-day drugs.''

No one spoke for a minute. Then Y said, "How sick?''

Poe wiped his face with a tissue. "Sick enough to need real help. Not that I'm putting anyone down. Give her the shaman, too. But Rukmani thinks that Mom has a good shot with Western treatment. Being as I'm a bettin' guy, I go with the proven odds.''

Y pulled in a straight against the machine's two pair. The contraption started dinging up a storm. "What does she have? Cancer?''

"Yes.'' Lucky guess? "She couldn't have told you.''

"No, she didn't tell me. I haven't even spoken to your mother. What you described . . . it sounded like cancer.''

Poe felt droplets pouring down his neck even though it was cool inside the casino. "She has some weird kind of leukemia. But Rukmani's optimistic.''

Y sipped vodka and said nothing.

Poe said, "She needs chemotherapy. Without it, she'll die. And please don't feed me shit that we all have to die eventually. I'm not in an existential mood.''

Y took out one of Poe's rolls of quarters. He could hear the desperation in the kid's voice. "I'll talk to her. No promises.''

A millstone was suddenly lifted from Poe's neck. He felt his eyes water. "Thank you.''

Y looked at the boy, handed him his vodka. Poe shook his head. "I've already had too much. I feel like my head's being attacked by a woodpecker.''

After dropping a quarter into the slot, Y dug into his pockets and pulled out a cellophane packet. "Take this. It'll make you feel better.''

"What is it?''

"A home remedy. You could get a vision, but don't pay it any mind.''

Poe looked at the powder, put the envelope in his shirt pocket. "Is this some kind of peyote?''

"A little peyote, a little mushroom, a few other desert plants, and cayenne pepper. Mix it with tomato juice and vodka for one hell of a

Bloody Mary.'' Y pulled in an ace-high against the machine's pair. He put another coin in the bottomless pit. "This is what you do. You take this shit, strip naked—it's warm enough—then go out into the desert and howl at the moon."

"There's no moon tonight."

"Then howl at the stars, howl at something. Beat your breast and be at one with the desert. I'm telling you, it works. Oh, you'd better wear boots. Lots of snakes out."

"Could you come by tomorrow to talk to Mom?"

Y managed a half-smile. "Tell Emma I'll come by."

"What time?"

"Daytime."

"Could you be a *little* more specific?"

"No. I'll come after dawn but before dusk."

Poe gave up. "Thanks."

"No promises." Another quarter into the machine. "I don't make promises, no one gets hurt."

From the moment his mother was admitted into the hospital, Poe ran in fast-forward. His life was a blur of death and disease, of decisions with consequences for which he was ill-prepared. At least, his brother and he became a united team, bombarding the doctors with questions, pressuring them until they got answers. They adopted a pugnacious us-against-them mentality, making them unpopular with the staff, causing Rukmani some heat. But neither cared, because too much was at stake. The animosity thrust against them reminded Poe of his painful youth. But along with the pain came the warmth of a revived fraternal relationship.

Remus lived a hellish commuter's existence, grabbing the last outbound plane from Reno, then flying back for work in the early morning. His energy seemed boundless, in stark contrast to Poe, who woke up every morning feeling exhausted and drained.

Pleasure became only a word in the dictionary. He spent all his conscious hours either at work or at the hospital—nursing, comforting, waiting to see what might happen next. Holding an old woman's hand as she slept fitfully, conked out on methotrexate. His mother's breathing was raspy, her breath stale and often fetid. Her hair turned brittle and cracked at the roots. Her skin was as parched as the desert floor. Rukmani was still puzzled by Emma's cellular presentation: the histology didn't quite conform to anything in the books. But the chemotherapy was working, and that was all that mattered.

For all his size and girth, Remus was able to adjust to sleep in a hospital room. Poe became an insomniac—restless and testy. After two weeks of frenetic hours, Weinberg ordered him home one sizzling afternoon. Three hours of blissful sleep in his own house, in his own bed. Alone with the world. It gave heaven a whole new meaning.

When he awoke, it was three o'clock and a scorcher. He was drenched, as wet and itchy as a Southern swamp. He ran cold water over his head, dressed in clean clothing, then stripped the soaked sheets, piling his linens and heading for the Laundromat. Pulling into a spot, he could see the heat rays emanating from the asphalt parking lot, feel the fire run through his shoes.

He stuffed his clothes in a washing machine, intending a quick trip to the hospital. But the thought of stepping through those doors, hearing the hushed tones in a room redolent with antiseptic smells. Life amid a sea of panicked, confused faces as white-uniformed staff scurried about like speed-driven specters. He couldn't muster the strength.

Instead, he made a detour for Records.

Bun-headed Madison was still manning the desk. She still wore the same distasteful expression. "You're back."

"Me and herpes—just can't get rid of us."

Madison screwed up her face. "Any specific reason why you compare yourself to a virus?"

"It's what I am—an invader." Poe rocked on his feet. "No, I haven't filled out the proper papers. But you're going to let me in anyway, because I outrank you and I'm feeling extremely violent. Next person who gets in my way is roadkill." He held out his hand. "The keys?"

Madison frowned, but stood up. "What year?"

" 'Seventy-three."

"Homicide?"

"Actually a suicide."

"Those are filed under Homicide." She pulled out a key ring, unlocked the door to the vault, and switched on the light. "This way."

"Madison, you deserve a raise."

"I deserve to win the lottery. But I'm not going to win any more than I'll get a raise, so why dream."

*　　*　　*

Born in Utah, Linda Joanne Hennick née Paulson had been thirty-eight years old at the time of her demise—three years older than Poe, which gave him pause. He had always thought of Alison's mother as a pretty but much older woman.

She had been found in a room at the Four Aces Motel and Casino. Poe knew the place. It was one of a quartet of cheap joints that sat in a dustbowl at the Nevada/California border. Twenty-five years ago, the casino hadn't been much more than a barn with tables and slots. When the wind blew, the rafters would rattle, and grit would coat the floor. Now the Aces was a hard-core gambling mecca for those who couldn't afford or couldn't wait for Vegas. Recently a grade-school child had been murdered in one of the motel's arcades. The father had been paged by security guards to take the kid home; the child had been crying and had wanted to go to sleep. But the lure of cards had been a powerful aphrodisiac, obliterating whatever little paternal love might have once existed.

He flipped through the microfiche.

A head-shot picture of the victim when she had been in one piece. Like her daughter, Linda had been beautiful. Alison had inherited her hazel eyes and blond hair. But Linda's face had been fuller, her lips not quite as lush. The snapshot showed a thirtyish woman with intense eyes. They were not only looking at you, but looking you over.

Another turn of the spool. Poe read on.

Cause of death was voluminous shock brought on by profuse arterial bleeding from multiple cuts and stab wounds to her wrists and arms. The postmortem black-and-whites showed a seminude woman sprawled on a bed, head thrown back, a pillow resting under her neck. One leg was straight, the other was bent at the knee. Her left arm rested by her side, the right draped across her wounded breasts. Her bottom torso and thighs were covered by a red dress. Her legs were bare.

About a half-dozen close-ups of the inflicted areas, the most notable being deep incisions across the wrists. There were also cuts and slashes across the belly and face. A head shot showed superficial crisscross slices on her cheeks, a swollen lower lip, and a couple of bruised eyes.

Poe winced, averting his eyes for a moment to catch his breath. It defied logic to classify the wounds as self-inflicted, as they were surgical in appearance. Yet homicide had been considered, then ruled out.

Why?

He continued scrolling through the chart on the sceen.

A snapshot of her stomach. It was also spiderwebbed with cuts, but they didn't appear to be as random. As he looked harder, a pattern emerged—a cross or at least something T-shaped. Faint but definite.

Again the wounds were meticulous in appearance.

Had she just gone crazy, or had she been undergoing some form of religious self-abnegation . . . some form of penitence? Or had the cuts been inflicted by the hands of another? Cults had been known to torture their subjects hideously for absolution.

He finished with the photos on the monitors, then scrolled until he came to the pathology report. Skimming through the details, he gleaned that when she was found, Linda had been dead for approximately ten hours. Rigor had come and gone, sped up by the intense desert heat. (The room temperature had registered at ninety-five.) Lividity had set in, the blood pooling to the lowest points of her body.

Poe flipped through the film until he hit upon the actual police report. She had been discovered by the hotel maid, who, having received no answer to her knock, unlocked the door to the room around ten in the morning. Linda had checked in at six the prior evening, listing herself as a single occupant. She had signed the register card, had given the clerk forty-nine dollars in cash for the room.

Checked in at six, found dead at ten. Narrowing her death between ten and sixteen hours—whatever good that did.

Articles found at the scene:

One leather handbag.

One medium-sized wallet containing a driver's license, a gas credit card, a picture of a little girl, and twenty-five dollars in cash.

One gold braided necklace chain.

One gold-and-diamond watch.

That got his attention. The Hennicks were not a wealthy family. A gold-and-diamond watch was unusual enough. Why wear something so pricey to such a cheap dive?

Unless she had met someone before her death. Someone she had wanted to impress. Or someone had given the jewelry to her before he had murdered her. A lover's quarrel gone bad? Yet, the death had been ruled a suicide. Why?

Other items:

One red dress.

One matching pair of red shoes.

One set of car keys on the nightstand.

One bloodied carving knife.

Poe shook his head.

The last item listed was a note left by the victim.

A *note*?

Poe's eyes widened. Alison had never made mention of any suicide note. Perhaps she hadn't known.

Frantically, Poe ripped through the microfiche trying to find the note's contents. Scrolling page after page. Where the hell was it? For some reason, it kept eluding him.

He really didn't want to have to dig up the original file. Where did they keep them? Did it even exist anymore?

Calm.

Another trip through the reel. And then he found it. A single sentence. *This is for what I did.*

Leaving Poe to figure out exactly what Linda had done.

TWENTY-FOUR

He couldn't ask Alison about it. If he did, she'd know he'd been snooping. Besides, how reliable was an eight-year-old's memory? The next logical choice would be Gerald Hennick. But, officially, the case had been closed twenty-five years ago, and Poe was reluctant. Hennick had suffered long before his wife's death. The humiliation as the ladies gossiped . . .

That poor man.

He's such a saint.

God will reward him his place in heaven for his devotion.

While men snickered . . .

What a cuckold!

Why does he put up with it?

The man has no pride.

Hennick the henpecked.

In truth, Hennick hadn't deserved the shameless pity or the callous scorn. His wife had been a victim of mental disease, and he had coped— just like millions of others plagued with tragedy, illness, and bad luck. God was a fickle dealer.

Without the Hennick family as sources, Poe was left with only one option.

He pulled out of the hospital parking lot at eleven in the evening, knowing that Y wouldn't hit the bars much before then. For the first time in several weeks, he felt upbeat. Emma would be discharged on Monday. Yes, she'd need more treatment, but her body required a break—a three-week interlude to build up strength for the next assault of chemotherapy. While Emma recuperated, she'd be living with him. Poe had also hired on a full-time nurse. Three people living in his clay oven. Privacy would be done Japanese-style.

His mother had completed her first round with flying colors. Her white cell count was close to normal, and her neoplastic neutrophils seemed to be in fast retreat. If only she could gain some weight. Every time Poe saw her stick frame, her frail movements and labored breaths, he felt a nagging twinge in his gut.

Enough of worries. Onto the streets, into civilization. He kept the windows of his car rolled down. The night was beautiful and balmy, studded with stars, colored by neon, and a full moon acted as a spotlight. He breathed deeply, savoring the air of freedom as he inched his way up the Strip. The sidewalks held people and laughter—a glorious city of anonymous millions.

Turning his Honda into the Luxor's driveway, Poe stopped, stepped out of the car, and handed the attendant the keys. He took another deep breath, staring at the holographic face of King Tut, who looked middle-aged, not like the fourteen-year-old boy-king he had been.

He went inside the towering black glass pyramid, his eyes immediately drawn to the up escalator, angled as steep as the Eiger. The triangular ceiling was pitched so high that it often gave momentary vertigo. A fantasy Nile riverboat ride encircled the lower casino like a moat. During the ride, tourists saw the various Ramseses and their consorts, adorning rock-coated walls speckled with graffiti in hieroglyphics. Poe often wondered what the words actually said.

For a good time, call Thutmose at . . .

Once again, Poe craned his neck upward. Suicidal people loved to leap from high places, and the Luxor had not gone unscathed. A few years back, a distraught woman had jumped from one of the top floors of the hotel and landed smack in the middle of one of the hotel's sumptuous buffet tables. The force of her fall had been so great it had blown off her fingernails. It wasn't one of the cleanest jobs Poe had ever seen, but it had been effective.

He started out by playing a couple of dollar slots, losing five hundred dollars in fifteen minutes. He then moved on to a table, nabbing a thou before being asked to go. Apparently his luck was pissing off the losers at the table. Before he left, Poe searched the bars; the old man was nowhere to be found.

Out the door, making his way down the Strip, the neon flickering in the warm breeze. The blocks were long, the traffic was thick, and Poe was happy to be counted among the living. From the Luxor he went to the Excalibur, from the Excalibur to the Tropicana. As the clock struck midnight, Poe began to feel restless. He had come on a mission and refused to admit defeat.

Moving north, into New York–New York. Built to simulate the Great Apple, the hotel and casino held the city's famous sights and buildings, including a replica of the Statue of Liberty scaled down to a third the true size. Poe supposed that the hotel had been meant to conjure up nostalgia in transplanted East Coasters. To him, it was an urban nightmare of noise, shadows, and graffiti, giving the impression of being dirty even though it wasn't. Choppy in design, the casinos were separated from one another by waterways, shops, and restaurants, making it difficult to spot people.

Poe's eyes traveled up, following a sizable flow of people being transported by the up escalator leading to the Coney Island Midway and Arcade. Lots of games and prizes, but the main attraction was a roller coaster which coursed through the entire hotel and casino. Those staying for the night were often wooed into slumber by the dulcet tones of grinding gears and blood-curdling screams.

Lighting a cigarette, Poe stopped in front of a concrete brook of water spangled with pennies. Behind him stood a restaurant reeking of garlic. Off to the left was a bank of dollar slots, to the right were shops faced in phony brick and covered with fake tagging. Whenever Poe examined the walls carefully, he'd inevitably find the real stuff mixed in with the ersatz defacing. Bloods and Crips logos . . . signs of the notorious L.A. Eighteenth Street Gang. In the city that hosted the shooting of rapper Tupac, he wondered about the wisdom of elevating anything associated with thugs.

Bouncing on his feet as he looked around. No sign of Y.

Instead, he caught a glimpse of the bowler.

He realized he was already moving in Hat's direction. His legs had processed the information quicker than his brain. Pushing through the crowd, he took off after the blip of felt. But the man tore away as fast and fluidly as a raging river, through the endless mazes of shops, stores, and restaurants. Poe kept pace with him, squeezing through the throng of people, darting down the casino's mock alleys and dingy side streets. The bowler jumped across his visual field, materializing, then disappearing. As Hat rounded corners, Poe saw flashes: the flapping motion of a loose double-breasted suit jacket and the hint of a rubber-soled shoe.

Running shoes with a suit.

Which made for an easy escape.

A few twists and turns and abruptly the hat was gone. Common sense dictated that Bowler was heading for the exit. Poe raced toward a side door nearby. Stumbling through the labyrinth, he felt blindsided. A chance meeting twice? Not in this solar system. Someone was playing games with him.

Poe bolted out the double glass side doors, into a *real* alley—a small lane meant as a conduit for taxis. He slowed and looked around. The roadway was sandwiched between two massive buildings which created a wind tunnel.

Dark . . . narrow . . . hidden.

Here the breezes had turned to menacing gusts, kicking up soot and dust, moaning a death dirge.

Brushing hair from his eyes, Poe blinked rapidly as he surveyed his options. To the left were the lights of the Strip. On the right were more narrow strips of asphalt and a web of service roads. A few lone souls in the distance, moving like finger puppet shadows against the walls. No hats. In these winds, a hat would have blown off anyway. Most of the foot traffic was headed east toward the Strip. If someone wanted to escape and blend, east was the way to go.

But something told Poe to turn into the bowels of the buildings. The gray night air blackened as the winds blew faster. Poe tightened his jacket around his body. Checking over his shoulder, he walked steadily until boulevard traffic had receded to background noise. He could hear his shoes against the ground. He became aware of his breathing.

A shout!

Poe jerked his head around, his heart doing double-time. Where did it come from? The right? The left? Another blast and suddenly a cab was upon him, honking like a foghorn. Poe slammed his body against the building, cursed the reckless driver. The car motor receded, replaced by the howling winds. Scraps of paper and debris glided through the air like vampire bats. Warm winds. Ominous.

He walked deeper into the darkness.

Stopping at the sight of something. White . . . fluorescent in the moon-light. He bent down and picked up the item.

A running shoe. Men's size eight.

Someone with a small foot.

Another shout!

More of a shriek echoing through the air. Poe ran toward the sound's direction, to the mouth of the alley as it emptied into the Strip. People had gathered around a spot. Poe could hear high-pitched wails—ululations that spoke words.

Get away!

No!

Nooooo!

"Police! Move back!" Poe shoved his way through the hordes as the woman moaned. "Back!" he screamed. "Back! Police!"

The crowd reluctantly parted. As her face became visible, Poe almost dropped to his knees as if he'd been sucker-punched.

The top of Alison's dress had been ripped away, exposing her breasts. In a weak attempt at modesty, she was hiding her chest with thin, scratched arms. Her stockings had been torn, her feet were bare. Her hair was loose, and her face had been dirtied and scraped. She was kicking aimlessly, lashing out as people tried to approach her.

Poe knelt down beside her, and was immediately smacked in the face by a fist for his efforts. He took off his jacket, tried to cover her, but she pushed it off, kicking with rage as she bayed.

"It's me, Alison," Poe shouted. "It's Rom—"

She caught him in the stomach with her foot. He gasped and screamed, "Someone call an ambulance!"

"Noooo!" She began to flail furiously.

"Alison, look at me!" With his left hand, he managed to secure her hands. He took her chin in his right hand and turned her face to his. "Look at me, Alison—"

She howled as he spoke. It sent chills up his spine.

"Alison! Look at me!"

"What's going on?" someone shouted.

"I'm a cop—"

"Where's your ID, bud?"

As if he had a free set of hands to show the fucker his badge. But people were getting nervous. On the surface, it looked like he was man-handling her. Last thing he needed was a riot on his hands. "Alison, look—"

Abruptly, she threw her arms around his neck and pressed her chest into his body. "Oh, Romulus!" She sobbed on his shoulder. "Someone pushed me! *Hit* me! I didn't do anything and he just pushed me down and started hitting and tearing at my dress. Oh God, it was awful!"

She wept bitterly. As she hung about his neck, Poe picked up his jacket and draped it over her nude shoulders. "Come on, baby! We've got to get you to a hospita—"

"Noooo!"

"Aliso—"

"Noooooooo!" She squeezed him harder, locking on his neck like a wrestler. "I can't, I can't, I can't—"

"Shhhhh." With a free hand, Poe liberated his badge, displayed it to the crowd. "Police! Break it up! *Now!*"

Another body kneeling next to his. A worried male voice. "My God, what happened?"

Poe looked over his shoulder. It was Y—out of breath and covered with a sweaty sheen. The old man had materialized from nothing. But Poe was too distracted to question him about his sudden appearance.

He said, "She was attacked. We need to get to a hospi—"

"Noooo!"

"Okay, okay," Poe soothed. He turned to the gawkers enjoying the show. Slowly, he stood up, Alison still hanging around his neck. His jacket fell off her back. "Pick that up," he ordered Y.

Y picked up the jacket and replaced it around Alison's shoulders. Gasping, the old man was still sweating hard. Poe hoped the old man wasn't contemplating a heart attack. Again, he flashed his badge. "Disperse now! Back away or you will be arrested!"

"That's talking tough," Y said.

Poe stabbed Y with murderous eyes. Alison continued to weep on his shoulder. Y clapped his hands several times. "Okay, folks. Party's over. Go home."

A pause.

"I said go home!" Y pointed to Poe. "Or he'll arrest you." He held up two fingers. "Scout's honor."

Slowly the lookie-loos began to break up, increasing their speed when they realized the freak show was over. After most of the people had gone, Poe spoke to Alison. "Sweetheart, I've got to get you to a hospi—"

"Noooo!" Saliva dripped from the corners of her mouth. "No, Rom. No, Rom. Please, please, no, no, no."

"Take her home," Y suggested.

"I've got to call Steve—"

"Noooo," Alison wailed. "Don't call Steve. I won't go home. I can't go home. Not like this. I can't . . . the kids . . . I can't see Steve—"

"Take her to your house," Y tried again.

"I can't do that," Poe retorted. "Baby, let me take you to this doctor friend of mine—"

"No!" She pushed him off and began to run down the taxi lane. Poe easily caught up with her, grabbed her to his chest. She hugged him and sobbed. "Please let me come with you. Please, I beg you, Romulus." *Crying like a wounded puppy.* "I *beg* you! Just this once. *Please?*"

Poe stalled. "Where were you attacked?"

Alison wiped her nose. "I was just walking . . . taking a shortcut. He just crept up on me."

Poe swallowed hard. "Did you see him?"

She shook her head. "He pushed me down. I fell on my face. For no *reason*, Rom! Then he . . . he began to rip off my clothes."

Again, the sobs. Poe said, "Alison, let me take you somewhere safe—"

"Take me to your house . . . just for a little bit. I swear I won't be a problem." A pause. "I'm *begging* you!"

Poe bit his lip. He looked down, saw the running shoe sticking out of his coat pocket. To Y, he said, "I'm parked at the Luxor. Get the car and take her to my place—"

"You're not coming?" Alison cried out.

"Baby, I have to look around—"

"Please don't leave me, Rom. Just this once, don't leave me."

Y said, "Call up one of your other detectives."

"Like it's *that* easy." Poe exhaled. "Y, get the car! We'll all drive to my place—"

"Thank you, Romulus!" Alison kissed him hard on the lips. "Thank you, thank you." She burst into tears.

"Where's your parking ticket?" Y asked.

With Alison hanging on, Poe couldn't reach his pocket. "In my pants pocket . . . in my wallet."

Y pulled out Poe's wallet, removed the parking ticket along with two twenties. He slipped the bills into his own pocket, ignoring Poe as he glowered.

Y said, "For chauffeuring money."

"Just get the damn car."

As Y jogged off, Poe tried to organize his thoughts. Alison was still clinging to him. He closed his jacket around her upper body, tying the sleeves around her neck. He said, "Just a few minutes and then we'll be off."

"To your house?"

"Just for a little while. I really have to look around. Try to find out something."

"Don't leave me, Rom."

"No, I won't. Don't worry."

It couldn't have been Bowler who hurt Alison. The timing doesn't fit. He couldn't have taken time out to attack a woman with me on his heels.

A pause.

Or maybe he did just that. Because Alison was one *hell of an excellent distraction. Certainly took me off his ass.*

Poe asked, "How long ago did the attack happen?"

"Maybe . . ." Alison sniffed. "Maybe ten minutes ago."

"How'd you get away from him?"

"I didn't. He suddenly stopped and ran away. Something must have scared him off." A beat. "Thank God it did."

He felt his eyes water. "I'm so sorry, Alison."

"It doesn't matter," she bleated out. "It's over. That's all that matters."

But he knew all of it mattered. He said, "We'll get you home soon—"

"Don't send me *home*!"

"I meant to my house." Poe bounced on his feet. "You can rest there."

"Thank you." Alison embraced him with force, whispering in his ear. "Don't leave me, Rom. Don't ever leave me."

TWENTY-FIVE

Alison had drifted into sleep within minutes. She had curled in a fetal position in the backseat of Poe's Honda, sleeping with her mouth slightly agape, eyes moving rapidly as she dreamed. Clearing a lump from his throat, Poe picked up his cellular and called Jensen's house. The answering machine picked up after three rings. Poe hung up and moved on to Steve's pager, but it, too, rang and rang. Thinking he had dialed wrong, he tried the beeper number again.

Again, it tolled continuously.

Poe disconnected the line. *Strange.* Steve didn't always answer his pages, but he always left his beeper on. Poe had always been able to leave a message. Again he phoned the house. This time he left word.

"It's Rom. Page me as soon as you get this. It's important." He clicked off and continued to drive along a lonely stretch of road. To Y, he said, "Steve's not home."

"That's not unusual."

"His pager isn't working. That is unusual."

"Maybe he didn't want to be interrupted."

Poe shook his head. "Something's going down. I don't like it." He paused. "I can't keep Alison at my place without her husband knowing. It doesn't look good."

Y said, "I'll vouch for you."

189

"No offense, old man, but that won't cut it. I'm dropping both of you off. I have to find Steve."

"What do I tell Alison when she wakes up? That you lied to her?"

Poe drummed the steering wheel. "Okay. *You* take the car and find Steve."

"What do I say if I find him?"

The car turned silent.

What the hell should he say?

Poe said, "Tell him I found Alison on the Strip and she seemed unsteady. When I couldn't locate him, I took her home to keep an eye on her. Tell him to contact me ASAP."

No one spoke.

Poe said, "Unless *you* want to tell him the truth."

"Me? Are you kidding?"

"So tell him what I told you."

"Okay, Romulus. I'm not arguing with you."

Poe drove the next few minutes in silence, a thought pricking his brain. "How'd you happen to come on us? Just walking by?"

Y kept his face flat. "Just walking by."

"Bit of a coincidence."

"Just like you being there when she was attacked."

Poe raised his brows. "Guess so."

But something was bothering him. The first time he had chased and lost Bowler, he had also bumped into Y. Poe reached into his jacket, fished out the running shoe. A small size. Y's feet were small. . . .

What on earth was he *thinking*? He'd known Chief all his life. He was tired. He was upset. Still . . .

He picked up the phone and dialed Patricia's number. A human voice actually answered.

"It's me."

"What's up, Sarge?"

She sounded sleepy. Poe wondered if she was alone. "Do you happen to know where Steve is?"

"Haven't the foggiest notion." A beat. "Why?" A yawn. "Did something go down?"

"His wife was mugged or attacked—"

"What? *Alison?*"

"Yes, Alison. By coincidence, I happened to be there. I don't think she was sexually assaulted, but I don't know for certain. She said she was pushed down. Then something scared off her attacker. She's scratched up, but she refused to go to the hospital or to her home. I can't find Jensen. Which is why I'm taking her to my place."

"I'll go look for him right now."

"First, I've got another assignment for you. Go back to the scene and see if the perp left anything behind." He gave her the precise location. "Check up and down the entire alley. And bring along help. It's dark and I don't want you nosing alone."

"I'll call up Marine Martin."

Poe waited a beat. "Patricia, I found a running shoe."

"A running shoe? Like an athletic shoe?"

"Exactly." He described it and gave her the size. "See if you can find its mate. And also . . ." He winced. "You might want to look for a bowler hat."

"A bowler!" A beat. "As in *the* hatted man in Nate's composite?"

"Possibly." Poe filled her in with the details. "It's unlikely that Bowler attacked Alison. He wasn't out of my sight more than five minutes before I heard the screams. If Hat did attack her, he worked at mach speed."

"Five minutes is long enough. It could have been him."

"True, but I'd like a better candidate. Go over there and let me know what you find."

Patricia said, "I'm leaving now."

"Page me when you get there. We'll maintain phone contact."

"Will do." She cut the line.

Poe glanced back at Alison. She was breathing deeply and unhurriedly. To Y, he said, "You know, I was actually looking for you tonight."

"Why?"

"What do you know about Linda Hennick's death?"

Y's face was stoic. "People hear things in their sleep."

"It's important."

"Not now it isn't."

Again, Poe drummed against the wheel. Antsy with a few minutes left to go, he tried Jensen's number once again. Hearing the machine kick in, Poe disconnected. Without thinking, he dialed Rukmani's number, realizing he just wanted to hear her voice. To his surprise, he got her machine.

"Ruki, it's me. Can you pick up? Ruki?"

Silence.

"Ruki, are you there? Guess not. I'll call your office."

He called her office. Three rings and her voice mail picked up. Rukmani didn't have lots of girlfriends. More likely than not, her companion was a male.

Her big get-even for his ill-fated encounter with Honey two weeks ago. Both of them as faithful as dogs in heat. Why bother with marriage . . . asking him to get down on his knees to propose? What the *hell* was that all about?

Y said, "As long as I got your car, should I look for Rukmani, too?"

"Not necessary," Poe answered too quickly.

"If I find her, I'll tell her to call you."

"No," Poe blurted out. "I've got Patricia hunting around the crime scene. Don't want to tie up the line for personal reasons. But thanks anyway."

"Sure."

Poe tried to appear casual, knowing Y could see right through him. He depressed the accelerator, speeding up the dirt road that led to the western foothills. Five minutes later, he parked the car in front of his clay pod. "Could you wait with her while I go make up the bed?"

Y nodded.

Poe returned several minutes later. It took some maneuvering, but between the two of them, they managed to carry Alison inside without waking her.

Poe walked Y back to the car. "You want to talk now?"

"Talk about what?"

"Linda Hennick."

"That'll take time."

"You're in a hurry?"

"I thought you wanted me to find Steve. Make up your mind."

Poe rubbed his face. "Yeah, go find Steve." He thought about the two twenties in Y's pockets. "You *will* look for him?"

"Yes."

"You won't get distracted?"

"I said I'd look for him." Y's face hardened. "You want me to write it out in blood, brother?"

Poe tossed him the keys, watched Y slip into the driver's seat and drive away. As soon as he walked across the threshold of his door, he remembered that his cell phone was still in the car.

His phone.

His lifeline to the world.

*   *   *

Settling down with his Scottish girlfriend and a pack of smokes, Poe felt himself loosen as the liquor worked its way into his gray matter. Ten minutes of staring at star-studded sky, breathing in fresh air, and drinking smoky firewater. When Mom moved in, he'd have to hide the Dalwhinne. But in the meantime, life was decent. His pager broke the spell. It was Patricia, but without his phone, he couldn't call her back. Y should return soon, *if* he didn't get involved with Mrs. Poker Machine and her daughter, Miss Vodka.

For the first time in his career, Poe turned his pager off. He was dressed in a tank top and beach pants, his toes wiggling in the warm sand.

The solitude gave him time to think about Alison . . . how she had just happened to stumble into that alley just as he appeared, looking for Bowler. There was a connection here. Maybe even one rooted in the past. Linda Hennick had been associated with the Bogeyman. Alison Jensen was now paired with Bowler—who might or might not be responsible for the deaths of Brittany Newel and Sarah Yarlborough—

"Rom?"

He startled, leaping up from the ground and wiping off his pants. "Yo. I'm here."

Alison stepped outside, looking absolutely edible. She had donned his gym shorts and a loose tank top. The side of her luscious breast peeked out from the open arm area. Her hair was wild, blowing in the warm breeze, and her feet were bare. A blink later, she was beside him, linking her arm around his. "Beautiful night."

Poe nodded.

She blinked back tears. "Hard to imagine that the same night can be so pristine, yet so . . . obscene."

Poe put his arm around her, drew her close. "I'm sorry." She laid her head on his shoulder. He could feel wetness on her skin. He said, "Would talking about it help?"

"Later. Why spoil the moment? You . . . me . . . it seems just like it once was." She nestled into his arms. "So innocent . . . so virginal."

Poe didn't speak. Waist down, he felt anything but virginal. He continued to stroke her head, his fingers tracing the rise and fall of her upper back. Graceful shoulders, delicate shoulder blades. His head pulsated as he wondered how to get out of it. At the moment, he was poking through his zipper.

She raised her mouth to his. "Kiss me, Romulus."

"Alison, this isn't right—"

"One kiss—"

"You're married—"

"For old times' sake."

He closed his eyes, pressed his mouth on hers. Her lips parted and he fell into her sweet abyss, their juices mixing in a heavenly dance as her tongue played upon his.

This couldn't go on.

Her lips caressing his as her hands snaked under his shirt, stroking his chest, gliding over his nipples. Then the fingers began to travel downward. Onto his belt, then under his waistband. Dipping between his legs.

Instantly, he broke off and backed away—erect, panting, and dripping sweat.

"We can't do this."

She moved toward him. "Yes, we can—"

"No, we can't." He moved backward. "You're married—"

"I don't love Steve," she spat. "I never loved Steve. It was always you—"

"Don't say that."

"But it's true, Romulus. You know I love you."

Bullshit personified. Still, Poe's heart jumped at the words.

She came closer to him. "And I know you love me."

He took a half-step back, still breathing hard. In a flash, it all crystallized. This wasn't a quickie round of head. Being with Alison meant the point of no return—a permanent wedge between Rukmani and him. Did he really want to screw up what he had?

Wiping droplets from his brow, Poe said, "I love you, Alison, but I can't. I'm in love with someone else."

Her face fell flat, her eyes turning hard and cold. Like lightning, she was instantly upon him, lunging at him, ripping at his shirt with long needlelike nails. He saw her raise her hand. He tried to snap his head back. She caught him on the side of his cheek.

He expected to feel the sting of a slap. Instead, he felt razor-sharp nails stab into his skin, raking his right temple all the way down until they gouged at his throat. His neck was immediately aflame. Brutally, he shoved her away, then grabbed his throat, blood oozing from the open wound. He screamed as his fingers clutched his wet Adam's apple. He yanked off his shirt and wrapped it around his neck. He shrieked, "Are you out of your *fucking* mind?"

Terror in her eyes as Alison moved away. Covering her mouth with her hands as tears poured from her eyes. She turned and bolted into the open space, toward the shelter of the mountains, tearing across the open terrain with winged feet even though she was barefoot.

It was a few seconds before Poe could react, get his hands to stop shaking and his feet to move. Mentally cursing her while he ran after her. "Alison!" he screamed at her speeding shadow. "Alison! *Stop!*"

Within moments she had disappeared behind a monolith of bedrock granite.

"Alison!" he bleated out. One side of his shirt had become soaked with blood. He turned it over, pressed the dry side against the raw cuts. His entire face throbbed, pain searing clear down into his throat. He could barely talk, let alone yell. "Alison, come out, for God's sake! I'm not mad! Just come out so we can go home!"

Silence greeted his pleas.

"Alison, please! I need help! And I can't get help unless I know you're safe. Please—"

His begging was cut short by a sharp howl. The reflection of a set of red eyes, the flash of pointed teeth.

A coyote, smelling the blood of the wounded. It inched forward. Poe was used to scrawny, mangy dogs. This one's coat was . . . thick . . . glistening. A good pelt of fur . . . like a short-haired wolf. Unlike any of the other wild dogs Poe had seen in the desert.

Elegant paws with long, tapered nails, the points gleaming in the moonlight.

Moving toward him, its red eyes bearing down upon him, staring him down with an almost human expression.

A look of intense desire.

Poe stepped back as the animal began to close in.

Do something!

Backing him into the mountain as it crept forward, bared its teeth— sharp and deadly.

Poe glanced around, picked up two large rocks. He hefted the lighter one, then hurled it at the dog, nicking it on the paw. He had expected the coyote to charge. Instead, it whimpered, eyes cast downward. Then it looked up with *melancholy* eyes.

Poe was momentarily stunned. Quickly, he regained his wits, tossing the heavier rock against a boulder. It shattered into bits of stone. Immediately, the doleful coyote retreated.

Disappearing into the mountain.

Poe continued to lean against the granite wall for support—panting, sweating, bleeding. A wounded animal himself. Swallowing had become difficult. He straightened up, peered behind the mountain wall, into a dark cave of rock and stone. He heard a slight whooshing. A whimper—as if the coyote was still crying.

"Alison, I hear you breathing! Come out *now!*" He took a couple of steps forward. "Alison, *stop* playing games. I need your help, baby. Please come out."

Whoosh, whoosh.

"I'm going to go back if you don't come out." Poe moved deeper into the blackness. "Alison, I can't see in here. And I don't feel too good. Please, please. I'm not . . ."

He exhaled forcefully. "*Please* come out!"

Whoosh.

Poe began to inch out backward. "Alison, I'm leaving now. If you don't come out, I'm not going to save you."

Whoosh, whoosh, whoosh.

He kept walking in reverse as he made his way toward the entrance. "This is it, kid! Your last chance!"

Then his ears perked up as hair pricked up on the back of his neck. He froze instantly. The whooshing sound had transformed. Now the rattling was unmistakable.

The weather had turned warm, and the rattlers were up from hibernation. He'd probably alarmed a denning female who was pissed at the intrusion.

Before him was a sea of nothingness, behind him his escape was blocked by a diamondback. He felt as if he'd just been assigned some Herculean challenge. Remaining paralyzed, he tried to think without panicking. Because panic killed faster than the known venom.

Listening to that ominous shaking, rattle and rolling. Just his luck that the reptile was behind him. Out of his direct line of vision. The sound grew in intensity.

This was *bad*!

His eyes frantically searched the dark for the glint of a weapon—a stick or a rock. But everything seemed out of reach.

He was going to get bitten; that was a given. The trick was to maneuver his position to accept the bite in the least harmful place.

The rattling became louder. He was barefoot. If he didn't move quickly, the sucker would take away his options and plunge into his ankle. The ankle wasn't good. A bite on the ankle would fuck up his ability to run home. The left forearm seemed to be the best of his bad options. He didn't need his arm to walk.

In one fluid motion, he turned and attempted to fling the rattler away with his left hand. Instantly, the snake sank its fangs into his wrist. Poe screamed as liquid fire shot through his veins. With all his strength, he squeezed the reptile's head until the rattler unhooked its evil jaws. Poe yanked the rattler upward and tossed it away.

He raced back toward his house, which appeared as only a small light in the distance. His heart hammering as his feet pumped, his head spinning as his breathing grew unsteady and more shallow. His gait was as wobbly as a drunkard's.

Don't freak out, don't freak out. You've got time—although not as much as you'd like.

Flying into his house, he tore through his kitchen cabinet, hoping to find an old bottle of antitoxin. Finding nothing, he fell into a rage, sweeping his arms over the shelves as bottles and dishes smashed onto the counter and floor. He quickly wrapped a light tourniquet around his wrist as it swelled with a speed that defied Einstein's theorems. He took a cold pack and laid it on the open bite.

Without a phone, without a fax, and without flares. No car and he was miles away from civilization. His left arm had grown to twice its normal size, his neck pulsed out stabs of pain. He felt as if he had just gone a round with the Grand Inquisitor. No sense sticking around waiting to die.

He threw off the wet shirt that had been wrapped around his neck and put on a clean one. Then he grabbed some fresh linens and gently draped them around his neck. He slipped on Nikes, then dosed himself with analgesics.

He had about an hour before the bite went from just being painful to life-threatening.

Stumbling, he started walking toward city life. He was dizzy and nauseated, but willed himself to remain upright, forcing his numb feet to go one step at a time, ordering his brain to remain conscious.

Breathe, Rom. Just keep breathing.

Fifteen minutes into his trek, he saw the priceless glimmer of headlights. Standing in the road, he waved the car down. His own Honda with Y at the wheel. The old man paled when he saw Poe's condition. He glanced at his bandaged neck, then at his gigantic wrist. Instantly, he knew what had happened. With a fleetness that belied his age, Y scooped Poe into his arms and placed him in the backseat. The Indian jammed the accelerator and the car flew forward.

Poe's body felt like molten lead. "Alison . . . still out there."

"Is she hurt?"

"Don't know." He swallowed hard. "She got pissed at me and took off. I followed her and that's . . ." His voice trailed off. He began to shake uncontrollably.

"I'll find her. But first things first." Y was going around eighty. "Your neck was bitten, too?"

"No . . . only my wrist."

"How long has it been?"

Poe muttered, "About a half hour."

"We've got plenty of time, son. Just hang in there."

Poe croaked, "No problem."

And then he passed out.

TWENTY-SIX

The nausea swept over like tidal waves, Poe's conscious moments punctuated by heaving and retching. Afterward, he fell into sweaty shivers that left him lifeless and disoriented. Sometimes he slept soundly. More often he dozed, hearing things in his semistuporous state. Disjointed voices reverberated in his head—sounds but no words. Eventually, the raging flames in his body quieted, choosing to flicker instead of burn. When that happened, Poe felt other things—needles in his arms, bandages ripping at his face.

Time passed. Then one day, he suddenly realized he was fully awake. Though the inferno had passed, his body still ached, his innards cramping, his muscles sore and rusted, his left arm painful to lift. He dared to open an eye.

Rukmani was sitting by his bedside, reading some charts. She looked calm . . . inscrutable.

He opened the other eye. He wanted to sit up, but he couldn't get his limbs to move. Panic enveloped his heart. Was he paralyzed?

Slow down, Poe. Move the fingers.

He could move his fingers and toes. If the digits moved, the limbs had to work. They were just "on strike."

Staring at Rukmani as memories flooded his pounding head. How long had she sat by his bedside? A while, he figured. Because someone had held the basin as he retched. He attempted speech. It came out as garbled sounds, but it got Rukmani's attention. She turned to him, wide-eyed. Her fingers touched his face, then stroked his brow, pushed hair from his face. "Hi, sweetheart."

Poe could make out her words, could almost see her features with clarity. He grunted out, "Where am I?"

"University Medical Center."

Ah, so he *was* intelligible. That was good. "What day is it?"

"Tuesday afternoon."

Poe did the simple mathematics. He had been bitten in the wee hours of Saturday morning. He'd lost about three days. Two things flitted across his brain—Alison and his mother, in that order. So much for filial loyalty. Rukmani kept petting his face. Specifically, one side of his face. The other side seemed as if it had been smashed with a meat tenderizer.

"My mother?" he got out.

Rukmani said. "She's doing great. I've set her up with the nurse at my place. I'll stay with her until you've recovered. Don't worry about a thing."

Rukmani continued to stroke him as though he were a cat or a talisman. He must have had one foot in the grave. "And Alison?"

Rukmani stopped caressing him for a second, then continued her loving movements. "What about her?"

"Is she all right?"

"Far as I know." She paused. "She hasn't come to visit, though. But Steve has. He sends his best wishes for a speedy recovery. So do the others—Patricia, Weinberg, Y, your brother . . . all of them were here."

How touching, he thought. Then wondered why he felt so cynical. Probably because he had been flattened by a steamroller. With effort, Poe managed to hoist his tortured body into a semireclining position. The back of his eyes throbbed as his visual field moved with each turn of his head. He took in the surroundings. Muted sunlight coming through orange translucent drapery. A curtain rod encircled his bed, an IV was hooked up to his arm, a tube from his body carried urine into a bag. He'd been catheterized.

He sensed his face going hot. Not only had he been intruded upon but demeaned as well.

No bad thoughts, Rom. Keep going.

The room held a ceiling-mounted TV, a bed, a nightstand, and a phone. He had a blanket over his legs. His left wrist and arm were bandaged, but his fingers were exposed. He could wiggle them, although it smarted when he did. There was tightness over the right side of his face. He touched his neck. His throat had been wrapped in gauze. He wore a hospital gown. He wondered who had undressed him.

Slowly, he turned his head until the phone came into view. He stretched out his right arm and picked it up. He pressed nine, but nothing happened. "How do you get an outside line in this place?"

"Romulus, what are you doing?"

"Making a phone call—"

"Give that to me—"

"Stop scolding me. Please just answer my question."

Her eyes rolled. More resigned than angry. "You press eight."

"Thank you." With calculated movements, he managed to dial Steve's pager. This time his beeper kicked in. "What's the number here?"

"Here? You mean your room or the hospital?"

"My room."

"Four seven two eight."

"What's the prefix?"

"Eight three three."

Slowly, Poe punched in the numbers. "Eight . . . three . . . three . . . seven—"

"*Four* seven."

Poe hung up and tried again. "Eight three three . . ."

"Four seven two eight."

"Four . . . seven . . ." He looked up and waited.

"Two . . . eight," Rukmani filled in.

"Got it."

He finished the number and pressed the pound sign. Jensen's pager started beeping. Success, albeit a limited one. He handed the phone to Rukmani, who laid it into the cradle on his nightstand.

"Got a mirror? I want to see what I look like."

"All I have is a small compact."

"Is it bad?"

"It's . . . extensive. It runs from your temple down to your throat. Luckily the facial wound is in your beard line. Y was really on the ball. He asked for a plastic surgeon. The work looks very clean and very precise. I'm sure that when it heals, you'll look very . . . masculine."

His line rang. Rukmani picked up the phone and gave it to Poe. He croaked out, "Poe."

Jensen spoke with false cheeriness. "Hey, buddy. Good to hear your voice."

"Is Alison okay?"

"Could you hold on a moment?" A half minute later, Jensen returned to the line, all pretense of merriment gone. "I can't talk long. I'm in the broom closet—"

"You're at the station house then."

"Yeah. I don't want anyone else hearing."

"What's wrong?"

"She had a breakdown, Rom." His deep voice cracked. "I had her committed on a seventy-two-hour hold. Doctor's orders. I didn't want to, but she kept talking about killing herself. And given her family history—"

"You did the right thing."

"She's racked with guilt."

Poe felt his heart sink. At least she was temporarily safe. "Is she coherent?"

"Who knows? She doesn't talk when I visit. Her shrink says she's profoundly depressed. They've pumped her up with pills, but it's too early to tell. She could be released as early as Friday. But that's doubtful, according to her shrink. Poe, I don't know what to do. I've got two boys at home who miss their mother. *I* miss her. I need her home, but I need her alive. I feel like *I'm* going crazy."

"Your sons are depending on you, Steve."

"I know, I know. I'll pull through."

"Would it help if I told her I wasn't angry?"

"I'll ask her psychiatrist to relay the message."

"If it's okay with you, I'd like to call Alison myself."

Jensen paused. "First you'll have to talk to the shrink. It's a her. I'll give you the number. Hold on."

Poe turned to Rukmani. "I need a pencil and a piece of paper."

Rukmani started rummaging through her purse. "Do us both a favor and dictate it to me."

Poe's head seemed split by a cleaver. As much as he wanted to tough it out, his body told him that she was making sense. He gave her the numbers as Jensen read the digits over the line.

Steve said, "Nice to hear you talking, Poe."

"Did you have a chance to speak with Patricia?"

"Yes. She filled me in. You chasing the hat, then losing him—"

"Just for a minute—"

"Then you heard Alison screaming . . . her . . . attack. Fat Patty and Marine Martin looked around the crime scene Friday night, then again on Saturday morning. I would have come down myself, but I was busy with Alison."

"Did they find anything?"

"Bits and pieces. No breakthroughs. You can deal with it later, Poe. First get better."

"You might want to check your beeper, Jensen. When I paged you Friday night, it wasn't working."

"Yeah, I figured that out after I got your message on my phone machine. The battery was gone."

"Gone?"

"Either I dropped it and the battery fell out, or someone took it out."

"Who would do that?"

A long pause. "Sometimes Gretchen gets tired of being interrupted. I'm not saying she did it, just . . . it won't happen again."

Poe said, "Talk to you later."

"For what it's worth, I've called it quits with Gretchen. I know I'm no angel. But if you walked in my shoes, you'd—"

"Jensen, right now, it's all I can do to keep my head above water. Let's forget about the personal crap and go solve some homicides. Just make sure your beeper works."

"Fair enough."

"I'm relieved to hear that Alison made it home."

"Cops found her holed up near Red Rock at four-thirty in the morning. She was crying uncontrollably . . . babbling. But at least she was talking." A beat. "I've got to go."

"Bye." Poe gave the receiver to Rukmani. He looked at the IV. "What are they shooting into my veins?"

"Glucose, antibiotics . . . Demerol as needed."

"That's probably what's making me nauseated. I don't do well with opiates."

Rukmani felt his forehead.

"Hot?"

"Maybe a hundred." She paused. "Not that I want to pry, but who clawed your face?"

He sighed. "Alison."

"What?"

"She wasn't in her right mind." Poe gave her some scant details. "She was shaken after her attack. I didn't realize how badly until it was too late. Jensen just told me that he had her committed. I need to talk to her. In person. I've got to get out of here."

Rukmani's voice turned hard. "The only thing you've *got* to do is get better."

"She's locked up, Rukmani."

"Judging by your wound, I'd say she's right where she should be."

"Look, I know you hate her—"

"I don't hate her, Rom. I don't even really know her." She took his good hand. "Dearie, you need to rest—"

He jerked it away. "I don't need your advice or your help, Florence Nightingale. I needed you last Friday night. When you *weren't* home."

Rukmani swallowed back a lump. "I'm sorry I wasn't around when you needed me. And if you don't need me now, I'll leave." She stood. "Call if you change your mind."

"Don't go." Slowly, Poe turned his head to meet her eyes. Too much effort. He sank back into his pillow. "Don't mind me. I'm just testy."

"Understandable." Rukmani kissed his forehead. "It's wonderful to hear you talk, Romulus. I love you."

Poe answered her words with a half-smile. Even that hurt as his facial muscles pulled at his stitches. He raised his hand to her thin, bony face, stroked her smooth cheek, then brushed long strands of black hair from her eyes. Rukmani rarely wore her hair down. Normally it was wrapped in a tight braid. Only when they made love did she loosen it. She had lovely thick hair. It softened her worn face, made her look younger than her forty-three years. He took her hand and brought it to his lips, lightly kissing her slender brown fingers. "I should probably buy you a ring."

"I've picked one out. I'll buy it, and you can pay me back."

"Such romance."

Rukmani kissed his hand. "The gods create some couples from the heart. Others are made from the genitals. Still others come from the head."

"I pick the second choice."

"Unfortunately, we're the third. We've always let brainwork intrude upon our personal life. Funny thing is I don't mind. And neither do you."

She spoke the truth. Poe said, "When do you think I can leave this place?"

"When you're afebrile for a twenty-four-hour period, when you're steady on your feet, and when you can pee without a tube."

"When do you think that'll be?"

"A couple of days," Rukmani answered. "Right now, the gouges are more of a medical concern than the bite. The toxin is pretty much gone from your system, although I'm sure you still feel some localized burning. For the future, you might want to keep a couple of bottles of antitoxin in your first-aid kit."

"Agreed. Think I can leave tomorrow? I really need to get back to work."

"You really *need* rest, Poe. Brittany Newel and Sarah Yarlborough are dead. Furthermore, they'll be dead tomorrow. That's how it works when you're dead."

Poe rolled his eyes. "Are you going to get me lunch?"

"I could get you some toast and tea—"

"That's a diarrhea lunch," Poe complained. "I want a real lunch!"

"First see how you do with the toast and tea." Rukmani pressed the nurse's bell. "Why did Alison lash out at you?"

"Because I told her I wouldn't sleep with her." He looked at Rukmani's curious eyes. "I told her I was in love with you. Well, what I actually said was that I was in love with someone else. But she knew who I meant."

Rukmani smiled, the tip of her nose turning red. "You told her that? Awww. I take back all my nasty thoughts about you."

Poe laughed, then winced.

A young nurse came in. Her name tag said Lilith. Rukmani ordered the food. When they were alone again, she said, "I probably shouldn't be bringing this up. Because it'll just whet your appetite for work."

"What?" Flinching, Poe brought himself to an upright position. "Tell me."

"Remember you asked me to type the grass under Sarah Yarlborough's fingers?"

Poe perked up. "What about it?"

"The blades were an unusual species. The botanist couldn't place it."

"Which means?"

She sighed. "I have been talking to local nurseries. Usual grass for the Southwest is Marathon grass—a commercial name for tall fescue grass. All of them down here only carry Marathon—in seed *and* in sod. So it looks like the grass under Sarah's nails came from a very esoteric source.''

''Could the botanist identify the components?''

''Perhaps.'' Rukmani organized her ideas. ''There are a couple of problems with further testing. First off, it's going to take a long time to get results. Second, I don't have a lot of sample to spare for testing. I've got to keep some bagged for evidence. That leaves very little left over.''

Poe plunked his head back into his pillow. ''You come up with important information. And now you tell me we can't process it into anything meaningful.''

''It's not all that grim.''

''It isn't?'' Poe sneered. ''Do you think my lunch is coming in this millennium?''

Again, Rukmani rang up the nurses' station. ''Maybe I wasn't assertive enough.''

Lilith reentered the room. ''Yes?''

Rukmani said, ''His lunch? If possible in this *century*?''

The nurse was taken aback. ''We're backed up, Doctor.'' In a huff, Lilith pivoted and left.

Poe said, ''Very good, Ruki. Let's hope she doesn't have easy access to potassium chloride.'' He paused. ''You know, grass is grown like any other plant, right?''

''Eugene, Oregon. The grass-growing capital of America. Highest pollen count in the nation.''

''Take a sample up to them.''

''And if they identify it . . . then what, Rom?''

''Well, we know it isn't the usual lawn grass, right?''

''Which means?''

''If it's a special grass, maybe it has a special purpose. And if we can determine what the grass is used for, then we can link it to a specific place.''

''Like a certain casino owner's office?'' Rukmani asked. ''Poe, you need a warrant for that, not a botanist.''

''I'd settle for a link to any golf course.'' He picked up the phone and dialed the station house.

Lilith returned, tray in hand. ''Lunch.''

''Just leave it,'' Poe dismissed her. ''Hey, Brenda, it's Sergeant Poe. . . . Thanks, I'm doing all right. Be doing a lot better if I was over there instead of here. Is Patricia at her desk by any chance? . . . Sure, I'll wait.''

He looked up. Lilith was still holding the tray.

Poe said, "Hey, thanks a lot. Just put it on the bed."

The nurse sniped, "How about opening the folding table?"

"What folding table? Where is it?"

Rukmani took out the folding table. "Happy, Lily?"

The nurse set the tray on the table. "You're quite the charmer, Dr. Kalil. I can see why you work with dead people."

"They never talk back." Rukmani smiled. "Thank you, Lilith. I mean that sincerely."

The nurse shook her head and left.

"Poe!" Patricia shouted over the line. "You can talk!"

"I can indeed."

"It's good to hear you. How are you doing?"

"I'll live. That's all that matters."

"Did you hear about Alison?"

"Yes. Terrible."

"Jensen left about ten minutes ago for lunch. Poor guy. Like Weinberg would say, Steve is such a schlemiel. You know what that is?"

"Yep."

"He's making an effort, but he's really out of it."

"Yes, it's a pity," he said quickly. "I've got an assignment for you."

"Working from a sickbed," Patricia stated. "That's true dedication."

"I want you to go around the local golf courses, *especially* those courses frequented by Parker Lewiston. I need you to pick up some grass samples."

"*Grass* samples?"

"Yeah, grass samples." Poe laughed. "The lawn kind of grass, Patty. The other kind is still illegal in our fair state even for medical reasons."

"That's too bad."

"Isn't it, though." Poe sighed. "Just my luck. Here I am laid up, sick and nauseated, and a little too far east and south to get legally buzzed. Instead, I'm stuck here with a snippy nurse and a diarrhea lunch."

TWENTY-SEVEN

Weinberg shifted in the chair, trying to hide his anxiety. Hospitals made him nervous. He wondered how long it would take Poe to make a full recovery. Or at least how long before the kid lost the bag. The lieutenant had decided it was the catheter that was making him squirrelly. Tubes belong in laboratories, not in bodies, especially not in private parts.

Another shift. He said, "Interesting theory, Rom. And it's good that you're thinking in . . . professional terms—"

"You're shining me on."

"Not at all." He was having trouble making direct eye contact. The bag kept getting in the way. "It's a good conjecture, but we can't *do* anything with it."

"Yes, we can," Poe insisted. "We can go into Parker Lewiston's office, take a sample of the grass, and see if it matches the scrapings taken from Sarah Yarlborough's fingernails—"

Weinberg interrupted, "Poe, you have nothing to link Lewiston to Sarah Yarlborough. It was Brittany Newel who had this quasi-doubtful link to Lewiston, according to her disgruntled boyfriend. And Newel didn't *have* any grass under her nails."

"Lieutenant, the grass from Yarlborough's nails seems to be unique.

Nothing like it is sold anywhere around here. If we match it to Lewiston's office, we have—''

''Circumstantial evidence.'' Weinberg forced himself to look at Poe's face. ''Say Lewiston's office is the only place in the city . . . hell, the only place in the entire country that has that kind of grass. It still isn't enough. If the samples match, then possibly you could postulate that Sarah Yarlborough was in Lewiston Parker's office. But it won't tell us if she died there. And even if she *did* die there, it doesn't tell us who committed the crime.''

''Sir, how many people are allowed into Parkerboy's office, let alone commit a murder—''

''Poe, first you need to tie Lewiston to Yarlborough through evidence—a witness or photograph placing them together. *When* you got something, we can continue the discussion.''

Weinberg had adopted a mulish look. Poe backed off. ''Maybe I'm moving too fast. Why don't we get a limited warrant for Parker's office, stating that we're there to get a grass sample—''

''On what grounds do we file the warrant?''

''Loo, Parker screwed Brittany Newel—''

''Sergeant, we're going round in circles. Brittany Newel did not *have* grass under her nails. You want a warrant, find something that can link Parker to Yarlborough.''

''I'd ask Yarlborough's pimp about it except Ali Abdul Williams died in a freak accident with twenty grand worth of fresh bills. Know what I think? After Parker popped Yarlborough, he paid Williams off to keep his mouth shut. But even with the payoff, Parkerboy didn't like loose ends.''

Weinberg said, ''And following your logic, Lewiston must have set up Williams's car accident?''

''Lewiston could have rigged the car.''

''Maybe he *did* rig the car. But even Lewiston couldn't guarantee Williams's death.'' Weinberg tried to remain patient. ''Poe, your head is full of conjectures. Nothing wrong with that. But I can't ask a judge for a warrant based on a fertile imagination. Being sworn officers of the law, we gotta follow due process.''

Poe said nothing.

Weinberg said, ''You know, Lewiston's been around these parts forever.''

"So what does that have to do with anything?"

"Don't get snappish," Weinberg whipped back. "All I'm saying is that *I've* never heard a rumor that he liked the underage set. Have you heard something different?"

Poe shook his head.

"So he's suddenly changed his taste in playthings?"

Poe regarded the lieutenant while he analyzed the question. The response came in a sudden rush of loose thoughts. He tried to organize his words. "Lewiston is a gambler from the get-go."

"So?"

"He's reached his pinnacle, sir. The man has gambled and won in the ultimate city for gamblers. Lewiston made it to the top in *Las Vegas*. He owns four casinos, he owns celebrities, he owns sports arenas as well as sports figures. He's got a slew of material playthings and hookers. The man has the Midas touch—everything turns to gold. A risk-taker like him, sir, a man who has built himself up on dares and challenges . . . what does he do for thrills now?"

"He plays golf."

Poe chuckled. "Right."

"You sneer. But he plays four days a week—"

"Golf may be a way for him to pass his time, but it doesn't get his blood pumping. Because in golf, you have to play by rules. Lewiston doesn't *follow* rules, sir, he *makes* them. The ultimate—playing by your own rules. And maybe that means raping underage kids *and* getting away with it. Especially thrilling because it's such a vile thing to do. And maybe even the underaged sex wasn't enough. To get the charge, he had to get away with murder—"

"You really don't like this man, do you?"

"No, I don't."

"Okay, Poe. Let's assume the man is trying to get away with something. Get me evidence. Then we get the warrant."

Poe was frustrated, but said nothing. His limbs ached and his head was swimming in a very choppy ocean. Plus, he still had to call Alison's shrink.

"I'm tired, Loo," he announced.

Weinberg stood, grateful to get away from the bag. "Anything I can do for you, guy?"

"No, I'll be fine. Thanks for coming out."

"My pleasure. You did me the favor, actually. As a Jew, I did my good deed for the day."

"What's that?"

"Visiting you." Weinberg patted Poe's wiry shoulder. "Heal up, Sergeant." He hesitated, then pulled a cigar from his pocket and tucked it into Poe's bedcovers. "When you're feeling better . . . a Cohiba."

"I must rate," Poe said. "Thanks."

"Get better. I mean that."

As soon as he left, Poe's head hit the pillow. He closed his eyes, trying to think about the case. Thinking about Lewiston's office . . . he needed to get a sample. A small sample of grass. Had to skirt the law. He had to find a link. . . .

The dungeon was driving her crazy. She *had* to get out.

Because there was work to be done. Her research files moldering. Had to get out, had to do it. If only she had the energy to do it with her powers. But they had sapped her with their binds. She was just too tired. Plus the moon wasn't right.

How to get out?

The most *expedient* way was to cooperate. Say the right things, and behave the right way. At least talk to the shrinks. But she didn't *want* to talk. Not to these idiots who didn't understand her powers and her quests and what she needed to do—

"Alison?"

The voice was in the medium range. Not the nurse's squeaky voice. It sounded like one of her shrinks. The new one—the redheaded woman.

Of course, Alison wouldn't answer her. She didn't even move, remaining immobile in her bed, swathed in a clean white cotton gown, staring at her mittened hands. They had done that to her, encasing her hands in padded gloves so that she couldn't hold a spoon even if she had wanted to eat. They tried to feed her, shoveling in food that she let drip out of her mouth. Claiming that they had been worried that she might hurt herself.

Again, the voice spoke. "Alison, there's someone on the phone for you."

She refrained from moving physically. But the fact that the shrink was allowing her to talk on the phone . . . to someone on the outside. It wouldn't be Steve. Steve would have come in person. And they already knew that she wouldn't talk to Steve. Not that Steve anyway. Not even any Steve—the new one *or* the old one.

Shrink was talking, "... is Romulus Poe. You know Romulus, don't you?"

Alison remained quiet. But her eyes must have given away something. Because Redhead continued talking.

"He wants to talk to you," she said. "Because he likes you, Alison. He's your friend."

Her heartbeat had quickened. If he was calling her, well then that was a good sign. It meant he wasn't dead.

"Would you like to talk to him, Alison? He'd like to talk to you."

Alison didn't respond; she wouldn't dare give that bitch the satisfaction of seeing her *want* something. This place had nothing to offer her. Nothing. For the millionth time, she cursed her husband. Why didn't he just let her ride it out? She *always* got better.

"... put it next to your ear. You don't have to talk if you don't want to. But it might help if you listened. You might like hearing a familiar voice."

Alison continued to be silent.

Then that awful pause. The shrink giving her that little exasperated sigh. She had to be new to the profession. Seasoned shrinks would never, ever sigh. Seasoned shrinks would have endless patience. Because her condition wouldn't be frustrating to them. Because they'd seen it all, done it all.

Why'd they give her someone so inexperienced? Maybe they didn't think she was sick enough to merit a real shrink.

"... don't even have to listen if you don't want to." Another sigh. "But since you're not talking, I can't know what you want or what you don't want. So how about if I just hold the receiver up to your ear."

Her heartbeat was racing. Did she really want to hear Rom's voice?

The shrink was approaching her.

No, don't hit her. Don't slug her, don't push her, don't scratch her. You can't do that. That would be bad. Just let her be, let her be, let her be.

The shrink put the receiver up to Alison's ear, leaned over, and spoke into the mouthpiece. "Sergeant Poe, I have the receiver up to her ear. You can talk now."

Poe saying, "I'm okay. Say something."

Alison stayed silent.

Poe said, "Dr. Braverman, can you hear me?"

"Yes, I can hear you."

"Do me a favor. I know her hands are protected. Can she hold the receiver at all?"

"Probably." Dr. Braverman put the phone to her own ear. "The thing is, Sergeant, I don't think she *wants* to hold the receiver."

"Then just drop it on the bed and leave. I'll shout and hope she can hear it. I need to talk to her in private."

"I really shouldn't do that . . . leave the phone here—"

"Alison won't talk if people are scrutinizing her. Give me five minutes with her in privacy."

"This is unorthodox."

"I realize that," Poe said. "But you're not having any luck. Give my idea a try."

"All right . . . but not too long."

"Agreed."

Dr. Braverman put the phone on the bed, but she remained in the room.

Poe shouted, "Is she gone?"

No response.

Poe said, "Dr. Braverman, I know you're there. Please give my idea a whirl."

He waited, then heard a robust sigh over the line. Footsteps, then a door slamming. Poe counted to ten.

Again, he said, "Is she gone?"

Alison muttered something.

"Pick up the phone, Alison."

Nothing.

Poe tried to be patient. The woman was fragile. "Alison, if you can, please pick up the phone and tuck it under your chin. I'll wait for you."

He heard nothing, then static over the line, loud crackling sounds as if the receiver was being manhandled. Then, abruptly, it stopped.

"Are you there?"

Nothing.

"Alison, listen to me. I'm not mad. Could I *ever* stay mad at you?"

Again silence. Poe decided to wait her out. He sat up on the mattress, changing position to avoid bedsores.

She whispered, "How are you?"

Poe said, "All right. It's good to hear your voice."

She started to cry. "They have my hands tied up. They won't let me see the boys. I'm afraid."

One of the few times Poe heard sincerity in her voice. Because Alison was terrified of losing her sons. He said, "Ali, listen to me. You're in on a seventy-two-hour hold. That means they're going to reevaluate you. You know the drill. If you want to leave, you have to talk to them. You have to convince them you're okay. That you're not going to hurt yourself."

She was silent. Poe could picture big tears running down her cheek.

"Look, you want to see your boys, right?"

"Steve's poisoned them against me—"

"No, no, no, no, no," Poe blurted out. "I don't have much time to talk before Dr. Braverman returns. You want to get out, you can't talk about people being against you. You have to be positive . . . say things like . . . like, 'The breakdown was good. Because now I realize how much I need help. And I intend to get therapy—' "

"But Steve has poisoned them against me. He's also poisoned the nurses against me. He's evil, Rom. He's out to get me. He's always been out to get me. Because he wants his whores and I'm in the way. He wants me out of the way."

Conveniently ignoring the facts: that she had torn up his face, and flown off in a rage. That she had been found babbling in the mountains at four in the morning. Did she remember any of it? Yet her accusations made sense on a superficial level. Jensen did have whores. He had always claimed that he had taken on women because Alison had never been available to him. Which was probably half true.

Alison said, "You know the man who attacked me in the alley behind New York–New York?"

"What about him?"

"*Steve* sent him. He did, Rom, honestly. He sent someone to *hurt* me. So he could have the boys and his whores and no more Alison. That's why he did it . . . sent the someone to attack me. He did, you know."

Poe felt his heart sink. She didn't want to get out. She didn't want to get better. It was beginning to dawn on him that just maybe she was *incapable* of getting better. Perhaps she was where she belonged. The thought threw him into a blue funk.

"He's behind it all." She was blabbering now. "It's all his doing. Everything. Even those dead girls."

Poe sat up. "What dead girls?"

"Your cases. His cases. *He* did it."

"Did what?"

"The murders. Your cases. *He's* the one you're after. I know about the hat, you know."

That got Poe's attention. "What hat are you talking about?"

"Don't play innocent, Rommie, because I know everything. You know who *owns* that hat? Steve owns that hat. He bought it for a costume party four years ago."

Poe realized he was breathing hard.

Not good. Slow it down. Think, Poe. Think!

Delving deep into his mind. Jensen *had* mentioned something about owning a bowler hat. Something about buying it for a party. Could Jensen have mentioned it to throw him off? Could she possibly be telling the truth?

Poe, you idiot! She's sucking you into her delusions. Mildly, he answered, "Really?"

Alison talked with animation. "Yes, yes, he did, he did own a hat! Check it out, Rom. It's *his* hat."

"Alison, I don't have a hat in my possession. Any idea where it might be?"

"Me? No, I don't know where the hat is. All I'm saying is, if you *did* have the hat, it would be Steve's hat! I swear to God, it's his hat. Find that hat and check it out."

She made a slurping sound over the phone.

"You know, Rommie, the man who attacked me wore a hat. So look where I was attacked. See if you can find the hat."

Poe said, "Alison, are you telling me that your own husband attacked you?"

"Oh no!" Alison responded. "Steve didn't attack me. He sent someone to attack me."

"So . . . someone else attacked you. Not Steve."

"Of course. He wouldn't be stupid enough to attack his own wife."

"And the person who attacked you also wore Steve's hat?"

"Yes. Steve gave it to him. After Steve murdered those two girls."

Weirder and weirder. Poe said, "Steve murdered two girls?"

"That's what I'm saying! *Steve* murdered those two girls! Mind you, not the Steve that I married. No, the man I married didn't kill the girls. It was my new husband, the evil Steve. *He* killed the girls."

"The evil Steve."

"Yes. The evil Steve. He murdered those two poor girls."

"Both girls?"

"Yes." A pause. "Well, I don't know about the second one. But the first one for sure—Brittany Newel."

Her delusions were peppered with facts which threw him for a loop. Why was she pinning Newel's death and not Yarlborough's on Steve? Poe licked his parched lips. "Are you saying that Steve killed the first one and not the second one?"

"Well, he *could* have done both. But I only know for certain about Newel. They had a thing going. Newel was pressuring him to marry her. Steve didn't like that. Brittany told me the whole story, you know."

Poe put the pen down. "When did you talk to Brittany Newel?"

"I dunno. Right before she died. Before he did it. He didn't want to be with her anymore." She dropped her voice to a whisper. "Maybe she was pregnant."

Poe bit his lip. If Newel had been pregnant, Rukmani would have discovered it. "Alison, you should have told me all this way back when. Why didn't you?"

"Why do you think? I didn't want to implicate my husband in murder. But now it's different. Because not only does he want to hurt all of them, he also wants to hurt me, too."

Hurt *all of them.* Poe said, "Who else does he want to hurt?"

"Oh . . . just me, Rom. I'm telling you. You've got to realize that he's trying to hurt me."

Crazier and crazier. Still, she was making some kind of bizarre sense. "Alison, if Steve wanted to hurt you, why would he lock you up? It would be easier for him to hurt you if you were under his roof."

"Rom, he doesn't want to *kill* me. I'm the mother of his children . . . of the *old* Steve's children. He just wants to tame me. Because I have the power. It's true. He's jealous."

"I see."

"He *is* jealous, Rom. He's always held the power. But now, *I* have it. You don't understand. He is really an evil person! Are you coming out to visit me?"

The last question said in the same breath as the accusations. Her mind was running wild. Poe answered, "I'll be out as soon as I can."

"Why can't you come *now*?" A pause. "What is it, Rommie? Got a date with your *girlfriend*?"

Her mentioning of Rukmani, even if not by name . . . it sent chills up his spine. "No, Alison, I don't have a date. I'm in the hospital. I'm still recovering—"

"I didn't scratch you *that* hard!"

So she did remember! His head felt like bursting. "I got bitten by a diamondback rattler—"

She gasped. "Omigod, omigod."

"Alison, I'm okay."

"Omigod—"

"I'm okay," he shouted over her.

She stopped chanting.

Blessed silence.

Patience, Poe.

Softly, he said, "I'm fine, Alison. I just need a little rest. Just like you. We both need to rest."

A long pause. Poe was about to give up.

Then she said, "So when do you think you can visit me?"

"Maybe in a couple of days."

"*That* long?"

"Maybe sooner. I'll do the best I can."

"I love you, Romulus. You know I love you."

"Take care, Alison."

"You're hanging up?"

She was whining. Poe lied, "They've got to draw some blood from me. I have to get off the phone."

"Will you call me back?"

"As soon as they let me. They're going to give me a sedative, which will knock me out for a couple of hours—"

"Don't take it!" she shrieked. "It's how they control you. What you do is pretend to swallow it, but then spit it out."

"Thanks for the warning. I've got to go."

"I love you, Rom."

"Bye, Alison. Take care." He hung up, heart-sickened by their conversation. A moment later, his phone rang.

"It's Dr. Braverman. You know, we monitor all our patients' phone calls."

"So I figured."

A pause. "You *knew* you were being taped? But you gave her instructions on how to get out."

"I knew I was being taped. She didn't." He was irritated. "She's in a mental hospital. You'd be derelict if you allowed her free use of the phone."

Another pause. "Oh."

"Besides, I'm a cop. We do the same thing."

"Are you having blood drawn now?"

"No. I'm tired. I wanted to get off." He sipped water from a glass. "You owe me. I got her talking."

Braverman said, "What are these murders that she's talking about? Is she making them up?"

"No. They're cases that her husband and I are working on. We work together—her husband and I."

"Who was murdered?"

"That's not really relevant."

"It may be relevant, Sergeant. Who is Brittany Newel? The one she claimed she spoke to?"

"A hooker."

"Could she have spoken to her?"

"Nothing is impossible. Is it likely? No."

"Was she her husband's mistress?"

Poe hesitated. Did Alison really know, or was it just a delusion? Because Jensen had claimed that Newel had been a one-shot deal.

Was he telling the truth? Was she telling the truth? Too much confusion. Poe said, "You know, I'm really tired."

"Could you find out if they were really an item? Because if they were, it might help us understand her delusions more clearly. Because all delusions have elements of truth."

"I understand your interest. But it's not in my best interest to pry into the personal life of my coworker." But Poe was going to pry. Because he had to make *sure* that what Alison had told him was indeed a delusion. "I need to rest, Doctor. Alison exhausted me."

"This attack that was made on her," Braverman went on. "Was it real?"

"I didn't actually see her being attacked. Just the outcome. But it looked real to me."

"So perhaps the actual attack set off the other delusions."

Poe's head was spinning. "Sounds logical."

Braverman said, "I've met Steve several times. I'm interested in your impression of him. It might help me understand Alison better."

Was she kidding? Poe said, "Doctor, I don't talk about my coworkers behind their backs."

"Don't you want to help?"

Poe repeated, "I don't talk about my coworkers—"

"I get the message, Sergeant." Braverman sighed. "We made a breakthrough. I'm just trying to follow it up."

We *made a breakthrough? I got her talking, lady. All you did was listen.*

"Follow up all you want, Doctor. As long as I don't have to talk about anyone, I'm willing to help."

"Just what is your relationship with Alison, Sergeant?"

"A very good question. I really need rest—"

"Sergeant, are you sure you're not using your illness to evade intimacy?"

"Doctor, I don't need illness to evade intimacy. I do it when I'm at the peak of health."

He hung up the phone, surprised by his own insight.

Not that the self-revelation would translate into any meaningful reform.

TWENTY-EIGHT

Poe brought the mirror in front of his face. Three neat, parallel lines running down his neck, dipping under his jawline, and ending at his Adam's apple, all of it tidily raked like a Japanese rock garden. It felt worse than it looked. Or maybe that was the snakebite talking. It was hard to separate the two. Still, he was drunk with newfound freedom and grateful for being tube-free.

Dr. Guenswite had put down the scissors and the tweezers and was now lecturing Poe on how to keep the wound clean and how to change the dressing. A plastic surgeon, Guenswite was in his forties, his face Vegas bronze and his nails manicured pink and perfect. He wore a natty tie under his white coat. He spoke professorially. If Poe didn't want scarring, he'd have to keep the area covered when he was outdoors. Sunlight was the wound's worst enemy. Sunblock was not enough. He'd have to—

"I don't care about scars," Poe interrupted. "I'm not going around with a bandage on my face. It puts people off."

The surgeon spoke authoritatively. "I understand the inconvenience. But I caution you against acting in a rash manner. You may regret it later."

"I'm sure I will," Poe answered. "In the meantime, leave it uncovered and I'll take my chances."

Rukmani broke in, "Paul, could you give me a minute with your patient?"

The surgeon twisted his wrist, flashing a gold Rolex. "I'm on a tight
schedule, Rukmani."

"You know, you're just about done. How about if I finish up?"

Guenswite liked the suggestion. He quickly charted his patient, then
left, giving them both a toothpaste-white smile. Rukmani waited a moment, then said, "He's a dandy, but a damn good surgeon. And he's right
about the scarring."

"I'm sure he is," Poe said. "Gimme a mirror again."

Rukmani complied. "You don't have to be wrapped like a mummy,
Rom. A simple gauze bandage just to protect—"

"I thought you said it looks masculine."

"It looks like a baby version of Brittany Newel's wounds." She
smiled. "Hey, where *was* Alison on the night of the murder?"

"Out," Poe replied. "How do I know? I've had Patricia check up on
her behind Jensen's back."

Rukmani paused. "I *was* kidding."

"I know. But I wasn't. Am I supposed to slap some antibacterial cream
on this?"

"I'll do it." Rukmani took a tube of ointment and applied it to her
gloved fingers. She dabbed it gently onto Poe's cheek. Instinctively, he
jerked away. One-time operant learning thanks to Alison's nails.

"Stings?" Rukmani asked.

"A little."

"Hold still." She smoothed balm over his wounds. "Do you honestly
. . . suspect Alison?"

"As you said, the wounds are similar. But that isn't the only reason."

Another application of topical. "What is it, then?"

He waited a beat. "Alison is just too familiar with the cases. I know
she hears Jensen talking over the phone. But even so, she just knows too
much."

"For instance?"

"She knew that Jensen had had an affair with Newel. We kept that
under tight wraps. Steve certainly wouldn't have told her. So how did
she find out?"

"Wives have ways."

"She knew about our suspect's hat. She also knew her husband had
owned a similar hat. Furthermore, she told me the man who assaulted

her wore the same hat. *If* she was attacked. Alison has a vivid imagination.''

''Didn't you see scrapes on her face?''

''They could have been self-inflicted. She might have done it to make her story more real or to get attention.''

''Even if Alison did fabricate the entire incident, it doesn't mean she *killed* anyone, Rom.''

''I'm not saying she did. But she knows *something*. Right now, I'm exploring everything.''

''Not that I'm defending the woman . . . can you tilt your head up?''

''Like this?''

''Perfect. Hold still.'' Gingerly, she applied ointment to his neck. ''How would Alison have had enough strength to subdue and murder Newel? Drag her out to the desert? Newel wasn't murdered at the drop.''

''She could have slipped something in Newel's drink—''

''The medicine would have kicked in quickly. Which means Alison would have had to drag Newel to her car. Then tie her up and mutilate her in a compulsive manner.''

''My scratches look pretty damn compulsive.''

''I thought you adored this woman.''

''I have feeling, yes. But I'm not blind.''

''Lower your head just a tad.''

Poe complied. ''Alison has always been different. So was I. If we were kids today, both of us would have been diagnosed with obsessive-compulsive disorder. She has been diagnosed with OCD, as a matter of fact.''

''Is she on medication?''

''Ruki, she's taken every kind of medication, had every type of therapy available. Everything has failed. Sure, there are times when she picks herself up, when she's almost normal. But they're getting fewer and much farther between. Right now, she's severely disturbed. I'm afraid she might have lashed out in a delusional state, thinking that Brittany was going to steal Steve away.''

''If she lashed out *specifically* at Brittany, she had to have some kind of organized thought process going.''

''Her shrink told me that delusions are often a mix of fact and fiction.'' He closed his eyes, feeling like a traitor. ''I need you to do something for me. When Alison was at my house, she used my hairbrush. If I give you a sample of her hair, can you extract her DNA from it?''

"You're wondering whether her DNA matches the DNA of the skin scraping from Brittany Newel's nails."

"Exactly."

"It would be better if the hairs were pulled from the root. But, yes, it can be done. Especially with this new process of extracting the DNA from mitochondria. But it'll take time and money."

"Alison isn't going anywhere. Neither is Newel."

"What about Sarah Yarlborough? You want me to compare her DNA banding as well?"

"My opinion? The two cases aren't related. Yarlborough is Parker Lewiston's baby."

"You've found out something new?" Rukmani's eyes widened. "The grass underneath Yarlborough's nails! You've matched it to Lewiston's office! Good for you—"

"Not quite."

Rukmani stared at him. "So what do you have on Lewiston?"

"Nothing, actually."

"So . . . you're jumping to conclusions without a shred of evidence?"

"Basically. But I'm right about this."

"Poe, why would Lewiston risk everything to kill a crack whore?"

"For the thrill of it. Or maybe it was a genuine accident. Everyone knows Parker has a thing for hookers—"

"*Call* girls," Rukmani corrected. "Sophisticated, beautiful showgirls that know how to service very wealthy men. Not crack whores like Brittany and Sarah. And if you think he did one, why not both?"

"You said the forensics didn't match."

"No, I didn't say that," Rukmani chided. "I said that *superficially,* the deaths don't seem related."

"Are you done with my face?"

"Just about." Rukmani capped the ointment and took out a cream. "You know, I've ordered DNA extractions from the transfer evidence pulled from both Yarlborough's and Newel's nails and vaginal swabs . . . see if anything matches up. Those results should be back within two, maybe three weeks tops. If you want to buttress your nonexistent case against Lewiston with some actual evidence, get me one of his hairs. I know you can't ask him for it. Maybe you can con a couple strands from his barber. The man does get haircuts."

"In order to process the hairs as indictable evidence, I need to take it directly from his head."

Rukmani said, "Well, if you get the samples, I'll send them off to the lab. When we get the results back, we can play mix and match. If you're willing to pay. No way *I* can justify ordering them to the county."

"No prob. I'll just dip into my readily accessible spare cash—"

"Don't play Hardluck Harry on me. I know you have mucho casino winnings squirreled away."

"More like *had*," Poe said flatly. "Mom doesn't have private medical insurance."

Rukmani was quiet. "She has Medicare, doesn't she?"

"Yes, she does. But you know these things, Ruki. Not everything is covered. Certainly not every doctor is covered. And at the time of treatment, you're not thinking in cost-analysis terms. Only what's best. Then you get the bills." He shrugged. "Hell with the money. Let's just get her healthy first. How's she doing?"

"Much better. She's starting to eat again. I think she even asked the nurse for a beer."

Poe smiled. "Never thought I'd say this. But I'm anxious to see her. How about if I move her to my place Sunday afternoon?"

"Great.

"Late afternoon."

"Putting it off as long as you can."

"You got it." He squirmed. "Aren't you done yet?"

"You really should let me put a bandage on. For protection as well as . . . aesthetics." She gave Poe the mirror. "Take a look."

The left side of his face looked like an oil slick with ski tracks running through it. "I'll grow a beard."

"I've never seen you with facial hair." She grinned. "Will it be as thrilling as my imagination leads me to believe?"

"Breathtaking." Poe laughed, then grimaced.

It still hurt to show emotion.

After signing a mound of discharge papers, he reached the Bureau by three in the afternoon. The two front-office secretaries—blue-suited Molly and black-slacks/white-shirt Brenda—gave him applause as he walked in. Each of them was trying not to stare.

"It'll heal," he assured their worried faces.

"You look great," Molly said.

"Terrific," Brenda agreed. "Very . . . masculine."

"A big dueling scar." Molly paused. "I don't think that came out right."

Poe smiled good-naturedly "Any messages while I was gone?"

"A few calls." Brenda handed him a thick pile of paper.

"A few?" Poe said, leafing through the stack.

"People care," Molly said.

"More like they want a favor."

Molly said, "Have fun, Sergeant."

Poe blew a kiss, then came into a near-empty squad room. After exchanging pleasantries with the other guys—who were also trying not to stare—Poe sat at his desk and busied himself in catch-up. One new homicide had occurred in his absence. A bar fight. Cut-and-dried.

The rest of the messages involved details and paperwork—court cases, files, evidence, witnesses, interviews. And a never-ending sea of phone calls. A couple hours later, he jumped at the tap on his shoulder.

Patricia asked, "Is this a ghost I see?"

Poe gave her a lopsided grin. "More like the creature from the black lagoon. Whaddaya think? Lon Chaney? Peter Lorre? Scarface?"

"You look great."

"Take pictures of my good side, baby."

Patricia pulled up a chair. "How do you *feel?*"

"Pretty good, actually." He drummed his desktop. "Got anything for me?"

She dropped her voice. "Alison's time frame."

Poe nodded, took out his pad.

Patricia skimmed her notes. "Here we go. On the night of Newel's murder, she went out to dinner in the early evening. Verified that from her credit card *and* the restaurant. The waiter remembered her. She sat alone, ate scampi and steak, and was very polite. Waiter said she tipped big, then left around . . . nineish."

Poe wrote in his notepad. "Go on."

"She didn't go directly home. But she made a phone call to her house at nine-fifteen. That I got from the phone records. She spoke to her father, who was baby-sitting." She cleared her throat. "That I got from him."

"Really."

"Yeah, Mr. Hennick was very nice, but . . . well, he seemed to be playing it pretty cagily. Why, I don't know. Maybe he's trying to protect his daughter, maybe he honestly doesn't remember. It was a month ago."

"What did he have to say?"

"He recalled Alison's phone call. She told him that she'd be home in a bit."

"How long was 'a bit'?"

"He said she came home several hours later. Which would have put her home around eleven . . . maybe twelve."

Poe said, "Big Ray, the bartender, remembered Newel leaving with Hatman around ten-thirty. If Alison came home at eleven, she's off the hook. Even in one of her manic stages, she couldn't have worked *that* quickly—picking someone up, then murdering her."

Patricia said, "But if she came home later, around midnight, then she'd have enough time."

"I'll call Hennick, see if I can pin down the time. What about Jensen? Where's his alibi?"

"According to the bellman who comped the room at the Big Top, Jensen met Gretchen there around midnight."

"The bellman comped Jensen the room?"

"Comped Gretchen the room. They have an arrangement."

"Gretchen pimps for him?"

"That was the implication."

Poe mulled over the facts. Newel left with Hat at around ten-thirty. Steve was unaccounted for from ten-thirty to one-thirty, when he finally answered his page—enough time to do something nasty. "When did the anonymous call come in from the Big Top?"

"Around twelve, maybe later."

Poe snapped the fingers on his right hand. Big Ray had remembered Newel leaving with a short, thin man. A *man* disqualified Alison—unless she was in drag. And a *short* man disqualified Steve—unless he did something to disguise his height. Maybe he was off-base in suspecting either one of the Jensens. Hell, maybe Lewiston did both of them.

Patricia closed her notepad. "Does this help at all?"

"Time will tell." A beat. "I've got a job for you."

"Just as long as it doesn't involve botany," she answered. "I must have contacted a hundred nurseries while you were sleeping off your snake attack."

"Anything productive?"

"If I'd found something out, I wouldn't be sitting on it. All the wholesalers in the western part of the United States sell the same three types of grass, seed, and sod. And they're all variations of Marathon—Bonsai fescue, tall fescue, medium fescue. It grows well out here.''

Another dead end. But he didn't expect anything, so he wasn't disappointed. "Deluca, I need you to go to Naked City and talk to the whores. I'd do it myself, but my face would scare them off.''

Patricia grew nervous. "When?''

"Tonight. Take a couple of plainclothes with you for protection.''

"What do I ask them?''

"If any of them were ever sold to Parkerboy.''

"Sir, if they were sold to Lewiston, he probably paid them off to keep their mouths shut.''

"If he paid 'em to be silent, then we'll pay 'em to talk.'' He handed her an envelope. "From my personal treasure trove. Use it wisely.''

Patricia looked at the bills inside. Around five hundred in twenties. "I can't take your money.''

She started to hand it back to him. Poe pushed it back against her chest. "If we get something, department'll reimburse. If any of the ladies have been with Parker, try to find out what his proclivities are.''

"And if I get nowhere with Lewiston?''

"Ask about Sarah Yarlborough. Find out if she had ever been with Lewiston Parker. Hell, you can even talk about A. A. Williams. See if any of them think his bang-up was more than just a bad accident.''

"And if they still don't talk?''

"If they don't talk, then I keep my money.''

Patricia winked. "If I don't abscond with it.''

"Sweetheart, if you break the law, you do it big-time. Like the old-time robber barons or Western outlaws or even D. B. Cooper. You remember him, don't you? The one who parachuted into nowhere with millions of bucks in his knapsack. Good old D.B. That's the difference between being a petty criminal and being a legend.''

TWENTY-NINE

When the pain overtook the productivity, Poe called it quits. By six, he was in his car, his destination being dinner at Rukmani's with Mom. Five minutes from her apartment, he turned around and headed toward Honey's. But as he thought about it, he wavered. His last encounter with the call girl had ended on a sour note. The way she had spoken about Rukmani . . .

She's so accomplished.

Sneering. As if one couldn't be accomplished and sexual at the same time.

He didn't really like Honey—she was vain and egotistical—but he needed to assuage this gnawing hunger in his groin. And he wanted it without complications. There were other call girls, but they required advance notice. Honey, on the other hand, always made time for him.

Yet his stomach churned as he neared Honey's apartment. He realized he didn't want a quickie. What he wanted was *real* sex. Naked, sweaty sex and lots of it with someone he liked. He wanted to take Rukmani into the desert, lay her down on a blanket, and chug vintage Cabernet from the bottle. Then he'd strip her naked, her body sprawled out like a centerfold, the setting sun beating onto her damp, nut-brown skin. Then he'd overturn the bottle and spill wine all over her stomach. Then, pinning her arms, he would slowly lick—

He braked hard, coming within inches of rear-ending the car in front of him.

Back in reality.

Hell with Honey! He reversed the car, and once again he headed toward Rukmani's. But as he neared the building, he became filled with dread. Seeing Mom so frail. As if he felt at the peak of health himself. *He* needed TLC; but Mom needed it more.

He picked up his cellular and punched in numbers. Rukmani answered. "Where are you?"

"Two blocks away from Alison's." A lie. "I haven't hooked up with Jensen yet." The truth. "He called in sick today." The truth as well. Two to one: Poe was on a roll. "I figured I'd just stop by—"

"Jensen doesn't have a pager?"

"It's easier to talk in person."

A long pause. She didn't believe him. Ironic, because this time he was being straight.

"When do you think you'll make it here?" Rukmani was irritated. "She's asking for you, Romulus."

Guilt, guilt. Poe said, "Give me an hour."

"Do what you have to do." She lowered her voice. "I miss you, Rom. I miss you in my bed."

Poe felt a lump in his heart. "Ruki, I feel exactly the same way."

"Do you?"

If she only knew. "Think we can steal a few minutes alone tonight?"

"I certainly *hope* so." She paused, then spoke pointedly. "And I certainly hope it's for more than a few minutes."

No one was home.

Poe stood on Jensen's doorstep, phone in hand, sweat falling from his face. The sun was dropping and its rays were cooking everything in their path. He mopped his brow with a handkerchief, then took out a tube of ointment and bathed his wound. The unguent felt gelatinous and dripped down his cheek. He dabbed up the excess, then popped a few Advils. His head throbbed, and his skin felt as pinpricked as a tough steak. After a half minute of baking, he decided that heatstroke wouldn't do anyone any good.

He went back to his car, turned on the air conditioner full blast, and paged Jensen, waiting for a callback. Fifteen minutes later, he knew it wasn't going to happen. He should have revved up the Honda and pro-ceeded directly to Rukmani's. Instead, he took out his lock picks.

Popping the catch to the front door within a minute, he stepped across the threshold and inside the personless house.

Hot and stuffy.

Someone had shut the windows, had turned off the air-conditioning. Around these parts, people didn't do that if they were only going out to dinner. Because it took more energy to recool the place than it did to maintain a set temperature.

But people *did* turn off the juice if they were planning an overnight. He checked his notepad for Gerald Hennick's number, then gave the old man a call. After fifteen rings, he hung up. Why didn't the old man answer? Was he out? Was he okay? Maybe Poe should stop by. Then he wondered why he was so concerned for Hennick's safety.

He paged Patricia. When she called back, he heard background noise. "Did I interrupt something?"

"I'm at Barry's Place, hanging out before Naked City."

"Sounds like fun."

"If you like your men bald and fat." She laughed. "I should talk. Nate's making up some subs. We stopped by Myra's for some authentic kosher deli takeout. She had lots of meat but no cheeses. So Big Ray added some provolone and Swiss from his personal stash. There's plenty if you're interested."

"I'd love to, but I need to play the dutiful son."

"How's your mother doing?"

"Better, thanks." A beat. "Patty, are you talking in privacy?"

"I'll call you back in five minutes."

More like two minutes. Poe said, "Did you talk to Jensen this morn-ing?"

"No. He called in sick."

"Who spoke to him?"

"I guess Molly or Brenda."

"He's not at home," Poe told her. "No one's home, as a matter of fact. Not even the kids."

Patricia said, "So maybe he's feeling better and took them out to dinner."

"The air conditioner's turned off. Why turn off the juice if you're only going to be gone for a couple of hours?"

"How do you know the air conditioner is off?"

"I'm in the house."

A pause. "I won't ask." Another pause. "Sergeant, maybe Jensen took the kids out to spend the day with Alison. He called in sick because it was too embarrassing to admit where he was going."

A perfectly rational explanation. Which would neatly justify why Hennick wasn't home. Jensen had taken Dad as well. Poe said, "Makes sense."

"Anything else?"

"Who's going with you to Naked City?"

"Marine Martin."

"Patricia—"

"He's very strong, sir."

"I have nothing against the man, but this isn't his type of assignment. He's got cop plastered across his face—"

"He *begged* me. He's itching for some real action."

"No one's going to talk to him. The man doesn't interview. He gives orders. And he salutes everyone."

"I told him to stay in the background and evaluate. Like a spy. He liked that. Besides, with Jensen gone, he's the only one I could get on such short notice. And he does have a good eye for detail."

"He's a fine detective as long as he doesn't work with people."

"I'll keep him under wraps." A beat. "Anything else? They're waiting for me. Sure you don't want to join us?"

"Positive. Thanks anyway. Page me when you're done with Naked City."

"It'll be late."

"I'll be up. Talk to you later."

He pushed the end button, slapping the phone repeatedly against the palm of his hand. He knew he should leave. But as long as he'd gone this far . . .

He started with the bedroom closet, giving the hanging garments a quick once-over. Lots of clothes, but there were some empty hangers on Alison's side. Maybe a dozen of them. More than he'd expected to find. Perhaps Jensen had packed up some dresses for his wife, so she could feel more at home during her hospital stay.

Poe checked Steve's side—some stray hangers as well.

So what? Steve had taken some shirts to the laundry, and hadn't had time to rehang them. Nothing to suggest that he had done a disappearing act.

On the floor sat ten pairs of shoes for him, around fifteen for her. Stashed in the closet corner was a pile of shoe boxes. Poe grabbed the smallest one—a female size seven shoe box—and brought it into the light. On the side was printed the word RESEARCH in bold black marker letters. He lifted the lid.

A ghost emerged from the closet—a brief history of Linda Paulson Hennick in pictures and newsprint. Poe spread them out on the bed, arranging them in chronological order.

There were several faded black-and-whites of Linda as a young girl. One was as a child of around eight in a long white confirmation dress with a dainty crucifix hanging from her neck. A big-toothed elder was handing her a Bible. When Poe squinted, he could make out the title— the Book of Mormon. He picked up another set of yellowed newspaper clippings. One was from the *Deseret News*, showing Linda after winning a statewide spelling bee. A big, goofy smile, but her hair had been perfectly curled. The second clipping was from a smaller paper in Utah—a picture of Linda displaying the red second-place ribbon she had won from a citywide LDS bake-off.

A good little Mormon girl.

The next set of photographs—no longer black-and-white, but rather faded, discolored snapshots—showed a coltish preteen dressed in jeans, wearing a sultry pout on her lips.

Alison's pout.

Another collection centered around Linda showing off a two-piece bathing suit. Most of her torso was covered—the way it was with two-pieces from the fifties—but the look on her face. It was hungry for love. Or more like hungry for lovin', if Poe had to put a spin on it.

Later snapshots included several of a lovely, burgeoning adolescent. A yearbook photo of a ponytailed Linda in an angora sweater with a string of pearls around her neck. A big newspaper article with a picture: Linda holding a wand and wearing a crown. The caption read:

The reigning beauty of St. George.
Linda Joanne Paulson: Hamilton High Homecoming Queen.

Then there were a couple of later pictures with Gerald Hennick. In one of them, she wore a light, sleeveless blouse and a paisley pair of capris and had a tented scarf over her head. He had donned a T-shirt and a pair of jeans. They were holding hands and scowling, she more than he, reminding Poe of a sanitized version of James Dean with a much hungrier Natalie Wood.

He continued to rifle through snatches of a dead woman's life. A faded newspaper photo from the *St. George Telegraph*. A group picture of twenty teenaged girls—one row of ten standing in the back, a second row of ten kneeling in front. A big black circle had been drawn around Linda Hennick. She was in the front, second from the left.

Poe stared at the picture, at the young adolescent faces. For some reason, it looked familiar, but he couldn't quite place it. The snapshot captivated him; the girls' wide smiles seemed so genuine: as if they had been having a really marvelous time. He pocketed the clipping.

His cell phone rang. It was Patricia, and she sounded tense. "I don't know if this means anything. But I thought I'd pass it along."

"Shoot."

"It's about Jensen. You made me curious, so I called up the hospital where Alison was staying—"

"Uh-oh!"

"I used my title and pushed and finally got through to a Dr. Rand, whose official title is senior administrator. I told him I was trying to locate Detective Jensen. I had an emergency." A pause. "Sir, Alison checked out this morning. Actually, Jensen checked her out against doctor's advice."

Poe started bouncing on his feet. "Did the doc know where they went?"

"No. But he said that even if he did know, he wouldn't tell me. Something about patient confidentiality."

"Is this guy an M.D. doctor or just a pencil pusher?"

"Haven't the foggiest notion." A beat. "Why would Steve do that, sir? First check her in. Then take her out against doctor's orders."

Why indeed?

Maybe Alison wasn't as delusional as he thought. Maybe she was telling the partial truth. That Jensen *was* trying to get rid of her. He had planned to transfer her to some faraway podunk loony bin so he could play with his whores. Perhaps he should have taken her words more seriously.

Then there was the flip side. Yes, Alison was delusional, but she was also highly manipulative. Somehow she had talked Jensen into pulling her out. Once free, she planned to escape so she could live in her own crazy world—psychotic and untethered, with a propensity toward suicide.

Both options stank.

Two women brutally murdered, and everyone involved was either untouchable or missing. To Patricia he said, ''You just concentrate on Naked City. I'll make a couple of calls.''

''Like I said, sir, I don't know if it means anything.''

''It means something, Patricia. What it means . . . well, that's the question of the moment.''

THIRTY

Weinberg stated, "These are the facts. He asked for some time off, and I gave it to him. Given the circumstances, it seemed like a benign request. End of facts."

Mentally, Poe counted to ten. "So you have no idea where they went?"

"I told you no."

As he stopped for a red light, Poe shifted the cellular to his other ear. "He must have given you a hint."

"He said he was taking Alison and the family away for some rest and relaxation."

"He didn't run down a list of possibilities?"

"Come to think of it, he mentioned something about scuba diving in Cabo de San Lucas."

Poe paused. "You're putting me on."

"Yes, I'm putting you on." Weinberg was irritated. "I'm not holding back. He didn't tell me a damn thing, and I didn't pry. Steve has been looking pretty bad. Tell you the truth, I was thinking of eighty-sixing him for a while. He hasn't been much use since she broke down."

Poe tried another tactic to keep the conversation alive. "I'm very concerned for Alison's safety. He took her out against medical advice. She needs medication when she's agitated. Jensen may not know with whom he's dealing."

"Poe, I'm *sure* he knows his wife better than you. As far as taking her out of the loony bin . . ." Weinberg scoffed. "Medical advice hasn't done a damn thing for that woman. She's been . . . unstable for years."

"That's why she should be watched by professionals."

"Look, Poe, if we were having a purely intellectual discussion, I'd say you were right. But I'm not Steve, I don't know what's running through his head, and I've never lived with a woman who had mental problems. The man asked for time to recoup, I told him go ahead. Time for you to move on and get a life."

Poe swallowed his superior's sarcasm. "She's an old friend, sir. I'm concerned."

Weinberg softened his tone. "I know that. But Alison is Steve's wife. If you want to keep your nose in one piece, you don't go sticking it where it don't belong."

Words of wisdom from Lieutenant Mick Weinberg. Poe said, "If you do hear anything, could you pass it along to me?"

"Sure." A beat. "How're you holding up?"

"Actually, I'm doing all right."

"Your face's okay?"

"It's ugly. But it doesn't hurt that bad."

Weinberg chuckled. "Get some rest." Then he clicked off.

Poe depressed the end button, folded his phone, and placed it in his pocket. It was close to nine. His erotic plans for the evening were being eroded away by worry and fatigue. And the prospect of dealing with Mom.

Nothing kills romance faster than a mom.

Despite Poe's reservations, Patricia was glad to have Marine Martin along. If not subtle, he was observant and alert. At six feet tall, Martin was lean, with a turkey wattle, but he had big arms, thanks to daily workouts at the gym. He was bald and very fair and was always on the lookout for skin cancer—one of the reasons he didn't mind working at night. For the assignment, he had dressed as casually as he could muster—khakis and a polo shirt—but he wound up looking more like a lost tourist than an underground man. As they approached the area, Patricia played upon his image.

"I'll do the talking." She wore black pants and a loose tunic top which hid her gun. Up ahead was the black hole. "Just walk around and try to look out of it."

"A tourist from the Needle taking a late-night stroll."

"Exactly."

He raised two fingers to his forehead and brought them down in a crisp motion. "Don't worry about a thing, Patricia. I have experience in surveillance."

"It's a good idea if you don't salute, Martin."

"Roger." As they approached Naked City, he whispered, "Just go and do your duty. I'll take care of the rest."

Patricia wasn't too sure about that. Still, she walked in the shadows and waited for her eyes to adjust. When they did, all she saw was fleeting figures. She'd have to start showing off the bread if she wanted results. Palming a twenty from her pocket, she made it suddenly visible. Immediately, a crack runner approached—a white girl in her teens. She wore a loose skirt and a halter top. She held up a finger, indicating a hit's worth of rock.

Patricia motioned her closer. The girl hesitated, and Patricia made her move. "I'm looking for an action girl."

The teen glanced at her shoes. "For twenty bucks?"

"There's more if I find what I want."

The girl studied her nails. Not making eye contact was part of the game. "For you?"

"For someone who could work a big man."

"Big as in fat?"

"Big as in money . . . power—"

Abruptly, the teen ran off to a slowing white Honda.

Patricia stood alone, wondering what had just gone wrong. Was it her breath? Not to fret. There were others. Within moments, she saw a young boy coming her way. She shook her head, and the kid did a turnaround and vanished.

Again she bided her time. She didn't have to wait long. Another white female teen approached. This one wore a black minidress. She held up an index finger, the unasked question being a single hit? Yes or no.

Patricia stepped up to her, gave her a once-over. So very young. "Need an action girl." A beat. "Good pay."

"What kind of thing?"

"Just have to be nice to a big man. Someone with *lots* of money."

The girl shook her head and took off. This time Patricia was upset as well as puzzled. What was she doing—or saying—that was putting them off? She trod deeper into the darkness, then took out a cigarette, exhaling lean wisps of smoke, watching them rise into the overcast nightime sky.

Waiting.

Suddenly she felt a presence. She jumped, then realized that Marine Martin was at her side. Angrily, she whispered, "What are you doing?"

"You disappeared from my visual field—"

"Martin, I'm miked up to your—"

"Visual contact is the most important factor in surveillance. Sounds are apt to be misinterpreted."

"I need room to work."

He wagged a finger at her. "Safety first, Deluca."

"Can you go now?"

"Your method hasn't met with success. A reexamination might be in order."

"*Go!*"

Martin tsk-tsked, then left her alone in nothingness. She was annoyed, but grateful for his caution.

She didn't want to wait for the next candidate. Instead, she wanted to make it happen. She replaced the twenty with two fifty-dollar bills. Her eyes swept the scene, caught some feral orbs looking her over. Stepping into the open, Deluca held up five fingers. The kid came forward. "Nickel's worth?"

Patricia showed her a fifty. "I need an action girl."

The girl looked over her shoulder. "What?"

"Routine stuff."

Again the girl's eyes darted about. "Gotta be quick. My man don't like me taking too long. Where's the car?"

"No car. Take a walk with me."

The girl shook her head. "Can't do that. I'm not back in two minutes, he fucks me up."

This time Patricia showed her two fifties. "You willing to be nice to someone?"

"Who?"

"A big man. Lots of money."

The girl's eyes narrowed. "Why me?"

"He likes them young."

"Nuh-uh." She turned to go, but this time Patricia followed. "Lots and *lots* of money."

"Won't do me no good if I'm dead like the other one."

She started to run. Patricia grabbed her arm. "Which other one? Talk to me."

The girl squirmed out of her grip. "Fuck off!" She sped away.

Patricia started after her, but stopped. She stood in the blackness, panting, wondering what the—She felt herself being jerked backward.

Something hard around her throat!

Choking!

Strangling!

No air!

Looking down . . . a pair of shoes . . .

Patricia pounded hard on the instep, grinding down with the full force of her weight. When the pressure around her trachea eased, she grabbed what was around her neck with both hands. Using balance and her weight, she flipped something forward.

Suddenly some jerk lay sprawled out on the ground. And there was Marine Martin, straddling the body, pointing a gun at the man's head. "Police!" he shouted. "Don't move! Don't move a single muscle! Freeze! *Freeze!*"

Dazed, Patricia was still panting. But her autopilot took out a pair of manacles and cuffed the creep.

"Good work!" Martin was breathing hard. "Good work!" He started reading the man his rights. Patricia cut him off in midsentence. She grabbed hold of the handcuffs and yanked the moron upward into a sitting position. Bending over his ear, she whispered, "Gun's at your head, asshole. You move, you're brain jelly."

The man nodded. Caucasian. Late twenties. Didn't appear to be tall, but *damn* he was fat. An enormous overhanging gut. How in God's name had she managed to flip him? Suddenly, her back felt sore. The scuzzball had long, straggly dirty-blond hair and a couple days' worth of beard. Patricia leaned in close. His breath stank.

She asked, "Why did you attack me?"

"Fuck you, pig!" He spat at her.

Patricia wiped the saliva from her cheek, then took the palm of her hand and jammed it upward into the guy's nose. He screamed as blood poured out of his nostrils.

To Martin, she stated, "Looks like our friend here fell down and met with an accident."

Marine Martin gave her a get-a-grip-on-it look. "I can take it from here, Detective."

Patricia ignored his warning. Instead, she grabbed the back of Scuzz-ball's collar and pushed his face back onto the ground and out of spitting range. Then she spoke slowly into his ear. "This is the deal. I can lock up your uglified face and let you rot. Or if you cooperate, you might even walk."

Sensing escape and possibly money, the man stopped cursing. Patricia pulled him back up and sat next to him, watching Scuzz lick his blood from his upper lip. Reaching in her pocket, she showed the fat boy several fifties.

"See this? Now let's see if you're talkative."

Eying the bills, Scuzz nodded. Marine Martin looked aghast. "I think we should bring him—"

"A minute, Detective." To Scuzz, Patricia said, "First off. Why'd you jump me?"

"You were fuckin' with my girls. You want business, you see me."

"I was asking around for a young action girl. But when I told them it was for a big man with money, instead of being excited, they played rabbit. Explain in ten words or less."

His beady eyes looked upward at Deluca's face. "Give me those fifties and mebbe I kin hep you."

Marine Martin was appalled. "This man is extorting money from you! He belongs in jail!"

"Probably. But I'm just an old softy." To Scuzz, Deluca said, "One fifty is yours if I like your answer, sport."

"I need a tissue. My nose is runnin'."

Patricia looked up at Martin. "Can you help him out?"

Grimacing, Martin pulled a tissue from his pocket and carefully wiped his nose. Afterward, he dropped the soiled paper in Scuzz's lap. "Keep it."

Patricia said, "I'm waiting for an answer."

Scuzz hocked up saliva and spit it off to the side. "A man with money who comes here . . . only one reason. He wants throwaway meat. Else he be shopping in a rich-ass store. He come here, he wants somethin' he kin toss when he's done. I like my ponies whole. I tell them to stay away from fuckers with promises. If they listen, they usually live."

"So which big man shops here, sport?"

"Don't got you no names 'cause I don't deal. Besides, it ain't the big man who ever shows up. The sale of young meat is all done through brokers. The big man uses his personal stash of whores as go-betweens."

"Who around here deals with the big man's brokers?"

"Stupid motherfuckers. The kind who die in car crack-ups."

Ali Abdul Williams. "I see."

Scuzz shrugged. "Accidents happen."

"Indeed they do." Patricia gave him the fifty and took out another. "Give me the brokers' names, sport. But make it righteous. Because I can nose a lie. Remember you're still cuffed and I'm still pissed."

Scuzz looked greedily at the money, then at Deluca. "Don't got any name. But for money, I can hep you."

Patricia slipped some bills into his pants pocket. "Speak."

"Nali Abousayed," Sport said. "Hangs around the Lady Slipper. You can't miss him. Fucker's a towelhead A-rab. Wears a big gold robe."

The Lady Slipper was one of Parkerboy's casinos. Deluca said, "Abousayed is the big man's broker?"

"No, he's a zillionaire. But the A-rab gets his women from the Slipper."

Meaning he gets his whores from Lewiston. "Go on," Patricia encouraged.

"One of Nali's *favorite* whores, I seen her around here, asking to buy young girls."

"What does she look like?"

"Blonde. All his whores are blondes. A-rabs like blondes."

"Can you give me more details than her being a blonde?"

"Get me some pichures. I'll tell you yes or no."

Patricia was skeptical. The guy was pure dirt and was probably talking from his ass. Still, it was a lead. "Slipper's a big place. Abousayed have any favorite spots?"

"He blows fat wads of cash on the tables."

"Dice or blackjack?"

"Baccarat."

Correctly pronouncing it as ba-ka-*ra.*

Only in Vegas.

THIRTY-ONE

It took five minutes for Emma to get out of bed, another five to slip on her robe. Her legs seemed to give way under her weight, but she was determined, slowly putting one foot in front of the other. First to the bathroom to empty her bladder. Proudly, she could now do that by herself.

Drained of her water, she suddenly felt parched. Which meant two things: either she could beep Rukmani or she could take a trip to the kitchen in the dark. She opted for independence.

Steady and slow. Keeeeeep going.

As she trudged into the living room, she squinted. Light was pouring out of the kitchen.

A burglar!

A *hungry* burglar?

More likely it was one of 'em with a bad case of insomnia. And even if it was a burglar, what could he do to her? Shoot her dead? Couldn't be much worse than living like this. Using all her strength, she managed to push open the swinging door.

Romulus looked up, then stood. "Ma? Are you okay?"

"Just a little thirsty."

Poe noticed that her eyes had turned to slits. He immediately shut off the light. "Let's go back in the living room. It's more comfortable—"

"This is fine."

"C'mon." He ushered her back into the grayness and sat her on the couch. "What can I get you? Water? Juice? Soda?"

"How about water?" She gave him a droopy wink. "A little firewater?"

"I wish I could, Mom. Be right back."

Emma closed her eyes and sank into the cushions. When she heard his footsteps, she forced herself to straighten up.

Poe brought a glass of water to her lips. "Here you go."

The water felt cool and fresh. "I'm tired, but I can't sleep."

"You always were a bit of an insomniac. This whole mess probably threw your schedule off completely."

"How do you feel?"

"Me?" He made a pshaw sound. "I'm fine. I went to work today."

"When are you taking me to your house?"

"Sunday."

Despite her fatigue, she brightened. "Sunday?"

"Yes, Sunday." He had already told her. She must have forgotten. "That's in five . . . well, now it's four days."

Her heart sank. "Four whole *days*?"

"It'll go quick." Poe smiled. "I'll even cook for you."

"Really trying to kill me off."

Poe gave her a small smile. "Maybe you should try to sleep—"

"This is the first time in a month that we're alone and already you're sick of me."

"I'm thinking of your health, Mom."

"Thinking of *your* health." She took a deep breath, then let it out. Spidery fingers inched their way up to his wound. She touched him gently. "How are you?"

Again, Poe answered, "I'm fine. Really. It looks worse than it feels."

"You should go to sleep."

"You're right. I will just as soon as I tie up some loose ends."

"I'll wait for you—"

"Ma—"

"I gotta finish my water first."

Picking up the glass, Poe again brought it to her lips. She took the tumbler away from him. "I can drink by myself."

He sat back on the couch. "It's a real pain in the ass being dependent on other people."

"Ain't that the truth."

He turned to her, kissed her wrinkled cheek. "You'll get better soon."

Emma bit her lip to keep it from trembling. "Maybe."

Poe said, "Doctors tell me you're doing terrific."

"I hate doctors." She locked eyes with her son. "When do I get my medicine man?"

"I'll remind Y. He visited you in the hospital."

"Twice, I know. When's Remus coming back out?"

Poe smiled to himself. She hadn't even officially lived with him and already she was missing her "good" son. "He'll be out on Sunday to help you move into my place." A beat. "You miss him, don't you?"

Emma shrugged bony shoulders. "He's put up with me for fifteen years. Now I suppose it's your turn."

Poe was silent.

"It scares you to take care of me," Emma stated.

"Not at all."

"Lying through your teeth." She laughed, but it was brittle. "Us Poes. We're all a pack of liars. I know I scare you. But you'll get used to it. Your father did." Her eyes moistened. "Although not for very long."

Poe looked away. He hated it when she talked about his father. How their lives might have been if he hadn't been driving that rainy night. "We'll get along fine."

"We'll fight like cats and dogs. I'm impossible to live with. But at least I'm honest." Emma coughed. "Give me my water."

Poe gave her the glass, watched her down the contents. Then he said, "How about bed now?"

Emma looked around. "Still trying to get rid of me."

"Actually, yes, I am."

The old woman managed a desiccated smile. "Now you're fighting fire with fire. Okay. Walk me in."

He helped her to her feet. Such an insubstantial body. He held her bony arm, guided her to her bed. When she reached the mattress, she let the robe slip off her frail frame, her nightgown hanging on her like a jacket on a scarecrow. She sat down and he lifted her legs over a pillow. Carefully, he brought the duvet to her shoulders.

"Comfy?"

She sneered, "I feel sick to my stomach, I'm as bald as an eagle, and I look like a witch."

"You look beautiful." He leaned over and kissed her cheek. With the moonbeams spotlighting her face she looked as gray as dust. "Good night, Mom. I'll see you in the morning."

She picked up a slip of paper from the duvet, looked at it, then at her son. "This fell out of your pocket."

Poe looked at what she was holding—the newspaper clipping he'd taken from Alison's house. "It looks familiar, doesn't it?"

Emma held it to the moonlight. "I know these people. The circled one is . . . was Linda Paulson . . . or Linda Hennick. This one is Elizabeth Adams. This is Abby Taylor. This is Helen Raymer . . . her brother was in my class."

"Linda Hennick was a year behind you?"

"Two years."

"Do you know when this picture was taken?"

"Probably mid- to late fifties. It looks like their senior class picture. I have one just like it. Back then, Mormons separated the boys from the girls."

And that's why it looked familiar. Poe had probably seen his mother in the same pose. "Where was it taken, Ma?"

"Probably in St. George High—" She squinted. "No, no, no. I remember this picture. This was on their senior field trip to NTS. Got themselves in the paper and everything. It was a big deal . . . not to go to NTS, but to get your picture in the paper."

"NTS?" Poe regarded his mother. "Are you talking about the Nevada Test Site?"

"Yep. Every year the seniors would take a one-week trip through southern Nevada and on to Las Vegas. 'Course, they didn't show good Mormon children the Strip . . . which wasn't much to look at back then. Though Vegas did have a few casinos. I wouldn't have minded seeing it. But they didn't take us there. They took us to the Mormon church and to the Desert Museum and the Paiute Reservation . . . to the shops where the women sold their baskets." She sighed. "They made such beautiful baskets and sold them for a pittance. After the reservation, they took us to visit the ghost towns and—"

"Mother, why in the *world* would your school take you to the Nevada Test Site?"

"The bomb was big back then. Our weapon against Stalin and the Commies."

Far as Poe knew, the bomb was still big. "What did you actually do there?"

"Where?"

"At the test site?"

"What do you think? We watched the bomb explode."

"Where? They took you underground?"

"No, no, no. We went in the days when they tested aboveground. After you were born, they moved underground. Finally figured out that radiation was bad for you."

Poe opened his mouth and closed it. "Your senior class trip was watching an *atomic bomb* explode?"

"Back then, Yucca Flat was a big tourist attraction."

Poe was stunned. Yucca Flat boasted the honor of being the most bombed surface on earth. It was pocked with craters from multiple bomb drops. In the sixties, the Apollo astronauts had used it as training ground because the terrain had become similar to the lunar surface. About as likely to find life there as well. The place was a sea of radiation.

Emma became entranced in her memory.

"They took us there very early in the morning . . . before dawn. It was dark and cold and a little spooky. We had to hunker down in these little troughs that the soldiers had dug a couple of years before. We were just these kids, giggling and telling scary things because we were all nervous. But we were excited, too. When we looked up, we could see the plane circling overhead. We knew we were seeing history."

"If you want to call it that."

Emma became defensive. "It *was* history, Romulus! Seeing the plane, knowing what was going to happen. And then they started the countdown . . ."

She took a breath.

"Over the loudspeaker. Clear as a bell. Ten! Nine! Eight, seven, six . . . finally down to zero. And then the plane dropped its load—the big one! We covered up our eyes, of course. You had to cover your eyes. Still, even with my eyes closed and covered with my arms, I still saw this . . . this fantastic burst of light shooting through my skin . . . like God creating the universe. And then . . . at the same time . . . you felt this big blast of heat . . . sizzling through your clothes. And when they said you could look up, you did. And there it was. Right there in the sky . . . that famous mushroom cloud . . . what a thrill!"

"If you call megatons of radiation a thrill—"

"You had to *be* there."

"I suppose."

"It was a big favorite with the schools and with the tourists. They'd bring in busloads of people at a time."

"Wonder who did the NTS public relations? Betcha it's the same guy who keeps selling that Brooklyn Bridge."

"You're being sarcastic, but it *was* a tourist attraction. You get an old poster from the Chamber of Commerce . . . well, I guess this would have to be the early, *early* sixties. The poster shows the Strip—let's see, back then there'd be the Hacienda at the south end. Then maybe the Flamingo and the Last Frontier and the Dunes and Sahara and Stardust, going down straight through to downtown Vegas. Which was pretty seedy back then. Before all this fancified stuff with Glitter Gulch. There was the Horseshoe, the Lady Slipper—"

"I know the hotels, Mom."

"Anyway . . . the poster has a pichure of the neon skyline with a big ole Vegas Vic tipping his big cowboy hat. Now this was before *he* went neon. Right there, right behind Vic, there's a mushroom cloud."

She nodded for emphasis.

"That was Vegas—bombs and gambling. Don't know which one is worse for your health."

"Bomb-watching for your senior class trip." Poe rubbed his face. "It's different."

"Well, you didn't look right at it. The light would blind you, it was that strong. You could see your bones through your hands—"

"That's because you were getting whole-body-X-rayed, Mom."

"They were careful 'bout it. There was this whole procedure. How you shouldn't get too close, how you shouldn't look. They passed out these booklets—"

"Who passed out booklets?"

"I don't recall. Maybe the government or maybe it was from the Las Vegas Chamber of Commerce. This isn't a big secret, Romulus. There were lots of articles written about the drops. Right there in all the papers. And being the good Americans we were, we all supported it. It's all part of Nevada state history."

"I know that. I just thought that maybe someone would think twice about taking a bunch of schoolgirls into a hot zone."

"This was the heart of the Cold War. If the government told us we needed the bomb to hold back the Reds, well then, it was our patriotic duty to test 'em, and we were honored to be a part of it. 'Course we didn't know back then that the government lies like a pack of thieves. And no one knew that the radiation was danger—''

''You know, it's a wonder that this city isn't full of mutants.'' A pause. ''I guess it is. We just can't see it.'' He waited a beat. ''Mom, when did we move here from St. George?''

''Here?'' She swallowed dryly. ''Nineteen sixty-four. You and Remus were three years old.''

''And when did they stop testing aboveground? 'Sixty-one?''

'' 'Sixty-three.''

''So I missed it.''

''Yep. Good thing, too. When those critters exploded, they made such a noise . . . I swear you could hear it clear down in St. George. Both you and Remus were poor sleepers. That's all you would have needed. Bombs going off.''

''You know, Mom, radiation hangs around for *years*—''

''What are you thinking? That the radiation has something to do with my cancer?''

''That's exactly what I'm thinking.''

''I thought about that, Romulus. But look at my friends here. Practically all of them are living and healthy to boot. Well, Bessy. She has breast cancer. Had it for years. And Katherine has diabetes. But she is over sixty and weighs about two hundred pounds. All in all, we don't seem like a real sickly crew.''

''Maybe they never got as close to the bomb as you did.''

Emma thought about it. ''You think we could sue the government? At least get them to pay my hospital bills?''

''I know there've been some class-action suits—victims with thyroid cancer. What would it hurt to look into it?''

''Well, I don't reckon you'll find too much. Lots of tourists came and went during those years. If they all got sick with leukemia, I think we would've heard about it. And I do think the NTS were pretty careful about the wind factor. If it was blowing too hard, they'd cancel the drop.''

''Like I said, radiation hangs in the air. Say they made a drop on a calm morning. Then a week later, the winds kicked up. And you know how the winds can kick up. Man, they'd spread that crap all over the place. You know, I never could understand why Las Vegas city officials would let NTS get away with aboveground testing when it's only, what . . . about sixty miles away from here. Talk about fouling your own nest.''

"They didn't know—"

"That's bullshit, Mom. They did know. They'd been testing the shit in the South Seas years before."

"Such language." Emma held her ears. "You don't understand the times back then. The Commies were our enemies—a *real* threat to our safety and welfare. The bomb was our safety net."

"A net with very big holes."

"Yeah, looking back, it was probably all smoke and mirrors. Life is funny." She handed him back the clipping. "You still want this?"

Poe took the picture. "I need to return it. It doesn't belong to me."

"Linda Hennick's been dead for years. Does it belong to Gerald or Alison?"

"Alison."

"You're still sweet on her?"

"A bit."

"That's too bad. I like your India Indian friend much better."

"Actually, I like Rukmani better, too."

The old woman smiled. "Actually showing some maturity. What's the occasion?"

"In your honor."

"Just as long as you don't get *too* mature." Emma winked at her son. "One Remus in the family is enough."

THIRTY-TWO

One-twenty remaining in the envelope. Poe said, "You gave a dirtbag who spit in your face over three hundred and eighty dollars?"

Patricia thought a moment. "No, I gave him one-fifty. The rest of the money went to other people. That averaged maybe fifty a pop. Sorry, but you can't buy anyone for less than a twenty." A shrug. "At least I brought something back."

Poe pocketed the bills, sat back in his desk chair. "You check the sheet on this jack— What's his name?"

"Lamar Larue," Patricia answered. "Fat guy. Must have weighed around two-eighty. I actually *flipped* him!"

"The woman doesn't know her own strength."

"He's got a rap sheet longer than a premium toilet roll."

"How long has he been in Vegas?"

"Two years."

"Long time," Poe replied. "Wonder why we haven't nailed him before." A beat. "He's probably done favors for some big boys. They've kept him loose. What about the Arab he mentioned? Did you run him through NCIC?"

"So far, Nali Abousayed hasn't popped up in any of the criminal databanks. But that doesn't mean anything. Rumor says he's royalty—a prince in some emirate. I'm sure he has diplomatic immunity.''

"Where'd you hear these rumors?''

"A couple of dealers . . . cocktail waitresses. I spoke to several Lady Slipper people around six this morning—*after* they got off shift. I'm *sure* Larue immediately ratted to Abousayed or his bodyguards that a fat broad cop was gunning for him. I didn't want to charge in without sizing up the situation. I wanted to be as discreet as possible.''

"Good idea, especially if Mr. Prince has bodyguards.''

"He has an entire entourage—wives, mistresses, kids, nannies, doctors, cooks, tutors, translators, guards—''

"So he's untouchable.''

"Appears that way.''

"Just like Lewiston.'' Poe drummed his desktop. "Too bad loathing a person isn't grounds for arrest. Now let me get this straight. Larue told you that the sale of underage girls was done through Lewiston's brokers.''

"Yes, through his whores.'' Patricia paused. "Actually, we never mentioned Lewiston by name. We kept referring to him as the big man.''

"No name?''

Patricia shook her head.

Poe sighed. "Did you feel that Larue was telling you the truth . . . or at least *part* of the truth?''

Patricia said, "You know, Sergeant, I hate to say this. But I'm very gullible. Someone could pass wind and convince me it's perfume.''

Poe laughed. "I think you're just being modest.''

Patricia smiled. "Sir, I believe there were elements of truth in Larue's story. Abousayed may be untouchable, but he isn't invisible. I think we should take pictures of his whores. Try to identify them. Maybe we could tie one of them as being the broker for Newel or Yarlborough. I know this town has an infinite supply of hookers. But when *two* of them get murdered, that's not good for the profession. Everyone talks.''

Poe nodded. "Go for it.''

"Uh, sir?''

"What?''

"Like I said before, I'm sure that Larue has warned Abousayed about me. There're probably dogging my heels. I think someone else should take the assignment.''

Poe drummed his desktop. "Who do I have? Jensen's on leave of absence, Marine Martin was with you last night. If Larue warned Abou-sayed about you, I'm sure he warned him about Marine, too.'' He blew out air. ''There's Grandpa Herrod. He's getting better, actually has a picture of the kid on his desk. Though if you mention it, he gets all pissed.''

''Sir, it's taking some photographs. Why don't you dress like a tourist and do it yourself?''

A good idea: a legitimate excuse to escape. A quick dinner at Ruk-mani's with Mom, then he'd hit the streets. Maybe he'd leave Mom with the nurse and take Ruki with him. Not only was Ruki good company, but she'd be excellent camouflage. Later, they could check into one of the hotels . . . or how about a sleazy *motel* . . . or better still, parking in a dark alley . . .

''. . . laroid if you want,'' Patricia said.

Poe was jerked out of his reverie. ''Sorry, I didn't hear you. I still get a bit foggy.'' He touched his temple. ''Residual effects from the medi-cation.''

''I have a Polaroid camera if you want.''

''Sure.'' He could think of *lots* of things to do with a Polaroid. ''Thanks.''

Patricia glanced at her watch. ''I've got a court case in a half hour. I should go over my notes.''

Poe started snapping his fingers, then stopped. He was tense and he knew why. ''Has anyone heard from Jensen at all?''

''Not a word. Hope he's sucking up sun and fun. Guy was a basket case, Sergeant. He really needed a break.''

''Everyone needs a break.'' He stood up. ''Lunchtime. I'm going to check in on my mother.''

''How's she doing?''

''Pretty good. She's a real survivor.''

''Yeah, you look like you're from strong stock.''

''Short but strong.''

''Your brother is short?''

''Once he was very short,'' Poe said. ''That was a long time ago. In another decade . . . in another century.''

Having picked the lock so many times, Poe was thinking about having a key made. He flipped the latch, walked inside, fanned away the stale odor, and started opening windows. Hot fresh air mixed with hot stale air. Poe loosened his tie and opened his shirt collar. He went into the master bedroom.

Opening the closet, he riffled through the clothes for a second time. Nothing had changed since he had been here. The same empty hangers, the same holes in the groupings of shoes. The Jensens had packed some clothes, but only a week's supply. Maybe two if they stretched.

He folded his arms across his chest and tapped his toe. Something was off. Nothing he could put his finger on, just some invisible vibration of impending disaster.

Now who was going off the deep end?

Alison's paranoid ramblings. Her grandiose manner and illusions of power. The good Steve. The bad Steve. The jealous Steve. Steve was trying to drive her insane.

No need to drive *anywhere, Alison, you're already there.*

She was delusional. In the midst of breakdown. So why was he getting such a weird feeling?

He flipped his wrist to his watch.

Twelve-ten.

If he left now, he could make it to Rukmani's, spend some time with Mom.

Just put back the clipping and leave.

He dug into the closet corner until he found the RESEARCH shoe box that contained clips of Linda Hennick's tortured life. Underneath that carton were two more RESEARCH shoe boxes. Bigger shoe boxes. Poe regarded the stamp on the end of the boxes.

Men's size eleven. Steve's size.

Poe took out the stacked boxes and brought them into the open, laying them on the bed. Linda Hennick's research was housed in a women's size seven shoe box. The other two were men's size eleven shoe boxes. The night Alison had been attacked, Poe had found a running shoe— men's size eight.

Too small for Steve. Too big for Alison.

Men's size eight.

Probably a little guy with a small foot. Because even Poe was a nine. His own running shoes were ten and a half. The heat from running caused the foot to expand, so he always bought roomy athletic shoes, at least a size big—

Women's size seven.

Poe looked at the box stamp. Once the carton had contained a women's size seven pair of black pumps. A women's size seven pump could easily translate into a men's size eight *running* shoe.

He rubbed his face.

Alison, what have you done*?*

Maybe nothing. Maybe he was letting his imagination . . .

He opened the Linda Hennick research box and put back the senior class picture taken at NTS. He replaced the lid and licked his lips.

He moved on to the next box and opened the top.

Newspaper articles—dozens of them—as well as magazine articles, photographs, and political cartoons. Nothing was original; they were all reprints or Xeroxes. They had nothing to do with Linda Hennick.

Instead, they centered around the Nevada Test Site and the atomic bomb drops.

Poe picked up the longest article—two pages stapled together and printed on plain white paper. It looked like something Alison might have picked up over the Internet. It was a history that traced NTS and Nevada's atomic history. He skimmed the sentences, knowing most of the facts.

Truman had established the Nevada Proving Ground (NPG) in 1950 because it was too far and too inconvenient to test the bombs in the Central Pacific. On January 27, 1951—eleven years before Poe was born—a one-kiloton bomb named Able was dropped above Frenchman Flat in the 860,000-acre area of the NPG later renamed NTS. More bombs followed, each one christened as if the government were birthing an infant. Some of the bombs were detonated at the surface of NTS, others were dropped from planes, mounted on steel towers, or suspended from large balloons. One was even fired from a cannon. From Able in 1951 to the last, Little Feller I, in July 1962. All in all, over a hundred aboveground or atmospheric detonations done in seven distinct series.

The Limited Test Ban Treaty forced the action down under. More charges were made—over eight hundred of them—but all exploded beneath the earth's surface. Still, radiation continued to spew into the air, because the charges had to be vented to release the pressure. Zillions of gamma rays and radioactive iodine particles shooting into the atmosphere, mixing with rainclouds, falling down only God knew where.

Poe tossed the article down on the bed, picked up a handful of clippings. He sorted through them.

A column from the *Deseret News* dated January 12, 1951. Fifteen days before Able:

The atomic tests planned for the Las Vegas bombing range will not endanger the health of area residents, Dr. John Bowers, new dean of the University of Utah College of Medicine and Atomic Energy Commission consultant, said Thursday.

A reprint of a handbill distributed by the Atomic Energy Commission dated January 11, 1951, sixteen days before Able:

From this day forward the U.S. Atomic Energy Commission has been authorized to use part of the Las Vegas Bombing and Gunnery Range for test work necessary to the atomic weapons development program.

   Test activity will include experimental nuclear detonations for the development of atomic bombs. . . .

Poe skimmed down to bold letters.

NO PUBLIC ANNOUNCEMENT OF THE TIME OF ANY TEST WILL BE MADE.

A Bruce Russell cartoon from the *Los Angeles Times*, dated 1951. A mushroom cloud labeled "U.S. Atomic Weapons Superiority." Next to it was a toad labeled "Soviet Aggression."
The caption read: "The mushroom that's deadly for the toad."
Mom's words echoing in Poe's brain.
This was the heart of the Cold War. If the government told us we needed the bomb to hold back the Reds, well then, it was our patriotic duty to test 'em, and we were honored to be a part of it.
A part of what? A guinea pig for radiation?
Another piece from the *Boulder News*. The streamer stating: "Our Atomic Alarm Clock Is the Talk of Boulder City."
Quotes about the bomb drops:

If it will help them make the peace and more security for our country, I don't care how many they shoot off.

I think it is necessary for national defense and it doesn't scare me in the least.

A young man "wishes the blast would go off every Friday morning at 3 A.M. to wake up his brother Mike to deliver papers."

From the *New York Times*, June 9, 1957:

The best view of the detonations can be obtained from Mount Charleston, which lies just east of US 95, only an hour's ride from Las Vegas, over good roads.

Mount Charleston was around fifteen minutes away from Poe's house. He sighed, remembering Mom's words from last night: *It was a tourist attraction.*

Article upon article. Support for the drops at first. And then came the criticism:

A cartoon by Herblock reprinted in the *Las Vegas Sun*, in June 1957. A chubby avuncular-looking man painting a mushroom cloud. The paint bucket read, "Keep Smiling." The paint ladder held a sign that read, "Atomic Energy Good News Commission." The caption read, "I'm painting the clouds with sunshine."

The details were interesting, but none of the content was new. As Mom said, it was part of the Silver State's dubious history—a well-documented, well-orchestrated, and nonconsensual dupe perpetrated on the American people and southern Nevada by the AEC. Because they really did know radiation was dangerous.

But did they know *how* dangerous?

And what did all this have to do with Alison?

Both Alison and he had been born in St. George, Utah. Poe's family had moved when he was three. Alison had moved when she was three, following the Poe trail several years later. Both of them had been essentially reared in Las Vegas, just an hour away from the test site.

A shoe box of her mother.

Another shoe box of NTS history.

Was she *blaming* NTS for her mother's illness?

Was she blaming NTS for her *own* illness?

To a warped mind, the conclusion might make sense. Her mother *had* become mentally ill shortly after Alison was born, after her move from St. George to Las Vegas. It was conceivable that the radiation had something to do with Linda Hennick's illness.

And while he was musing, maybe it had something to do with Alison's illness as well.

Or with his mother's cancer.

Or maybe his and Remus's height problems, while he was on the subject. Not to mention the sterility.

But the testing had been moved underground *before* he moved to Vegas. In the overlap between his life and the atmospheric testing, he had been miles from the action.

Poe thought a moment.

As he had stated to his mother, radiation hung in the air, was kicked around by the winds. And everyone knew about the desert winds. Also, there was the venting of the underground charges.

Still, as his mother had so aptly pointed out, her Vegas buddies were a pretty healthy bunch. And his classmates from school—no big problems so far as he knew.

His eyes returned to another political cartoon.

Dated much later . . . 1984. Mike Smith and the *Las Vegas Sun.* A side-by-side diptych photo.

The left cartoon showing a mushroom cloud. In front of the cloud, two men were talking to each other, the first one saying: ''Don't worry. Someday this'll all blow over.''

The right cartoon showed the same cloud. The second man answering the first man, saying: ''Over Utah, over Nevada, over Arizona.''

The caption stated: ''Government not negligent in aboveground testing. U.S. Court of Appeals.''

Poe stared at the cartoon.

Over Utah, over Nevada, over Arizona.

Why not over *California*? NTS was just as close to the California border as it was to Utah. He racked his brain, trying to bring the cartoon's appeals case into memory. Scrambling through the articles. He vaguely recalled an appeals case. He had been relatively new on the LVMPD force, so it must have been around the late eighties.

He opened the third shoe box.

More NTS articles. As he sifted through them, he found what he was looking for. The U.S. Court of Appeals had overturned the case against the government, clearing the AEC of negligence for all the billions of radiating atoms it had exploded into the air.

People had sued the government for their ailments. But they had lost.

What were the details of the original case? Poe thumbed through more clippings. He found a piece in the *Reno Gazette-Journal*. Headline: "People 1, Feds 0."

It took a long time—far too long, in fact—but at last a federal judge had said what many Nevadans have long believed: that the above-ground atomic tests of three decades ago endangered the lives of people downwind from the Nevada Test Site.

The original case against the government had been brought to trial right about the time Poe's mother had moved to Reno. The case had been adjudicated a couple of years later, after Poe had moved back to Vegas.

Another article. This one was dated in 1991. It was actually an official legislative document—the Radiation Exposure Compensation Act of 1990. Poe skimmed the legalese, concluded that it had something to do with compensation for high-risk people with illnesses linked to radiation exposure in general.

He paused.

That certainly could include Mom.

He read further.

People at high risk included uranium miners (Mom was out of this category), subjects of human radiation experiments (had Mom ever been an experimental subject?), military personnel involved in weapons tests (to his knowledge, Mom had never been in the military), and the down-winders.

The *downwinders*.

Poe hit his head.

Of course, you *idiot*! The *downwinders*!

Because weather moved *down*wind—from west to east. Which meant that the fallout also moved from west to east. Land due east of NTS was at extremely high risk for excess radiation: eastern Nevada . . . Arizona . . . Utah. And east of NTS was forgotten land—sparsely populated areas, lots of grazing ground, and small towns of good Mormon stock. Especially in the 1950s when Mom had been a teen.

God, apple pie, and Chevrolet.

Patriotism.

America: Love it or leave it.

God bless the USA.

Unimportant, expendable people.

Bunkerville in Nevada. In Utah, there was Cedar City, American Fork, Ephraim, Kanab—and St. George.

When Poe had lived in St. George, aboveground testing had still been going on. Huge clouds and winds of radiation enveloped the air he had breathed as a baby. And Emma, a young mother taking out the baby stroller for long walks with her sons through the countryside. Her two tiny infants—little babies with developing brains, and developing thymus glands, and developing thyroids, and developing *pituitary* glands. The three of them, breathing in mouthfuls of radiation with each gentle, passing breeze.

What had it done to Remus and him?

What had it done to his mother?

What had it done to Linda Hennick?

And what *has* it done to Alison Jensen?

THIRTY-THREE

Not that it was now or never. Things could always be changed . . . or altered . . . or redefined physically and mentally, as it were. But being that the old man and the boys were settled in Los Angeles, it left long stretches of time alone to assess the situation.

No one knew where they were. And no one even bothered to look for them. Because of the temporary leave of absence.

A smile on the face.

It just worked out perfectly. Long days and nights to make things right . . . to do things correctly.

It was good to be correct.

It was very good to be perfect.

Because perfection was an asset in this world. So few people are really careful . . . really observe.

So the time was right.

Now all that was required was balls to do the deed.

Go out in style. Like that oldie song.

Good-bye cruel world, I'm off to join the circus.

Because life was a circus—a crudely constructed theater of the absurd. Living in a cesspool while fending off blows from insignificant people who pummel and smash your self-esteem. Until you get so sick and tired of all of it that you lash out and—

Well, what does it really matter?

Because . . . because . . . *all the world's a stage.*

Or at least a bad Hollywood movie.

Lights! Camera! Action!

And here were the director, the producer, the writer, and the star—all wrapped up into one.

Now for the title.

How about "Predators of the Night."

Or "Night of Prey."

Or "Death Under the Moonlight."

Or "Moondance Death."

Or "Moon Music."

Dancing to the rhythm of the nightcall.

Be it alive or be it dead, I'll grind the bones to make my bread.

"I've got a job for you, Y."

The old man said nothing as he put a dollar token in the poker-machine slot.

Poe stared at the Chief's silvered fingers. "Why don't you use a money card, guy?"

"Too sterile," Y responded. "Don't feel like you're playing the machine."

Poe chuckled, but understood exactly what Y was saying. He said, "Anyway, my job's a simple one. I'll even pay you."

"You always pay me." A beat. "How's your arm?"

Poe rotated the limb, flexed his wrist. "Still intact. You know, Mom's waiting for her medicine man."

"I'm negotiating."

"Negotiating?"

Ping! went the token as it plunged into the machine's infinite coin cavern. "These things take time. Lots of charlatans in the business. Even the good ones . . . they smell money, they get greedy. Tell her a couple more days."

"Will do."

Suddenly the machine started singing as its lights flashed strobic blips of blue and pink. Y gave out a small smile which seemed to crack his leathered skin. "Look at this!" He pounded Poe's back. "Royal fucking flush!" He jabbed Poe's ribs. "How much is that?"

Wryly, Poe said, "As if you don't know—"

"How *much*?"

"How many coins did you put in?"

"Five."

"Then it's four grand. Unless you're playing progressive."

"Four fucking grand!" Y grinned. "Pretty good, huh?"

"Very good."

"Where's my ticket?"

"You've got to wait for an attendant to clear—"

"Where's the fucking atten—"

"Here I am!"

A chipper forties-plus lady in black slacks, white shirt, black tie, and striped vest took out a key. She inserted it into a lock, opened the slot, and pressed several buttons. In a moment the machine was cleared.

She handed Y a ticket. Her smile was friendly and inviting. It said: *You're on a roll. Try again. Play back those winnings.* Aloud she said, "Congratulations, sir. Can I get you a celebration drink?"

"Vodka straight up for me, a beer for my friend—or you want a scotch, Rom?"

"Beer's fine."

"One vodka straight up and a beer. Any particular kind, sir?"

"Heineken."

"Right away."

As soon as she left, Y put another dollar into the machine.

Poe said, "What are you doing?"

"I still got a half roll left."

Poe took the coins from the old man. "What do you say you quit a winner tonight?"

"I can play off everything in my pocket and still be a big win—"

"Let me tell you about this job."

Y kissed his ticket. "Don't need your job."

"Then do me a favor."

"A favor I'll consider." He faced the kid. "What?"

"I need you to take some pictures. Private . . . discreet."

"Porno?"

Poe rolled his eyes. "No, not porno." A beat. "What do you know about Nali Abousayed?"

Y shrugged. "Some kind of Arab sheik."

"Dangerous guy?"

"Anyone with power and money is dangerous."

Poe rolled his wrist a few times. "Beyond the usual hanky-panky, has he even been implicated in serious crimes?"

"Such as?"

"Sex with kids?"

"Beats me."

"You're just a wealth of information tonight."

"The wealth part is true." Again, Y kissed his winning ticket. "Why are you curious about Abousayed?"

Poe leaned over and spoke softly. He went into his story, starting with his suspicions about Parker Lewiston, ending with Nali Abousayed and his whores provided by Lewiston. As Poe spoke, he saw Y's face darken and turn stony. Alarming. Poe knew he had struck a nerve.

Still, he continued. "According to this scuzzball, one of Abousayed's hookers has been in Naked City acting as a broker for a power guy."

"Lewiston?"

"I'd assume Lewiston, since Abousayed gets his whores from Lewiston. Maybe one of the whores brokered Sarah Yarlborough. Or at least someone who knew Yarlborough or even Brittany Newel. I'm just looking for some kind of connect—"

"Give it up," Y interrupted.

"What? *Why?*"

Chirpy cashier came back with the drinks. Y nudged Poe. "Tip her a C-note."

"Me?" Poe stared at the old man.

Y said, "I'm good for it."

As she laid down the drinks, Poe slipped a hundred-dollar bill into her pocket. When she'd left, he said, "Look, Y. It's just some pictures of Abousayed's whores. No big deal."

"Then you do it."

"They know me at the Slipper. As soon as I walk through the door, I'm marked."

"And these same people won't figure out that you sent me?" Y rolled his tongue in his cheek. "Romulus, you're the only one left who still talks to me."

"Just go in there and play your machines. When you go to the john, snap some photos."

"I never play in Lewiston's places."

Poe paused. "Why not?"

"I don't like the man." Y downed his vodka in a single swig. "Let's get out of here."

He bolted from the chair. Poe had to fast-walk to keep up with the old guy.

"Think you should claim your winnings before you leave?"

Y stopped walking. "I suppose that would be a good idea."

Together, they went over to the cashier's cage. After ten minutes of waiting and ID checks, Y left the casino with a $4,100 check. They walked along the Strip, underneath a modern art canvas of neon and moonlight. The night was mild, and Poe took off his jacket.

He said, "I don't like Lewiston either. So let's get him."

Y shook his head. "You're gonna lose, Rom."

"Why do you say that?"

"Because it's true."

Poe placed his hand on the old man's shoulder to get him to stop walking. Carefully, he evaluated Y's expression. "You've gone up against him before, Chief?"

Y muttered, "Back when I was spitting mad, I didn't have the balls. Now I have the balls, but don't have the anger."

"What did he do to you?"

His eyes grew distant. "He stole a woman, turned her into maggot meat."

Maggot meat. Interesting choice of words. There had been only one woman in Y's life who fit that description. "Linda Hennick."

Y said nothing, chewed on nonexistent tobacco chaw.

"Did he have something to do with her suicide?"

"He killed her, Romulus."

Poe absorbed his words. "It was an unusual suicide—"

"' 'Course it was *unusual*!" Y snapped. "Because it wasn't a suicide. It was a homicide! Four Aces had been one of Lewiston's babies. A big moneymaker in chump change. Later, the Gaming Commission made him sell it off after he bought the Bucking Bronco. Regulations about one person not owning too much. And something about antitrust. But back then, twenty-five years ago, Aces was his. Everyone was paid off, Romulus. From the cops to the clerk to the room service man to the witnesses. Everyone."

The two of them resumed their walk at a slower pace.

Poe rubbed his forehead. "You get me some names, I'll press to reopen the case."

"What's the point?"

"The *point*?" Poe was incredulous. "The point, Y, is to bring a killer to justice. Now, I know it happened twenty-five years ago. Some of the parties involved might be dead. But certainly others would be alive—"

"Leave the dead in peace."

Poe stopped walking. "You can't be *serious.*" Y kept on going. Poe jogged a few steps and caught up with him. "You just accused Lewiston of murder."

"I did."

"Now you're telling me to let it go."

"Linda Hennick's dead. Stirring up the pot won't bring her back to life."

Again Poe stopped Y in his tracks. "I thought you *loved* this woman!"

Y's face turned to stone. "I did."

Poe waited for an answer.

"I caused Gerald Hennick enough heartache." Y looked up at the sky. "Don't want to cause him any more grief."

Poe let out a small snort. "Well, I'll be damned. You're actually capable of guilt."

Y walked away. Poe caught up with the old man and grabbed his arm. "Stop being so damn touchy. Are you going to help me or not?"

"Not if you drag up Linda's memory."

"This isn't about Linda Hennick. It's about nailing Lewiston for chewing up young girls. . . . Slow down, Grampa. You're going to give yourself a heart attack."

"Then everything I own is yours."

"Cash your winnings first. Then you can die."

Y slowed. Poe sighed. "Look, if you don't want to help me out, I'll do it myself. And if I fail, it's no big whoop. Failure is an old friend. Now, what about Abousayed? Are you going to help me? Yes or no."

Y licked his dry lips. "Just for tonight?"

"A week would be better. Once I have pictures of his women, I'll take them to Larue. See if he can identify any of them as Lewiston's broker."

"Going through all this trouble on the word of a piece of buffalo turd."

"Yes, informants are shits and unreliable, but they're all we have. Just a few measly pictures, Y. Please?"

"Give me the freaking camera."

Poe stopped walking. "It's in my car."

"Where's your car?"

"In the opposite direction." They reversed their steps. "Thank you, Gramps."

Y didn't answer.

Poe said, "Hold your check for safekeeping?"

Y took out the slip of paper and gave it to him.

"You want me to come with you to the bank tomorrow?"

Y nodded.

Poe said, "Have you heard from Alison at all?"

"Gonna ask you the same thing," Y said. "Guess the answer is no."

Neither man spoke.

Poe said, "Not good."

Y answered, "Not good at all."

THIRTY-FOUR

Molly stuck her head in the squad room. "Is Sergeant Poe in?"

Patricia looked up from her desk. "He went to develop some film. He should be back in ten minutes. What is it?"

"Phone call."

"I'll take it." Patricia depressed the blinking light. "Detective Deluca."

There was a pause, then an old man's feeble voice. "Sergeant Poe, please."

"He's out at the moment. Can I help you?"

Another hesitation. "Maybe I should call back . . . y'say he'll be back in soon?"

"Yes, sir, he should be. Who is this, please?"

"Uh . . . Gerald Hennick."

Patricia sat up in her chair. "Hello, Mr. Hennick. What can I do for you?" A beat. "Is everything all right?"

"Y'see, I'm not . . . I was wondering . . . have you heard from my son-in-law, Stephen? Stephen Jensen?"

Patricia felt a jolt through her spine. "Mr. Hennick, we thought that Stephen and Alison were with you."

"Well, they were, but . . ."

Poe stepped into the squad room, cup of coffee in one hand, cigarette in the other. Frantically, Patricia waved him over. Out loud, she said, "Mr. Hennick, Sergeant Poe just walked in."

"Gerald Hennick?" Poe jogged over to her desk, spilling coffee onto his fingers. Irritated, he set the cup down and shook his wrist, wiping his hand on his pants. He took a hit on his smoke, then stubbed it out on his shoe and tossed the butt in the garbage. Patricia gave him the phone.

"Hello, Mr. Hennick. How are you?"

"Well, I'm fine . . . just fine, thank you." A pause. "I'm not the problem. Y'see, I was just wondering if you'd heard from Stephen or Alison."

"They're not with you, sir?"

"They *were* with me, Sergeant, but not now. Y'see, we all started off going on vacation. To give Alison a little breather. She hasn't been feelin' too good lately."

"I know."

"So Stephen thought that she needed to get away . . . just Alison and the family. We were going to go campin'. Then Stephen decided that he should spend some time alone with Alison. Just the two of them. So they took off—"

"Did they say where they were going, Mr. Hennick?"

"No . . ." A pause. "No, they didn't. Stephen said something about makin' it a surprise. I told him I didn't know if a surprise was a good idea. But Stephen seemed so pleased, I didn't want to spoil anything. Y'see, times haven't been so good between them."

"I understand," Poe answered. The old man sounded as courtly as Jimmy Stewart. "Where are you now, sir?"

"Stephen dropped me and the boys off with my brother and his wife. Now, we're okay. We're having a good time—"

"What *city* are you in, sir?"

"Los Angeles."

"And you're fine?"

"Yes, Sergeant, we're all fine. Not to worry about me or the kids. But my daughter . . . she and Stephen left two days ago. And I haven't heard a peep from them. I'm gettin' a bit concerned."

"But the boys are okay?"

"The boys are fine . . . just fine. They went to Disneyland with my nephew and his wife and their kids. Everyone's gettin' along fine. But I didn't go in case Alison called. My brother has an answering machine, but people don't always leave messages. I was hoping that maybe you'd heard from Stephen . . . that he called in to work."

"No, he hasn't called, but that's expected. He's on vacation." Poe drummed the table. "Mr. Hennick, why don't you give me your phone number in Los Angeles. I'll make a couple of calls. If I find out anything, I'll give you a ring. And if you hear from them, please call me as well."

"All right." Hennick recited the number. "Thank you, Sergeant. Hope I didn't bother you too much."

"Not at all."

"Bye now."

Hennick hung up. Poe placed the receiver in its cradle. "Apparently, Steve took Alison on a 'surprise' getaway. Just the two of them. Hennick has no idea where they went and hasn't heard from them in two days. He's worried."

Patricia gave a weak smile. "So he's being spontaneous—"

"C'mon! Taking your mentally ill wife for a *surprise* vacation? He knows the score with her. At best, she tolerates him. At worst, she detests . . . it's a recipe for suici—" Poe paused. "Maybe that's exactly what Steve wants."

Patricia gave a startled look. "Sir, to me it seems like a harmless and sweet gesture."

Poe grunted. "Steve is *not* harmless, and he certainly isn't sweet." Poe went to his desk and took out his lock picks. "I don't like it. There are children at stake. We need to do something."

"Like what?"

"Like finding out where they are, for starters." He crossed the floor, sitting at Jensen's spot. He examined Steve's desk drawer, tried to shake it open. Patricia looked around the squad room. Just Marine Martin and Herrod at their desks. The rest were out in the field. Marine's eyes darted between Poe and her, giving Patricia a curious "What's going on?" look. She answered him with a shrug.

She went over to Jensen's desk. Poe was attacking it with his picks. "Sir, what are you doing?"

"I'm breaking into a desk."

Patricia tapped her foot, unsure what to say. "I don't think you should do that . . . sir."

The lock clicked. Poe pulled out the top desk drawer and began rummaging around in the mess. He found a couple of loose credit card slips and pocketed them.

"Sir, this is an invasion of privacy," Patricia persisted. "If you did this to me, I'd be furious."

"Then it's good I'm not doing it to you." Poe closed the top drawer and opened the side file drawers. Racks of case folders, all of them neatly organized. They appeared in order. "If Steve wants to be furious, fine with me."

"Sergeant, what exactly are you looking for?"

Poe showed her a credit card slip. "If I have his card number, I can call up and pretend I'm Steve. Find out when and *where* this card was last used."

"I believe they ask you security questions—like your mother's maiden name and Social Security number."

"I know. And I'm sure all that information is listed in Jensen's employment records."

"What you're doing is illegal."

"Call the cops."

"This isn't right."

"So sue me." Poe slammed the drawers shut, then stomped off to his desk and picked up the phone. Patricia followed on his heels.

She said, "There's no indication of any problems—"

Poe shoved the phone into the receiver. "Look, maybe *Steve* wouldn't call to find out about the kids. But *Alison* would. She may be off her rocker, but she loves those boys."

"Are they in danger?"

"No, the kids are fine. But neither of them knows that."

"I don't understand—"

"Detective, I'm just going to find out where they are. Once I'm sure that everyone's safe, I'll back off." Again, he picked up the phone. "Molly, can you connect me with the Personnel Department, please?"

Patricia threw up her hands. "So what happened last night?"

"Last night?" Poe was puzzled. "What was supposed to happen last night?"

"Abousayed. You were going to take pictures of his women."

"Oh, that! I sent Y as my proxy, since I didn't want to be spotted. He took a couple of rolls of film. I hope they came out. Chief's not exactly a techno-guy."

"It's pressing a button and waiting for the snapshot to eject."

"Yeah, uh . . . we decided against the Polaroid. It made too much noise. Instead I gave him Rukmani's Canon."

"So where's my Polaroid?"

"In my car. I owe you a pack of film."

"What happened to the film?"

"I used it up." A grin spread across his face. "Family photos."

Patricia eyed him skeptically, but didn't further the conversation. "That was a good idea, Sergeant. Sending in Y."

"A decent thought does flit through my brain every millennium." He drank his now-tepid coffee. Into the phone, he said, "This is Detective Sergeant Romulus Poe from Homicide. I've got an emergency situation here and I need to see a personnel file on one of my men. He's on vacation and his mother died. His records should have a list of close relatives— No, I'd rather you don't give any information over the phone. I'll come down in per—I know it's an unusual request, but like I said, it's an emergency. . . . All right. All right. I'll be down in ten minutes."

He hung up the receiver.

"Photographs won't be ready for an hour. Might as well try to get a fix on Steve and Alison."

"I'm sure they're fine, sir."

Poe stood and finished off his coffee. He took out his car keys. "Must be nice to be *sure,* Deluca. But I'm from a dysfunctional family. Ergo, I'm *never* sure of anything!"

Following a trail of credit-card charges Poe found out that the Jensens had last eaten at a chophouse in an outpost called Vista de la Mesa, where they had taken a room at the Dunes Inn Motel. Looking for the name on a map, Poe found the speck—a high-desert hole in the wall about fifty miles from the Nevada/California border. It was also around twenty miles from Highway 15, the main artery linking L.A. to L.V. Maybe the couple were headed home.

When Poe called the motel, a young, dull male voice informed him that the Jensens had checked out about two hours ago. Poe asked the clerk, "Have you cleaned the room yet?"

Silence. When he finally *did* speak, he seemed to be working hard. "I dunno."

"Could you check for me?"

Another protracted pause. "I suppose."

"Could you do it now?"

"Want me to check the room?" A beat. "Or want me to find out if the room was cleaned up?"

Simplicity, Poe. Not everyone understands complex sentences. "Just check the room, please. See if it has been cleaned up."

"Can you hold on? I gotta find someone to watch the desk while I check the room."

"I can hold."

Poe heard the clunk of a receiver being placed on a hard surface, followed by the sound of receding footsteps. In the background, he heard a voice shout, "Kathy? Kathy, are you around?" The wait seemed interminable. Poe drummed, snapped, rocked on his feet, took out a cigarette he had bummed off Y last night, then put it back in his pocket.

It took ten minutes for Mr. Dull to return. He sounded shaky. "Uh, the room's a real mess."

"A mess?"

"Yeah, a *real* mess. There's blood on the sheets—"

"Oh God!"

"I think I should call the cops."

"Good idea."

"Where you callin' from again?"

"Las Vegas Metro Police Department. What police department services your area?"

"Police department?"

Poe enunciated each word clearly. "I want to call up your local police. Who do I call?"

"Who?"

"Yes, who. What is the name of *your* Police department?"

"Vista de la Mesa Sheriff's Department."

"Thank you. That's good. Now. Do you have a phone number?"

"Uh . . . sure." Another wait. Finally, Dull came back and slowly spit out the number. He said, "If *you* call 'em, then the line'll be busy when I call."

"Give me a minute to call first. Then you go ahead and call. Please make sure the room isn't touched."

"I already touched the doorknob."

"That's fine. But *don't* touch anything else. I'll make that call real quick."

"That's good. Because it's a real mess there. Spooky."

"Bye now." Poe cut the line, called the Vista de la Mesa Sheriff's Department. An upbeat, elderly female voice answered the phone.

"This is Detective Sergeant Romulus Poe from the Las Vegas Metro Police Department. I need to speak to someone in Homicide immediately."

"We don't have a homicide department," she answered. "Don't need it."

That's what you think. "Anyone in charge who I could talk to?"

"How about Sheriff Bruckner?"

"Sheriff Bruckner would be fine."

A short wait. Then a deep male voice. "Bruckner. Who's this?"

Poe introduced himself, explained the situation as succinctly as he could.

Bruckner said, "Thanks for calling. I'll get right over there."

"Could you call me as soon as you get there? If it's as bad as the kid says, I'll want to come up."

"That's nice of you to be concerned, but it's not necessary. Our guys know this town pretty well. Think we can handle it locally."

Marking his territory. Poe kept his patience. "Of course. But Jensen is one of our men. There's a personal interest here. Hell, if it was one of yours, you'd do the same, right?"

A long pause. Then Bruckner said, "Sure, come on up. Just don't bring a big-city posse with you. We're low-key here, do things differently than in places like L.A. or Las Vegas."

"I wouldn't even bother you except Jensen is a colleague." Poe thought a moment. "You know, if I leave now, I can be there in two hours. Maybe you could hold off—"

"Not for two hours."

"Okay. I understand. The investigation will probably take time. The clerk described the room as a real mess . . . lots of blood. Sounds like you're going to need your techs."

The line went quiet. Then Bruckner said, "If it's real bad, I'll wait. Do you the courtesy, since it's one of yours."

Cold feet at the sight of blood, Bruckner? Or just no techs?

Poe said, "Thank you, sir. I'll see you later." He hung up and grabbed his car keys. As soon as he pulled out of the parking lot, he paged Weinberg. The lieutenant called back a minute later and Poe recapped the situation.

Weinberg said, "I'm at Myra's. Pick me up. I'll get me a couple of sandwiches to go."

"I'd like to bring Rukmani Kalil along."

"Good idea. What kind of sandwich does she like?"

"She's a vegetarian."

"Does she eat eggs? I could get her an egg salad sandwich."

"She eats eggs as long as they aren't fertilized."

"No fertilized eggs here, Poe. They aren't kosher."

"Sir, what about Alison and Steve? Should we put out an APB for them?"

The loo said, "This is the plan. First, we hit the road. As we ride, we call up the motel— What's the name of the place?"

"Dunes Inn Motel."

"In what town?"

"Vista de la Mesa."

"Never heard of it."

"Me either. Sure doesn't sound like an ideal spot for a second honeymoon."

Weinberg hesitated. "Let's not jump to any conclusions. We'll talk to Bruckner directly. See what he has to say. If it's really bad, I'll issue an APB. You say this town is near Highway 15?"

"About twenty miles away."

"And they left the kids in L.A."

"Yes."

"So they're driving southeast. Could be they're coming back here."

"I thought about that."

"Maybe we'll pass them as we drive up."

"Wouldn't that be nice."

"You bet," Weinberg answered. "Save us all a lot of speculation."

THIRTY-FIVE

They congregated in the motel's parking lot—Poe, Weinberg, and Rukmani, along with Bruckner and Byron, the dull desk clerk. Heat sizzled off the blacktop, the sun relentless in the open terrain. The sheriff wasn't what Poe expected. About fifty, he was tall and thin— his khaki uniform hung on his stick frame—with a pencil mustache and clipped hair which had silvered at the temples. A beanpole with a radio announcer's mellifluous voice.

"Lieutenant?" Bruckner asked.

"No, I'm Sergeant Poe." The two men shook hands. Bruckner's grip was firm, but not overbearing. Poe cocked a thumb toward his superior. "This is Lieutenant Weinberg."

Mick stuck out his hand. "Thanks for waiting for us."

"Since it is one of your own." Bruckner glanced at his watch. "You made good time."

"Driving with a speed demon," Weinberg answered. "This is Dr. Kalil. I hope you don't mind. I've asked her to come."

Rukmani held out her hand. "Pleased to meet you."

Poe noticed Bruckner hesitating a fraction of a second before taking her hand. The sheriff said, "Likewise. Hope no one will be needin' your services, Doctor."

"I hope not, because I'm from the coroner's office."

Weinberg wiped his face with a handkerchief as he scanned the one-story dive—a gray stucco bunker. A long time ago, the motel had been painted white. There was some residual blue window trim, but at least half of it had chipped away. All the rooms—twenty-four total—were under one tar-paper roof. The check-in office held two vending machines—one with soda, the other with snacks. No other food establishments were in sight. The town was nothing but parched desert terrain. Why in the world would Steve take Alison here?

Poe seemed to read his thoughts. He mopped sweat from his forehead and said, "Byron, can I take a look at the guest book?"

Byron looked at the sheriff. The clerk was in his early twenties, of medium stature, with a round face and a flabby stomach. He had a circular button nose and wore glasses which dimmed his dark blue eyes.

Bruckner said, "Show the sergeant the book, Byron."

Without a word, the clerk turned and headed toward the office. Poe shrugged and followed.

Weinberg asked, "Which room was it?"

"Twenty," Bruckner answered. "In the back. I gave the inside a quick once-over. Byron wasn't lying. There's blood all over. But no bodies."

"You checked?" Rukmani asked.

"Yes, ma'am," Bruckner responded. "Had to make sure that someone wasn't lying in there, injured."

Rukmani noticed the condescension in his voice. "So you walked around?"

Bruckner smiled. "For about thirty seconds."

Poe came back. "Someone checked in under the name Stephen Jensen with a wife named Alison. Spelled the right way—with one L. It looks like Jensen's signature. Could it have been forged? Sure."

"It doesn't make sense," Weinberg said. "Steve taking Alison here."

"No, it doesn't."

No one spoke. Then Rukmani said, "I don't know about you gentlemen, but I'm ready to have a look."

Bruckner smiled. "Yeah, it's mighty hot out here for a lady."

Rukmani smiled back. "In Punjab, Sergeant, this weather is called springtime." She started forward. "The unit's number is twenty, correct?"

"Correct," Bruckner answered.

They hadn't taken more than a few steps when Poe felt the presence of another person. He turned around, saw a video camera pointed his way. Bruckner looked backward as well. He shouted, "Byron, get that damn thing outta our faces."

"A couple of shots, Sheriff—"

"Byron, we're doing serious business," Bruckner shouted. "Now turn that off before I crack it over your head."

Byron lowered the video camera.

Rukmani said, "Can I borrow that?"

Bruckner paused, beckoned Byron over. "Give it here."

"But I'm not doing nothing—"

"This lady wants to borrow it."

Byron looked at Rukmani with suspicious eyes. She held out her hand. "I'm from the coroner's office. A video camera would be helpful for my official business. If I can, I'll even send you a copy when I'm done."

"Give it to her," Bruckner pushed.

Reluctantly, Byron handed her the camera.

"Thank you," Rukmani said.

Bruckner said, "I think you should go back to the desk, Byron."

"Kathy's watching the desk."

"Well, go back and help her out."

Poe said, "I don't mind if he tags along. As long as he doesn't come in the room with us."

Bruckner stiffened, displeased by Poe's undermining his authority.

"C'mon, Sheriff. Be a sport."

Through a clenched jaw, Bruckner said, "I suppose it's all right."

Byron smiled. "Hey, thanks, Sheriff. Promise I won't get in your way." To Rukmani, he said, "Are you really gonna send me a copy of the tape?"

"No."

Byron was taken aback. "No?"

"Against regulations." Rukmani gloved up and broke a yellow crime ribbon that had been taped across the door. She turned the knob. "Ladies first, right, Sheriff?"

Bruckner told Byron to stay back. They entered single-file with Poe coming last.

His stomach dropped.

He had expected lots of blood—on the crumpled sheets, on the furniture, on the threadbare pink carpet that covered the floor. But he hadn't expected so much spray. Big, crimson abstracts on the walls and ceiling as if shot from an aerosol spray can. His eyes swept over the inkblots, then scanned the room. A rickety queen-sized bed, a worn pink spread batiked in red and brown blood. Two cheesy plastic wood-grain nightstands. Reading lamps attached to the walls. Across the bed was a dresser supporting a twenty-six-inch TV and its movie box. The TV was bolted to the dresser, the remote control was attached to one nightstand by a chain. Everything was nailed shut as a control against theft.

He swallowed dryly, felt his hands shaking. To cover his nervousness, he took out his pad and began to take notes. A mild stench permeated the stuffy room. Enough to wrinkle the nose, but not quite enough to upset the stomach.

Weinberg was unnerved by the horror. To Poe, he said, "You're *sure* the signature was legitimate?"

Poe looked up from his notebook. "No. But someone checked in under Jensen's name, and used his credit card."

"Christ!"

Rukmani had come out of the bathroom. She lowered the camera. "No body in the shower à la Hitchcock's *Psycho*." She sniffed, took out a mask. "But it smells pretty rank. Anyone look for a body in the closet?"

Poe dabbed some VapoRub under his nose. He opened the small door, gingerly peeked in. "Looks harmless to me."

"Let me get a shot of it." Rukmani started the tape rolling as she studied the closet. "Indeed, there's nothing dangling from a coat hanger."

Bruckner winced.

Rukmani stepped out into the open. "It's clean inside." She shut off the video camera. "Well, it's dusty, but there's no blood."

Poe pointed. "See those drip marks on the wall? They're coming from the seam between the north wall and the ceiling."

Rukmani said, "There's a crawl-space entrance in the bathroom ceiling."

The men eyed each other. Poe said, "Get me a ladder. I'll do it."

Bruckner said, "I can do it."

"Fine," Poe said. "It's your territory."

Bruckner paused. "But it is *your* man. It's up to you."

"I'll do it," Poe repeated.

"I'll get you that ladder."

As soon as he left, Rukmani said, "Ain't he a love?"

Weinberg said, "Have a little pity. He's probably never worked a homicide . . . probably scared shitless." He turned to Poe. "Are you up for this?"

"It's what they pay me to do."

"Not when there was a personal relationship," the lieutenant answered. "You know who could be up there."

"I know." No one spoke. Then he said, "It could be her, it could be him. It could be both—"

Rukmani interrupted, "On the surface, it doesn't look like enough spray for two people."

Poe said, "Alison couldn't possibly be strong enough to shove Steve into the crawl space. That would require her to lift around two hundred and twenty pounds of dead weight over her head. Not to mention that the crawl space is above her reach. So she'd have to find something to climb on. She couldn't do it." He shook his head in disbelief. "She couldn't do it."

Rukmani took his hand. "Romulus, I hope to God she's all right. I really mean that."

Again, Poe swallowed dryly. "I know you do. Thanks." He snapped his fingers, then stopped himself. "Maybe you should take another sweep of the place with the camera."

"I have enough." Rukmani looked around. "What we really need are some techs."

Weinberg said, "If we find a body and it turns out to be . . . either Alison or Steve or someone from Vegas, then I can make a case for jurisdiction. One thing at a time."

Rukmani said, "By the way, Rom, how'd the pictures come out?"

"Pictures?" Poe asked.

"The snapshots that Y took last night."

"I haven't had a chance . . ." He rubbed his face. "Who do you have to fuck to get a ladder in this place?"

"Patience, Poe," Weinberg said. "Look, if it's too much, let Bruck-ner—"

"I'm not letting that bozo touch anything." Poe stomped out of the room, saw Bruckner schlepping a ladder. He was as thin as the implement he carried. Poe jogged over to help him.

Bruckner said, "Who is that woman?"

"Dr. Kalil? She's the deputy coroner."

"She any good?"

"Is she any *good*?" Poe glared at him. "You talking personal or professional?"

Bruckner turned red. "Look, I just . . ."

Poe let him retreat into embarrassment. They brought the ladder into the bathroom and steadied it under the crawl-space entrance. Bruckner was suddenly obsequious. "Are you sure you want to do this, Sergeant?"

No, I don't want to do this, you asshole. "I'm fine. I'll need a good strong flashlight."

"Right away." Bruckner left.

Poe started up the rungs as Weinberg held the ladder. When he reached the opening, he pushed the cover to the side. A rush of blood came streaming down, landing on Weinberg's head.

"Shit!" the lieutenant groused. But he kept a firm grip on the ladder. "Will someone get—"

"—a towel," Rukmani finished his sentence. "Right away." She rushed out and came back holding a pile of linens. She wiped Weinberg's bald pate and face. "It's fresh blood."

"I figured that out, Doctor."

Rukmani smiled. "Sorry, Lieutenant."

Bruckner came back with the flashlight, wrinkled his nose. "Goddamn, that's . . . let me help you out, Lieutenant."

"If you could hold the ladder for a moment so I can wipe—"

"You bet." Bruckner gave the light to Poe. "Is this okay?"

"Perfect."

Weinberg released the ladder, dabbed himself off. "Whenever you're ready, Sergeant."

Poe took a deep breath, let it out, then stuck his head up into the steamy crawl space. He cringed at the smell: overripe meat in the beginnings of the decay process. There was also a heavy, metallic stink that hung in the hot, idle air. He shined the light into the vast cavern between the ceiling and roof. In the dimness, the floor appeared wet and shiny as if coated with tar. Poe could make out puddles. As he circled the beam around, he saw the lifeless lump lying about five feet from Poe's head.

He came down for air, into the bathroom. After taking a couple of breaths, he said, "There's something up there. But it's out of my reach while standing on a ladder. I'll have to go in to retrieve it." He eyed Weinberg. "Which means I'll trample on evidence . . . maybe muck up some shoe prints. The proper alternative is to come in through the roof. Take about half of it off—"

Weinberg said, "Poe, look at this place. You start mucking with structure, it's going to fall down like a house of cards."

"That could very well be."

"Go in and do what you have to do."

Rukmani said, "Let me get you goggles and a mask—"

"I'm okay. I've got my VapoRub."

"Please, Poe," Rukmani insisted. "Besides the blood and the smell, there's probably years' worth of dust and bat and bird guano. Believe me, you don't want to breathe it in, nor do you want it in your eyes."

"She's right," Weinberg said.

"All right." Poe waited for her to give him the protective devices. As soon as he was masked up, he said, "Here's to nothing."

"Be careful," Rukmani called out.

Hoisting himself upward, Poe squeezed his body into the limited space. Sometimes it was good to be short.

With a throbbing head and a stomach filled with acid, he crawled into wet, sticky liquid. The goggles cut the light even further. He could hear himself breathe, smell the rot through the mask. It was scorching and humid and as pleasant as wading in a cesspool.

Inching his way over to the lump as his gloved hands splashed up blood. Trying to keep his lunch down as he reached out and grabbed a lifeless arm. He began dragging it back over to the crawl space.

Light. Definitely not Steve. It was a woman.

His heart took off. He felt the room spin around him, a smothering sense of vertigo.

Don't faint, you schmuck!

Towing it closer to freedom. But he couldn't make out the face in the grayness. When he got to the crawl-space opening, he shouted, "I can't carry her down—"

"It's a her?" Weinberg shouted.

"Yeah, it's a her," Poe answered back. "I don't know who, though. The face is messed up, and it's way too dim. I'm going to lower her down and you have to catch her."

To Bruckner, Weinberg said, "Why don't you hold the ladder? I might as well catch her. I'm already bloodied up."

Bruckner nodded. "Sounds like a good game plan."

Weinberg had noticed that the sheriff had gone pale.

Poe clutched the body around the torso, felt his fingers dig into soft, raw flesh. A wave of nausea shot through his gullet. "I'm going to bring her down."

"Slow, Poe."

"As slow as I can."

He lowered her down, feet first. "Got her?"

"Not yet—"

"Now—"

"A little more . . . to the left."

"Now?"

"More."

"I'm slipping—"

"Got her," Weinberg said. "You can let go."

With an audible sigh, Poe rid himself of the body. For good measure, he shone the light around the attic space for a second time. This time, no lumps caught his attention. But he knew that something could be stashed in the corners. Later on, he'd make a more thorough check.

Later on . . .

Just as soon as he identified . . .

Weinberg shouted, "It's not Alison."

He answered back, "You're sure?"

"Positive."

Relief shot through Poe's body. He waited a second to compose himself, then began his climb downward. As his feet touched the floor, he ripped off his goggles and studied the corpse.

He grimaced.

Like Brittany Newel's, half the face was untouched, with the other half neatly raked in raw furrows. Not unlike his cheek. Poe forced himself not to touch his face, to concentrate on the job.

Unlike Newel's, this one's body had been devoured, eaten away, with whole chunks missing from the torso. All that remained was a massive lump of torn flesh and tissue. Her legs had been gouged and, in some places, skinned to the bone.

"Dear God!" he said.

Rukmani took his hand. "At least it isn't her."

"I know." A breath in and out. "Thanks for giving a damn."

"Even a damn and a half."

He blew out air, studied the face. And then it hit him. "Oh my God! I know who this was! Gretchen Wiler!"

All eyes went to him.

"Who?" Weinberg asked.

"Gretchen Wiler!" Poe repeated as he bounced on his feet. "You know Gretchen. She was Steve's mistress!"

THIRTY-SIX

Room 24 had been designated the "hospitality suite," although the fleabag had plenty of vacancies. As soon as Poe stepped inside the room, he ripped off his gloves and goggles and slammed the door with his foot. Beelining it to the bathroom, he turned the taps on full blast and splashed tepid water over his dirty face. Head pounding, he popped pain pills, then peeled off his clothes and showered, drying his body with a towel as absorbent as cheesecloth. The unit was hot and stuffy, but still he breathed deeply, thrilled to be away from the slaughterhouse. At present, the crime scene was thick with techs and black from fingerprint powder.

An APB had been put out for Steve and Alison.

Sitting on the bed, he dabbed his injured cheek, then wiped his face and towel-dried his hair. He was smearing ointment over his wound when the door opened. Rukmani stepped inside, mopping her sweaty face with a sleeve, oblivious to his presence. When she saw him, she took a step back. "My God! It's a naked detective!"

Poe raised his eyebrows. "Take a shower, babe. Soap'll do you good."

"And you'll still be here when I get out?"

"Are you kidding?"

She smiled, went into the bathroom, and shut the door. A moment later, Poe got up and walked into the steambath. He slipped his arms around her dripping, bony body, his hands traveling up to her firm, small breasts, his fingertips grazing her nipples. Her hair was braided but soaked. He could see her ribs. She looked like a waif. "When was the last time you ate?"

"I'm Indian. I'm used to starvation." She faced him, water pouring off her face. She stood on her tiptoes and kissed his lips, then licked the tufted line of black hair that ran down the middle of his chest. "God, you're beautiful when you're wet. Like burnished leather." She sucked his nipples. "You also taste wonderful."

"Likewise." He brought her lips to his and kissed her hard, their mouths mixing with the fresh, running water. He moved down to her neck and breasts.

He turned off the water.

They made frantic love on the shower floor.

They rinsed off anew. This time they didn't even have the luxury of dry towels. Damp and hot, they began the arduous process of redressing in dirty, sticky clothing.

Slipping on her bloodied surgical pants, Rukmani said, "There's got to be a better way to shoot this."

Poe looked up, his fingertips oily from his face salve. "Pardon?"

"If this were the movies, we'd have clean clothes."

Poe put on his sweat-soaked shirt flecked with bits of serum and tissue. "When we sell the story to Hollywood, we'll put clean clothes in the script."

The doorknob jiggled.

Poe shouted, "A minute."

"S'right." The loo's voice. "Take your time."

"How are they doing over there?" Poe asked.

"Still got ground to cover. You almost done? I want to take a shower. Somebody should supervise."

"I'll be out in a few minutes."

"Did Rukmani go back with the body? I can't find her."

They eyed each other. She giggled like a schoolgirl. Out loud, she said, "I'm here, Lieutenant. I'm going back with the two of you. That doesn't mess anything up, does it?"

"No, no," Weinberg said. "It's fine, it's fine."

Silence.

She whispered, "Stop smirking."

"Like he doesn't know—"

"That's not the point. Being obvious is crass."

Poe put on his dirty pants, turned flat-faced. "Better?"

"Very professional."

He opened the door, smiled dryly. "It's all yours. I'll get Byron to find you some dry towels."

Weinberg looked over their faces. "Thanks."

As soon as they stepped outside, they broke into peals of laughter—an expression of release more than joy. It was late afternoon and the heat had become even more oppressive. It took effort to breathe.

"Shit!" Poe exclaimed. "I left my mask—"

"I've got extras."

He stopped walking, held her shoulders. "I've got to get this out, all right?"

"Uh-oh—"

"No, no, no. It's nothing about us. It's about the case. If this mess is Steve's doing, then I'm not as concerned. But if it's Alison . . . Ruki, I'm very worried about you."

"Me?"

"It seems to me that Alison is attacking women who she believes have hurt her . . . have taken away her men. Newel was Steve's fling. Gretchen was Steve's mistress—"

"And now that she's finished with Steve's women," Rukmani interrupted, "she's going to move on to you, or rather your women—meaning me."

Poe nodded. "In the past, when she has brought you up . . . it wasn't fondly. I'd kill myself if anything happened to you."

"That would be a waste. Who'd avenge my honor?"

Poe licked his lips. "You're not taking me seriously."

She grinned. "Does this mean you care?"

"Yes, I care very much. Are you hearing me at all?"

She turned serious. "I hear you. I'll be careful." They started walking toward the death scene. "I've been doing a little thinking myself."

"And?"

"These killings . . . they have a ritualistic aspect to them, don't you think?"

"What specifically?"

"For instance, only half of the face was destroyed."

"Could be ritualistic. And it could be for ID purposes. That Alison—or whoever did it—wanted us to know who the victim was."

"Good point."

"Still, I don't disagree," Poe said. "The meticulous raking. Appears as if someone was dressing the body." He stopped walking. "Gretchen was mutilated more severely. Know what that says to me? That the killer was really *pissed* at her. If the killer was Alison, that would make sense. Because Gretchen wasn't a casual fling. She was viewed as a real threat."

"Or perhaps Alison has completely decompensated."

He nodded. "That's possible, too."

Again, they started inching toward the bloodbath.

Rukmani said, "It's not the rakes, Rom. It's the chunks that bother me. It's the big gouges in her legs, particularly the insides of the thighs. From a shrink's perspective, I could interpret it as Steve lashing out at Gretchen sexually. Because the inside of the thigh is very sexual. You know, I always felt that Steve had a weird attitude toward women. Deep down, I think he despises them."

"Really?"

"You don't think so?"

"Honestly, no. I think he just loves pussy." He stopped walking and stared at her. "Has he ever come on to you?"

Rukmani blushed. "Once."

Poe felt a stab of anger. "What? *When?*"

"Six, seven months ago. Right after we started dating."

"Why didn't you *tell* me?"

"Why bother? At that time, things weren't serious between us."

Abruptly, she stopped speaking—the unsaid line being: are things really serious now?

She shrugged. "You work with the man, Rom. If I had gotten in the way, I would not only have screwed things up between you and Steve, I would have messed up our relationship. Anyway, he wasn't persistent. He suggested we go out for a drink. I told him I was swamped with work, and he took it as the rebuff it was meant to be."

"Great," Poe muttered. "Now I'm *really* worried about you. Both Steve and Alison have a vendetta—"

"You're overstating my worth."

He brushed her lips. "I don't think so."

"You must be worried," Rukmani said. "You're acting very sweet. Can we talk about the body? Particularly the wounds in the inner thighs."

Poe wiped his forehead. "Go on."

"Rom, I've seen bite victims—"

"So have I."

"Then you know that while they ain't pretty, they don't resemble what was on Gretchen—big, jagged holes in the flesh. I've got to say this. It looks to me like the body was being eaten—"

"I don't want to think about this—"

"Yet the body didn't have the typical signs of cannibalism."

Poe paused. "It wasn't butchered or dressed as edible meat."

"Exactly."

"Maybe he/she/they ran out of time to do it properly."

"So why eat the flesh *raw*?"

"I don't know, Ruki."

She bounced on the hot ground. "There's no shade in this place. How about we take a little ride?"

Poe ran his hand through his now dry hair. "I've got to supervise the techs."

"Okay, I'll try to be brief. Have you ever heard of the psychological disorder called lycanthropy? You may know it better by its common name: werewolfism."

Poe digested her words. "You think Alison's a werewolf?"

"No. I think she thinks she's a werewolf."

"I've got to disagree with you on that one."

"Why?"

"Be ... because ..." Poe stuttered. "I just don't think that she ... how common is this delusion? It is a delusion, isn't it?"

"Yes, lycanthropy is a psychotic delusion. How common? Depends on where you live. In Scandinavia, werewolf tales were very common. If you lived in England, werewolves were unheard-of."

"No werewolves in England?"

"No legends, for some reason. I can't figure out why exactly. There are plenty of wolves in English forests. The Brits had a different perspective. I'm sure there were some English people who believed they were animals. But their forays weren't written down as folk legends, rather viewed as an aberrant psychological state akin to insanity."

"Where'd you learn all this?"

"I was a psychiatric resident before I went into pathology. I decided I liked my people dead rather than crazy."

"And I'm supposed to take you seriously?"

"I wrote an impressive, erudite thesis on this very subject—the *Panchatantra,* which is a Sanskrit book of fables. I related its tales to DSM-listed psychological disorders like lycanthropy—wolves—or kuanthropy—dogs—or boanthropy—cows and bulls. All of this is a *very* strange concept to you Americans, but a very common idea to us Indians. The ability to switch corporeal identities is inherent in our religious tenets. Hence many of us are vegetarians. The belief in metempsychosis combined with our mainstay of reincarnation means we don't eat flesh because we don't want to eat Aunt Benazir—''

"You are truly sick." A beat. "What's metempsychosis?"

"Transformation from a human form to an animal, and vice versa. For some unlucky souls, it's an involuntary act. Others can do it at will. We've hundreds of fables about people turning into wolves or wild dogs or bulls or bears. But this is all beside the point.

"Rom, the one common factor all these fables and legends have is the need for fresh kill. It is imperative to the well-being of a wild animal."

"So Alison thinks she's a wild animal."

"Why not? She's got all the signs."

"And in this delusional state, does she actually e . . . e . . . eat the person? Or does she just think she's eating the person?"

"Judging from the gouges, I'd say someone was definitely dining. I'll look at the skin under the microscope for distinct teeth marks." Rukmani wiped her face with her surgical smock. "God, it's hot. Even I'm sweating. I'm going into the office. Want a Coke and a bag of Chee-tos."

"You can *eat* Chee-tos now?"

"You said I should eat."

"The idea of Alison . . ." He covered his face. "Why would she . . . be susceptible to *that* kind of delusion?"

"Anyone's guess." Rukmani began to walk toward the office. "Could be she had what she perceived as a meaningful experience with an animal: a dog, a cat, or even a coyote. We live in the desert. She has seen coyotes."

Poe thought about the scratches on his cheek—how she had turned into something feral. He said, "What about a snake?"

"Snakes are big in fables," Rukmani answered. "Look at your own religion—Adam and Eve and a giant talking serpent with hands and feet. You have myths just as we do. Only difference is, you defy logic and insist it's the truth. Sure you don't want some Chee-tos?"

"Positive."

"Suit yourself." Rukmani kissed his lips. "Love you."

She walked away before he could respond.

As if he would have responded.

Emotionally stifled guy that he was. But she accepted him anyway. That was the wonderful thing about love. It sanded down the rough spots, turned everything into fine lacquered furniture.

Poe watched her sway as she bounced toward the office. His groin was still fixated on her ass. But his mind was elsewhere—thinking about the claws of a possessed woman, a howling coyote with doleful eyes, and a rattler with a bite as painful as rejection.

THIRTY-SEVEN

As the sun sank, the techs packed their bags. Even though Bruckner had cordoned off the room as an official crime scene, business was booming at the Dunes Inn. The murder was less than a half day old, and already Byron was leading tour groups of locals, explaining it all in gory and inaccurate detail. Of course, no one could go beyond the ropes, but one could use imagination. The clerk talked about wild orgies and high-pitched screams in the middle of the night. Not that he mentioned any of this to the police. So Poe took it with a grain of salt. The owner of the Dunes Inn—one Roy "Mac" MacDonald—was delighted, hauling in a tidy profit in drinks and snacks.

By eight in the evening, Poe was back on the road. Weinberg sat shotgun; Rukmani had fallen asleep in the backseat within the first ten minutes of the ride. The loo made a few weak stabs at conversation, then succumbed to slumberland. Heavy blankets of exhaustion pressed down on Poe's brain. He thought about the case to keep awake.

Alison and her breakdowns. Alison as an animal. She sure had acted like one the night she'd gone after his face. More than just a jealous woman, she had had a feline quality.

Catlike in action as well as in her beauty. A sleek, muscled woman with magnetic eyes. And her legs—long and slender. He remembered a time that they had wrapped around him as they panted in the backseat of his claptrap Buick.

So young.

Twenty years ago.

Where had the time gone?

Where had Alison gone?

That night he had searched the cave, the coyote looking at him with doleful eyes—human eyes. How it had howled—as if in deep psychic pain. . . .

He shook his head, trying to clear his thoughts.

It was his own imagination working overtime. So absorbed with fear and dread, he had chosen to anthropomorphize a wild beast to make it more palatable. Besides, why would Alison imagine herself to be a beast?

Rukmani stirred, opened her eyes. "My mouth feels like sandpaper."

Poe handed her a bottle of designer water. She downed it in three gulps. "Thanks."

"Have a nice nap?"

"Yes, I did, thanks. Where are we?"

"About an hour from home."

"I've got all this dictation to go over." She blinked several times. "And since Bruckner was kind enough to release the corpse to Clark County, I should start the autopsy."

"Are you up for it?"

"I'm sure I'll be fine as soon as I eat. I'm hungry."

"I'll take you out to dinner."

"What about Mama Emma?"

What about her, Poe? He felt his head throb. "I should peek in on her. Do you mind a late dinner?"

"Actually, it would be preferable. Fewer chemical changes in the corpse. Let's go out afterward. Would you mind Indian?"

"As long as you don't mind me eating tandoori chicken in front of you. I don't want you to feel I'm eating second cousin Shoba—" He stopped talking, then said, "Rukmani, in your thesis, did you only analyze the werewolf legends? Or did you actually study people who had werewolfism?"

"I related myths of the *Panchatantra* to medical case studies of lycanthropy."

"In these myths, did the people turn into beasts? Or did they just *think* they were turning into beasts?"

"Depends on the legend." Rukmani gave the question some thought. "Some actually transformed their whole form at will. Some needed a concrete object to bring about the transformation. Usually it was an animal skin. If I remember correctly, skins were pretty much a cross-cultural requirement for transformation. As a matter of fact, the word 'berserk' comes from the Berserkrs—old-time marauders and murderers who wore animal hides and went on spree killings in Scandinavia. They were objects of intense fear, and the subjects of many a scary ghost story. *Ber* means "bear" and *serkr* means "shirt"—they wore bear skins."

"These Berserkrs were real people then."

"Yep."

"And they'd don bear skins and go around killing people, believing they were bears."

"Exactly."

"Ed Gein's predecessors."

Rukmani wrinkled her nose. "Yes, Gein did flay his murder victims and wear their skin."

"I suppose he got the idea from somewhere." Poe paused. "I didn't see any kind of animal skins in Alison's house."

"Which means?"

"She doesn't fit the mold."

"Romulus, there's no mold. There are only legends to explain medieval psychosis. As long as Alison believes she's a wolf, she's a wolf. Besides, didn't you say something about Alison dressing up in men's clothing? That she might be the guy who was in Nate Malealani's bar?"

"I *suggested* it as a possibility—"

"Seems to me she's already in the process of doing some kind of transformation."

"Ruki, it's speculation."

"If she's delusional enough to believe she's a man, she's delusional enough to believe she's a wolf."

"Maybe." They rode in silence for a couple of minutes. Then Poe said, "I never stated explicitly that Alison dressed up as the ponytail man."

"But you did say something about finding a sneaker belonging to your mysterious hat man—"

"*Maybe* it belonged to him—"

"And it was Alison's size—"

"*Maybe* it was Alison's size. I was tossing out ideas."

"Fine. We'll leave it at that."

Another moment of silence. Then, Poe said, "Don't laugh at me, okay?"

"I'd never laugh at you, Rom. What's on your mind?"

"The ni . . . ni . . ." Poe took a deep breath. "The . . . night I got bitten by the snake, there was this coyote." He tapped on the wheel of the car. "It looked very human to me, especially the eyes."

"The eyes looked human?"

"Yes. Human . . . and very familiar."

"Alison?"

"Ruki, it was very dark and I was in a lot of pain. I could have been hallucinating. But yes, the eyes looked like Alison's eyes. That same color, and the same expression." He hit his forehead. "Maybe I'm going nuts."

"You were under stress, Rom. You were frantically searching for Alison, and you found her wherever you could."

He exhaled forcibly. "You're probably right."

"On the other hand, Alison bolted as soon as she gouged you," Rukmani continued. "Maybe she had been to that cave before. Maybe she kept her skins there. Someone should go back and check."

"There're rattlers in the cave, girl. Remember?" Poe blew out air. "I suppose I could go back wearing boots and gloves."

Rukmani patted his hand. "You've just pulled a body out of an attic. The cave can wait."

"But it should be checked out. Worse comes to worst, I confront my own demons." Again he blew out air. "Maybe Alison's mother acted that way . . . like an animal? Linda *was* involved in the Bogeyman murders."

Rukmani said, "But as the victim, not the killer."

Poe thought about the note.

This is for what I did.

What if she had murdered Janet Doward? Later, in a more lucid moment, she had realized what she had done, had come to regret her deed and couldn't go on knowing what she had done?

This is for what I did.

Poe said, "When I broke into Alison's house, I found a shoe box filled with articles about her mom."

"Did Alison ever mention her mom in connection with animals?"

"No. But she rarely spoke about her mother, period."

The car turned silent except for Weinberg's gentle snores.

Poe said, "She had three shoe boxes, actually. One concerning her mom. But the others dealt with the Nevada Test Site."

"Well, there's a non sequitur."

"Not really," Poe said. "I think in her demented mind, she blames the NTS and the atmospheric testings for her mom's mental condition— all the radiation and fallout. I think that's why she was collecting articles on the bomb shots."

"Mostly the fallout has been linked to thyroid cancer from I-131." Rukmani shrugged. "Of course, we're only at the tip of the iceberg. The complete NTS story hasn't even begun to be told. There was so much bureaucratic lying and paper-shredding we'll never know what really went on."

"I agree. As a matter of fact, I truly believe that the fallout caused my mom's cancer. She was a downwinder."

Rukmani sat up. "She was?"

"Yep. St. George, Utah. Right in the downwind path."

"That could explain her atypical leukemia."

"So I'm right? The fallout could have caused her cancer?"

"Certainly."

Poe said, "I found out that the government had passed some kind of downwinders' compensation act in 1990. Maybe I can get some money from them to help defray her medical bills."

"I think you have a legitimate case." She paused. "Rom, you said that Alison blamed the tests for her mother's condition?"

"I *suggested* it."

"Was her mother also in the line of fallout?"

"Yep. She was also from St. George. She was two years younger than my mom."

"What about Alison? Where was she born?"

"St. George."

"Same as you. Your families go back, then."

"Yes. Except Linda Hennick was a white Mormon, Mom was a brown Mormon."

"A little discrimination."

"Just a tad."

"And Alison and you . . . you two were . . . an item."

"Yes, we had sex. It lasted about six months. After she started high school, she blew me off. Mr. Brown Tic Boy was cramping her style. I understand how it is . . . the need to be popular . . . but . . .'' He threw up his hands. They landed back on the steering wheel. "It still gets to me. That was almost twenty years ago. I'm such a doofus."

"We're all prisoners of our past."

"I'd settle for parole."

"You, me, Alison." Rukmani shook her head. "Look at Alison and her shoe boxes of her mother."

"One shoe box of her mother. But *two* shoe boxes of NTS."

"Meaning?"

Poe smiled. "More people wrote about NTS than about Linda Hennick."

Rukmani paused. "I think you've hit on something."

"Good." A beat. "Fill me in."

"The boxes of the test site material. Maybe she was blaming the tests for her mother's condition and for her *own* condition as well."

Poe paused. "That seems logical. Radiation does have this mystical, mutative aura—"

"Borne out by science," Rukmani added.

"Definitely borne out by science. That's why it would fit perfectly in delusions of a twentieth-century woman. It would make complete sense for Alison to incorporate the bomb shots into her psychosis. Hell, for all we know, she could blame fallout for turning her into a werewolf."

THIRTY-EIGHT

The old man appeared droopy, aimlessly plunking quarters down two poker machines, alternating from one slot to the other. His sand-colored shirt was wrinkled, his jeans sported a big brown stain, and his moccasins were coming apart. He hadn't shaved in a while and he looked like a bum. Any other establishment would have thrown him out. But in this town, as long as you had money . . .

Poe took the stool next to his. "How much have you played back, Chief?"

Y didn't answer, instructing the machine to deal him two electronic cards. "I want my money back."

"What money?"

"The money you took from me."

"I didn't take any money—"

"My winnings."

Poe smiled patiently.

"You want to end up on the streets, Y?"

"I'm already on the streets." He drew a pair of sixes, losing to the machine's pair of nines. "The money's mine. I want to piss it away, it's my business."

"Do we have to go through this every time?"

Y hit a three of a kind. Poe said, "There you go, old man. Chump change to blow. That should last all of ten minutes.'' He regarded the Indian's haggard face. ''How long have you been here?''

Y didn't answer, dropped another quarter in the slot.

''Have you eaten in the last twenty-four hours?''

Again no answer.

Poe called over a waitress, gave her a fifty. ''Roast beef sandwich on rye to go, please. Keep the change.''

She pocketed the bill. ''Thank you, sir.''

''You know what? Bring me a beer—a Heineken.''

''Right away—''

''And a vodka,'' Y grumped. ''Straight up. And make it Stoly. None of that bar crap.''

She smiled. ''Certainly, sir. For you, it's complimentary.''

After she left, Y said, ''You can't eat in the casinos.''

''That's why I asked for it to go.''

''I'm not going anywhere.''

''What about my job?''

''What job?''

Poe brought his hand to his eye, pressed down on an imaginary shutter button.

''Already done that.'' Y stopped playing. ''Did the pictures help?''

''By the time I came back from the motel, the processing places had closed.''

Y placed another quarter in the machine.

Poe said, ''You can ask me about it.''

Y played with his braid, twisting the end around his pinkie. ''Nothing to ask. If you knew something, you'd tell me.''

''And if you knew something, you'd tell me.''

The old man pushed the draw button. ''You think I'm holding back?'' Y ended up with a king high.

''Where do you think they might have gone—'' Poe covered the machine's quarter slot. ''Y, I'm talking to you. Look at me.''

''I'm looking. You're ugly.''

Poe said, ''I think Alison may be trying to imitate her mother.''

Y fed the machine.

''You've got to talk about it, Chief.'' Poe became grave. ''Too many people have died. I can't cut you any more slack.''

''Can't help you, Rom.'' He asked for three cards. ''I never understood Linda, let alone her daughter.''

"Then tell me what you knew about Linda."

"Not here."

"So let's leave."

"What about my sandwich?"

"Fine. We'll wait for the sandwich."

"So I'll play while we wait." He put in a coin and drew up a two-pair hand.

The waitress returned with the to-go sandwich, the vodka, and the brew. Poe sipped suds, watching Y nurse his drink and play out his hands. This time the old guy won twelve dollars.

"You're doing fine," Poe said.

Y polished off his booze, picked up his winnings and the sandwich bag, then got up. Poe took a last guzzle, then put down his beer and followed the old man outdoors. They walked down the Strip, neither speaking. Just two guys enjoying the night. Y took out his sandwich and took a bite. "Myra makes them better."

"I'll tell my boss."

Another bite. Y said, "She should put a poker machine inside the restaurant. Right now all she has is a couple of dinky slots. One-coin odds. Typical tourist shit. You want a bite of my sandwich?"

"No thanks. I'm doing Indian with Rukmani in an hour."

"So late?"

"She's working."

Y finished his food and tossed the bag into a garbage receptacle. He bent down and picked a vibrant red flower from one of the hotel's lavish frontside plantings. He gave it to Poe. "For Rukmani. A true Indian."

Poe smiled, took the bloom. "How gallant. Talk to me about Linda Hennick."

Y slowed his walk. "She wasn't happy in her marriage."

"What in particular?"

Y looked up at the cloud-covered sky.

Poe said, "Gerald didn't do it for her?"

"Gerald's a good man. A good Mormon and a good father."

"But she was looking for someone more interesting."

"She seemed fascinated by Paiutes. Thought we were different."

"Exotic."

"She told me we had bigger penises."

Poe started coughing. Y pounded his back and said, "I didn't debate her impression. But it gave me an idea of what was wrong with Gerald. We didn't last as an item too long. She was beautiful. She moved up quickly.''

"Why did she marry Gerald in the first place?"

"Why do you think?"

"She was pregnant?" Poe paused. "So Gerald wasn't such a good Mormon after all."

"Who said it was Gerald's?" Y started walking. "Still, he married her, took in Alison as his own. She might even have been his own. Alison's kid looks just like Gerald."

"Harrison. Yes, he does."

"Linda had it narrowed down between Gerald and two others." Y licked his lips. "But she wasn't no fool. She could handle her men. She came and went as she pleased, no questions asked. She'd still be doing it today if it wasn't for Lewiston."

Poe stuck his hands in his pockets, looking at his feet as he walked. "You've left out Linda's mental illness."

"Her mental problem was Gerald. She didn't like him. He wasn't any fun."

Poe cleared his throat. "Putting it bluntly."

Y shrugged. "To Gerald, it was easier to have a sick wife than a bored wife. So he made up all these stories to explain her nighttime exploits. Told the world she didn't remember. . . . Well, that could be true. When Linda tripped the light fantastic, she drank herself comatose."

"She was under psychiatric care, Y. You don't become institutional-ized for being a party girl."

"You did back when. Housewives were supposed to be meek and mild, not randy women. *Gerald* checked her in. He thought her problems were in the head. 'Course, the minute she got out, it started all over again."

"So where did Parker Lewiston fit in?"

"Linda was beautiful. He had an eye for beautiful women."

"So they had an affair? How does that add up to Lewiston murdering her?"

"I don't know *why* he did it. I just know he did it. Like I told you, anyone who knew anything was paid off."

"So why are you against me reopening the case?"

"On what grounds?" Y asked.

"That's my problem. Just give me some names—"

"No." Y picked up his speed. "It's past history."

"Slow down." Poe held his arm. They walked slower. "You know, she left a suicide note."

Y stopped. "That's bullshit."

"No, it's not."

"Then it was planted."

"It was her handwriting."

"Then it was forged!"

"Would you like to know what the note said?"

The old man looked down, didn't speak.

"It said: *This is for what I did.*"

Again, Y became agitated. "That's bullshit, Rom. The note was put there by the cops to take the heat off Lewiston. He paid them to do it!" He started jogging away.

Poe went after him, grabbing his arm, forcing him to stop. "Assuming you're right, how do you know all this?"

Again, Y looked away. "I just know."

"How? Some mystical god came down and whispered the facts in your ear? C'mon. Don't you want to find out what really happened?"

"I know what happened. Lewiston killed her. Now let go of my goddamn arm."

Poe held his hands in the air. "Happy?"

Y hailed a cab. "Where's my fucking camera?"

Poe pulled a disposable out of his pocket. "I'll walk you in—"

"I can do it *myself.*"

Y got in the cab and slammed the door, leaving Poe in limbo, as if stood up for a date. He took out his portable phone and paged Patricia. A minute later, she phoned back. Party noises in the background. She was probably at Barry's eating ziti marinara with Nate.

Poe said, "Have you heard anything concerning Jensen?"

The question brought her down. "No, sir, not a thing."

"No whereabouts on the car?"

"Nothing."

"Gerald Hennick didn't call back, did he?"

"Sir, if he had, I would have told you right away."

Poe let out a sad laugh. "Yes, I'm sure you would have. Take care. If I learn anything I'll let you know."

"Vice versa."

She sounded glad to get off the horn. First, Poe made the obligatory call to Rukmani's house and spoke to Emma's nurse. Mom was sleeping—tired, but otherwise fine. Then Poe phoned Rukmani at the coroner's office. "How close are you to dinnertime?"

"Pick me up in a half hour."

"How about if I come down now and just wait for you?"

A pause. "If I didn't know any better, I'd say you sounded lonely."

"I am lonely. I miss you." A beat. "The only redeeming feature of this otherwise miserable day was being with you."

Another pause. "You're waxing sentimental. I like it." A laugh. "I really do."

"I'll be there in ten minutes."

"I'll be waiting."

Poe paused, then he cut the line. He had almost said it. Had come *this* close to uttering those three words. So close. He was very proud of himself.

And, at least this time, he had thought it.

The phone rang, waking him out of that groggy state of almost sleep. He reached for his cellular, then realized it was Rukmani's line that was ringing. She answered, her voice heavy with slumber. Eyes half closed, she stretched out her arm, hand clutched around the receiver. "For you."

He took the phone. "Poe."

"You know any place that develops pictures at this time of night? I think I got something that might interest you."

"What? Y?" Poe sat up. "Where are you?"

"Right outside the Slipper."

"I'll be right down—"

"No, don't come down here. I'll take a cab to Havana. I'll meet you there."

Y hung up. Poe started dressing.

"What?" Rukmani asked.

"It's Y. I sent him to the Lady Slipper to take pictures of the Arab guy . . . Abousayed. Actually, pictures of his women."

"So what does Y want?"

"He wants to develop the film. At this moment! He obviously wants to show me something. Y sounded serious and sober. To me, that's dangerous. Know any twenty-four-hour processing places?"

"Not offhand. The phone book's on the kitchen counter. Want me to come?"

"No, you sleep."

She rolled over and shut her eyes.

Poe finished dressing, then went into the kitchen. After thirty seconds of searching her paper-strewn kitchen counter, he found the phone book under a pile of old medical dictation. A moment later, he heard padded footsteps. He glanced over his shoulder. Her form seemed more erect. Her face not quite as white.

He said, "Hey, Mom, how are you doing?" He stopped his frantic search. "Get you some water?"

"Yes, I'll take some water." Emma sank into the kitchen chair. "What are you doing?"

Poe gave her a filled glass, then went back to the phone book. His finger slid down a list of photo shops. "I'm looking for a twenty-four-hour film-processing place so I can develop a roll."

"Are you still planning to move me on Sunday?"

Poe forced himself to stop. He managed a smile. Slow down. Mom's more important than a case. "Of course I'm going to move you in. Just as soon as Remus gets down—"

"I want to go home, Romulus."

"Home?" Poe licked his lips. "You mean back to Reno?"

The old woman nodded, her eyes leaking tears. "I miss the boy. Why did he kick me out?"

Poe took her hand and sat. "Remus didn't kick you out. You know how much he loves you. He's just very busy—"

"Not nearly as busy as *you* are."

Guilt stabbed Poe's heart. "Mom, you started treatment here. Finish up the treatment. Get your strength back. And then we can talk about you going back to live with Remus."

"I haven't been easy, Romulus. You think he'll take me back?"

"Of course he will."

"I'll be good—"

"Mom, he loves you just the way you are." A pause. "If you could cut out the drinking, it might be helpful."

"I know. If I live through this . . . this thing, I'll try."

"Of course you're going to live. You'll probably outlive us all, driving us crazy along the way."

A slight smile. "Maybe."

"You want more water, Mom?"

"I'm fine."

"I'll walk you back to your room."

Emma nodded. Poe put his arm around the frail woman's waist and slowly escorted her back to bed. He pulled the covers up to her chin. "Comfortable?"

"You're going out?"

Poe nodded and kissed his mother's forehead. She wrinkled her nose. "What'd you eat for dinner, Romulus?"

Poe's taste buds still buzzed from the spicy chutneys he had eaten last night. "That strong?"

"Loaded with ginger."

"That's true. Have a good sleep." He paused. "Mom, how well did you know Linda Hennick?"

"Not that well. She was white and I was brown. We ran in different social classes."

"Did she have . . . a reputation?"

"She had her share." A sly smile came to her lips. "Didn't we all."

Poe laughed. "I don't want to hear this."

"She was worse than most, better than a few. But she always held herself classy. Like Natalie Wood in *Rebel Without a Cause*."

Poe remembered the photographs. "Yeah, she went through kind of a sullen stage, didn't she?"

"Sullen 'cause she didn't get what she wanted."

"What did she want?"

Emma's smile became a broad grin. "Your father."

THIRTY-NINE

If Mom had kept her secrets, he might have been excited about Y's call. Instead, Poe was plagued by a niggling suspicion. He knew his father had made occasional trips back to St. George after the family had moved—purportedly for business. He knew his father had died in St. George in a one-car crash . . . on a lonely stretch of icy road. But that was about all he knew. Despite repeated questions, Poe had never understood exactly what business his father had done. Mom had always been vague: something about arranging bus junkets from the Rockies states to Las Vegas. At the time, both Remus and Poe had believed everything Emma told them. Back then, their mother had been their hero. Maybe in a way she still was.

Poe stopped at Flamingo Avenue, his eyes fixed on the strobic flashes of colored lights.

Mom had rarely talked about his father. All Poe's information had been gleaned from biased relatives. Dad had been a charmer but a scamster, a ladies' man and a thief. He had been a failure as a gangster, being as he had only been part Italian. He had spent whatever money he had on trinkets. He had often turned mean when he drank.

Then when Emma walked into the room, they would immediately hush up, as if someone had pushed an imaginary mute button.

The traffic light turned green. Poe depressed the accelerator.

A ladies' man making trips back home. Back to where a beautiful lady awaited him.

Linda had it narrowed down between Gerald and two others.

If Linda Hennick and his father had . . . then that would mean that he and Alison were . . . which would mean that he had . . .

A very distasteful thought.

Better to think that nothing had happened. And with Harrison Jensen looking exactly like Gerald Hennick, it probably was the truth. Still, he was enough of a detective to be curious, even if it was in bad taste. A pity that the only two people who could tell him positively were six feet under.

He wondered if his mom had known something. The glee on her face when she told him that she had bested Linda Hennick. But if she had known, she had never made any move to stop the relationship between Alison and him.

Certainly Gerald Hennick had never said anything.

Which left only one unanswered question in his mind.

Did *Alison* know something?

Could that have been the reason why she had broken off with him once she had reached high school?

He thought a moment.

Now he was using cheap rationalization. They had broken up because she hadn't wanted him anymore. She had simply dumped him.

While waiting for the film to be developed, they smoked cigarettes and drank tepid coffee at the counter of a nearby diner. Making idle chitchat because Y didn't want to talk about the pictures. Poe didn't push him: everything in due time. They talked about Emma, they talked about Alison.

No idea where she could be?

Y always answered with a shrug.

When the requisite hour had passed, they got up, paid the waitress with a twenty (keep the change, ma'am), and went back to the nearby strip mall which held the processing store—a hole in the wall that doubled the normal charges for nighttime developing. But beggars don't look at a gift horse's dental work, so Poe paid the price without flinching.

He started sorting through the pictures as they walked to the parking lot. "What am I looking for, Chief?"

"You'll know it when you see it."

Poe regarded Y. "That obvious?" He unlocked the car, slid into the driver's seat, and turned on the dome light. Y sat next to him and shut the passenger's door. From his pants pocket he pulled out a flask of vodka.

He took a long drink. "At last."

Poe had gone through four pictures. He decided to start again from the beginning, this time studying the photographs instead of just scanning them. "Been waiting for me to show up before you got soused. How thoughtful of you."

"I pass out, you'll take care of me."

Poe smiled. "I'll find the cleanest Dumpster this side of the Mississippi."

Y took another swig. "You're not as bad-ass as you think."

"I'm not bad-assed at all. Some have even called me a sucker." Poe pointed to a man dressed in a kaffiyeh. "I take it this is Nali Abousayed?"

Y looked at the picture. "You've got a nose for detail."

Again, Poe smiled. He examined the face—a dark-complexioned, good-looking man with crisp features. "You take clear photographs. Want to do my wedding?" A beat. "If there *is* a wedding?"

"For Rukmani, I'd do it."

Another flip of the snapshot. "Nali's a handsome guy." Poe raised his brow. "Rich and good-looking. Wonder why he pays for it?"

"Why do you pay for it?"

"Convenience." Poe let out a small laugh. "It's nice to know at the outset that you're going to score."

"Maybe he feels the same way."

"Maybe." Poe discarded another snapshot. "I really wish you'd tell me what I'm looking for. Will you at least tell me if I passed it?"

"You won't pass it."

"That sure of yourself." Poe took out a cigarette, sticking it in his mouth but not lighting it. "Who are these wom—"

Y took the cigarette out of Poe's mouth. "I can't understand a damn thing you're saying."

Poe said, "Who are all these women with Abousayed? I don't recognize any of them. You know how many hours of gumshoe work I'm going to have to do to identify them?"

"You're doing it personally?"

"Well, Deluca and me. I'd have Jensen on the job except I don't know if he's tied up. I mean that literally."

Y didn't speak. Then he said, "You suspect her more than him, don't you?"

"I'd like to think it's him. I really want to believe it's him. But I'm honest enough to admit maybe it's her."

"Or both."

"Or both," Poe echoed. "I'm keeping an open mind. I'd sure like to find—" Abruptly, he stopped talking.

That face. That goddamn face!

Y said, "I told you you'd know it when you saw it."

Poe started sweating. As clear as daylight. And that was probably why she'd been so damn defensive when he had first approached her with the photograph of Newel. She didn't want to think about throwaway hookers. "Why didn't you just tell me over the phone?"

"And taint your meticulous police work?"

Poe muttered, "I bet she *pimped* for him, the bitch!"

"You know that for certain?"

"I'm going to find out." Poe wiped his forehead on the sleeve of his shirt. "Where do you want to be dropped off?"

Y looked at the car's clock. "It's three in the morning."

"I know. Naked City should be wide awake. I hope Lamar Larue's in the mood for some ID work."

"Let me go with you—"

"No way, José."

"Romulus, you look and smell cop. You'll clear the place out before you get anywhere. Me? I look like a desperado. They see me, they think a gomer with a welfare paycheck."

"A gomer?"

Y said, "You've never heard that expression? Get Outta My Emergency Room. Doctors call us indigents that behind our back."

"You're not indigent." Poe regarded the old man. "Exactly how do you make ends meet?"

Y took a final gulp from his flask. "It's not so hard when you don't own anything."

Poe waited until seven in the morning for the wake-up call, spending several restless hours dozing in his Honda. He'd dropped Y off at the

Havana, rented him a room, and given him fifty bucks spending money. Why he paid for the old man when Y had a bank account was anyone's guess. Something to do with tribal loyalty coupled with genuine affection.

When he knocked on the door, Honey asked who it was. He identified himself, and she greeted him in a flowing lavender robe which was open to reveal a sheer, short nightie. There was something feathery and fuzzy on her feet. Her aqua eyes were sleepy and half hooded, her lips were pink and puffy. No makeup. He wasn't a client who was worth the effort. She cocked her hip, scolding him with a look.

"It's customary to call."

"Can I come in?"

"Can I stop you?" She stepped aside and he walked in.

Looking intensely at her face. She was probably thirty by now, without so much as a line on her brow. It was as if a worrisome thought had never passed through her brain. She was gorgeous and arrogant. As carefree as a butterfly as long as men wanted her to spread her legs.

She spoke with conceit. "I *knew* you'd be back."

"Have a seat," Poe said.

She gave him a seductive smile. "Shouldn't I be saying that to you?"

Like a Pavlovian dog, he felt himself go hard. "In a few minutes. First, you sit." A beat. "Please."

"You're acting awfully distant." Honey's expression hardened. "Oh God! You aren't going to start in on that girl, are you?"

"Brittany New—"

She was disgusted. "Poe, it's seven in the morning. Either drop your pants or get out of here."

Poe remained rooted to his spot. "I wasn't going to ask you about Newel."

Honey tapped her foot. "So what do you want?"

Poe pulled out a postmortem shot of Sarah Yarlborough. "Do you know her? I've got a witness that says you do."

Immediately, Honey grew angry and turned her head. "I'm not looking. Get out before I throw you out!"

"I'm not leaving. You don't like it, call the police."

Honey closed her robe and stomped over to the kitchen phone. "You know, even cops don't have a right . . ." She punched in for directory assistance. "You can't get away with strong-arming—"

"I haven't touched you, Honey. Nor do I want to."

She jerked her head up, a stunned expression on her face. Someone was talking in her receiver. She faltered, then said, "Yes, I want the number of Las Vegas Metro Police . . . I don't know which station! Any station!" A moment later, she slammed the phone down and started dialing.

Calmly, he waited out her bluff.

"This is going to be a blot on your perfect record. A cop being arrested here . . . barging in on me. You can't get away with this!"

Someone at the front desk spoke in the receiver. Honey paused, then again slapped the receiver back into the cradle. She stood there with her arms folded tightly across her chest. "What do you *want* from me?"

Poe went into the kitchen and spoke softly. "Just take a look at this photo—"

"No!"

"Why not?"

"Because I don't *want* to." She glared at him. "And you can't force me!"

He pocketed the picture. "Then that tells me something."

"Like what?"

"Like you're scared to death."

She paled. "No, it tells you that I don't like looking at dead girls!"

"Especially if you had something to do with their deaths."

"You're acting crazy, Romulus!" She licked her lips seductively. "Maybe you need something that you haven't been getting from your doctor friend. So what do you say?"

"Honey, this is *serious.* If you don't start listening to me, you're going to go down for murder."

She stomped off. "I don't know what you're *talking* about! Get out of here!"

"Let me explain it as briefly as I can," Poe said. "See, there was once a very young and beautiful girl who tried to make it in this godforsaken town. Well, she didn't exactly make headlines on the marquee, but she was a star under the sheets—"

She slapped him hard on his bad cheek. "Fuck you, Scarface!"

Poe forced himself not to flinch. He bit back pain and went on, "She managed to hook up with the big boys, specifically Parker Lewiston. They did the nasty for a couple of years and then he unceremoniously put her back on the streets. And there she was. A has-been at the ripe old age of twenty-one—"

She attempted another slap. He caught her wrist and gently lowered her arm. "You hit me again, I'll arrest you, darlin'."

Tears were running down her eyes. She started to run away, but he held her arm tight.

"She was a has-been," Poe said, "but she wasn't stupid. Moreover, she was *persistent*. Although she knew Lewiston was no longer interested in her physically—at twenty-one she was just too damn old—she asked him if she could work in other capacities in exchange for being set up. Being as she wasn't the typical dumb bimbo, he struck a bargain with her. She'd work for him as a call girl for his important clients. Also, she could be one of his arm girls—someone above legal age to have dinner with. So he wouldn't look so perverted—"

"Why are you doing this to me?" she cried out. "I was always so *nice* to you!"

"Parkerboy kept his word and set her up. Later, as she began to age, he didn't want her anymore as an arm girl. To keep a roof over her head, he told her, she had to start doing some real work—like pimping. Because he wanted very young girls . . . more like *children*—"

"Stop it!"

"And she agreed, bringing him young, damaged goods—"

"Stop it, stop it, stop it!" Her eyes were deep overflowing pools. She gasped as she spoke. "Please stop it! Please let me go!" Out of breath. "Please! Let me *go*!"

She was wailing now. He took her in his arms and hugged her tightly as she sobbed uncontrollably on his shoulder. At first, her emotions seemed real—deep moans of sadness and regret. But soon she turned them into something manipulative. She wound her arms around his back and pressed her hips into his groin, feeling for an erection. It was there.

Pavlovian dog.

She quieted, wiping her eyes with her hand. She whispered, "This is all so ugly, Romulus. Why have ugliness in your life when you could have pleasure—"

He broke away and held her at arm's length. "Honey, listen to me. You set Sarah Yarlborough up with Parker Lewiston and he killed her—"

"No—"

"Know what that makes you? It makes *you* more than an accessory—"

"No! You're wrong—"

"You could be charged with *first-degree* murder!"

She moaned out, "But you don't *understand*!"

Immediately, Poe thought about reading Honey her rights. But everything he'd done so far had skirted the bounds of legality. If he were to start getting official, he knew she'd lock up tighter than a bank vault. Instead, he asked her to explain it to him.

She dried her eyes and looked at him with a baleful expression. "It wasn't supposed to happen!"

Poe waited.

"It was . . . an accident."

Poe nodded, signaling for her to continue.

"Parker . . . he sometimes gets . . ." She looked away.

"He gets rough?"

She faced him and nodded. "But you've got to understand. From the beginning, I always asked for girls who could take it rough. Because if they can, there's money. Money for their pimp, money for them. If they were good, Parker always made sure the girls got their fair cut. It's all part of the package."

Poe paused. "Was Parker rough with you, Honey?"

She nodded.

"Tell me."

She broke away from him and lit a cigarette. Her hands were shaking. "Is it necessary to talk about me?"

"The more you can tell me, Honey, the better it is for you."

She puffed hard, blowing smoke in his face. "He likes tools." She glared at him. "Do you need more details?"

"I'm getting the idea." He lit his own cigarette and blew smoke away from her face. "What happened between Sarah Yarlborough and him?"

"Sarah Yarlborough was the crack girl with the pink hair?"

"Yes."

Honey continued to smoke. "I never knew her name. Her pimp just told me she could do the job."

"Sarah's pimp—Ali Abdul Williams."

She seemed shocked at the mention of his name.

Poe said, "Yes, Honey, I do actually work as a cop. Know what happened to A.A.?"

She looked at him expectantly. He drew a line across his throat. Her hands migrated toward her own neck. For the first time, Honey's eyes seemed concerned. "How?"

"Car accident."

Instant relief. "Oh, well, it happens—"

"A *rigged* car accident."

She became defensive. "How do you know that?"

"See, it's this big chain-reaction thing. You mess with one part of the car, it does other things to other parts of the car. And that makes cops real suspicious. Kind of like Sarah Yarlborough. You start cutting her up with knives, all of a sudden—"

"It wasn't my *fault!*"

He felt like saying tell *that* to a jury. Instead, he said, "Okay. It wasn't *your* fault. So let's see how we can get you out of this mess."

Instantly, she smiled. "You still have a thing for me, don't you?"

"Honey, I'm going to have to read you your rights now."

She walked away. "Then I'm not going to talk to you."

"It's just a formality."

"Bullshit!" Her self-preservation suddenly kicked in. She spun around. "I want a law—"

"Okay, okay." Poe took in a breath, let it out. "Listen to me, girl. I want to help you. I want to get you a deal, and I think I can. I want to get you immunity in exchange for your testimony against Lewiston—"

"No *way* I'm going up against him!" She shook her head vehemently. "You can bring me down in chains and I won't say a word. I'll take my chances with the courts."

"He's not untouchable, Honey. I've already got evidence against him in the murder."

"What kind of evidence?"

"I wouldn't be much of a cop if I told you that." He paused to for-mulate his tall tale. "Suffice it to say, I've got strong, indisputable evi-dence. I've also got witnesses that put him with Yarlborough."

"So what do you need me for?"

"Your corroboration would be the icing on the cake!"

"Forget it!" Honey stomped her cigarette butt in a crystal ashtray. "I'd rather eat a gun."

Poe was surprised by her adamance. "Honey, Lewiston is going down. Do you want to drown with him?"

She broke into vicious laughter. "You arrogant little twerp! *Maybe* you could hang something on *me*. But Parker isn't going anywhere. You're a runt in his world, Poe. He eats guys like you for breakfast."

"You're not leaving me much choice, Honey." Poe threw the butt of his cigarette into her sink. "If I don't get Lewiston, I'll have to come after you. You'd be surprised how tenacious I can be."

"You won't last any longer at this than you do at sex."

Poe smiled. "Just doing you a favor. I thought whores liked it fast—"

"Get out of here."

Poe grabbed her robe, the fabric ripping under his force. He shoved his face against hers. "Remember this face, Honey. Because you're not going to eat, sleep, fuck, or even take a crap without seeing me pop up out of nowhere—"

"You *can't* harass me! I'll have your badge for this! Get out of here!"

He let her go with a shove.

Honey picked up the phone. "I'm calling your superior! I'm going to ruin you!"

"Good luck to you!" He opened the door and stepped outside. Just to let her know that she hadn't gotten to him, he shut the door gently.

FORTY

It had been a long haul . . . a heavy haul. But at least *that* part of the job was finally done.

Done and done away with. What a *relief*!

Now it was solo time. For the first time to be completely self-reliant.

Enough to make a being giddy.

Independent after an entire life of beings bossing you around, telling you what to do and what not to do. Of souls who were stupid trying to convince you that they weren't stupid, that they were right, when you *knew* that they were at fault. And helpless to defend yourself. Being beaten down by people inferior to you.

A lifetime of drudgery and tediousness (was that even a word?).

Poe would know the right word. He was good at those trivial kinds of thing. He had the brain, could have made something more of his life. But he made mistakes. He had a temper. He was impulsive. He could be easily led.

Smart but definitely beatable on his own turf.

Just look at what was happening.

The deaths were still unsolved. And that made him look like a jackass.

The thought brought on a smile.

The smile of the wolf.

Because when animals smiled, they were anything but friendly.

Sweating from the heat, Remus lugged in the biggest of the two trunks, set it down on Romulus's dirt floor. It took up almost half the room. Poe followed a moment later, toting the lighter trunk in his arms. He regarded his invaded space with a frown.

"This isn't going to work."

Remus relieved his brother of the weight, set the smaller trunk on top of the larger. "I just threw her stuff in randomly. If I were you, I'd leave it packed up. She won't miss anything in there."

"If she doesn't need the stuff, take it back with you." Poe wiped moisture from his forehead and started snapping his fingers. "*Look* at this place! I can barely find any room to walk, it's so crowded."

"She wants her belongings—psychological crutch."

"What she *wants* is to go home."

Remus paused, his massive body heaving from the exertion. Deep rivers of perspiration ran down the giant's face. He mopped them with a damp handkerchief. A troubled look passed through his deep-set eyes. "Are those your words or hers?"

Poe cursed himself for speaking impulsively. "Doesn't matter."

"Tell me, Romulus."

Poe stopped snapping, clasped his hands together. "She told me she wanted to go home—home being Reno."

"What'd you tell her?"

"To stay here until she was done with her treatment. Then we could reevaluate." Poe looked upward. "I guess I flunked the son test."

"Right," Remus remarked. "And just as soon as I take her home, she'll want to come back."

"It's a moot point anyway," Poe said. "You've got a palace to build. When that's done, we'll talk. Besides, she isn't going anywhere until she's done with her chemotherapy."

Remus regarded his brother—the heavy scratches etched into his face, the stress lines stamped on his brow. "Thanks for the help, Romulus."

Poe shrugged. "Least I could do."

"I read about that horrible murder in California. The one where a mutilated woman was found in the motel attic . . ."

Poe said nothing.

Remus said, "Are you investigating it?"

"Why would I be investigating a California case?"

"Because it's connected to Alison."

Poe did a double take. "Why do you say that?"

"She and Steve were mentioned as suspects in the article."

"You're kidding!" Poe swore. "What paper were you reading?"

"Reno Times."

"Christ!" Poe began to pace. It was hard because he found himself sidestepping the trunk. "Dammit!"

"You were keeping it a secret?"

"I was trying to keep it secret. We thought that Alison and/or Steve might be headed back here. Here meaning Vegas. We didn't want to scare them off, so we left out . . ." He kicked the trunk, then hopped as pain shot through his foot.

Newton's third law, idiot! Action, reaction!

Limping, he groused, "Where the hell are Rukmani and Mom?"

"She took Mom shopping so we could settle in."

"Don't women have anything better to do than shop?"

Remus said, "Your pantry is pretty bare. You should do some shopping yourself."

Poe was still swearing to himself.

Remus put a hand on his brother's shoulder. "Come on. Let's buy grub for your kitchen. What's life without salsa and chips?"

"Fine," Poe muttered. "Fine, fine, fine." He picked up his keys.

"I'll drive," Remus said. "I can't fit into your car."

"I've still got to lock my house." Poe looked at his keys. "I wonder why I even bother with this dump. Nothing here is worth stealing. You want the outhouse, it's yours."

"Does Rukmani have a key to your house?"

He paused. "No, she doesn't."

"Then you leave it open so they can get in. If we step on it, we'll get back before they arrive."

Poe's cellular went off. He answered the call. "Poe."

Remus saw his brother turn bright red. "Everything okay?"

Poe gave him an irritated wave as he bounced in place. Remus could hear an irate male voice screaming on the other end. Rom said nothing, just took it for about a minute.

Finally, Poe said, "That's unadulterated bull—If you'd let me explain—" He rolled his eyes. "Now, that's not—Look, let's meet at the Bureau. . . . Yes, I know it's Sunday. I'm in the middle of moving my mother into my house. But obviously you think this is important. And if it's important to you, it's important to me—"

Again, Poe sneered.

"*No,* I *don't* think it's important. If you'd let me—All right. . . . All right. . . . No, it's no problem, sir. My mother's doing much better, thank you. I'll be down in twenty minutes, okay? . . . Okay."

Poe clicked off the phone. He sank into his couch. "I'm in deep shit!"

"What'd you do?"

"Intimidated a whore."

"That doesn't seem so terrible."

"She's Parker Lewiston's whore. She must have called him up and he must have made some calls. Someone high up in the brass told my lieutenant that I tried to strong-arm a call girl into giving me some freebies."

Remus stared at his brother. Rom's jaw was working overtime. "Did you?"

Poe gave him a sour look. "No. But I have . . . had a prior working relationship with her."

"Uh-oh."

"On top of that, I did muscle her. God knows it wasn't for a lousy fuck. It was for information about a murder."

"The girl in the attic?"

"No, someone else."

Remus wiped his face. "I'm sure you'll . . . you'll work something out."

"Worse comes to worst, I get suspended pending an internal investigation." He cursed under his breath. "I'm so damn *frustrated!* That bastard Lewiston murdered a *child.* And I'm this close to him, Remus." Poe pinched off a centimeter between his index finger and thumb. "But I can't get him!"

"Patience, bro."

"Patience is highly overrated."

"It has its good points." Remus sat down, practically flattened the couch. "I'm a patient person. Learn something from your big brother."

"Big brother." Poe regarded his brother's face. "I'm seven minutes older than you, guy."

"I meant in size. And you know what they say. Size is all that matters."

Poe laughed at the old joke. Not that he knew anything about Remus's genitals. As freakish children, they had both suffered from an overly developed sense of modesty. With a twinkle in his eye, Poe said, "You know, I've always meant to ask you—"

"I know what you're going to say." Remus grinned. "Don't. You're already depressed. I don't want to add to your misery."

Poe stood, threw up his keys, and caught them. "I have to go. But there's nothing to prevent you from going shopping."

"Still getting me to do your dirty work."

"What else are giant, well-endowed brothers for?"

Sweat was pouring off Weinberg's face. The air conditioner had been turned off because it was a weekend. The room temperature must have been close to ninety. He fanned himself with a folded piece of paper, then pointed to Poe's desk chair.

Poe sat.

The loo said, "You've got ten minutes."

Poe said, "I've never mooched freebies. I always pay my debts. Ask anyone. I don't even own a mortgage."

Weinberg was trying to be patient. "So what did you do that made Lewiston's whore mad?" He pulled up a chair. "More important, what did you do that made Parker Lewiston mad? Because someone with clout put in the phone call."

Poe looked at the ceiling. "You're not going to like it."

Weinberg grimaced. "What?"

"Cutting to the chase . . . I had reason to believe . . ." Poe cleared his throat. "I believed that this call girl, Honey Kramer, was involved with Parker Lewiston in the murder of Sarah Yarlborough." Again he loosened his vocal cords. "Actually, Honey admitted . . . that Lewiston had killed her."

"What?"

"Off the record. As soon as I tried to read Honey her rights, she stopped talking."

"I can't believe . . ." Weinberg licked his lips. Patience. *Patience!* "I need some details, Sergeant."

Slowly, Poe went through the entire story. From Deluca's first visit to Naked City, to her talk with scuzzball Lamar Larue, to Y's snapshots of Nali Abousayed's women—one of them being Honey Kramer. Then Poe returned to Naked City, where Larue had identified Honey as the whore who brokered underage girls for a good price for some unknown client. She never said, but everyone *knew* it was Lewiston.

"The next step," Poe said, "which seemed eminently logical at the time, was a visit to Honey—"

"Completely ignoring due process."

Poe smiled sheepishly.

Weinberg said, "Poe, why . . . *why* didn't you give the assignment to Deluca? Not only is she a woman, which would have protected you and the department against possible harassment complaints, but also she was the one who *started* the Naked City investigation."

"Yes, that would have been the smart thing to do."

"Anyone other than you! Especially since you had a prior *relationship* with this woman." Weinberg got up and started to pace. "What the hell gets *into* you?"

"I fucked up," Poe said. "But that doesn't diminish what I learned—"

"You can't use any of it."

"I'm not saying I can. But don't tell me we can't use the information as a springboard to *something*."

Weinberg sighed, rubbed his forehead. He muttered to himself. "Okay, okay, okay. First things first. How to get you out of this mess."

"Has she lodged a formal complaint?"

"Nothing in writing," Weinberg said. "Could be it was just a warning call."

"Someone is trying to scare me off?"

"Exactly. Which means you go within a mile of Honey Kramer, you're fair game for any and every kind of legal or disciplinary action. And no one—and I mean *no one*, Sergeant—will rescue you. You understand?"

"Got it."

"Let's hope this whole fiasco ends here." He gave him a dismissive wave. "Get out of here. Take care of your mother."

Poe stood. "Can I say one more thing?"

"Can I stop you?" the loo barked out.

"Lewiston killed this child in cold blood. Shouldn't we be doing something about it?"

"If you had come to me in the first place with your theories, I might have been able to do something." Weinberg thought a moment. "Lewiston isn't going anywhere. Let's meet at Myra's at ten o'clock Monday morning. We'll do some brainstorming—you, me, Patricia, and . . ." He looked at Poe. "With Jensen gone, who do you want to bring in?"

Poe winced. "I guess Marine Martin. He was with Deluca when they took Lamar Larue down. He actually did a good job."

"Call him up."

Poe's beeper went off. He looked at the number. Dispatch. He called, using his desk phone. A moment later, Weinberg saw Poe's eyes go wide as he scribbled down information.

"What?"

"They found the car."

"What car? Jensen's car?"

Poe nodded, spoke into the receiver. "Put me through to the cops at the scene. . . . Try, anyway. . . . Yeah, I'll hold."

"Where?"

"About seventy miles northeast. Lincoln County."

"Another Sunday shot to hell." Weinberg picked up another phone and called his wife. "Two reasons why I continue to flush money down the toilet for that restaurant. One, it's her love. Two, at least we get a chance to take meals together."

Into the phone, Poe shouted, "Yes, call their unit number, then call me. I know it's staticky out there, but—you must be able to reach them somehow. . . . Yes, I'm aware of interference because of the military base, but—Yes. . . . Look, keep trying to reach them. . . . Yes, patch them through immediately. But first tell them to pop the trunk. . . . That's right. They should open the trunk to make sure—Break the lock if they have to, just get the trunk open."

Poe hit his forehead in frustration.

"Yes, I know they were told not to touch anything, but this is—Yes, Sergeant Poe has given out an *order* to open the trunk. We're leaving right now—Lieutenant Weinberg and I. Yes. . . . Yes. . . . Keep trying. Thank you." Poe hung up the phone, looked at Weinberg's doleful face. "Myra's not too happy?"

"Irked. But she's still making us sandwiches."

"What a gal!"

Weinberg's expression softened, his eyes grew distant. "She's a wonderful woman. I'm a lucky guy. Let's go."

FORTY-ONE

"It's locked up tighter than a drumskin. I tried jimmyin' it with my knife, but the tip broke off. Now I could try shootin' it off. But if there's someone in there, I could be doin' more harm than good."

"Don't *shoot* anything!" Weinberg could just picture the bullet ricocheting off the trunk's steel surface and hitting one of Lincoln County's finest smack in the face. "We're about a half hour away."

Poe pushed down on the accelerator, straining the car to the max. He said, "Do you think there's someone in the trunk?"

"Well, it is saggin'," the officer responded over the radio. "I pushed it down coupla times. Feels like somethin' heavy's inside. But whatever it is, it sure ain't movin'."

The Honda flew upward as it hit a sudden dip, landing with a thud back on the road. Weinberg felt the impact clear up his spine.

He snapped, "Slow down!"

Over the line, the officer said, "Beg your pardon?"

Poe answered, "Nothing. We're fretting because they don't make shocks like they used to."

Weinberg said, "I'll call your desk sergeant. Let him know what's going on. Thanks for calling."

"No problem."

"Be there as soon as we can. Over and out."

Poe took another dip at speed. The car bounced on its tires.

"You're making me seasick," Weinberg groused. "Besides, you heard what the man said. Whatever is in the trunk isn't moving."

"But it still could be alive."

"How about if *we* make it there alive? Slow down!"

Poe tried to get hold of himself. He gripped the wheel, forced himself to reduce his speed. His eyes scanned the vast stretches of monotone desert—flat, sand-drenched terrain, parched and foreboding. Tufts of clouds drifted through the marine sky. The sun was beginning its descent. Within the hour, they would be housed under a canopy of brilliant oranges and roses. The crickets would come out, the air would become balmy, and a serenity would drape and soften the searing air as harsh as sackcloth.

Weinberg hung up the mike. "A pleasure to have some real interdepartmental cooperation. Someone in Lincoln County reads state bulletins." He sipped water. "We got lucky."

Poe nodded. "What do I do when I get off of the 95?"

"I'll tell you what to do when we're at the turnoff. We're about ten minutes away."

They rode in silence, the vista whizzing by them like an endless bolt of jaundiced cloth—a lifeless blur of sand and grit. Poe noticed the car's temperature needle creeping into the red zone. He turned off the air-conditioning and opened the window. A blast of heat slapped their faces.

He smiled apologetically. "Don't want to have car trouble."

"It's fine. We're close to the spot. Turnoff's about a hundred yards."

Poe dropped the speed. Weinberg squinted from the glare. "We're not far from the Nevada Test Site."

"This is true."

"The place gives me the creeps. Like I'm breathing in radioactive iodine 131."

"You probably are."

"You know, Poe, you have this uncanny knack—"

"Here?"

Weinberg consulted his notes. "Here."

Poe screeched as he rounded the turn.

"You take a right on the second service road," Weinberg said. "About a half mile. The car was dumped about two hundred feet from the pavement onto the floor. Whoever made the drop couldn't have gone far on foot. In this heat, you can't walk more than a few yards without drying up.''

Poe didn't say anything.

''I wonder if they had a pickup waiting. I mean, you wouldn't just junk the car and take off on a hike.''

''A pickup makes sense.'' But Poe was thinking: *metempsychosis*. What if Alison's delusions were more than delusions? If logic was suspended and the laws of physics were abandoned, anything could happen.

A big *if*.

Her delusions are getting to you, guy. The month's events combined with the desert sizzle were doing strange things to his mind.

''Here it is,'' Weinberg said. ''Turn right.''

A moment later, the rented Buick came into view. Next to it was a highway patrol car with its doors open. Poe parked the Honda off-road, the contraption wheezing as he shut the motor. He popped the front hood, allowing the steam to vent, then got out with his picks in hand. He jogged over to the plum-colored sedan.

Immediately, he started in on the trunk's lock, burning his fingertips on the fiery metal. His hands were shaking and sweat fell in big droplets off his nut-brown face.

Two khaki-uniformed men emerged from the patrol car. Weinberg put on a panama hat, stepped from the Honda, and greeted the officers. One was named Beal. He was a stocky redhead. The other was called Polk, and he looked to be American Indian.

As Poe worked the lock, the lieutenant peered inside the backseat of the Buick. The upholstery was dark red, but Weinberg could make out a few darker-stained areas. He put on gloves and felt those specific areas. They were still damp—tacky actually—even in the heat. Something had soaked the velvet through and through. He glanced at the fingertips of the latex gloves. They were smeared with iron-brown glue.

Sticky plasma.

Weinberg shouted, ''How's it going, Sergeant?''

Poe was soaked with perspiration. *Get a grip on it,* he yelled at himself. ''It's jammed,'' he answered back. ''I think someone stuffed putty inside the lock.''

''Can you get inside?''

''I think so. I can feel the tumblers, but . . .''

Silence.

"Keep working," Weinberg encouraged him. He put his latex gloves into an evidence bag, then wiped his damp face. He took off his hat and mopped his head as well. He donned his hat, then unbuttoned the top portion of his shirt. It was all useless. Nothing was going to cool him off.

Poe shouted, "One more tumbler . . . here we . . . got it!"

The trunk popped.

Poe stood up, looked inside, and gasped. A flushed, florid face cooked medium-rare stared at him with a black expression. Puffy lids and swollen blue eyes floating in a sea of pink. His heart hammering, Poe felt for a pulse. He screamed, "He's alive! Help me get him out!"

The four men lifted the two-hundred-pound-plus body. Poe shouting, carrying his portion of the weight. "Bring him into the backseat of the Honda. It's cooler—"

Beal saying, "I got a blanket in the trunk. Protect his head."

Weinberg saying, "Poe, get the ice chest from the trunk of the Honda. We've got to bring his temperature down."

"I've got a jug of water with me," Polk answered.

Beal saying, "I'll call in nine one one."

Weinberg saying, "Just hang on, Stevie boy." The lieutenant was breathing hard. His face sweaty and pale. "We're gonna take good care of you."

Gingerly, they placed him down. Weinberg barking, "Put the blanket under his head to protect him from the heat."

"You got another blanket?" Beal asked Weinberg. "If you cover the windshield, you'll keep the rays out."

Poe lugged the cooler to the backseat. Inside, the ice cubes had turned into tepid water. He peeled off his sweat-soaked shirt, dipped it in the lukewarm liquid, and wrung out the excess. Gently, he draped it over Jensen's forehead. Instantly, the material turned hot. Poe repeated the process. Over and over and over. It would have been great to be able to cool Steve's entire body in the same manner. But their water supply was precious.

Working silently, quickly, mindlessly. Poe's heart thumping against his sternum. Dipping the cloth, wringing the excess into the ice chest, draping it over a heat-smacked face. Dipping, wringing, draping, dipping, wringing, draping. After Weinberg covered the windshield with the extra blanket, he took off his own shirt and helped Poe cool off Jensen. He checked the vital signs—an irregular, fragile pulse along with faint breaths.

Beal and Polk were contacting emergency services.

Weinberg spoke softly, encouraging Jensen to keep breathing. As if it were a voluntary act. Poe licked his cracked lips. "Did those guys say something about having a jug of water? We're running a little low here."

"I'll get it."

Within moments, all three men returned to the Honda. Polk handed the jug to Poe, who poured its contents into the ice chest.

Beal said, "Ambulance should be here in . . . ten, maybe fifteen minutes."

An eternity. Poe nodded, kept dipping, wringing, and draping.

Beal raised his eyebrows. "Miracle the guy's alive. Cramped in the trunk in *this* heat." A pause. "If I'da known, I would have shot the lock out."

"You might have killed him," noted Weinberg.

"Still, sitting on it while he was burning . . ." Beal wiped his face. "I shouldn't talk. Sometimes they can hear."

Poe said, "You're doing great, Stevie. Just hang in. Just . . . hang—" Abruptly, the big body convulsed, loose limbs shaking as if made out of straw, the bottom jaw slamming against the upper. He said, "Give me something to keep his mouth open."

Polk took his club from his belt, and together they gently inserted it between Jensen's upper and lower back teeth. The big man continued to shake for another minute.

Weinberg said, "Well, we got brain activity."

Poe felt Jensen's forehead. Though still too hot, he seemed cooler. "Can somebody check on that ambulance?"

"It's only been a few minutes since we called," Polk said.

"Just to make sure." Poe looked up for a moment. "It's going to get dark."

"I'll do it," Beal said.

"Here he goes again," Polk stated.

Jensen spasmed uncontrollably, his teeth biting into the billy club. Poe took the moment to stretch, rotating his shoulders and touching his toes. His back ached from bending over Steve in an awkward position.

After Steve quieted, Weinberg said, "Keep working on him, Poe. I'm going to go call and ask for some guys to comb the area. We got about a half hour before it's pitch black. Like I said before, whoever dumped the car couldn't have gotten very far on foot."

"Car could have been dumped hours ago," Beal said.

Poe shook his head, looked down at Jensen. "No way. He couldn't have lasted hours in the trunk."

Weinberg said, "We're going to look for Alison, Rom. We're going to look for her and we'll find her—dead or alive."

Poe nodded, knowing in his gut that she was very much alive. Alive and absolutely crazy if she did this. But even if she was physically responsible for this horror, she wasn't to be blamed. Her sickness had reached the point of no return. She was helplessly out of control. She'd probably have to be institutionalized for life.

But Alison's emotional guiltlessness was of scant comfort to him. It didn't make Gretchen any less dead or Steve any less moribund—stricken by sunstroke or dehydration.

Dipping, wringing, draping.

Working and working. Hot and exhausted, the near sun beating down on his wet back, sending his melanin-producing cells into overdrive.

After ten minutes came the answer to Poe's prayers—the distant song of a siren's wail. To Beal, he said, "I'll keep working on him while you fetch the paramedics."

Twenty minutes later, as the sun dipped below the wasteland floor, Jensen was being loaded into the ambulance. An IV had been placed in his arm and his temperature had been brought down to a livable 103 plus. Two Lincoln County highway patrol cars had appeared on the scene, having been assigned to cruise the area. But there was little to see as the night crushed out color vision, reducing visibility to shades of gray, fuzzy shadows under starlight, moonlight, and the narrow beams of flashlights.

As his own shirt was soaked, Weinberg had donned a blue medic's tunic. He gave one to Poe. The lieutenant took a deep breath, dabbing his neck with a handkerchief. "I'm going with him to the hospital. Lincoln County has given Clark County permission to tow the Buick to our impound. You wait here and direct traffic. Set up a dozen flares. That should get their attention."

Poe nodded.

"You've got enough water?" Weinberg asked.

"Now I do." Both he and Weinberg had downed around a half gallon of bottled water given to them by the medics. No sooner did Poe drink than he felt himself sweating it out. Even in the dark, it was still around ninety.

"What about your car?" Weinberg inquired.

"I topped off the radiator. I should be able to make it back without a hitch."

"You got your phone?"

Poe lifted his cellular.

Weinberg said. "Keep in touch with Patricia. If she doesn't hear from you within the hour, I've instructed her to send someone after you."

"I'll be fine."

Weinberg placed his panama on his bald head. "Just in case."

Though it was Monday morning, it felt like a Friday. Poe dangled an unlit cigarette between his fingers as he stared at lukewarm coffee. Myra had turned on the air conditioner and the restaurant was beginning to cool off. She was in the kitchen scrambling eggs. He sat across from Weinberg and Deluca, and all of them seemed to be having trouble getting into gear. At least, Poe had slept in his own bed. He knew the lieutenant had spent the night at the hospital. True dedication.

Poe pocketed his smoke. "Did they say they'd call us?"

"If there's any change in his condition." Weinberg drank coffee. "When I left this morning, they seemed to have the seizures under control."

"But he was still unconscious?" Poe said.

"Yes."

"What do the seizures mean?" Patricia said.

"That his brain was fried," Poe said. "Jesus Christ, what a mess!" He looked at Weinberg. "There was blood on the upholstery."

Weinberg said, "We'll type it, but I'd be surprised if it was Steve's. The doctors I talked to didn't say anything about large wounds. Just a few nicks and cuts here and there." He regarded Poe. "And don't jump to any conclusion about Alison. She could be alive and well."

"I think she is alive and well."

Weinberg was taken aback. "So you don't think the blood is hers?"

"No." Poe applied lip balm to his desiccated mouth. "I think the blood either belongs to Gretchen Wiler—"

"The body in the attic?" Patricia asked.

Poe nodded.

"Steve's former mistress."

"Yes." Poe hesitated. "Or just maybe the blood isn't even human."

Again Weinberg made a face. "Why do you say that?"

"I think Alison is into weird stuff. Which is clear if she killed her husband's mistress and stuffed her husband into a car trunk."

Weinberg made a face. "You think Alison did it."

"I'm not discounting it."

"And the blood in the Buick?" Patricia asked.

"Maybe some kind of animal sacrifice . . . just a feeling." Poe downed his coffee. "So what do the doctors think about Steve's waking up?"

"They're cautiously hopeful."

Patricia frowned. "What does that mean? Thirty percent, forty percent, fifty percent? Doesn't anybody believe in statistics?"

"Doctors aren't about to go out on limbs," Poe said. "Not their fault. Expectations take on a whole new meaning when you're talking about life and death."

Patricia said, "Anyone want to talk about Honey Kramer's admission?"

Poe glanced at Weinberg. "Any more complaints?"

"I haven't called in for my phone messages," Weinberg answered. "Has anyone paged you?"

"Not yet."

"Then you're probably safe for the moment, Sergeant. Just keep your nose clean."

"And Lewiston walks—"

"Don't guilt-trip me when *you* fucked up," Weinberg scolded. "You have anyone else besides Lamar Larue puts Honey Kramer and Sarah Yarlborough together?"

"There was A. A. Williams," Poe said. "But he's dead."

"So you know what you've got to do, Rom. You've got to find someone else who saw them walking into Lewiston's hotel. Where does he keep his main office? The Lady Slipper or the Laredo?"

"The Laredo."

"You need another witness. Start hunting."

"Breakfast time," Myra chirped. She laid down a platter of eggs and onions, a basket of fresh kaiser rolls. "Don't tell me that this doesn't look good."

"It looks like heaven," Poe said, meaning every word.

"Well, dig in!"

Myra gave her husband a Weinberg yarmulke. The lieutenant used it to cover his bald head. He scooped some eggs onto his plate. "Are you gonna join us, Myra?"

"I've got some kugel in the oven and soup on the burners. You eat."

Patricia sank her teeth into a kaiser roll. "Man, this is great!"

"Isn't it?" Myra said. "I've got an order for six dozen. I'm catering a bris in two days. You know what a bris is?"

"Yeah," Patricia answered. "They lop off the foreskin."

Poe winced. "Another tribal rite of passage."

Myra hit his shoulder. "The baby doesn't feel a thing."

"Has anyone ever asked the baby his opinion?"

Again, Myra hit his shoulder. Laughing, she disappeared into the back of the restaurant.

Weinberg adjusted his yarmulke as he bit into his roll. "We've got to establish two things if we want to make Honey Kramer's off-the-record confession work. First, we've got to establish a definite relationship between Honey and Sarah Yarlborough. That's your job, Poe—"

"You're repeating yourself, sir."

"Shut up and listen." Weinberg sipped coffee. "Deluca, I want you to keep an eye on Honey. See how often she visits the Lady Slipper or the Laredo or any of his other places."

"She isn't going to visit Lewiston," Poe said. "He's going to keep her away from him."

"Well, see if you can establish a relationship between Honey and one of Lewiston's lackeys. Keep a camera on you. Snap pictures." Weinberg's beeper went off. He checked the number. "It's the hospital!"

Patricia put down the roll. Suddenly her stomach felt like lead. "Please make it be good news."

Weinberg called. After five minutes of being transferred, he finally was put through to the right place. He identified himself, listened for a moment, then sat back in his chair. "Great!"

"He's conscious?" Poe asked.

Weinberg nodded. "He's talking."

"All right!" Poe gave his hands a loud clap. "Yes!"

Patricia brought her hand to her chest. "Thank God!"

"Shhh!" Weinberg scolded. He nodded as he listened to the doctor on the other end of the line. "Yeah, he's right here." To Poe, Weinberg said, "Doc wants to talk to you."

"Me?"

Weinberg handed him the phone. "That's what he says."

Poe took the cellular. "This is Sergeant Romulus Poe." He listened, then said, "Not a problem. I'll need directions."

"To the hospital?" Weinberg asked.

Poe nodded.

"I'll give them to you. We'll go together."

Poe said, "I'm coming down with Lieutenant Weinberg. We should be able to make it in around an hour . . . hour and a half."

Weinberg said, "Deluca, you check impound, find out if the techs have discovered anything new with the Buick."

"Will do," she answered. "Then should I follow Honey? Just in case?"

"Yeah, do that," Weinberg said. "What could it hurt?"

Poe said, "I'll be there as soon as I can. Thanks. Bye." He stood. "Steve's asking for me."

"For *you*?" Patricia said. "What about?"

"He wouldn't say." To Weinberg, he said, "I think we should take a couple of gallons of bottled water with us." He pocketed a couple of rolls. "And some nutrition while we're at it." He took out a twenty, laid it on the table. In answer to Weinberg's quizzical look, he said, "A tip."

"You don't have to do that."

"I'm not giving it to you, sir. I'm giving it to your wife."

FORTY-TWO

Two days since the kill for fresh meat.

The craving was getting stronger. Moist, tender meat, rich in blood and protein. A necessary part of a balanced diet. All the requisites for healthy eyes, strong teeth, and a gleaming coat.

Resting in the cave with the head nestled in the crook of the forelegs. Cool and dark. The bright sun was streaming past the entrance. Bright sun hurt the eyes.

So did the tears.

Once she had been normal. Once she had lived and laughed and loved. Once the craving was satisfied with a cup of coffee or a pint of cottage cheese. Eating meat meant barbecuing a steak on the Fourth of July.

How had she gotten into this state? How, how, *how*?

She knew how. It was all there in her research. Once she had been interested in the research. Now even that didn't matter. Only meat.

Raw meat.

Her fur drying out from the intense desert rays, brittle from dehydration. So parched her haunches looked as bare as regular thighs. Her hocks resembled her former calves. Her chest was sunken and bony. She felt junkyard-mean. A wild, mangy animal with red eyes and sharp teeth.

But it hadn't always been like this. Once she had eaten to live. Now she lived to eat. Needing to gorge herself on recent kill. A requirement of her new body. Steve didn't understand, though she had tried to explain it. He couldn't see past his blind eyes, never examining what was underneath until it was too late.

And it was too late.

So she'd done what she'd had to do.

Anyway, she *really* didn't want him to raise the children, turning the boys into dolts like him. Better she should raise them and turn them into what she was. Legitimate beasts driven by instincts—blameless in all they did and how they acted.

Better still was to let the old man do the job. He would teach them about the beauty and wisdom of God. Because that was the only difference between what she had been in her former life and what she was now. Because once she had stopped her instincts because God said.

God said it was wrong to steal.

God said it was wrong to commit adultery.

God said it was wrong to kill.

God said it was wrong to eat live animals.

But all these "God saids" applied to humans, *not* to animals. And now that she was one of them, all the "God saids" didn't matter. Animals could steal and mate with whoever and kill and eat and didn't have to feel guilty about anything. That's what animals were. That's what animals did. Everyone accepted them and their needs because all they were was animals. And it was well known that carnivores needed fresh kill to survive.

The only question that remained in her mind: how had she actually become one? She knew it was all there in the green book. The official government pamphlet on the initial bomb drops. In all those boxes and papers. Her research.

If she had just looked a little harder . . .

She shifted position and closed her tired eyes.

It was good to be an animal . . . completely unaccountable for your bchavior . . . instinct-driven instead of conscience-driven.

If only the *tears* would go away.

The tears were the last vestiges of her old world. That horrible transitional phase of her living in two worlds—one as a human with morals and ethics, the other bestial, dictated by drives, acting with acuity and wiles.

There were times she felt like returning to what she had been. If she could figure out how to do it . . . to go back and forth between the two worlds, making the transition with ease and finesse.

She knew it could be done. Something to do with atomic and anatomical structures. Manipulating the particles, conserving the mass but rearranging the molecular alignment. And then there was entropy and enthalpy and the physical concepts. If she just knew, then *maybe* she could transform.

It was all there in the research . . . the way to go back and forth. But right now the research seemed very far away.

More important was her need for fresh meat.

The smell in the hospital was making Poe sick—that dizzying combo of antiseptic sprays and death. His heartbeat sped as he walked down the endless hallway, his armpits drenched and his forehead wet and clammy. Abruptly, dots of light danced in front of his eyes. He stopped and leaned against the wall, covering his face with his palm.

Weinberg halted in his tracks. "Are you all right?"

"I'm—"

"Hold on." The lieutenant looked around for a chair. Finding a spare one in an empty, open hospital room, he dragged it out and placed it on the floor. "Have a seat."

"I'm okay—"

"*Sit!*"

Poe didn't argue as a black screen slowly closed off his line of vision. He sank into the chair and dropped his head between his knees.

"You need a doctor, Rom?" Weinberg asked.

He mumbled through his hand, "More like a psychiatrist."

Weinberg found another chair and sat beside him. "Nah, you're fine. Just take a couple of deep breaths."

Poe said nothing, ashamed by his physical weakness. Weinberg seemed to sense his embarrassment.

"It's nothing, Rom. You've just been to too many hospitals, that's all. I remember when my mother was dying of cancer. Right before I came out here . . . to Vegas. I was still in Chicago, working CAPS. Whenever I had a spare moment—which wasn't too often—I rushed over to visit her. See, my mother and I were real close. My old man died in World War Two, so she raised me and my sister by herself. She and the rabbis. They wanted me to be a rabbi. Can you imagine me as a rabbi?"

Gingerly, Poe lifted his head. The room undulated, but he managed not to pass out. "I could imagine more absurd things."

Weinberg laughed. "Right in the middle of that whole ordeal, I thought I had a heart attack. I was hospitalized and the docs couldn't find anything wrong. When they sent in the shrink, I knew I had to pull myself together. Even so, for years, I couldn't look at a doctor's stethoscope without breaking into a cold sweat. You're looking better already. Can you stand up?"

Poe got to his feet, wiped his face. "Yeah." He rotated his shoulder and bounced on his feet. "I'm fine now. Let's go."

The two men walked in silence until they found Jensen's room. Weinberg tiptoed in first, Poe followed on his heels. At his bedside, they observed Steve's sleeping form. He wore hospital pajamas open in the front. His head was thrown back, blond hair strewn all over his face. He was emitting deep snores. An IV had invaded his arm, and his head was replete with electrodes. A monitor continuously read out his brain waves from an EEG machine.

Weinberg whispered, "Get us some coffee and the newspaper. Who knows how long he'll be sleeping?"

Poe studied Jensen's sickly pink complexion—a miracle he had survived. "Be back in a minute."

An hour later, after they both had polished off two Nevada dailies and a couple of car magazines, Jensen stirred. His eyes fluttered and the EEG's needles started spiking as if his cerebral cortex were having an earthquake. Weinberg and Poe stared at each other, wondering if he needed medical attention. But Jensen opened his eyes and the needles settled down.

"Hey there, Detective," Weinberg said softly. "Recognize me?"

Jensen slowly rotated his head in the direction of the sound. He blinked a couple of times, staring at Weinberg for several seconds. Then he nodded.

"Do you need anything, Stevie?"

A large hand crawled out from under the hospital cover. It inched its way to a cup on the nightstand and grasped the paper receptacle. Jensen brought it to his mouth, and water dribbled down his chin.

Weinberg wiped him, but Jensen moved his head away. The big man said, "Ice."

Poe stood, then returned with a cube wrapped in a napkin. He put it in Steve's hand. The big man sucked until the napkin was soaked with cold water, then placed the wet paper on his head.

"Do you want a cold compress, Steve?" Poe asked.

Jensen shook his head no.

"More ice?"

"Yeah."

Poe wrapped another cube in a napkin. A moment later, Jensen spoke. "I've got . . ." He sighed. "I've got one motherfucking headache. Can't take anything." Another sigh. "Until my brain's normal. Guess I'm gonna wait a long time."

Poe smiled. "You're doing great."

"Think so?" Jensen croaked out.

"Yes, I do."

Weinberg said, "Between yesterday and today—a world of difference."

"You look any better," Poe added, "you're going to distract the nurses."

"So trade places with me, cocksucker." Jensen bit his lip. "More ice."

Weinberg pressed the nurse button. "Can we have some more ice here, please?"

"Right away," a disembodied voice answered.

"That means thirty minutes," Jensen growled out.

Weinberg stood. "I'll get it."

As soon as he was gone, Jensen asked Poe, "Have you found Alison?"

Poe shook his head. "We're looking—"

"She's crazy." Jensen swallowed dryly. "Violent." He let out a dry cough. "You've got to find her . . . before the police. Otherwise, she'll get herself . . . killed. Or kill herself."

He paused. "Where do you think she is?"

"In the desert."

"California? Nevada?"

"Nevada. Southern Nevada."

"Near NTS?"

Jensen looked away, his brain waves on overdrive. "Probably. She's . . . over the edge. Completely insane."

Poe told himself not to snap. "Steve, I think Alison believes that NTS is at fault for her insanity."

"The radiation . . . she keeps talking about the radiation." Jensen's breaths were shallow. "Her thyroid is *fine*. It's her brain that's . . ." There was a very long pause. "Somehow, she's become strong, Rom. Real strong. She's gotta be taking something . . . steroids. She can . . . do damage."

"Like kill Gretchen Wiler. We found her body."

Jensen closed his eyes. "It was . . . was too late by the time I came back."

Weinberg returned with the ice. Poe said, "We were talking about Gretchen Wiler's murder. Steve says the killing was over by the time he came back." He paused. "Came back from where?"

"Came to," he corrected. "I must have passed out in the night. I'd been drinking . . . tequila shooters. Polished off about a bottle. Still, I usually don't . . . don't pass out."

"She could have slipped you something," Poe said.

"Probably. It was all Alison's idea, you know."

Weinberg wrapped ice and gave it to Steve. "What idea?"

Jensen sucked on the ice cube. "Bringing in Gretchen." A beat passed. "For a threesome." He looked away. "I knew something was . . . wrong. But I didn't want . . . I just . . . I was trying . . . I should have—"

Weinberg interrupted, "Steve, we can always talk about it later."

"No!" Jensen became agitated. "Later means another corpse. You've got to find Alison now!"

"We will. I promise, Steve, I promise." Poe waited a beat. "Who called Gretchen down to the motel?"

"I called her . . . on the phone," Jensen said. "I even offered her money for it. She accepted, of course. I drove back down to Vegas and picked her up." He let out a weak breath. "Drove her to the motel." Another hesitation. "We partied. I knew it was weird. But Alison seemed to like it."

He closed his eyes. Tears leaked from the shut lids.

"Sometime . . . during all the partying, I passed out. When I came to . . . blood was all over. She . . . Alison . . ." He composed himself for the confession. "Alison was eating Gretchen's corpse."

Poe tried to keep his face flat. "She thinks she's an animal, doesn't she? A wolf or a coyote."

Jensen looked wide-eyed. "She told you?"

Weinberg looked at Poe quizzically, saying: *How'd you know that?*

Poe said, "She didn't exactly tell me. But I'm right, aren't I?"

The big man nodded. "When I woke up, she had on this wolf costume

. . . covered with fur from head to toe. And she was acting like a wild animal . . . growling . . . snarling . . . her face . . ." He started panting. "Oh God, her wolf face was covered in blood!"

The needles began going haywire. No one spoke, Weinberg and Poe looking at their laps as Jensen cried. After the big man had calmed down, Poe tried to save Jensen's dignity with another question. "Had you ever seen the costume before that night in the motel?"

Jensen dabbed his eyes and shook his head no.

Weinberg said, "What happened after you woke up and saw all the blood?"

"I was still groggy . . . too shocked to speak. Suddenly . . . she attacked me. Just jumped me, and bit me on the neck." Jensen turned and showed them the puncture marks on the side of his throat. He eyed Poe. "Sound familiar?"

"The attacking part, yes. Except she scratched me." Involuntarily, his hand moved to his marred cheek. "Did you fight her off?"

"I couldn't . . . *hit* her. No matter what she had done. I was . . . I just let it . . ."

He looked down.

"While she was biting me, she must have stuck me with dope or something. Because then I don't remember anything else. Not a thing. Not until I woke up this morning. I do remember going in and out in this hazy blur. But not really *seeing* or *hearing* anything."

Jensen took the ice and placed it over his forehead. "I called you, Rom, because I think she's out to get you. I think she's out for revenge on anyone who she *thinks* has . . . wronged her."

"Thanks for the warning."

Jensen sucked more ice. "Somehow I made it. Maybe God knew that someone had to take care of the boys. But you . . . you may not be so lucky." He stared at Poe with concern. "She's violent. Be careful . . . not just you, but Rukmani. I don't want *more* death . . . on my conscience. Please!"

He was wrought with anxiety. Poe patted his shoulder. "I'll take extra special care of both of us."

He sighed. "I'm very tired."

"Go to sleep," Weinberg said. "We'll come tomorrow. Ask more questions if you're up to it."

Jensen said, "First go find my wife. Please, Rom. Find her before she finds you."

FORTY-THREE

"This delusion . . . that Alison thinks she's a wolf," Weinberg said. "Sounds to me like Steve's making an excuse for his wife's killing spree."

Poe answered, "Sir, I think she's truly psychotic."

"Not all psychos are cannibals." The lieutenant sipped from his water bottle. "Parading around in a wolf's costume, eating a corpse. If Steve's memory is to be believed."

"Actually, Rukmani told me that delusions of being an animal are as old as time. Look at all the werewolf legends."

"So now Alison's not only a wolf, but a werewolf? She comes out when the moon is full and murders hookers—one who just happened to be her husband's mistress." Weinberg looked disgusted. "She lured Gretchen by having Steve bring her down to the motel. Don't tell me that isn't premeditated murder."

Nervously, Poe tapped the wheel of his car. "Actually, sir . . ." He cleared his throat. "Both Gretchen Wiler *and* Brittany Newel had had sexual affairs with Steve."

"*What?*" Weinberg coughed. "Where'd you hear that? Are you *sure?*"

"Yes."

"When did you find this out?"

Confession time. Poe said, "I knew it from the start . . . Don't say it—"

Weinberg snarled, "Poe—"

"Steve told me it had only been a one-night stand with Brittany. And since he had fucked half of the city's hookers, I didn't see the relevance."

"*You* didn't see the relevance—"

"I know I should have—"

"Yes, you definitely *should* have!" Weinberg said. "You deliberately withheld vital information from me, Poe. And for what reason? For *what* reason?"

"I didn't want to embarrass Steve."

Weinberg slapped his forehead. "You're out of control. I should pull you off the case. You're way too overinvolved!"

"Sir, I—"

"Just *shut up*! I don't want to talk to you!"

They drove without talking for ten minutes. Then Weinberg said, "What were you talking to Steve's doctor about?"

"Just his condition."

"Stop bullshitting me and answer the fucking question."

Poe licked his lips. "I wanted to know if he took a picture of the bite on Steve's neck."

"Why?"

Poe stalled. "I wanted Rukmani to have a look at it."

"Go on, Poe."

"I want to make sure that the mark was *Alison's* teeth."

"You doubt Steve's story, then?"

"Sir, I don't doubt Steve was attacked. But by his own admission, he was doped up most of the time. He may have missed something. For all we know, that bite mark may have been given to him by Gretchen." A beat. "Just trying to fill in the gaps."

Weinberg thought as he drank water. "Did the doc have a picture of the bite mark?"

"Several. I have a snapshot in my backpack."

"The doctor just . . . released part of Jensen's medical chart over to you?"

"The doctor took several pictures. Steve assigned one of them over to me."

"So you don't suspect Steve of anything?"

Poe shook his head. "Not at the moment, no."

Weinberg said, "I still can't figure out how Alison could do that much damage by herself. Killing Gretchen and carrying her into the attic. Then stuffing Steve into the trunk.'' He rubbed his eyes. ''Even if she was taking steroids. Even if she believed she was *Hercules*. It spits in the face of logic. There had to be a second party.''

Poe spoke prudently. ''Possibly.''

''But you're not committing to anything. No wonder you never got married.'' Weinberg redirected the air-conditioning vent away from his face. ''So you tell me how she could lift Gretchen into the attic.''

''Alison's around five-seven or -eight. If she had been taking steroids—''

''Okay,'' Weinberg interrupted. ''So maybe she could lift Gretchen. Let's even assume that she could. Tell me how she could have lifted Jensen into the trunk.''

''Leverage.''

Weinberg looked dubious.

Poe said, ''With enough adrenaline pumping through your veins, and a wheelbarrow and ramp, it could be done.''

''She left the car in the middle of nowhere. So you're telling me she takes off with a wheelbarrow and ramp in tow. And if she left them behind, where's the wheelbarrow? Where's the ramp? Does that seem logical to you?''

''No, it doesn't.''

''Do you know if she had a lover on the side?''

''I don't know.''

''A good-looking woman like Alison, even if she is cuckoo, she could attract men.''

''Absolutely.''

''So, she could have roped someone into helping her do the murders.''

''Yes.''

''I want you and Patricia to go question the neighbors,'' Weinberg ordered. ''Find out who came and went from the house.''

Poe sighed. ''Okay.''

''What's the sighing? You sound like a love-struck goose. What's the *problem*, Poe?''

''Nothing. I'll go question the neighbors.''

''I know you want to look for Alison. Forget it! I don't trust your judgment when it comes to her. She could sweet-talk you into doing something dumb.'' The loo paused. ''I don't know if I trust your judgment period. Between not telling me about Steve and Brittany Newel, then your manhandling of Honey Kramer, I should suspend you.''

"You'd be within your rights.''

"Maybe the snake toxin went to your brain. Maybe it's your mother's illness. Whatever the reason, let the highway boys look for Alison. You just piece together something logical from what Steve told us.''

"I'll do what I can.''

Poe's cell phone started ringing. He picked it up. "Yes?''

The female voice said, "God! *Finally!* You've been out of range for what felt like hours.''

"Patricia?''

"You've got to come back right away.''

"We're on our way. What's up?''

"I'm outside Honey Kramer's apartment. Or what once was her apartment. It blew up about ten minutes ago.''

"Oh my God!''

"What?'' Weinberg asked.

Poe handed the lieutenant the phone.

"Weinberg here. What?''

"Honey Kramer's apartment exploded around ten minutes ago!''

Weinberg swore silently. "Where are you, Deluca?''

"Right outside the place.'' A pause. "I saw it, sir. I was watching the place . . . and then there was this loud bang . . . the place just . . . detonated.''

"What's happening now?''

"Fire trucks arrived immediately. So did the ambulances. I've called someone down from the Arson—''

"Good thinking—''

"Scariest fucking thing I've ever seen!''

"We'll be there in a half hour,'' Weinberg said. "Should I bother to ask this?'' A pause. "Was Honey inside?''

"Sir, I saw her enter the building. That's why I was watching the place.''

"Any possibility that she could be alive?''

"I don't see how.''

The apartment was belching dark plumes of smoke, but Patricia couldn't make out any more active flames. The fire department had stopped spraying, but a half-dozen fighters were still chopping through blackened siding. Hoses lay curled along the ground like sleeping cobras. Several ambulances had arrived to transport victims to the hospital. Arson had started to do their thing. The mixture of water and ash choked Deluca's throat. She was trying to figure out her role in all of this when Poe's dirt-coated Honda chugged its way through the ropes. She felt relieved when Lieutenant Weinberg stepped out and immediately took over.

Retreating across the street, she observed the inferno with her arms folded, her face covered in black soot. Poe walked up and stood next to her, smoking a cigarette. Together, they watched the ambulances flash and wail as they sped down the street. Neither spoke, taking mental notes on the commotion. Finally, Patricia asked how Steve was faring.

"Back from the dead," Poe answered. "Amazing."

"What'd he tell you?"

"That Alison murdered Gretchen Wiler. She used Steve as bait to lure her down. Gretchen went, thinking Steve wanted a threesome. They partied. Steve drank and passed out. Next thing he knew, the room was covered with blood and Alison was munching on Gretchen's corpse."

Patricia winced. "Steve doesn't recall anything about the murder?"

"He says no."

She paused. "Do you think he's holding back?"

"Honestly, I don't know."

"Do you think . . ." She paused. "Do you think he was involved in the actual murder?"

"He was a heartbeat away from death when we found him. I'm inclined to believe his story and his innocence."

"Does he have any theories as to *why* she did it?"

"Just that she's crazy."

"Not that crazy," Patricia replied. "She purposely picked out Gretchen."

Poe nodded, gazing at the blackened structure. "I caused all this." He took a deep drag on his smoke. "I should have . . . if people died—"

"No one died," Patricia interrupted him. "Even Honey Kramer's still hanging on."

"You're kidding."

"She's not in good shape, but she's alive." Patricia looked at her feet. "I was surprised. Man, that explosion." She let out a breath. "They say it was lucky that I was watching the place and called it in immediately. Fire chief said a few more minutes and the flames would have reached the central heating system. Then the entire building would have been torched.''

"Honey Kramer is actually *alive*?"

"Alive but burned." A pause. "*Badly* burned."

Poe licked his lips. "It's all my fault. I should have handled it better."

Patricia stared at him. "You blew up the building, sir?"

"You know what I mean."

"And here I thought that only women had the capacity for irrational guilt."

"What about the other victims? How bad off are they?"

"I don't know the medical details, Sergeant. But like I said, the fire department was here in a flash."

Poe took a final drag. "I should have figured that she'd run to Lewiston ... tell him I strong-armed her. I should have known he'd do something like this." He crushed out his cigarette with too much force. "Too late now."

"Sir, even if you hadn't done anything, Lewiston probably would have gotten rid of Honey as soon as the investigation started gaining force. Look what happened to A. A. Williams. You know someone monkeyed with the van."

True enough. He faced her. "Was Honey conscious when she was brought out?"

"I don't know. They took her to the University Medical Center."

Poe said, "I want a twenty-four-hour guard on her hospital room." Eyes fixed on the action, he saw Weinberg break away from the crowd and head toward them. "Uh-oh!"

Patricia said, "Looks like the lieutenant has something on his mind."

Probably my dismissal, Poe thought.

Weinberg stomped over to them, attempting to brush wet ashes off his clothing. All he did was streak his pants gray. He spoke in a grave manner. "No deaths yet. Even Honey Kramer is alive."

Poe said, "Patricia told me. What a relie—"

Weinberg interrupted, "Patricia, you stay here and tag along with Arson. See what you can find out from them. I've also ordered a police photographer to come down to take extensive pictures of the damage. You can tag along with her also." He turned to Poe. "They took Honey to the burn unit at the University Medical Center. C'mon."

"Me?" Poe asked.

"Yes, you."

"Sir, you told me to keep away—"

"That was then, this is now." Weinberg coughed. "She kept calling your name out as they loaded her into the ambulance. I don't know if she was asking for you or cursing the day you were born. Let's go find out."

FORTY-FOUR

))   Hard to believe that there was a breathing person beneath the shroud of bandages. Honey's arms and chest were completely dressed, her legs probably wrapped as well. Poe couldn't tell, as they were covered by a lightweight sheet. Her head was also swathed in gauze. If she made it, she'd be in for a long and painful haul.

Poe watched over her as she slept fitfully, wondering why it had been cosmically ordained that the summer of his thirty-sixth year should be spent in hospitals. He stared at Honey's swaddled face, her eyes moving underneath bright red eyelids. Her lips were bluish and covered with something sticky. The skin above had been blistered red.

An hour passed before he heard signs of life—a soft, whispery moan. In another context, it could have been interpreted as erotic. Here it suggested agony. Her eyelids fluttered, opened, then closed. Poe was almost hoping she'd fall back asleep. Instead, with effort, the lids reopened, then widened when she saw him. Slowly the eyes moved and took in Weinberg's face. He nodded, glanced at Poe, who turned on the tape recorder strapped across his chest.

Poe spoke softly. "If you want, I'll go away."

Honey whispered a no.

He spoke softly. "Someone said you were asking for me. Blink once if that's a true statement."

"Don't have to blink." She breathed laboriously with each word. "I can . . . talk."

Her words were muffled, but Poe could make them out. He said, "Do you need more pain medication?"

She nodded. "But it'll . . . knock me out. So wait until . . ."

Poe said, "I have a tape recorder running now, Honey. Is that okay?"

"It's . . . good." A long pause. "I want to confess."

Poe's brain started racing. "About what we talked about?"

She nodded. "Yes."

Poe coughed into his fist. "All right. Mind if some other people hear it? Witnesses? So certain people won't say I'm making this up?"

"I'm tired. Now . . . or never."

"I need to tell you your rights."

"Quick." There were tears in her eyes. After Poe advised Honey of her rights, she started talking in a raspy hush.

"He did it." A pause. "Parker Lewiston. He killed that girl . . . with the pink hair . . . Sarah Yarlborough." Another hesitation. "I saw it . . . saw him do it."

She took in Poe's expression, her own eyes now dry.

"He was . . . screwing her, said he was gonna give her . . . the ultimate high. She thought he meant drugs."

More labored breathing . . . her voice was as soft as a sable brush.

"As she started to . . . climax, he . . . choked her. Don't know if he meant to kill her . . . but . . . but the end was the same."

Three deep breaths, a moan of agony.

"When she stopped breathing, he knew. He didn't . . . give a shit. He reached into his pocket . . . pulled out a knife . . . slit her throat. Did it to make it look . . . look like . . ."

Her words became unintelligible. Poe said, "He slit her throat to make it look like what, Honey?"

"The other one. The other girl . . . in the picture you showed me."

"Brittany Newel?"

"Yes." More toiled breathing. "Yes, Brittany Newel."

"Parker Lewiston choked Sarah Yarlborough to death. To masquerade her death, Lewiston slit her throat."

"Yes."

"So the police would think that Sarah Yarlborough and Brittany Newel were murdered by the same person."

With great effort, she told him yes.

Poe said, "Where'd he kill her?"

"In his office . . . in the Laredo." She looked away. "I'm tired. I want my dope now."

"Right away." Weinberg called the nurse. "You did a great service, Ms. Kramer. You really did."

Honey didn't respond. A doctor came in and monitored her vitals. Within minutes, artificial harmony shot through her veins. She drifted back into a restless unconsciousness. Eyes closed, Honey murmured, "Now . . . I can finally . . . sleep."

Weinberg finished off the last bits of his pastrami sandwich, threw the napkin in the backseat of Poe's Honda. "Get your car washed. I'll pay for it."

Poe turned out of the hospital complex's parking lot. "What now?"

"Good question," the lieutenant responded. "What we got was more like a confessionette than a genuine full-scale confession."

Poe said, "She said he did it. She said she *saw* him do it. She said *how* he did it. She said *where* he did it. I've got a witness that'll link Honey and Sarah together the night of the murder. I think we've got a lot."

"It won't stand up before a grand jury."

"Agreed," Poe answered. "But maybe it's enough to convince a judge to issue us a search warrant for Lewiston's office at the Laredo."

"What's in his office? The knife?"

"If we are magically lucky. Actually, what I had in mind was a sample of grass."

"Grass?"

"Lewiston's entire Laredo office is floored with grass for golfing—"

"The sample found under Yarlborough's fingers. The odd-type grass." Weinberg thought a moment. "Okay. We probably have enough to get a warrant."

"It's a start."

Weinberg said, "That confession will be contested in every way, shape, or form. It was done while she was drugged, it was done under duress, it was done without her having legal representation. No way it's going to be meaningful unless she stands by it once she recovers. Especially since she lodged a complaint about you three days ago. His legal eagles are going to accuse you of coercing her, tear into you like—"

"I'll take a polygraph."

"It won't stand up in court."

"So let's get the warrant for his office and maybe if the grass blades match, that'll stand up in court." Poe paused. "We should move on it now, sir. Before Lewiston finds out she's still breathing."

"I'll contact the judge. Where's the tape recording?"

"It's in my knapsack."

Weinberg reached around and lifted Poe's knapsack from the backseat floor. He started rummaging through its contents. "She was hard to understand in person. Tape makes her sound even more muffled."

"You can make out the words if you listen hard enough." Poe thought a moment. "If you want we can take it down and have it enhanced—"

"Better straight off the brisket." Weinberg paused. "A deli term. It means we don't do anything fancy unless we have to."

"I agree."

Weinberg pulled out the tape recorder and slipped it into his briefcase. "You go back to the office and work with Deluca on the explosion. I'll send in Baylor and Herrod to search Lewiston's office—"

"What?" Poe was appalled. "You can't lock me out now! This is my moment of glory."

"Exactly. I need people who are dispassionate and professional. You're not either when it comes to Lewiston. Baylor and Herrod'll work out fine."

"At least give it to Marine Martin."

"Serious?"

"Yes, go ahead and give it to him." Poe raised his eyebrows. "Talk about dispassionate. Anyway, Marine works well with Herrod."

"All right. Herrod and Marine Martin." Weinberg picked up the cellular. "Drop me off at City Hall. You go back to Homicide Bureau and prep the duo about Lewiston." He started making calls and was immediately put on hold. The lieutenant regarded his sergeant. "Poe."

"What, sir?"

"Lewiston has power. Watch your butt."

With his hair slicked back and garbed in a brown suit, short-sleeved white shirt, and string tie, Marine Martin looked more like a Vegas junket passenger than a cop. But the giveaway to his profession was the eyes, scanning the crowds, noting the doors and exits, observing the motion at the Laredo. With the warrant stowed neatly in his coat pocket, he was ready for action. His partner, Kurt Herrod, had donned a dark blue suit over a wrinkled white shirt. Herrod was around the same height and age as Marine. And like Marine, he had milky blue eyes, as well as a large, bald pate ringed with gray. But Herrod was much stockier. Together, the team resembled a before-and-after weight loss picture.

Herrod's eyes swept across the casino. "You have a name of someone who will take us up to Lewiston's office?"

"Asking for someone would ruin our tactic of surprise," Martin responded in a clipped cadence. "We go into this mission unannounced."

"Martin, it isn't a mission, it's an assignment." Herrod stuck his hands in his pocket. At least Marine didn't call him Grandpa. "It's a job—"

"Mission, assignment, or job, the semantics don't matter. Only results." Marine glanced at his watch, set to display military time. "It is now precisely twenty-one hours—"

"Don't salute."

"Ready when you are."

"Sure, let's do it."

With that Marine marched up to the information desk and butted in to the front of the line. He laid his badge on the desktop in full view of the information lady. She was in her early twenties—a blonde with pale green eyes, two beats away from being pretty. She picked up the badge and studied it as Marine spoke.

"Detectives Martin Donaldson and Kurt Herrod from Las Vegas Metro Police Department. Homicide Bureau. We need to see Mr. Parker Lewiston immediately." He held out his hand. "The badge please?"

The woman handed it back, confused by what was going on. Herrod came to the rescue.

"If you could, ma'am, please call down your floor supervisor." Herrod took Marine out of earshot from the crowd. "Martin, we're gonna have to do this in steps."

"It will ruin element of surprise—"

"There's a system here. You can't just waltz in and expect the Red Sea to part."

"If the Red Sea doesn't part, then we'll swim across." Marine's eyes narrowed. "She's using the phone."

"That's because I asked her to call her supervisor."

Marine went back to the desk, holding position as sentry until he got some satisfaction. Within moments, the floor boss materialized. He was broad and well-muscled, with a fleshy face. He stuck out his hand, pulling them off to the side—away from the line and from playing customers. He was all business.

"Bobby Guard. What can I do for you, gentlemen?"

Herrod presented his badge. "We're here to see Mr. Lewiston."

Guard's eyes glanced at the gold shield, then he motioned them to follow. He took them through the casino, past the flashing lights and beeps of cacophonous sound, past the soft shuffle of cards and the cheers from a table as the dice came up seven. Into the back of the casino, up to the cashier's desk. Then he stopped at a side door which blended with the wall and was keyed as well as alarmed. Guard disengaged the bells and buzzers. Then he led them through a series of mazes, and into an air-conditioned suite—a hermetic sitting room which held several leather couches and four wingback chairs placed around a poker table. The area also had a bar, a miniature craps table, and a couple of slot machines. Off to the left was an attached office, which held multiple TV monitors scanning the casino floor. Guard tried to settle them into the chairs. Herrod took up residence on the sofa, but Marine elected to stand.

Guard said, "A drink, gentlemen?"

"No, thank you, Mr. Guard," Herrod answered. "We're here to speak to Mr. Lewiston. The sooner the better."

"Mr. Lewiston isn't in." Guard poured himself a finger's worth of scotch—Glenmorangie. "If you had called—"

"Sir!" Marine broke in. "We do not need Mr. Lewiston for our operation." He whipped out the paper from his jacket. "We have a signed and sealed search warrant for his office here at the Laredo. It gives us the authority to conduct a complete and thorough property search and seizure of the entire twenty-sixth floor. Which we understand is Mr. Lewiston's private office—"

"What are you talking about?"

"We are on a tight schedule, sir. We'd appreciate it if you would take us there immediately—"

"Lemme see that!"

Marine handed him the warrant. "You may read it on your own time, sir. We have our work to do."

"How do I know this is legit?"

Herrod said, "Take it to a lawyer if you want. But we know it's legitimate and we don't need to wait for your permission. Direct us and we're out of your hair."

"You're gonna have to slow down here." Guard sipped his drink and settled into the couch's overstuffed pillows. "Even if this was on the up-and-up, I'm not quite sure who could help you with the office. Are you sure you don't want a drink—"

"Sir, you are stalling," Marine stated. "This is unacceptable!"

"No, I'm not stalling, Detective," Guard answered lazily. "You see, I have a job here. And that's protecting Mr. Lewiston's property, both down at the casino and in his offices—"

"Sir, you do your job, we'll do ours!" Marine looked down at his wrist. "Shall we go?"

"See, that's what I'm trying to tell you," Guard answered. "Even if I wanted to, I couldn't help you. Mr. Lewiston's office is in a private locked wing. It's alarmed and I don't have a key. Now I'm gonna help you out. Mr. Lewiston has always maintained a very good position with the police department here. You just ask your captain—"

Again, Marine interrupted. "I'm going to have to insist that you take action now, sir. Either *you* do it or *I'll* do it."

"Detective, I intend to make some calls. But it's going to take a while. So why don't you wander around the casino, and I can have you paged when—"

"That is not acceptable," Marine announced.

Guard smiled. "Detective, it's the best I can do. Take it or leave it."

"Consider your option discarded. Obviously, you are not the man for the job. I'll look elsewhere." Marine turned on his heel and started to exit the room.

Guard jumped up, his drink splashing over the rim of his glass. "Hey! Where're you going?"

Marine was out the door. "To find someone who has some authority."

"Now wait a minute!" Guard grabbed his arm. "You just can't—"

"Let go of my arm, sir!"

"If you want my help, you just hold on a goddamn moment—"

Within a second, Marine had flipped Guard onto his back and had him pinned against the floor. The glass flew out of his hand, hit the floor, bounced, then rolled until it was stopped by the leg of the couch. Herrod stared with admiration at the old-fashioned tumbler. Good, strong crystal. Must be expensive stuff.

Glaring down at the restrained floor boss, Martin formally stated, "The next time you grab me, I will arrest you for assault upon a police officer.

Now, you have a job to do, sir. If you can't do it, I'll do it in good old all-American Marine style!''

Two bouncers came storming into the office. Guard shouted, ''Don't touch them! Don't touch them!''

The bouncers halted in their tracks. Marine offered Guard a hand, then yanked him to his feet. He lectured, ''Your protection is late. If I had been someone dangerous, you would have been in serious trouble, Mr. Guard.''

The meaty duo glared at Marine, then at Herrod, who smiled back at them. Guard glowered at his so-called protection. He snapped to them, ''Get out of here.''

The two leadweights looked at each other, then left.

Marine said, ''With or without you, I'm going to the twenty-sixth floor—''

''Read my lips, Detective.'' Infuriated but hog-tied, Guard took a deep breath. ''I *don't* have a key to Mr. Lewiston's private elevator, I *don't* have the key to Mr. Lewiston's office, I *don't* have the key to Mr. Lewiston's private wing—''

''Unacceptable!'' Marine said. ''I'll find my own way to get the job done.''

Guard had a noticeable strain in his voice. ''Detective Donaldson, you can't get up to Mr. Lewiston's office unless you use the proper elevator with the proper elevator key—''

''There must be a fire escape staircase somewhere.''

''I'm sure there is, but that's probably hidden as well as locked.''

''Find it for me.''

''That's also gonna take time.''

Marine felt his face go hot with anger. ''You leave me no choice. I take it Mr. Lewiston's office has windows?''

''Well, yes, but—''

''Then I can get into the office, Mr. Guard.''

''They're *picture* windows, Detective. They're glued into place.''

Marine flexed his biceps. ''A cut or two doesn't deter a good soldier, sir.'' He picked up the phone and asked for emergency services—the fire department. ''They'll help me find the fire escape staircase. And if not, they have equipment to take me to the twenty-sixth floor and axes to smash glass.''

Guard's stomach was drowning in acid. ''You've *got* to be kidding.''

"I never kid!"

Guard believed that. He said, "Detective, you start smashing windows, I'll have your *job!*"

"It is a chance I'm willing to take." A pause. Then Marine spoke into the phone. "Hello, this is Detective Martin Donaldson of LVMPD. I need ASAP a ladder truck and a half-dozen of your finest men."

"I don't fucking believe—"

Playing his part, Herrod broke in, saying, "This isn't going to be good for business, Mr. Guard. Having a bunch of wailing fire trucks pull up in front of your place. It might even start a panic reaction."

Guard grabbed at the phone. The man was fucking crazy! "If you'd just wait a goddamn minute—"

"There is no need for profanity." Into the phone, Marine said, "New developments. I'll have to call you back." He disconnected the line and handed the phone to the floor boss. "Five minutes to get something going. Starting . . . now!"

Guard rubbed his forehead. Keeping his bile down, he activated the cellular and talked softly into the receiver. He hung up and punched in another number. Did it a third time. Finally, he turned back and faced the detective duo. "Someone will be here in fifteen, twenty minutes—"

"Unacceptable!" Marine brought his wrist up to heart level, his eyes fixed on his watch. "I will give you seven minutes and not a second more. If no one appears within the allotted time, I'm calling back the fire department—"

"Detective, the woman's *not* in the casino. She has to come from down—"

"Then get someone *in* the casino who has the keys!" Marine kept his eyes on the watch. "Ready . . . set . . ."

Guard was getting desperate. To Herrod, he said, "Talk some fucking *sense* into him."

Herrod said, "Give him eight minutes, Martin."

"All right. Eight minutes. Go!"

Guard said, "This is crazy! *You're* crazy—"

"Seven minutes, forty-two seconds remaining—"

"You should be in a *loony* bin—"

"Seven minutes, thirty-seven seconds . . . thirty-six seconds—"

"I don't need a goddamn town crier!" Guard popped a handful of Tagamet and Maalox, washing them down with scotch from the bottle.

Once again, he started making calls. When the supervisor hung up, Marine announced that he had two minutes and twelve seconds left on the clock.

Guard opened the door. "By sheer luck, I found someone. C'mon, we'll meet him by the elevator."

"Good job, Mr. Guard. I knew you could do it." Marine opened the door. "You lead, sir, as you know the way out."

Guard sneered, punching his right fist into his left hand. But he reluctantly led them out the door. His balls were between a rock and a hard place. He knew that letting these two yahoos up into Lewiston's office was gonna cost him his job. Worse than that, Lewiston never forgave, let alone forgot.

But what was his choice? To let some loose cannon smash up Lewiston's office windows, creating a wind tunnel between the outside and inside, hurricaning half of the boss's office contents up into the ozone layer?

What could he do?

What could he *do*?

But what if the motherfucker had been bluffing?

What if?

Who could tell a bluffer better than Guard, who had seen millions of bluffers try to outsmart the pros? The floor boss studied Marine as they walked over to the bank of mirrored elevators. The cop's face revealed nothing except the crazed look of will and determination.

Bluffing or not bluffing, the cocksucker would have made one hell of a fine poker player.

FORTY-FIVE

Honey had taken a turn for the worse, her condition downgraded from serious to critical. Though Poe had stopped whipping himself for the explosion, guilt still tugged his conscience. Sifting through the wreckage at the call girl's apartment, Arson had come up with some physical evidence of explosives, but none of it name-called Lewiston. Poe knew it would take months to assess the exact cause by making a methodical examination of ashes and soot and debris.

Still, he retained some minimal hope of nailing Lewiston. Last night, Marine Martin had brought back bags of grass from the casino owner's Laredo office. The blades were now being processed in a specialized lab in Reno. As odd as Marine was, he had done a fine job.

No sign of Alison, yet Poe sensed she wasn't far away. Alison—his longtime, suffering friend, his ages-ago lover, his possible half sister . . . a possible serial killer. Steve's ominous warnings playing in his brain . . .

Burying himself in the mundane details of work, Poe was glad to see the day end. He gunned his Honda and sped to his private hive in the middle of nowhere. After settling Emma down for a predinner nap, he donned his gym clothes and took off for his run, feeling the constricting ties loosen as he dripped in sweat. The sun was heading toward the horizon, gilding the desert floor with its soft late-afternoon rays. The air was clear and quiet, the only disturbances being the scuffling of his soles

355

against the arid ground and the dust that swirled up from under his athletic shoes. Overhead, a hawk circled, casting an elongated, dancing shadow on the desert floor.

He took the final fifteen minutes of his five miles at a steady, fast walk. Winded and wet, he mopped his face with his shirt, his skin flushed and pulsating with heat. He rotated his head and shoulders, hearing his bones creak and crack. From a distance, as his house came into view, Poe saw a dark blue Lincoln Town Car, its chrome trim reflecting hot light. Immediately, he slowed his pace, his nervous system flashing Code Red. A moment later, he saw two loitering figures wearing Hawaiian shirts, beach pants, and sandals. They were around five-eleven, maybe six feet. Very stocky, with round, thick faces, heavyset arms, and meaty hands.

Goons.

And here Poe was, dressed in gym shorts, a tank top, and running shoes with rubber soles, *and* without his gun. He might as well have been naked. They stiffened when they saw him approach, straightening as if someone was about to take roll call. Both were swarthy, with dark eyes and lots of facial shadowing. One Hawaiian shirt was a blue print of waves and surfboards, the other was woven with ukuleles, leis, and bikini babes sitting in a red background.

Poe kept fifteen feet between himself and the beef. He dabbed his damp face. "Can I help you, gentlemen?"

Folding his arms across his chest, Red Shirt blocked the door to Poe's house with his girth. His legs were spread apart, his feet rooted to the ground. "Are you Sergeant Poe?"

"That would be me."

Blue Shirt's hand sidled under the hem of his Hawaiian masterpiece. No doubt his fingers were wrapped around the butt of a revolver. He said, "We're from Mr. Lewiston's office. He wants to talk to you."

"So if you just hop in the car," Red continued, "we'll take you right over."

Poe regarded the Lincoln. No plates. And he couldn't read the number off the temp license affixed to the car's windshield. The glare was too strong. He said, "He wants to talk to me now?"

"That's right, sir." Red took a step toward him.

Poe backed away. They were still talking nice, but how long would that last? He knew he could easily outrun them. And even if they put the pedal to the metal in that dinosaur car of theirs, they could never steer it once it got off-road. Too many sinkholes. Poe could easily lose them in the mountains. Escape wasn't the problem.

Mom was. The nurse wasn't due back until nine tonight, and Emma was alone in his house. Poe was almost certain that they weren't aware of her. But what if he ran away, and the goons came back? What if they broke into the house to rummage through his things? What if they saw her? What if they decided to get nasty?

What if, what if.

He had left Emma taking a nap on the couch. He prayed she'd stay there, but he knew she was a light sleeper. Worse than that, she was curious. What if she heard voices and decided to have a look for herself? He didn't want her walking out in the middle of *High Noon*. Especially because Gary Cooper was without his six-shooter.

How to get them off the property ASAP?

Poe said, "I'm afraid you've come at an inconvenient time. I've got a busy schedule."

Blue came closer. "Sergeant, you left work an hour ago. Even if you plan to go back, it's only six. This shouldn't take too long."

Poe inched away. "No, I don't think so."

Red said, "Don't make problems for us, Sergeant."

Advancing on him like schoolyard bullies. Poe said, "Hate to be a nuisance, guys, but get the fuck off my property."

"Now you're gettin' nasty," Blue replied. "You could even say that you're provokin' us."

"The man knows polysyllabic words." Poe took two long strides away from the duo. "I'm impressed."

"You're backing away from us," Blue answered. "Are we makin' you nervous, Sergeant?"

"You clowns?" He chuckled. "Have you gentlemen looked at your guts lately? You two couldn't run fifty feet without keeling over. I suggest you leave before you melt!"

"Such a big mouth for a public servant," Red said. "Someone should report you." A beat. "Or at least teach you a lesson."

"You're leavin' us no choice, Sergeant," Blue said. "C'mon. You cooperate with us and I promise you'll be with a coonskin piece of ass before dinner."

Poe felt his entire body go rigid with anger. "Look, you assholes, maybe I can't get you right now. But you sure as hell can't get me, either.

Which means you *lose*, big-time. 'Cause on foot, you cocksuckers don't stand a chance in hell of catching me.''

Blue brought out his famous ally, a .44 Magnum.

"Brilliant," Poe sneered. "Shoot a cop. Fucking *brilliant*! I see that Parkerboy hires real brainwork."

Blue waved the gun at him. "Get in the car, faggot."

Poe spat back, "Shoot me first, asshole."

Blue fired at Poe's feet. "Next shot'll turn you into a girl. Now get in the car!"

A sharp, loud boom echoed as smoke belched from the desert floor. When the dust cleared, a stick woman was poking out of the doorframe.

Emma Oakley.

She was holding Poe's shotgun, pumping in a new shell with a pro's ease. She brought it up to her eye and pointed it at Blue Shirt. It probably weighed as much as she did. She said, "Ten seconds to clear out before I give two jackasses some permanent air-conditioning."

Blue and Red eyed each other. Mom pulled off another round, the pellets whizzing perilously close to Blue's cranium. "Five seconds just passed."

The Shirts backed up and opened the Lincoln's doors. Emma kept the gun on the car, hoping they wouldn't try anything funny like running them over or ramming the house.

Right before he closed the door, Red yelled out, "If I was you, pal, I'd keep an eye on your little darkie friend."

"Get out of here, you foul-mouthed louts!" Emma bent her trigger finger and ripped off another cartridge packed with both ball and buck. Although the load hit the ground, some of the pellets caught the Lincoln's rear passenger tire.

At that point, Blue Shirt peeled rubber. Emma watched them go, then lowered the gun. Her jaw was working furiously, chewing more gums than teeth.

Poe realized his hands were shaking. He stuck them into the waistband of his running shorts. "Good shot."

"Once you have it, you never lose it." Emma wiped her forehead. "Haven't felt *that* good in years." A beat. "I wish I could scare away the critters in my body like that."

Referring to her leukemia. Emma had been doing so well, Poe had almost forgotten she was sick. He said, "You must be scaring them to death, Mom, because you're doing great with the treatment." He walked over to Emma, relieved her of the shotgun, then kissed her cheek. "You saved my life."

"Ach!" She waved him off. "Just being a mother hen."

Slipping his arm around her, Poe escorted her back into the house. "I owe you."

"Nah, you don't owe me nothing." She paused. "Well, I suppose we could celebrate with a beer."

"How about a Virgin Mary instead?" Poe picked up his cellular and dialed Rukmani's number. While he waited for her to answer, he opened a can of tomato juice and added a strong dash of Tabasco.

Of course, the machine picked up. Poe started imploring the contraption, "Ruki, it's me. Pick up the phone. It's an emergency. Pick up the phone. Pick up the phone. Pick up the phone. It's an emergenc—" He disconnected in disgust and punched in her office number.

Emma sipped her spiced juice from the can. "You're worried about her?"

Poe tapped his foot as her office line rang and rang. "I'd like to hear her voice."

"They're blowing smoke, Romulus."

"Yeah. Smoke from a .44 Magnum." Again he cut the line. "Goddammit, where is she?"

"Maybe she's out for an evening stroll."

"Why do people always call when you don't want to talk? And they're never in when you *do* want to talk." This time, Poe called the morgue's general number. "Someone *please* answer!"

Finally someone did. An elderly male who sounded winded. Poe identified himself. "Can you please tell me if Dr. Rukmani Kalil is anywhere in the building? She doesn't seem to be answering her phone in her office."

"Rukmani Kalil?" the shaky voice repeated.

"Yes." Poe tried to keep the panic in check. "She's the Indian pathologist—"

"Oh yes, yes. Sure. She's a very nice lady."

"Yes, she is. I have an emergency and I have to speak with her immediately."

"Oh, so this is urgent?"

"Yes, it's very urgent!"

"Hold on then. I'll go take a look."

Poe heard the clop of the phone receiver being placed on a hard surface. He startled at the touch of his mother's hand. She patted his shoulder. Emma said, "I'm sure she's fine, Romulus."

"I'm sure you're right."

"Let's have a beer in the meantime—"

"No beer, Ma."

"*One* beer. It'll calm you down."

"As grateful as I feel, the answer is still no."

Emma clamped her lips together.

Five agonizingly slow minutes passed. Then the jostle of the phone being picked up. The elderly voice saying, "Hello?"

"Yes, I was asking about Dr. Kalil?"

"Yes, I know. She's not in—"

"Shit!"

"Pardon?"

"Nothing . . . nothing. Thank you." Poe disconnected the line and started snapping his fingers. Then he called Patricia. When she answered, he said, "I can't believe I got you in."

"What's up?"

"Two things. First, I just got shot at by two goons hired by Lewiston—"

"You're kidding!"

"Wish I were."

"Hiring men to shoot at a cop? Lewiston can't be that stupid."

"No, he's not. If questioned, he'll deny sending them over. Or at the very least, he'll say he sent them merely for my convenience and they acted on their own with the guns. The upshot is there are two maniacs out there driving a midnight-blue Lincoln Town Car with no plates. The only thing I could decipher was that the car came from Desert Rose Lincoln."

"I'll try to locate them right now."

"No, I've got another assignment for you. I need you at my house— ASAP. Before they left, one of them made threatening remarks about Rukmani. I've tried calling her, but she isn't at home and she isn't in her office. I want to look for her, but I need someone here to watch over my mother. Someone who's trained in case they come back—"

"I can take care of myself," Emma cried out.

"I can look for Dr. Kalil," Patricia said.

Poe said, "No, let me do it—"

"Do what?" Emma asked.

"Mom, I can't hold two conversations at once."

"I thought you were talking to me—"

"Sergeant?"

"Yeah, I'm here," Poe answered. "I'll look for Rukmani. I know some of her spots, but I don't know exact addresses. I'd like you here with Mom."

"I'll be there in ten minutes. What about the Lincoln?"

"I'll phone it in." Poe hung up and dialed Dispatch. After he fed them the information, he called up Marine Martin and brought him up to date.

"I'm on the lookout," Marine answered. "From which direction were they coming?"

"They left heading east. They're probably going back to the Lady Slipper, or maybe the Laredo. Frankly, I don't care where they are as long as they're not anywhere near my house or Dr. Kalil."

"I'll try to establish visual contact with the Lincoln, sir."

"Good." Poe waited a beat. "I heard you did a terrific job executing the warrant, Detective. Good going."

"Thank you, Sergeant. Over and out, Sergeant."

"Over and out." Poe clicked off, his mind on a thousand different things. He quickly dressed in a T-shirt, jeans, and boots, strapping his holster and gun around his waist. He started pacing. Moments later, he noticed Emma nursing her drink. He smiled at her and said, "How's the Virgin Mary?"

Emma finished the can and licked her lips. "Too spicy. It'll probably give me an upset stomach." A beat. "Rom, you're as nervous as a cat. Go out and look for her before it gets too dark. I'll be okay until what's-her-name comes."

"Detective Patricia Deluca." Poe bounced on his feet. "Are you sure?"

"Yes, I'm sure," Emma snapped. "I still have a couple of rounds left in that old thing." She nodded toward the shotgun. "I'll be just fine."

Still, Poe hesitated. "Be careful, Mom."

Emma wrinkled her nose. "Look who's talking."

FORTY-SIX

He raced the Honda, trying to guess Rukmani's moves. If she wasn't home and she wasn't at work, where would she be at six-thirty in the evening?

She could be doing her laundry, or shopping, or out getting some dinner.

Or out socializing.

When they spoke, she had given no indication that she had made dinner or date plans. But Rukmani could be spontaneous.

His first stop was the local Laundromat. The two of them usually went together about twice a week. A large whitewashed place with fifty industrial machines and a dozen dryers spinning rainbows of cloth-colored swirl art. At first glance, she wasn't there. Poe checked the faces hidden by newspapers, then checked the faces peering at the vending machines.

Not one of them was Rukmani.

He went next door to the storefront called the Coffee Hut—a hangout of the laundry people, a good place to pick up women. Lots of Gen-Xers with uncombed hair and two days' worth of beard growth. Girls with spiked hair and pierces. Rukmani wasn't among them.

Poe returned to the Honda and drove another two blocks. He pulled into the parking lot of Beeny Boy's Coffee Shop. A favorite spot for the homeless who wanted to fill their stomachs with grease, fat, and something hot. It had a selection of dinner specials, Poe's favorite being a starter of clam chowder followed by a pork chop smothered in mushroom gravy with a baked potato and sour cream and peas, all for just $2.99. Rukmani called it Heart Attack on a Plate.

Poe searched the counters, searched the worn and torn red Naugahyde booths. He even asked a customer to peek into the ladies' room. She came back, reporting that both stalls were empty. One of the regular waitresses—a thirties-plus brunette named Hallie—noticed Poe scurrying by. "Sergeant, have a seat."

Poe whipped around. "Hi, Hallie." A nervous smile. "By any chance has Dr. Kalil been in today?"

Hallie shook her head. "I haven't seen her."

"If she comes in for a bite, will you tell her to call me? It's important."

"Sure, right away," Hallie answered. "Is everything all right?"

"Could be better."

"Coffee to go?"

"Uh, no." Poe waited. "Maybe I'll be back in an hour or so."

"I'll save you one of my tables."

Poe smiled. Hallie liked cops. They were big tippers. He left and jumped into the Honda, racing off to a second coffee shop. Again he came up dry. Then his phone rang.

Please be Rukmani.

It wasn't.

"I made it alive." Patricia paused. "Barely."

"What?" Poe was filled with concern. "Are you okay?"

Patricia whispered, "Maybe you can persuade your mom to give me the shotgun."

"Oh Christ! What happened?"

"Nothing. Which was very good. She just pointed the thing at me—"

"God, I'm sorry!"

"I scared her. Not that I blame her, but . . ."

"Put her on the phone."

Poe heard Deluca say, "He wants to talk to you." Then he heard his mother's protests. But she came on the line anyway. "What is it?"

"You pointed the shotgun at Detective Deluca?"

"I thought it was them returning."

"Mom, you did a great job. Now please give her the gun."

"Rom—"

363

"Mom, you have a professional watching you. Please don't argue. Just give her the gun."

Emma sulked, "You weren't yellin' at me an hour ago when I chased away those louses."

"Mom, you were *terrific*. Now just relax and let Detective Deluca take over. *Please!*"

Emma didn't answer.

"Mom—"

"I heard you, I heard you." A pause. "Well, all right."

"Thank you, Mom. We'll talk later. Now could you hand the phone back to Patricia?"

Emma grumbled. Then Patricia came back on the line. "Thank you, Sergeant."

"Is my mother doing all right?"

"She's squirrelly, to say the least."

"Patricia, please be careful. The goons could be coming back. You have the shotgun. Use it if you have to."

"I'll keep my eyes open."

"The nurse is due back soon. Still, I'd appreciate it if you'd stay put until I get back."

"Absolutely. Did you find Dr. Kalil?"

"Not yet. I'm going to check her apartment."

"Good luck."

"Thanks."

Five minutes later, Poe was opening Rukmani's front door. Everything seemed in order. Nothing was overturned or out of place. The bed was neatly made, no dishes in the sink. But as his professional eye digested his surroundings, Poe felt nervous. The muscle under his eye began to spasm.

A full pot of fresh coffee sitting on the warmer of her coffeemaker.

Some kind of curried potato casserole warming in the oven.

The evening paper had been unfolded and was resting on the dining-room table.

The curtains had been drawn for privacy.

The air conditioner was on.

Poe's heart sank. The place seemed as if she had stepped out and was planning to come back. Where the *hell* was she?

Don't panic, don't panic.

Emma's words: *Maybe she's out for an evening stroll.*

Made sense. It was a beautiful evening.

Back in the car, he began to cruise the side streets.

Up and down, down and up.

Nothing but empty cement and rows of still-life apartment buildings looking gray in the twilight.

Come on, come on. Be *here! Show your face.*

Those bastards, Poe cursed mentally. *Those son-of-a-bitch assholes. That motherfucking Lewiston. If anything happened to her, if* anything *happened to her . . .*

One pass around the block.

Lewiston was dead-ass roadkill as far as Poe was concerned. That son of a bitch had bullied and pushed his weight around for too long. His days on this planet were numbered. The bust last night . . . it had been a good one. Handfuls of grass. Now all they had to do was match it up. Unusual grass with unusual grass. And if Honey pulled through, they'd have an eyewitness to the murder as well as her verbal confession. Even without Honey, he still had it all down on tape. And he had Lamar Larue to link Yarlborough to Honey.

It all hinged on that grass—if the grass scrapings under Yarlborough's nails matched the grass in Lewiston's office. Ruki had sent the samples to the lab this morning.

Ruki, where the hell are you?

His head pounded like bongo drums. He wondered where she could be as he made a third pass around the block.

Please, let her show up.

Let her show up!

He just wanted to see her face, wanted to hear her voice and touch her soft skin—

Abruptly, he caught sight of flowing fabric as a figure turned the corner.

Thank you, thank you, thank you!

As Rukmani came into focus, she had never looked so beautiful. So beautiful and so wonderfully *alive*!

He blinked wet eyes, then suddenly froze.

A hidden presence . . . eyes on the back of his neck. He jerked his head around, but saw nothing.

Nothing.

But he couldn't shake the ominous feeling.

Damn you, Lewiston!

She was wearing a traditional kiwi-green Indian sari embellished with thread. Her hair was damp and loose—she must have just washed it—and it swayed as she walked. She was holding two shopping bags. Poe pulled the Honda to the curb and leaped out of the car. She jumped back in fright, almost losing her groceries.

She glared at him. "You *scared* me, Romulus!"

Poe took her bags and placed them in the Honda's backseat. Rukmani said, "You're upset. What's wrong?"

"Nothing." Poe leaned against the car, suddenly feeling light-headed. "Everything's fine."

He slipped into the driver's seat. Rukmani came around to the passenger's side, got in, and shut the door. "What is it?"

He looped his hand behind her neck and gave her a long, hard kiss. Suddenly he broke, whipping his head around. That dreadful being-watched feeling. "Where *were* you?"

She stared at him with concern. "Just went out to do a little shopping. Want to join me for dinner?"

"Anyone follow you?"

Her eyes narrowed. "Romulus, what is going on?"

"Did anyone follow you?"

"Look around. Does it look like anyone followed me?"

Poe took the opportunity to sweep his eyes over his surroundings. Staring out of the windshield, desperately trying to see signs of life. But the area was colorless and deserted. He craned his neck upward. Nothing except a lone hawk circling right above them. A magnificent bird, one he rarely saw in the burbs. Birds of prey, when they came this far south, did their hunting in the desert, where there were snakes, rats, rabbits, and lizards.

He buried his head in his palms, then yanked his head up. "What was that? I heard something."

Rukmani shrugged. "What'd you hear?"

"Like a thump . . . or a pop." He rubbed his head. "More like a pop . . . like a gun going off . . . kind of." Again he eyed the bird. "Maybe it was coming from Sky King up there."

"Romulus, you've been working too hard."

"No, I'm fine." Again he kissed her. "I'm great!"

Rukmani smiled at him in a tutorial sort of way. "Let's examine the evidence. You parachuted out of your car to relieve me of two bags of groceries. You've been kissing me like you haven't had sex in a while. When in fact I know from personal experience that you have."

"No argument there."

"You keep asking me if someone is following me." She grinned. "You thought something bad had happened to me. And now you're very glad to see me."

"I'm very happy to see you."

She pointed to her chest. "Are you going to clue me in?"

Poe related the events of an hour ago.

Rukmani said, "God, that's awful." A beat. "Good for Mom."

"Speaking of which, I have to go . . ." He glanced over his shoulder. "I swear someone is *watching* us."

"No one's here, Romulus."

Again, Poe looked out the window. Empty. Nothing caught his eye. Even the hawk was gone. He sighed. His brain was quickly transforming from creative imagery to paranoid hallucinations. "I just feel this *presence*—"

"In view of what you just told me, it's a normal feeling. It's just not accurate." She took his hands and kissed them. "I'm safe, and so are you."

Poe rubbed his forehead. "Maybe I'm going nuts."

"Maybe you need some nourishment." Rukmani smiled. "If you indeed broke into my place—"

"I didn't break in. I had a key."

"—you would have seen a fresh pot brewing and *gobhi matar rasedar* in the oven—"

"I wasn't thinking of *that* kind of nourishment."

"One type of nourishment is *not* exclusive of the other."

Poe smiled wistfully. "I left Patricia with Mom duty. I told her to stick around until I got there. And the nurse isn't due for another hour."

Rukmani didn't say anything.

With a shrug, Poe picked up his cellular and called home. "Hey, Patricia."

"Have you found Dr. Kalil?"

"Yes."

"I could hear it in your voice. When are you coming back?"

Poe said, "Patricia, if you don't mind, I was thinking of running over to the Bureau and looking over last night's haul from the Laredo. I wanted to go over a few details with Dr. Kalil about the . . ." *Shut up, Poe. Cellular lines aren't restricted.* "Well, all sorts of stuff."

A few details, Patricia thought. *Like bedroom details.*

Poe added, "If you have other plans, I can work with Dr. Kalil later."

"It's no problem, sir."

"Thank you, Detective." Poe paused. "Look, Patricia, I don't think they're coming back, but . . . just watch your *derrière*." A pause. "I keep feeling that someone is watching me. So just be extra careful."

"Being shot at will do that to you, sir. Besides, I have Emma Poe for backup."

"She's telling the truth," Poe said. "She saved my ass."

"What else are mothers for?"

Poe laughed. "I'll see you in a bit."

Patricia hung up her phone and stowed it in her pocket. Emma said, "He isn't coming back, is he?"

Such disappointment in her voice. The woman saved the guy's life and all he could think about was his groin.

Patricia put on a brave smile. "Actually, he wants to go over some crucial evidence with Dr. Kalil—"

"Goin' over crucial evidence?" Emma snorted. "Is that what they're calling hanky-panky nowadays?"

Patricia stumbled over some words, then just threw up her hands.

Emma said, "That's okay. A mother's love is forever." She paused. "I don't know why that is, but it's true. How 'bout if I fix us some chow?"

"Sure." Patricia patted her belly. "I love to eat."

Slowly, Emma inched her way over to Patricia. She stopped in front of her, and with bony fingers, the old woman stroked Deluca's face. "I would have loved to have a daughter like you."

Patricia was stunned. "Thank you."

"You be proud of what you are . . . *who* you are."

"Thank you, I . . . I actually am proud . . . of myself."

"Good." Slowly, Emma trudged over to Poe's tiny pouch of a kitchen. She lit a kerosene lamp and started warming the hot plate. "It's much milder now. Why don't you go take a walk. Be back in twenty minutes. You won't believe what I can do once I get a fire going."

"After hearing about this morning, Mrs. Poe, I think I'd believe anything about you."

Emma smiled. "Go."

Patricia chuckled as she stepped out of Poe's pod. Walking a few paces, she tried to clear her head. So much to think about: Alison on the loose,

Steve recuperating, Gretchen in the morgue, Honey in the hospital, Lewiston sending goons after Poe . . . threatening both Rukmani and him. It was she who had found the information that linked Yarlborough to Lewiston. Was she next in line for an ominous phone call?

Then there was Nate. Was their relationship moving too fast?

Don't think about anything, Patty. Just enjoy the fresh air.

Fresh, hot air.

She wiped her brow, realizing she must have been walking faster than she thought. Poe's house was now about half its size. The sun had baked the sand all day, and now the heat was rising up through the desert floor. She could feel warmth up through her shoes. In half an hour or so, the place would be magnificent—quiet and dark and warm and peaceful.

She turned her eyes upward to the darkening sky. The stars were beginning to come out, and the moon was magnified as it stepped out from the horizon. No civilization impeded. Only a hawk circling overhead. A big mother thing; beautiful in its athletic prowess, with a massive wingspread that looked to be over six feet. Suddenly, the bird dipped as if it sensed Patricia's vibrations, almost as if Deluca's presence were an intrusion on its privacy.

Dipping, then soaring upward in a perfect arc. It caught the wind and glided through the air. The big birds usually hunted at this time of the evening. There was still enough visibility to see, and their prey usually came up for air after sleeping through the hot day.

It circled lower down this time. Patricia could see how truly *big* it was. More than big. The bird was *enormous.* She could discern the creature's talons, feel the wind as it flapped its wings and hovered overhead. So large it loomed like a caped vampire silhouetted against the moon.

Without warning, the bird once again dipped. As it pulled back up, Patricia could see a trapped desert rat squirming in its beak. Swallowing its prey in midair, the bird shot back upward and started circling anew. One big gulp and the rat was history. All within a matter of moments.

Patricia was mesmerized. It was as if the hawk were showing off for her, displaying its awesome aviation skills, its fearsome talent as a hunter.

Now the bird was directly overhead. For a moment, Patricia felt paralyzed, helpless and small against nature's hunters. But then again, she was human. What could a bird . . . even a big, big bird . . . possibly do to her?

Still, a cloud of inexplicable dread passed through her body.

Then the bird swooped down.

FORTY-SEVEN

Just as Poe slipped into that blissful state of tingle, glow, and slumber, his cellular rang. Too exhausted to move, he murmured, "S'probably a wrong number."

Rukmani reached over his half-dead body to the nightstand. "Sergeant Poe's phone. This is Dr. Kalil."

"It's Emma."

Rukmani sat up, pulled the covers over her lap. "Emma, are you all right?"

His mother's name caught Poe's attention. He grabbed the phone and tucked it under his chin as he put on his pants. "What's going on? Are you okay?"

"Patricia's gone."

The adrenals started squirting. A millifraction later, the heart began hammering. Poe said, "What do you mean, she's gone? Where'd she *go*?"

"I don't know. I sent her out for a little stroll while I fixed us some dinner. When I went outside to call her back in, she didn't answer. I called and called. Then I noticed that her car was gone."

"Mom, stay in the house—"

"Is your mom okay?" Rukmani asked.

Poe nodded yes. "Deluca's gone." To his mother, he said, "I'm sending out a cruiser. They'll reach you faster than I—"

"Are you coming down?"

"Of course." He slipped on his T-shirt and asked Rukmani to call 911. "Tell them to send a black-and-white out to the house with full sirens and lights. Do you need exact directions?"

"I know the route."

"Also, call up Dispatch. Ask them if they've sent Deluca out on an emergency. It's an improbable long shot, but just in case. I don't want to look like an idiot." On the line, Poe said, "Mom, where's the shotgun you used on those jokers?"

"I got it right here."

"You know where I keep the buckshot?"

"Yep."

"Good. Just don't shoot the police when they knock at the door. Next question. Think carefully. When Detective Deluca left for her walk, did she have her purse with her?"

"I'm not . . ." A beat. "She left me her phone. That's what I'm callin' you on. Lemme look around for the purse. Right now I don't see it."

"Look for it, Mom. I'll wait."

Rukmani had donned a pair of scrubs. "A cruiser's on its way."

Poe said. "While you've got Dispatch on the line, tell them to patch you through to Lieutenant Michael Weinberg. Explain that it's an emergency—"

"I can't find her purse, Romulus," Emma said. "Come to think of it, I think she did leave with it."

Poe was somewhat relieved. If she had her purse, she had her gun. "Mom, did you see anything strange? *Hear* anything?"

"I had the radio on, Romulus. It wasn't blasting, but I wasn't paying much attention. I'm sorry—"

"Don't be sorry, you didn't do anything. I'm leaving right now. Be there in around ten minutes if I speed."

"Don't speed. It's not worth you crackin' up your head. Besides, in a true emergency, buckshot travels faster than you ever could."

Poe jerked the wheel to the right, swerving to avoid a head-on. The car screeched, but remained on all four tires.

Rukmani said, "Maybe I should drive—"

"I could have gone straight home. But *noooo*, I have to fuck around when my own mother is in danger—"

"You didn't do anything wrong—"

"I should have gone straight home after I found you!" Poe whipped himself. "If anything happened to Patricia—"

"Poe, she's a cop, same as you." Rukmani kneaded her hands. "She had her purse, she had her gun, and she certainly knew what was going on. You told her everything in detail. If something . . . bad happened to her, I'm sure it was unavoidable."

"I know the area better than she does. And I'm a faster runner—"

"You can't outrun a bullet."

Overhead, they heard the machine-gun clacking of a police helicopter heading toward the western end of the mountain ring. Poe's turf. Mick had ordered the full artillery.

Patty drove a maroon Saturn. Whoever was at the wheel couldn't take the car off-road because it could never make it through the numerous desert sinkholes—the wasteland's own natural field mines. Which meant that if her car was in motion, it had to be on a road either heading back toward town—so far they hadn't passed any maroon cars—or tooling along the vast open space of Nevada's desert. In either scenario, it could be spotted, even at night, in the bright searchlights.

If the driver was using the main roads. Trouble was there were scores of tiny mountain back roads. They weren't *good* roads—unpaved and often rutted—but they were great escape routes for the experienced native.

Rukmani said, "Romulus, why would Lewiston kidnap a cop, leaving himself open like that? It makes no sense."

"It makes about as much sense as his sending out goons to hunt *me* down."

"True." Rukmani sat cross-legged in the seat beside him. She placed her hands on her knees, took in a deep breath, then let it out slowly. Yoga breathing. She must really be nervous. Which made Poe even more nervous.

"Could you light me a cigarette?" he asked her. "I've got a pack in the glove compartment."

She exhaled and opened her eyes. "Sure." She lit up a smoke and stuck it in his mouth.

Poe inhaled, then placed the tobacco between his fingers. "My mother said Deluca's car was gone. But she didn't make mention of another parked car. If they forced Patricia to drive her own car, and there's no other car out there, where'd the kidnappers come from?"

Rukmani pulled out Poe's cellular and dialed for him. He took another drag on his cigarette and stubbed it out. Emma picked up the line. ''No one's here yet, but I hear a siren—''

''Mom, is there another car out there?''

''What?''

''If someone kidnapped Detective Deluca and took *her* car, they had to get to the house somehow. Is there another car parked outside the house?''

Emma said, ''No other car, Rom. But I do hear the police coming down.''

''Just don't shoot anyone, Ma. I'll call you back.''

Rukmani said, ''No other car?''

''No,'' Poe said. ''Either they were lying in wait—which doesn't make sense, because the terrain is flat and there's nowhere to hide—or someone dropped the goons off, or there were two men in one car, and one of them kidnapped Patricia along with her Saturn.''

Rukmani shrugged. ''If this was Lewiston's doing, he didn't plan too carefully. I thought he was a smart man.''

''You know what Lewiston is? He's a very *arrogant* man. He got away with murder twenty-five years ago—''

''What was this?''

''Linda Hennick,'' Poe said. ''Y's convinced that he killed her, and paid everyone off to cover it up.'' He waited a beat. ''I will say that kidnapping a detective isn't a slick move. The guy must think he can get away with anything. His guys did shoot at me.''

''Yes, that was *really* stupid.''

''Lewiston thinks that ordinary laws don't apply to him. And with good reason. No one wants to tangle with a billionaire who brings beaucoup bucks to the city's coffers. Especially the city attorney's office, since Lewiston has money to keep an expensive slander suit alive for years. Not that he's untouchable. We did get a search warrant—''

''That was pretty nifty.''

''Mick Weinberg can pull strings.'' Poe drummed the wheel. ''It's the Wild West out here. The local law challenges Lewiston's authority, and now he's demanding a showdown.''

Another police helicopter whizzed past, heading toward his house, its searchlight streaking across the ground like a shooting star.

Rukmani said, ''Why does Y think Lewiston murdered Hennick?''

"I don't know. He did tell me they were lovers."

"Who? Y and Linda?"

"I meant Linda and Lewiston, but Y and Linda were lovers as well. According to Y, Linda dumped him for Lewiston. Then Lewiston proceeded to dump her. The police report said Linda checked into the hotel alone and committed suicide. But if she did, it wasn't an ordinary suicide. The woman had gone after herself like a crazed maniac."

"She was mentally off, Rom. I've known patients who have flayed themselves to death."

"Well, she didn't do that, but her face and belly had cuts all over them. She also had a couple of black eyes, indicating she had been beaten up. Now Y sees conspiracy in everything, but in this case, I give the story points."

"It does sound violent for a suicide."

In the distance, Poe saw the strobic flash of blue lights. The cops had made it and Mom was safe. From out of the windows of the house came jaundiced light, courtesy of kerosene lamps and candles. Circling copters roared overhead as spotlights swept over night-covered, dusty roads. Sensitive to loud noise after working a decade in dead silence, Rukmani held her ears.

She said, "Why are they looking so close to your house? They should be searching the mountain roads."

"You're right." Poe pulled up next to the two cruisers. The night nurse's car was also there. He got out and turned on a high-powered flashlight, arcing the beam across the dirt as if sweeping for mines.

"What are you looking for?" Rukmani asked.

"Tire tracks." Poe used the beam as a pointer. "These impressions belong to the cruisers. See, they stop right where they parked. These over here obviously belong to the nurse's car."

"Those are from your Honda," Rukmani said.

"Yeah, those are mine."

Poe shined the beam on still another set of indentations. "These go from the road to here. . . . They're partially obliterated because one of the cruisers pulled up over them. But you can still see how they circle around back to the road. I think these were made by Patty's Saturn. I'll want a plaster impression of these."

Slowly, he walked to the road and back, then circled the house inch by inch, shining the light on the hard, packed sand. Lots of pebbles, desiccated plant matter, rat and snake burrows, and a few stray feathers, but no tire tracks or human footprints other than his own.

"I know it's dark, but I don't see any tire prints from a strange car." He regarded Rukmani. "So how'd the kidnappers *get* here?"

Emma came out to greet her son. Poe was about to respond when the two uniforms and the nurse emerged from the house.

Showing his badge, Poe said, "Thanks for coming out. I can take it from here. When you pull out, I want you to stay clear of this area." He indicated the spot. "I want to get an impression of these tire prints, so try to avoid kicking up dust when you leave."

"Will do." The officers climbed into their respective police cars and spun out as little dust as possible. Once they hit the road, they sped off. The nurse stood in place. She was in her late twenties, part Hispanic, part Native American. She had a broad brown face and wide dark eyes. Her name was Anya. She said, "Am I in any danger?"

Rukmani broke in before Poe could. "Why don't you and Emma camp out at my place for the evening."

"Fine with me." Anya looked pointedly at Poe. "Her apartment's got *air*-conditioning."

Emma pouted. "What about Remus? He's coming in tonight."

"Tonight? As in *now*?"

Emma looked sheepish.

"What? Mom, did you call him?"

"Yes, Romulus, I did. I asked him to take me home. I'll take my treatment up there. Too much going on down here." She looked down. "Besides, I miss Aunt Shirley."

Meaning: I miss the booze she gives me on the sly.

Another helicopter roared overhead.

Patricia, where are you? Absently, Poe said, "When is Remus coming in?"

"Eleven o'clock. He'll stay for the night, then I'm going back to Reno with him tomorrow morning."

"Ma, we'll talk about this later. I've got a missing detective."

She kissed her son's cheek. "There's nothing to talk about. I'm going." Emma held Rukmani's hands. "You're a louse, Romulus, but you picked a good woman. I musta done something right. I'm going in to pack."

Anya remained rooted to her spot. Rukmani said, "Maybe you could help her?"

"Why not?" Anya snarled. "I need my dose of daily insults." She stomped back into his pod.

Poe took out his portable phone. First he rang up the crime lab office, asking the techs to bring out the material needed for casting plaster impressions. Then he contacted dispatch and asked to talk to the helicopter pilots. Once he got through, he told them to search the back roads in the mountains. The last call went to Lieutenant Weinberg. He brought Mick up to date.

After he hung up, he said to Rukmani, "The loo's called an APB on the Saturn with the highway patrol as well as the local law in the bordering Nevada counties. So far no one's spotted anything. I bet they're taking back roads and driving with the lights off." He exhaled, looking up into a full-moon sky. "Weinberg and the captain went over to the Laredo *personally*. Guess who had to leave on an emergency trip . . . in his private jet?"

Rukmani clasped her hands. "I'm sorry, Rom."

"Honey's blown up, goons are taking potshots at me, and Patricia's gone. How convenient for him to be out of town." Poe shook his head. "At least you're okay, thank God." Again, he shined the light on the ground. "How did those suckers get to Patricia?"

"She was taking a walk, Romulus. Maybe they found her up the road. The car dropped off a couple of guys, then it sped off. Then the thugs forced her at gunpoint back to her own car and they all drove away."

"Deluca wouldn't have let them get that close. She had her gun—she would have opened fire."

"Well, maybe she did. Maybe there was a shoot-'em-up."

"Sound carries out here. I think my mother would have heard gunfire, even with the radio on." Thoughts flitted through Poe's brain. "Why would Patricia, knowing that I was shot at, take a long hike away from the house? I must be missing something crucial."

Neither spoke. Rukmani followed Poe as he took another trip around the house.

"Offhand, I don't see any big bloodstains. There could be drips I can't see in the dark. But definitely no bloodbath."

Poe took out his pad and started to jot down notes.

"So this is what we know. Patricia and her car are missing. It appears that Patty had her purse and gun. So if she was attacked, someone sneaked up on her like a ghost. But sound travels out here, and there's no place to hide because this terrain is as flat as a tortilla. So how did someone sneak up on her without making noise and without being seen?''

Poe waited for an answer. When it didn't come, he said, ''What'd they do? Drop from the sky?'' Again, he regarded the ground, hoping it would come forth with a clue.

Rukmani said, ''Emma said that Patricia went out for an evening stroll, right?''

''Correct.''

''I know the ground is hard, Rom, but maybe she left some footprints.''

Duh! Poe smiled. ''Good point, Doctor.'' He stepped away from the house, moving the flashlight over the packed sand, hoping to pick up a trail. The full moon was higher in the sky, adding extra illumination. But basically it was Poe and his rods, everything sketched in blacks, whites, and grays. Peering carefully, seeing nothing, but giving himself a monster headache.

The seconds passed, then minutes went by.

''Here!'' Poe shone the beam on a tiny impression of swirled sand. ''See this? Could be the heelprint of an athletic shoe.'' He studied the immediate area. ''Okay, here's another. I think we've got a trail.''

Rukmani squinted at the dent in the ground. ''Guess you've got to know what to look for.''

Poe said, ''We're lucky. Winds haven't kicked up yet.''

Methodically, they followed the tiny blips in the sand. The impressions stopped around a hundred yards from the house. Where they ended there was a shallow crater around six feet in diameter, looking almost like a snow angel.

''She must have fallen here,'' Poe said. ''Either fell or was knocked down.'' He moved the light around the area. ''I don't see any other prints. No tire tracks, no footprints. So what am I missing?''

''You're asking me?'' Rukmani answered.

''What'd she do? Fall into the earth?'' He stared at the crater, his mind fogged in confusion. ''If someone took Patricia at gunpoint back to the car, we'd see another set of footprints. Did I miss a set of footprints?''

''Not that I can tell.''

''So what's going on? We've got Twinkle Toes for a kidnapper?'' Poe bent down and examined the indentation in the sand. He pushed his fist into its center, expecting to hit rock. Instead, his hand sliced through a pit of sand.

"Did she hit a sinkhole?"

He began to dig furiously, scooping sand out of the crater, only to be frustrated by sand filling the hole as fast as he could remove it. Rukmani bent down and dug as well. Impatient and sickened, he stuck his hand and arm down into the ground, burrowing through the grains as far as he could go. Past his elbow, halfway up his biceps, he hit compact dirt.

"It's about two and a half feet deep."

"How wide?" Rukmani asked.

Carefully Poe moved his arm around the sinkhole. "I'd say about two feet in diameter. I sure as heck don't feel a body under there."

"Do you feel anything other than sand?"

"Yeah, there some junk—"

"Be careful of snakes."

"Yeah, you're right. It could be an animal's den." He brought his hand out, bringing up a fistful of feathers. Poe spread them on the ground.

Beautifully marked long tail feathers. The kind used in Indian head-dresses. From a big bird. Like an eagle or a hawk—

Poe blanched.

"What is it?" Rukmani asked.

He had turned speechless. The image—that massive *hawk* circling above when he was with Rukmani in the car. Squawking at him. As if it wanted to intrude upon his privacy.

Absurd thoughts raced through his brain.

Lashing out at him like some kind of animal. Lashing out at Steve in the same way. Eating Gretchen's raw flesh while costumed like a wolf.

Was it a costume?

The red, pitying eyes of the coyote.

The fierceness of that snake's bite.

The man with the ponytail who repeatedly outran him.

It was too weird to contemplate. Yet, he did.

"Romulus, you're white!" Rukmani said. "What is it?"

"It isn't Lewiston." Poe started to pace. "It isn't Lewiston at all. It's *Alison*! Steve Jensen owns a four-wheel-drive—an Explorer." He spoke quickly and animatedly as he walked in circles. "Somehow, Alison managed to kidnap Patricia in her own car."

"How could she do that?"

"Same way she got Steve in the trunk of his car," he said, speed-talking. "Alison carries Patty back to the Saturn, drives her off to a hidden spot, then switches to a four-wheeler. Once she's in an off-roader, she can go anywhere . . . do anything . . .''

"How'd she get Patricia back to the car without leaving footprints?"

"Metempsychosis!" Poe's eyes were wild. "She *flew* back."

"*Excuse* me?"

He grabbed Rukmani's shoulder. "Don't you see? She *shape-shifted.* She was that hawk that we saw—"

"Rom—"

"She flew Patricia back to her car, carrying her in her talons. Which explains why she used the car. She couldn't carry Patricia a long distance. Too much weight. So she shape-shifted back into Alison or some other human form and kidnapped Patricia in her own car."

Rukmani stared at him. "Rom, I don't know *what* you're talking about!"

"I'm right about this." Poe clutched her shoulders, digging his fingers into her skin just below the point of pain. "I know it sounds insane, but I'm right!" Breathing hard, his clothes drenched in sweat. "It's just like Steve said. She's out to destroy anything she perceives as dear to me. And somehow she's got this magical power to do it. Shape-shifting just like in your legends—"

"Rom, they were *legends*! Which meant they're not *real*—"

"But what if it *is* real? All the radiation fallout from the atmospheric shots. I mean, radiation . . . especially huge concentrations of radiation . . . it can work havoc on the cells."

"Yes, it renders them useless."

"Not in Alison's case! In her case, it gave her some kind of unimaginable ability to change form." He let go of Rukmani and looked up at the sky as he bounced on his feet. "And that's why the legends always came with a full moon. I mean, just look at what a full moon does. It controls the ocean waves."

"Rom, that's gravity-related, not radiation."

But Poe wasn't listening. "You take massive fallout from an atomic bomb and couple it with radiation from a full moon, who knows what you could produce?"

Again, all Rukmani could do was stare at him. Talking as if he were having a full-blown manic episode.

Still pacing. He said, "We don't have a clue as to what all this atmospheric radiation did to us. Not a clue. The Department of Energy has never been honest with the bomb's long-term effects. They've got thousands of pages of classified documents that we can't even touch."

"I agree with you," Rukmani said calmly. "We haven't been told the full story—"

"I mean, look at all this cloning shit," Poe exclaimed. "Big mammals being duplicated in test tubes. So what's the next logical step . . . shape-shifting, right? Turning the cells not just from one mammal to another, but turning them between species. Maybe all those legends weren't . . . legends. Maybe it wasn't lycanthropy at all. Maybe they knew something we didn't."

Again, he grabbed her shoulders.

"I've got to find her, Ruki. I've got to find her, and fast! Before she destroys Patricia!"

Rukmani looked at Poe with intense concern. He was uncontrollably agitated, sweating and ticcing and shaking. Rukmani had seen that look before, the same set of neurological impaired behaviors in mentally disturbed patients right before they took their Thorazine. How could Rom be so logical one moment, searching out footprints with a cold, rational eye, then speak such lunacy?

The scope and breadth of human behavior.

Remain calm.

She said, "Romulus, I'm not debating you. What you're saying . . . makes sense—"

"In a crazy way, it does, doesn't it?"

"But if Alison's out for you, we should leave the search to someone who's not personally involved—"

"No, no, no, no, no." Poe backed away, spasming as he talked. "I've got to face her. I'm *part* of it. It's what made me what I am, made Alison what she is." He headed back toward his car. "We're all victims, don't you see?"

"Rom—"

"You take my mother and Anya back to your apartment and lock the doors!" He broke into a jog. "I'm off to see the wizard. I'll call you from the car."

Rukmani had to run to keep up with him. "Romulus, where are you going? Please talk to me—"

"No time—"

She pulled at his shirtsleeve, but he shook her off. "Romulus, please! You're scaring me!"

He jerked open the car door.

"Poe, you're in no shape to drive. You're going to have an accident!"

"Call backup for me." Poe revved the engine. He rolled down the window. "Take care of yourself, Rukmani. I love you."

Had the words registered in Rukmani's mind, she would have been even more frantic. Instead, she cried out, "At least tell me where you're going!"

"Where it all started!" he shouted as he peeled rubber. "Nevada Test Site!"

FORTY-EIGHT

)) *I want you to know that it's not personal.*
    Had Patricia been able to talk, she would have told Alison:
Fuck you, you crazy bitch. Instead, she lay mute on the floor of the
maniac's four-wheel-drive, secured with a rope to the back bench. Her
hands and feet were tightly bound, her mouth had been taped shut. The
bitch had provided a pillow for her head and had left her eyes alone. As
Patricia tried to get comfortable—her fists were digging into her spine—
she appraised the situation in stark terror. After the hopelessness subsided,
she started to think. How to get out of this mess?

How had she gotten *into* this mess?

She still wasn't sure. Last thing she remembered was being knocked
down by the mammoth-sized bird—a strange avian creature with a half-
human face. She hadn't had time to examine the oddity with scientific
coldness, because she had lost consciousness. When she came to, she had
already been in this horrid fix—restrained and helpless. Alison had used
plastic ties instead of rope, making it virtually impossible to break free.
She was emitting a constant stream of babble—a crazed woman who
seemed to possess enormous strength and endless chatter.

"It was never personal," Alison prattled. "Not with any of them. They
were just a way of getting attention. You know how that works, don't
you?"

As if Patricia could answer her. The lack of response didn't stop her psychotic twaddle.

"No, never personal, never personal . . . well, maybe with *Steve* it was a little personal. I mean, how could it not be with those floozies he'd been seeing. Not that I blame him *completely*. I haven't been hot in the sack for a long time. I mean, I could be hot in the sack, but not with Steve, no, not with Steve. Never with Steve. And not with the kids around. You know how kids are. They come in at all the darnedest time— whoops!"

The four-wheeler bounced over a rock and landed on its tires with a thud and thump.

Alison giggled. "Must be hard on the butt, huh? I'll try to be more careful. I owe you a nice ride. Not too good on my spine, either. You know who's fault it really is? It's Rom's fault. You're just a way to get to him. If he had been more observant, none of this would've happened. You guys call yourselves policemen, but you're awfully slow. A man's mistress is sliced and dumped in the desert and no one even questions the wife. That's a little dense, don't you think?"

Yes, Patricia thought. *It was very dense.*

"Totally Rom's doing. He didn't want to get Stevie in trouble for my sake. He has a blind spot when it comes to me. He still loves me . . . still loves me very much."

A breath.

"Even if he doesn't realize it. I realize it. He's trying to fight it. Whoops . . . hold on!"

Again, she giggled as the car flew into space and landed on the dusty ground with a jolt. Alison lessened the pressure on the accelerator, dropping the speed to around sixty.

"Someone should pave the desert, get rid of all the sinkholes. Just mop the whole thing up with asphalt. Make it one big parking lot—with transportation into the hotels, of course. It'd sure save the city on a mound of traffic. Good idea, huh? I'm surprised that some rich, greedy contractor hasn't bid for the job. Paving the desert. Well, that would be interesting, huh?"

She paused for another inhalation of air.

"Well, I think it would be interesting. Pave the whole state of Nevada. Nevada as one big blacktop. One big circus. Because really that's what it is. The circus of a lifetime, starting with the silver rush, then the gambling. I mean, even the bombs were one big circus. That's what they were, all for show. I mean, what? We explode something like a *thousand* bombs into our atmosphere after exploding only *two* bombs in enemy territory. Now you tell me, who came out better, huh?''

Neglecting to mention that the bombs exploded in Japan had fallen on civilian populations. Why let logic enter into paranoia? If she would only shut the fuck up, then maybe Patricia could *think*. She tried to raise her head. A feather tickled her nose. Resting on the backseat was an oversized Indian headdress, along with a hairy gorilla mask and a brown derby just like the one Big Ray had described on the hatted man.

No one even questions the wife!

Alison must have noticed her looking at the paraphernalia, because she started talking again.

''You like my feather hat . . . the bird bit? I thought it was clever. I can do all sorts of clever things. By now, you must have figured out that I've got this power . . . this unbelievable power given to me courtesy of Uncle Sam. Because Uncle Sam poisoned the well. You know what I'm talking about, don't you?''

A pause.

''*Radiation,* Patricia. Radiation with a capital R. I mean, you guys— meaning the American People—you don't know the half of it. Or the third of it, or the quarter of it. Or even a teaspoon of it. It's like measuring cups. Uncle Sam gives you a quarter cup of sugar here, a teaspoon of vanilla there. But he never bakes you the whole cake. So you never put the entire puzzle together. Just like Rom. He thinks the stuff he found in my house was the whole picture.''

A snort.

''Like I'd show him the whole picture. Let him figure it out for himself, that's what I say!''

Shut up!

''I left him with just enough to get a scent. A hint. Gotta play fair, gotta play fair, that's what I say. But I don't think he's figured it out yet. I mean, he's figured out *some* of it—''

Think, Patricia. Think!

''. . . have faith in Rom. Eventually he'll get it. Unfortunately, not soon enough for you. The poor boy is dim-witted sometimes. You should have seen him in high school, twitching like a flea on a griddle. But it never, ever dawned on him *why* he was twitching. I mean, wouldn't you be curious why you twitched when no one else was twitching?''

Again, Alison paused for air. If Patricia could just get the ties off. Or even get the tape off her mouth. Then maybe she could *talk* her down. She grunted as loud as she could, but Alison didn't seem to notice.

"I just want to reiterate, Detective. It isn't personal."

Fuck you!

"...blame anyone, blame the government. Do you honestly think they're telling you everything? They're not telling you *anything*."

Patricia groaned.

Alison made a face. "Are you doing okay?"

Patricia shook her head and made sounds.

"You want to talk, don't you? You think if we talk, we'll be buddies, and then I won't do what I have to do. No go, Detective. I'm very sorry, but you're about to become another statistic."

Patricia groaned again.

"Now, don't you get all pissy at *me!* Just remember it's Uncle Sam's fault. I'll be showing you why in a matter of maybe . . . ummmm, ten or fifteen minutes. We got a very good jump and I made excellent time. We left LVMPD way behind, the boys back there all bogged down in looking for your car. Well, good luck to them. I know the caves, they don't. I know the desert, they don't. Rom knows the desert. Maybe he'll figure it out. Anyway, forget about them. You won't believe where we're going."

Alison heard Patricia desperately mumbling.

"All right, all right. *Maybe* I'll take the tape off. If you're good. Like I said, it's nothing personal. You know where we're going?"

"Waaaa?" Patricia muttered out.

"To the beginning, Detective. A United States of America original creation. That's what it is, you know. A new creation. Just like God. Only this one is evil. Nuclear evilness. No one can debate that!"

Patricia nodded. Not that Alison saw it. She was too busy speeding across the desert floor, hugging the mountains as she drove without lights. It was a miracle that she didn't crack into the granite wall, exploding them both to smithereens. Patricia looked out the back window, at a black sky flecked with silver. Suddenly, it seemed so beautiful. Tears ran down her face.

No, no, no. You can't give up! You can't *give up!*

Alison took a deep breath and let it out. "A new creation, but done not by God, but by man. See what happens, Detective, when man tries to imitate God? He messes it up and creates hideous life forms. You know why? Men just don't know when to stop. They just keep going and going and going until they finally say: 'Oh no, I went too far.' You've known guys like that, haven't you? *I* certainly have.''

Patricia answered with a muted grunt.

''I mean, look at all this cloning, Detective. Do you really think that they've only cloned a mere sheep? I mean, if they admitted to cloning an adult sheep, what aren't they admitting to? I mean, look at that madman . . . what's-his-name, who wants to clone people.'' A snort. ''And they think a few laws'll stop him. Boy, is the American public naive!''

Patricia said, ''Ooor . . . iiiite.''

''Sure, I'm right! I mean, what is the government *really* doing? Cloning *man*. It's already *cloned* man, only no one's saying anything. You know what the next step is? Cloning cross-species. Animal to animal, which *I know* they've done. Next, of course, is animal to person. Then it's male and female and then who knows what else. And it all started because some overzealous scientists decided to nuke half of Japan. Then who do we give the power to? Some Nazi . . . Werner von Beethoven or something. His secret way to get back at the Americans for spoiling Hitler's dream. And didn't we just buy into it hook, line, and sinker. I mean, can you think of anything more absurd than putting a Nazi in charge of America's nuclear power? You just wait. I'm going to show you everything.''

Again, Patricia glanced out the window. Sudden swirls of translucent clouds were passing over the full moon. They were moving fast, indicating winds were moving in.

Alison prated, ''If Rom had been faster on the pickup, he could have saved you. I'm *sure* he's out there looking for you. But the big question is, will he know where to look? Maybe he'll figure it out, but I doubt it. You see, the whole thing with what's-his-face—the casino guy almost blowing his head off?''

The car felt as if it had suddenly been pushed.

''Oh nuts!'' Alison exclaimed. ''Of all the times! Ah well, you go deep into the desert, you're going to hit winds. Where was I?''

The car was blessedly silent for about ten seconds.

''What were we talking about? Oh, yeah. Romulus and the trigger-happy jerks sent by Parker Lewiston. Let me tell you something, Detective. I tried to warn Rom. I tried to let him know. I was looking right at him, but did that stop him? No, of course it didn't. Because the brown tart came walking down the street and spoiled *everything*.''

Again the four-wheeler was buffeted. If the winds got any stronger, they'd slam it into the mountainside.

". . . they went back to her apartment. I'm sorry, Detective, but I got a little angry!" Alison hit the wheel for emphasis. "Because I was trying to tell him something, and the floozy couldn't wait to get her pants off. I mean, it's truly disgusting how licentious she is."

Patricia made sounds.

"Just wait a minute!" Alison suddenly felt annoyed. Like this woman was actually making *demands* on her. All these cops were alike. "Anyway, I'm taking you to the most ghastly laboratory on earth. We're almost there. Can you see it?"

No, Patricia thought. *I can't see a fucking thing except clouds.* The sky had gone from black to charcoal as the moon's light dispersed among the clouds. She could feel sand scratch the car's surface like cats tiptoeing across the roof.

Alison said, "The security there is absolutely appalling. Not that anyone just pops in. I mean, it isn't exactly the Hawaiian Islands. Can you imagine someone writing the PR for this place? Get your daily dose of gammas—faster than UV and just as effective. The test site's just like Las Vegas, you know—both of them slow death. Wastelands."

"Ahhhhh. Oooo uuuh ake iii offf—"

"I'll take it off in a minute. Let me just explain a few things first, okay?"

Patricia didn't answer.

Alison said, "I've got to orient you. So you know what's going on. Have to know what's going on. Now, if you *could* look out the window, you could see Highway 95. You take 95 and get off at the Mercury Highway to travel through the test site. You know how big this place actually is?"

"Oowww iiigg?"

"About the size of Rhode Island. That's a lot of square miles. I forget the exact number. I used to know it. Ah well, memory's going. Part of middle age. Or maybe it has something to do with my powers. Gain some powers, lose others. It's all about conservation of matter. That was what the bomb was all about. Conservation of matter, or energy, which really is matter. Just ask Einstein. E equals MC-squared. E is energy and M is matter and you can convert one to another and that's why I have my powers. The bomb did it to me. You understand now, don't you? It's not hard to comprehend. Just a matter of going back and forth between the states of matter and energy. The key is to make sure you do your conversions properly. Because if you don't, you lose the energy to entropy, which is wasted cells that you'll never get back. And entropy, let me tell you . . . it's the kiss of death. What you want is enthalpy—matter to energy, and all of it conserved. Good rule of thumb. Enthalpy conserves, entropy dissipates. Dissipates, and it's gone, gone, gone.''

A second of silence.

''What was I just talking about before all this?''

Patricia muttered under the tape.

Abruptly, Alison braked and yanked the tape off. Patricia's mouth felt as if it had been planed by a sander. Calmly, she said, ''Thank you.''

''*De nada,* Detective. What were we talking about? We talked so much. You know, I must admit. I am enjoying this conversation.'' She paused. ''I know! We were talking about the test site.''

''The geography,'' Patricia answered. ''You were going to orient me.''

Alison shrieked, ''You were actually *listening* to me. No one ever listens to me. Certainly not my husband.'' She hesitated. ''I'm really sorry about this, Detective. But I have to do what I have to do.''

Patricia said, ''You haven't done anything yet. If you don't start now—''

''I'm sorry, but I do have to do it. And probably sooner rather than later. It'll be easier for you and me.''

Great job, Patricia. You did better when your mouth was taped shut. She said, ''Alison, you were telling me about the test site?''

''Right! Normally, if we were regular people, which we aren't. Which *I'm* not, you know that, don't you?''

''Of course.''

''Anyway, if you wanted to get through, you'd go through Gate 100— the main entrance—through security courtesy of Wackenhut Services, Inc. And then you'd get badged and all that rigamarole. Me? I'm cutting to the chase. I'm taking you straight onto Mercury Highway via the cattle guard, which doesn't have any fence to speak of. We'll parallel the highway, off-road because we're less likely to be seen. Now, there is this one sorry-looking trailer right as you enter the cattle guard, but it's almost never manned. We'll just plow straight through. We'll pass the pen. You know about the pen, don't you? Or was that before your time? Probably was before your time. Definitely before your time. Know what it was used for?''

"What?"

"The nuke *protesters*. The authorities confined them in the pen before they took them into the nearest city for booking. There used to be lots of protests here—during the sixties and seventies and even the early eighties. But then everything just..." She sighed. "Everything died away. My mom even went to some of the early ones. That was back in the days before..."

Alison stopped talking, then resumed.

"Lots and lots of protests. If you could see, you'd notice that right below the pen, outside Gate 100, is or *was* the Peace Camp. Ever been out there?"

"No."

She sighed. "The place is a ghost town now, like so much of Nevada. So sad. Once it was a thorn in the side of good old Uncle Sam, but now it's a pathetic reminder that we failed, Detective. We failed!"

"That's very sad," Patricia answered. *Think! You dummy!*

"The grounds are still littered with tons of rocks painted with peace signs," Alison went on. "It's also got all these half-buried broken shrines to brotherly love. The hippies used to come and decorate the rocks with feathers and turquoise and other things. Know what else is there?"

"What?"

"The old Shoshone sweat lodges. Or what's left of them. Now they're nothing but frames. They look like big geodesic domes—the gym equipment that kids climb on? The Shoshones are related to the Paiutes. Rom's part Pauite. But you know that, right? So sad. Once we had Indians, then we had protesters. And now all of it—going, going, gone! You know what Uncle Sam has left us?"

"What?"

"The army bunkers. Hundreds of them right past Gate 100. They're lined up, one right after the other, end to end, looking like Monopoly hotels. Row after row after row. The soldiers used to live in them during the drops. Now even most of the soldiers are gone. I mean, nothing's left in this toxic waste dump except a few schnooks in Mercury. Could you imagine living so close to all that gamma radiation?"

"Alison, my back's hurting a bit. Could you prop me up, please?"

"Detective, what do you take me for? I'm not dumb."

"I'd just like to be out of pain, that's all."

"... start giving you too much freedom, you're out like lightning."

She isn't buying anything. Still tethered to the seats, Patricia was out of commission. *You'll have to do better, Patty. Either better or start praying for a miracle.*

Alison said, "Now do you want to hear more or not? Because if I'm boring you, we could get this over right now."

"How could I possibly find this boring?" Patricia tried to sound indignant. "Of course, go on."

"Right, Detective. You just don't want me to do it."

Patricia sighed. "Alison, do whatever you want. I'm in no position to stop you."

A long pause which lengthened to about a minute.

Finally, Alison said, "Tell you what. I'm going to let *you* choose where."

"Choose what? Death by stoning or death by fire?"

"No, not the method, just the place." Alison went silent for a moment. "Okay, I just went past the guard's van outside the cattle guard about two minutes ago. We're officially inside the Nevada Test Site. Now where do you want to go to have it done?"

"How should I know?"

"Want me to tell you the choices?"

"Sure, Alison! Empower me."

"You're getting testy."

"It's all the radiation."

Alison thought over her statement. "You're probably right. Radiation does do strange things to the psyche. Tell you what. First let's get out of Mercury. The town's nothing but a two-bit government base—a bank, a steak house and a bowling alley and a couple of stores. Steve once knew a guy who worked at the sheriff's substation in Mercury, right here in Nye County. He was a real jerk. He made a pass at me. I wouldn't have minded, except he was uuuugly! How about Frenchman Flat? You know about Frenchman Flat?"

"No."

"That's where they dropped the first bomb. Everybody thinks it's Yucca, but it's Frenchman. I checked it out in my research. Frenchman Flat. *Able* was the shot. Like in Cain and Abel. I *told* you this place was trying to imitate the Bible. Even named it after the first family. Want to see it?"

"Alison, I can't see anything."

"Don't worry. I'll describe it to you in detail." Alison smiled to herself. "In lots and lots of detail."

FORTY-NINE

As Poe boarded one of Wackenhut's white Jeep Cherokees, security guard John Keeper handed him a map of the Nevada Test Site. The winds outside were strong, and visibility through the windshield was poor.

Keeper said, "I don't understand entirely what's going on. But if you think you're looking for a fugitive here, I suppose you'll need a map."

Translation: Keeper thought he was crazy.

Poe couldn't look him in the eye without a tinge of embarrassment. Feeling so justified an hour ago, he was now playing a part in some loony play, an obsessed man driven by an insane hunch. But Patricia had been *his* responsibility, and as long as LVMPD was looking for her in town, he might as well search NTS. Weinberg and the Nye County Sheriff's Department had helped him cut through the red tape. But Poe could tell that the loo was more than skeptical, even though Mick was acting supportive. However, there was that nagging feeling that Weinberg was only helping Poe to get him out of the way.

Keeper looked to be in his twenties, athletically built, with iron pumper arms and a wide neck. His hair was sparse and amber in color. His pink cheeks held the remnants of acne pitting. He said, "We called in the description of the car to Nye County. They're looking around the town of Mercury."

"I guarantee you that if they're here, they're not in any populated area." Poe regarded the map, commenting on the enormousness of the site.

"Eight hundred and sixty thousand acres," Keeper announced. "We're a state in a state. What is visible is just the tip of the iceberg. Mercury's completely surrounded by mountains. Beyond that ring are miles of empty land. It's also where all the action is . . . or was. Still some stuff going on, but not like in its heyday." He cleared his throat. "So where to?"

"Nye and not Wackenhut patrols the Mercury vicinity?"

"Nye does the town, we patrol everything else." Keeper started the motor, turned on the windshield wiper to remove a layer of dirt from the glass. "Sure you don't want a copter? A good beam of light would make your search a lot easier."

"It would also alert my fugitive. I wouldn't want to scare her off . . . make her do something nasty." He added under his breath, "If she's even here."

Keeper raised his eyebrows. "So what looks interesting, Sergeant?"

Poe studied the map. The Nevada Test Site seemed to be divided into seven major areas. Directly north, via the Mercury Highway, was the Frenchman Flat area, then Yucca Flat, and finally Rainier Mesa. If he backtracked south and headed west on Jackass Road, *then* went north, he'd hit Jackass Flats, Buckboard Mesa, then Pahute Mesa—the most northernly area of NTS and the highest in elevation.

"What's in Jackass Flats?" Poe asked.

"Mostly old research facilities, although some are still currently in operation."

"Alison wouldn't be there." Poe rubbed his eyes. "She'd be out in the open space."

"It's all open space." Keeper paused. "Sergeant, we've got about two hundred security vehicles, and they've all been alerted. If your fugitive's out there, someone'll find her. I don't know what we can do that they can't do."

I can outthink her, guy, that's what I can do.

Poe said, "Where did the Department of Energy do its bombing? All over?"

"All over," Keeper repeated. "The underground shots were mostly up north in Buckboard and Pahute Mesa. Majority of the atmospheric shots were done in Yucca Flat, although the first bomb was dropped in Frenchman Flat. You have to go through the Frenchman acreage to get to Yucca.

So if you're not interested in the Jackass vicinity, we might as well go due north.''

"Sounds good.''

Keeper put the Jeep in first gear. The machine bucked, then jolted forward. Immediately, Poe felt the force of the wind against the four-wheeler. What a night to be out. A full moon shining down its rays while the wind made radioactive dust boogie in the breeze. By the time Poe returned home, he'd probably glow in the dark. He kept his eyes glued out the windows. Back and forth, his vision scanning across the open plains like radar. He said, "Tell me about the place.''

Keeper hooked onto Mercury Highway and said, "What do you want to know?''

"I'm not sure. But I'll know it when I hear it.''

"I could point out things of interest for you.''

"Sure. But first, how about if we get off the highway?''

"Why?''

"Because most likely my fugitive wouldn't be driving on the road—too visible. She has a four-wheel-drive.''

Keeper said, "You know, Sergeant, to get into Frenchman Flat, I'm going to have to cross through the mountains. Which means I'm going to have to use the road. I care more about your safety than I do about your fugitive.''

"How far is it to Frenchman Flat?''

"Around two miles.''

"Okay, if you have to use the road, use the road.''

They sat in silence as the Jeep wound its way through tight mountain curves. When it exited, it sped along a flat, desolate wilderness.

Poe said, "Can you move off the road now?''

"I suppose. Although in this wind, it's not a good idea." Keeper licked his lips. "How about if I take you on a tour via some smaller roads? I know the paths, and it'll give you a good cross section of what's here.''

"Fair enough.''

"Hold on." Keeper gripped the wheel as the car made the transition from smooth road to unpaved terrain with little fuss. "We take a lot of visitors to this area, since there's leftover debris from the shots. Mostly from Priscilla, which was detonated in the late 1950s. If you look to your left and squint through all the grit out there, you might be able to make out a big dome.''

"I see it."

Keeper said, "Those were experimental. If the visibility was better, you'd see remnants of a two-inch concrete dome which collapsed under the pressure of the shot. The dome still standing is six-inch-thick concrete, and that held up just fine."

"I'll keep that in mind the next time I build a bomb shelter."

Keeper smiled. "You're cynical now. But back then, the nuclear edge was what this country was all about. The facilities here still do a lot of important scientific research. Right here in Frenchman Flat, we have the largest spill test facility in the world. We shoot all sorts of toxic material into the environmentally controlled rooms and wind tunnels to study its dispersion into the atmosphere. That way we can devise modern and efficient cleanup protocol."

Poe said, "NTS got you doing some PR work, Mr. Keeper?"

The guard smiled. "People think in black and white, and that's never reality. The liberals all think of NTS as some Frankenstein laboratory. They don't have a clue to what NTS and the Department of Energy are doing here *now*."

"Uh-huh." Poe kept his eyes peeled to the muddied air, looking for any signs of motion and disturbance, any flicker of light. Whipping himself for his inadequacies.

Think, you asshole!

If Alison was going to butcher Patricia as she had the others, she'd need a working surface. It was too windy to work outdoors. Which would mean she'd either have to do her slaughtering in her car or find a preexisting domain that would protect her from the wind.

"Any way to go into those domes?" Poe asked.

"What?"

"Can you get inside the bomb shelters?"

"The domes? No, they're strictly off-limits. Boarded up. You never know about the internal structure. They may collapse at any minute."

So the shelters were out.

How far would she travel into the test site? Would she take Steve's Explorer all the way up those mountains to the highest elevations? Poe doubted it. It would take her too long to get there, and every moment she drove on open ground made her more vulnerable. Poe guessed that Alison would play it close to the entrance, not riding too deep into the site. If for no other reason than to decrease the likelihood of her car breaking down.

If I were Alison, and I didn't want to go far, where would I go to do my dirty work?

Poe said, "How many bombs were dropped here?"

"Here? Meaning Frenchman Flat?"

"Yeah."

"Not many compared to Yucca Flat. Here, maybe you had around fifteen, twenty drops. But the first shot—Able—it was dropped here. That was back in 'fifty-one. The Operation Ranger series. Ever heard of it?"

Poe shook his head no. Would Alison go to the place of the first bomb drop, figuring that was the start of her and her mother's ills?

Alison hadn't even been *born* in 1951.

Something twinged his gut. He knew she wasn't here. If she was anywhere, she was in Yucca Flat. He stated, "Yucca Flat was where most of the bombs were detonated?"

"Yes, sir."

"So what's there today?"

"Mostly subsidence craters. Lots of Yucca looks like the surface of the moon. The ground falling inward under the intense pressure of the bomb—"

"Anything original left?"

"Original?"

"Structures from the time of the bomb drops."

"Mostly it's open spaces with lots of craters."

"How about the army bunkers used to house the soldiers?"

"Gone. The News Knob is still there, the place where the reporters watched. And we do have some of the original viewing bleachers—"

"But no original buildings?"

"We have the control point facilities, where the engineers controlled the bomb shots. They're still in use."

"So you have security around those facilities?"

"Tight security."

"What else?"

"In Yucca Flat . . . as far as existing buildings . . ." Keeper thought a moment. "There're some plutonium storage and radioactive waste facilities. Uh . . . there's the Big Experimental Explosive Facility."

"Keep going."

"Oh, there's Japan Town—"

"What's that?" Poe sat up in his seat.

"NTS built Japanese-like buildings and dropped bombs on them. Then they measured the radiation that remained in the houses. It helped to give the government some base levels for Hiroshima and Nagasaki.''

"Does Japan Town still exist?"

"The framing's still there, yes."

Poe was disappointed. "All that's left is the framing?"

"Yep." Keeper gripped hard on the wheel to keep the winds from knocking over the car. "You might want to take a peek at the 'typical American homes.' NTS built this typical American town—you know a café, a movie house, a library, a school, a town hall—then bombed it with the Annie II shot. They did it to measure the effects of radiation on a typical American small town."

Poe broke in, "And most of what's left is framing as well?"

"Actually, we still have the two prototypes of the typical American houses. You know, a two-story structure with a living room, a dining room, a couple of bedrooms, and a kitchen. Some of them even had food—"

"And they're still standing?"

"More or less. They're pretty rickety by now."

"But the structure is intact?"

"Yes."

"And you can go inside them?"

"Yeah, I can give you a quick tour."

Poe wasn't interested in a tour. He said, "How far away are we from this typical American house?"

"About twenty minutes."

A lifetime in murder years.

Poe said, "Are we the nearest car to the place?"

Keeper said, "I can check."

Poe waited as the guard made the call, driving the Jeep at the same time. He repressed a compulsion to snap and fidget and bounce through the vehicle's roof. Finally, Keeper hung up the mike. "We're the nearest. Got another car about ten minutes farther. Should I tell him to meet us there?"

"Yes, please."

"So you think that's where she is?"

"Maybe," Poe answered.

"How 'bout we give it a shot, then?" Keeper grinned at the pun.

Poe, however, remained stone-faced.

*   *   *

It was . . . happening . . . any minute . . . any second. Bits and pieces . . . happening. The last . . . she knew . . . fight it . . . fight it . . . don't . . . let her . . .

Horribly, she knew what was going on. She knew it would be the last time . . . the last . . .

The urge to give in . . . the urge to fight . . . fading, fading, fading.

The urge to sleep . . .

Sleep . . . sleep . . . wonderful sleep.

FIFTY

Patricia was out cold, so the desire was overwhelming. True, she had promised that she'd be dead first, but flesh tasted so much better when eaten as the heart still pumped flowing, warm blood. Besides, would she really know the difference?

The detective's eyes were still open. Open but not focusing. Alison held up a feather and tickled her nose. Then she tickled her feet, hit a couple other areas, then ended up with the hatpin-through-the-palm test. No response—not a twitch, flick, or blink. Doped to the max, she shouldn't be feeling a thing.

So why not relinquish to a higher order? Let the powers turn her into that luscious state—from rational being to a beast programmed by instinct. She stared into Patricia's vacant eyes and once again told her it was nothing personal. Then she poked her stomach—rich and ripe with lots of juicy fat.

Females always tasted better.

Sitting on the wooden floor of the deserted house. The plan was to do her here, then leave the note for Rommie, telling him where he could find Deluca. Give the woman—or what would be left of her—a decent burial. She'd also give Poe a few more pieces of the puzzle. It was up to him to figure the rest out. Not that she believed he would ever get it. Eventually, she'd have to show him through demonstration.

The thought made her smile.

Detective Patricia Deluca—all laid out on a white linen tablecloth—a tasty meal for the typical American family in the typical American house. She would have laid her out in the dining room, but the living room was bigger—a comfortable area with a fireplace and big windows. Or what once had been windows, because the glass was gone, and all that remained was the holes. The furious winds were blowing in sand and gravel, coating Patricia in dirt. No matter. Grit was good for digestion. That was why animals ate bones.

No furniture in here. Not that she needed it. Everything in this old wreck was broken-down and old. But it reminded her of her grandmother's place back in St. George, Utah. She wondered how Granny was doing.

My, Granny, what big teeth you have!

All the better to—

The house had come in handy. Inside NTS but not *too* remote. Isolated, but not hidden. She had parked the four-wheel-drive against the building, but it remained very visible. Even with the sand blowing—which gave the car some camouflage—she'd have to work quickly. The ritual took such a long time, but she had no choice.

Shivering as gusts of wind and dirt coughed over her, she stripped naked. Her eyes directed upward, toward the lunar light.

First a simple howl, just to get things started.

With each subsequent ululation, the changes progressed.

It took four wails to thicken the musculature of the thighs. Another eight bays to swell and elongate the arms.

Faster now.

Louder now.

Deep cries to get the spirits going.

Go, spirits, go.

Her toes started to stretch as hair sprouted from hidden shafts, covering her feet with a coarse auburn carpet. The nails—narrow and sharp—lengthening until they extended beyond the digits and touched the ground before them. Her claws—painted blood red because she had polished her own toenails yesterday. Dragging her foot along the floor, she raked the wood in neat, parallel lines. Next came the hands, the fingers retracting as the nails turned into implements of torture. The fine, downy hair on her arms grew denser and steel-wool rough.

More wails, more moans.

Vocalization from the pit of her throat, from the cavern of her gut. Her spine bending, humping, pushing her down to all fours—a force beyond her control. Her head rocketed to the floor with a thump, and within moments she became unable to stand erect.

The powers were coming fast now, racing with each piercing aria that reached the heavens—

She suddenly stopped baying.

Did she hear a sound?

The rushing of the wind?

Her heart galloped. She knew wind sounds. And she knew mechanical sounds. Like the sound of a car engine. . . .

No, no, no. It couldn't . . . it couldn't, it couldn't, it couldn't!

But there it was.

The hum of a distant motor, growing louder with each passing second.

Louder, louder, louder!

It couldn't be!

Headlights spreading over the desert floor, coming closer, closer, closer, until they stabbed through the open holes that had once been picture windows.

Who? But it can't . . . not Rom. Not so soon. It couldn't be. No . . . no . . . it couldn't, it couldn't, it couldn't!

Her eyes frantically searching around, looking for help which didn't exist. She was on her own. Gazing at Deluca. To abandon such a tasty prize . . .

But it was all happening so fast. She couldn't take Patricia with her. Enough energy left to remorph? Barely enough power for her own body. The choice, the choice, the choice.

What was the choice?

Escape or battle? And which form? Animal or human?

No choice.

Humans shoot animals.

If only she had a gun. She had *had* a gun. Patricia's gun. But she had left it in Patricia's car!

Why had she done that?

A hint for Poe . . . that she didn't need a gun. That had been her rationalization at the time.

Well, sister, you sure could use one now.

The lights . . . brightening. Then suddenly there was darkness. The motor had died. Two car doors opening—closing.

No choice but to shape-shift back.

Her spine had already begun to straighten as she felt her toes and hands contract and shrink . . . her beautiful red claws returning to ordinary nails.

No matter. She'd beat the bastards in any form!

Opening the front door, then taking everything in at millisecond shutter speed. Poe saw something half-human leaping through the open window frame. His immediate instinct was to follow. But Patricia was lying on the floor, her skin as gray as dust.

A split-second decision.

No decision, you idiot! Patricia is lying on the floor!

Poe ran to her, bent down and felt the right carotid for a pulse as he stared into empty eyes. His hands were shaking and his palms were sweaty. His breathing had turned shallow and irregular.

"C'mon, sweetheart . . ." he muttered.

He felt the left carotid for a throb. "C'mon, Patty, baby. Give me a sign, sweetheart, give me a sign!"

Keeper was at his side. "Is she alive? Should we start CPR?"

A slight vibration. Through gasps of air, he choked out, "I feel something!" Horribly slow, but it was something. "I got a pulse—I think it's a pulse." A weak, dragging beat. But it was there. "I've got a definite pulse, it's a pulse. Is she breathing?"

Keeper was holding a mirror up against Patricia's mouth and nose. "She's breathing! Not very strong, but there's something on the mirror."

"Thank you, God!" Poe muttered. "Patricia, listen to me, sweetheart. You are safe, baby. Safe, safe, safe. You're going to be fine—"

Abruptly, Poe stopped talking. From the outside came the whinny of a stalled engine trying to kick in. Poe's brain registering: someone was out there trying to get away!

Flood it, baby, flood it.

Suddenly, Poe rose to his feet. "Keeper, is there a doctor in Mercury?"

"Sure—"

"Some sort of hospital?"

"There's something at the base—"

"Can you take her in by yourself?"

"I think so. Why? Where are you—"

"Hear that car engine? That's where I'm going. Backup's coming for you. Radio for help for me! And this time, get a *copter.*"

"How will I contact you—"

But Poe was out the door. Keeper screamed, "I'll get you backup!"

Racing through the wind as grit stung his eyes. He pumped his legs in hard, long strides as he tore toward the noise of the engine, which was running smoothly now.

Only moments before the car took off in flight.

He heard the engine roar, felt the heat of the exhaust.

Charging through clouds of grit kicked up by the Explorer's spinning tires.

Vaulting upward as the four-wheeler jerked into gear and bolted forward.

Grabbing onto whatever he could, his hands gripping something hard and metallic. His feet were dragged against the ground as the car sped off. An acrid smell hit his nose as rubber burned away from his shoes.

Being towed like a dead carcass.

Uh-uh, baby! You're not gonna get away with it!

Using all his strength, Poe hoisted himself upward and brought his feet up onto the rear bumper. Plastering himself against the rear window, he suddenly realized he was clutching the Explorer's stock-item rooftop luggage rack. He prayed that the bolts and welding would hold as dirt and sand blasted his face.

She veered sharply left.

Trying to shake him.

"Not nice, Alison," he screamed. "Not a nice thing to do to an old friend—"

This time she swerved to the right.

But he held on.

"You're going to kill us both!" he hollered, though he doubted that she could hear him. So maybe she could lip-read. He knew she saw him. She kept peering into her rearview mirror.

Speeding up, then slamming on the brakes. The mechanism locked as the Explorer teetered perilously on two wheels, Poe riding it like a windjammer. Luckily, the wind was blowing in the appropriate direction. The car sailed, then slowly came upright, landing on the ground with a thud. It careened out, then spun in a circle, throwing gravel into his face. Poe felt something sharp dig into his palm—a screw or a bolt. He winced but kept his grip.

"Nice try, baby, but no cigar—"

She floored the acceleration pedal and bulleted forward, checking the rearview as she flew. Poe pressed his face against the glass and smiled at her.

Alison shouted, "You're dead meat, Romulus."

Poe blinked, not sure if he'd heard her correctly, or if he'd heard anything at all. But out in the open—with the wind on your side—sound traveled. Which meant if he could hear her, then she . . .

He yelled back, "Honey, eventually you're gonna run out of gas."

"Not in your lifetime!"

Again, she angled and turned sharply.

Behind him, in the distance, he heard the beautiful symphony of wailing sirens. Seconds later came the rotary churning of a helicopter, its jeweled beam sweeping across the dirt floor. Grasping the rack tightly with his left hand, Poe freed up his right and waved like the Rose Parade Queen. The tip of the beam caught his frantic gesturing. A beat later, he was in the spotlight.

It was all over for Alison. She was screwed, blued. What Poe sincerely didn't want was for her to go out with a bang, taking him with her.

How to jump off a moving train.

The sirens became louder as they moved in closer.

Alison racing faster.

The spotlight shining down, forcing him to squint.

Only a matter of time before she hit something.

Sirens closing in, a megaphone barking out directions: *Stop immediately! You are in a Hazardous Radiation Zone!*

In other words, Poe was eating gamma rays.

For your own safety and protection! Stop now!

His brain barking its own orders: *Jump before you flip and go flying headfirst into nuclear fallout.*

The sirens kept getting closer and closer.

The ground underneath him whizzing by.

Jump, you idiot! Before she does something suicidal!

A security jeep almost at his bumper.

Very close.

Way *too* close. If Alison braked suddenly, he'd be pressed duck.

Jump! JUMP!

Alison continued to speed, breaking through a loose rope and some old metal fencing. Abruptly the sirens seemed to be losing ground, almost as if the pursuing vehicles were pulling back.

He blinked.

They *were* pulling back!

They were actually *slowing . . . stopping!*

He screamed out, *"What the fuck are you doing?"*

The cars becoming specks of light as Alison dragged on. Suddenly, she started to brake, spinning out dirt and pebbles. The Explorer began to slow.

Slower and slower.

Then finally it stopped.

Poe didn't move.

Neither did Alison.

The flashing lights of the police and security cars a good six hundred feet away.

Why the fuck aren't they moving in?

Why are they hanging back?

All Poe could think was that he must be sitting on some real deadly shit.

He remained glued to the back window, the wind streaming sand into his eyes. The helicopter was hovering overhead. All of them were waiting for Alison's next move.

Without warning, the ground rumbled, then gave way, the car dropping down a couple of feet. Poe's stomach lurched. Looking down at the earth's floor. Underneath him, the sand was moving as if it had been scooped out by a big, invisible spade, funneling toward the ground's lowest point.

He was sitting on some *very* unstable land.

Alison got out of the car, the gusts blowing her dress over her knees, her hair flying in the wind. Poe watched her advance. She was moving slowly . . . carefully. He took directions from her lead. With meticulous care, he got down from the bumper.

Immediately, the earth shifted downward. This time around four feet. No doubt about it. They were sinking.

As Alison approached him, her feet descended deeper and deeper into the ground until she was wading knee-high in sand.

Again, the earth fell.

Poe was now eye-level with the ground's surface.

He stood rock-still. So did Alison. The helicopter continued to spotlight them as it hovered above.

To Alison, he shouted, "Quicksand?"

She shook her head no. Then she came forward.

"Don't move!" Poe screamed.

Alison smiled. "So what's new, Romulus?"

"Stop moving!"

Alison complied. "Know where we are, Rommie?"

Poe clenched his hands. "No, Alison, I don't know where we are!"

She cocked her head to the side, and actually had the nerve to bat her eyelashes. "This was an underground test area, Rommie. Know what that is?"

Wind was blowing fast and angry. He had to shout to be heard. "I have an idea."

Alison brushed hair from her eyes, looked up, and squinted. "Tell them to go away. They're making so much noise!"

"Alison, why are we sinking?"

"NTS shot an underground bomb directly below us—right where we're standing. Doesn't it feel weird to be standing in the same spot where a nuclear bomb once exploded?"

"I feel privileged," Poe yelled. "Alison, why is the ground giving way under our feet?"

"Well," Alison said, "usually when you shoot a bomb down below, the ground above caves in."

Neither spoke.

She said, "It's from all the pressure. That's why there're all these craters in Yucca Flat. They must have detonated hundreds of underground shots here."

Poe licked his lips. "You said *usually* the ground above caves in."

"Yes."

"Usually," he repeated. "But not always."

"Well, at least not right away—"

Again, the ground rumbled and dropped.

Alison said, "This area where we are . . . know what it's called? A *potential* crater area."

"Which means . . ." Poe felt his balance wavering as sand sifted beneath him. "This land has a potential for craters."

"Big craters, Rommie. Very, very big craters. Hundreds of feet wide and a thousand feet deep. Burying everything with radioactive dirt as the ground sinks. The process can take days or weeks or even years. Or it can take seconds."

From up above, the helicopter's megaphone barked: *You are in an unsubsided underground test area. There is a potential for sudden craters. Do not move! We will send someone down to pull you up.*

Alison grinned. "How about doing some jumping jacks with me, Rommie?"

"Alison, please—"

"Up and down and up and down."

She attempted to wade in the sand and instantly, the ground sank. She shot her hand upward and grabbed onto him as they both struggled with the submerging ground.

"Stop moving, stop moving!" Poe shouted. "Just stop *moving,* dammit!"

Alison immediately became inert. By this time they were both waist-deep in sand. She was inches from his side, clutching his arm.

She said, "We're intertwined, Romulus. That's how it's always been with us. This push-me-pull-you relationship. We can't escape each other's clutches now. I realize that I'm dependent on your goodwill. But just as important, you're dependent on *my* goodwill. So, Rommie, what are you going to give me if I'm a good girl and don't move?"

Poe squinted as he looked up into the copter's bright beam. For a moment, he wished the metal bug would go away so he could see the sky. The moon might be the last thing he'd ever see, because the wind kept burying them deeper and deeper—

"Rommie, you're not with me."

"I'm with you, I'm with you."

"Rommie, I don't like that woman you're with."

Poe bit back the urge to bounce on his feet. "What woman?"

"If you're going to play games, I'm going to move—"

"Rukmani?" he said quickly. "What's wrong with Rukmani? She's no threat to you, Alison. She's old, and not a fraction as pretty as you. What's your problem with her?"

"You!" Alison shouted. "You're the problem—"

Again the ground growled and shifted. Now he was buried to halfway up his chest.

Alison giggled. "Won't be long now!"

Poe felt a rush of many emotions—fear, terror, hopelessness, an intense appreciation for life, and a frantic need to survive. The air, though poisonous and contaminated, was as precious to him as rubies.

Please God! Just a few more seconds!

Another copter was moving in. They both looked up, watching as the chopper's door opened and a rope tumbled down near their hands.

''So near.'' Alison grinned. ''So near, yet so far away.''

She broke into boisterous movements. The ground moaned, then caved in. Poe's hand springing upward as sand swept over his shoulders. Over his mouth and into his eyes. Covering him like a tsunami. Up his arms.

Just as the earth was making its final effort to bury him, Poe's fingers grabbed rope.

Clasping it with unseen strength from unused muscles, he felt himself rising upward. As he ascended, his other hand became liberated and it, too, seized the rope.

Pulling him upward. Hc held on fast and refrained from coughing. He gaspcd for air as his nose and mouth were yanked out of the ground. First, he was waist-deep in sand, then it was just his knees . . .

Tears stinging his cheeks.

His grip beginning to weaken as the chopper continued tugging him upward. His body felt heavy, even leaden. Then he realized that something below was yanking him down.

Alison had emerged from the deep, clutching his legs.

Was she trying to pull him down? Or was she trying to save her own soul?

Sweat spilling from his body as she kept her arms clasped tightly around his thighs. His palms became pools of perspiration as his hands began to slide down his towrope to life.

Hold on, you jerk! Hold on!

Alison smiling at him. Grinning at him with satanic evilness. With an uncontrolled viciousness, she bared her teeth and sank them deep into his thigh.

He screamed and kicked, trying to shake her off. But with each movement, he lost inches off his tenuous hold.

He forced back the pain and stopped kicking. Then she bit him again. Agony coursed through his body, stabbing white lights of pain behind his eyes. He squeezed them shut, opened them, looked down.

His eyes widened in horror. Alison's smile was gone. Her mouth was gone. Her entire *face* was gone!

Replacing it was something hideous with fur and snout and needle-sharp fangs, glinting in the helicopter's hot white light. Her hands werc claws, piercing his flesh.

The copter gave a hard, final tug, and seconds later, they were both liberated, sailing through the air, buffeted by strong winds. The chopper inched upward.

Searing pain continued to rip through Poe's thigh. The monster bit off another chunk of his flesh. His screams echoed as he violently flailed his legs, unwittingly kicking the beast off. Hearing ululations and shrieks as the monster freefalled through the air.

With terror, Poe looked down as the ground below roared, then gave way with tremendous force and sudden swiftness. Poe watched as Alison plunged into the swimming sand, heard her screeches through the bellows as the earth suctioned her inward, pulling her down into its airless chambers as mercilessly as water diving down a drain.

Free of her weight, he tightened his watery grip on the rope as the helicopter rapidly carried him to safe ground, the winds blowing him helter-skelter like a balsa glider. His lips were cracked open, his skin as brittle as parchment.

Lowering him until he was in jumping range.

Dry and dehydrated, he dropped to the earth, kissing the radioactive dust as if it were the Blarney Stone.

Never had poison tasted so sweet.

FIFTY-ONE

The change in Romulus was evident, though his nuances conveyed more than words. Rukmani had sensed it the first time he had actually taken her hand for support as he hobbled along, giving himself permission to lean on her physically if not emotionally. At the moment, Rom was walking normally, the only sign of his discomfort being an occasional wince whenever he misstepped. Still, he *chose* to stand close to her, his hand atop hers as they watched the casket being lowered into the grave. Although his eyes were focused on the coffin, his mind was adrift, no doubt thinking of a woman he had once known. When Alison had died, she had buried a piece of him with her.

Her committee chair in psychiatry had once told Rukmani that therapy was more art than science. The key was timing, and all the knowledge in the world was useless if the client wasn't ready.

After Patricia had recovered fully, after the network and tabloid news had died down, after the endless reports and paperwork had been filed and processed and thousands of questions had been answered, Romulus had confessed to her what he had perceived that night in an hour-long manic spill. They had been alone in her apartment, Romulus limping as he paced, grimacing with each strained movement. But he had refused to sit still.

You think I'm crazy, don't you?

Not at all—

Rukmani, I know *what I saw.*

I'm sure you do—

What? You think I was seeing *things. You probably think I need to see a shrink. I* knew *I shouldn't have told you.*

She considered it a very positive step that he had confided to her anything at all. She answered his agitation with calm seriousness.

Rom, why in the world should I doubt you? You're a perfectly rational man with two functional eyes. There are many hidden forces we don't know about, even more things we see but don't understand. And no, I don't think you need to consult a shrink. I don't want or expect you to do anything except heal up. *And you're doing a fine job at that.*

He stared at her, and said nothing. A moment later, he announced that he was hungry. Did she have any leftover *palak paneer* from last night's dinner?

One day, Rom would sort it out, separate fact from delirium, sift out what had happened in reality from what had occurred in the recesses of his terror-struck mind. He'd reach his own conclusions.

The gravediggers had begun to shovel dirt atop the wooden box. The service was officially over. Not that there was much by way of a eulogy; some generic clergyman speaking blank words to a half-dozen people. The others were walking away from the site, but Poe remained paralyzed, his eyes transfixed on the two behemoths who were sweating and grunting as heat baked their necks red. They worked tirelessly toward the end goal: covering Honey Kramer's casket with six feet of earth.

Rukmani felt jittery: a switch, because usually it was Rom who was all twitches and tics. To bleed off her restlessness, she scanned the grounds. Spotting Lewiston off to the right, she poked Romulus lightly in the ribs. His spell broken, Poe glanced in Lewiston's direction, his eyes locking with the casino owner's.

Good old Parkerboy. The billionaire with a flair, garbed in a black silk suit and white linen shirt. He did retain his signature string tie and boots. His fingers gripped a black Stetson, the hatband hammered in silver. The pate on the crown of his head glistened in the sun, covered in sweat. He was flanked by two goons. They were different apes from the ones who had taken potshots at Rom, but they were equally big.

Lewiston caught Poe's eyes and nodded.

Poe nodded back.

Taking the acknowledgment as a sign of encouragement, Lewiston made his approach. Rukmani would have liked to conveniently disappear. But as she started to move away, Romulus clutched her hand tighter.

Of all the times for him to show that he needed her.

Lewiston stopped and stood in front of them, tipping his hat to Rukmani as if he'd been wearing it. "And who might this beautiful woman be, son?"

Without missing a beat, Poe answered, "This beautiful woman is my fiancée, Dr. Rukmani Kalil. She works in our own coroner's office. When I'm stalled on a case, I consult Dr. Kalil. She's LVMPD's best-kept secret."

Rukmani answered, "Sergeant Poe is talking in hyperbole. I'm a bureaucrat—a lowly public servant." Rukmani's eyes rested on Lewiston's face. "But I do my job."

"I bet you do, little lady," Lewiston said. "I bet you do." He wiped his perspiration off his forehead with a silk kerchief, then returned his attention to Poe. "I think I owe you something of an apology, son. Those men who so rudely disturbed your privacy have been dismissed from my service. I fully admit sending them over to provide you with transportation. But I promise you, it is not my policy to strong-arm anyone, let alone a cop." He chuckled. "Man has to be insane to try a stunt like that. And I'm not crazy."

Poe said, "I agree with you, sir. You're anything but crazy."

"Just the same, Sergeant, you'd be within your rights to whop me with a civil lawsuit. The men were in my hire, I admit it. Now it's been a couple of months . . . I don't know what you're brewing up. But *if* you're thinking of slamming me with some kind of legal action, do yourself a favor and talk to me before you consult one of those bloodsucking attorneys-for-hire. I could save us both hundreds of hours of legal work, and tens of thousands of dollars in fees."

Poe's voice was flat. "I have no intention of suing you, Mr. Lewiston. I'm not interested in your money."

In other words, I can't be bought, you bastard.

The casino man studied Poe's eyes with his own squinty knobs. "I'm glad to hear that. So let me do something for you, son—"

"I don't need your favors, either."

Lewiston chuckled. "You've got a hair-trigger reaction, boy, you know that?"

"Hair-trigger reactions can save a cop's life." Poe mopped his face with his shirtsleeve. "I repeat, I'm not interested in your favors."

"It's not really a *favor,* son. More like a pledge of mutual cooperation. Now, I know you're investigating me for something. I'm not sure *what*—"

"The murder of an underage child prostitute named Sarah Yarlborough," Poe answered.

Rukmani nudged him in the ribs.

Again, Lewiston laughed. "Well, thank you for informing me of the charge. That's right neighborly of you."

"Considering our sides are a hundred and eighty degrees apart, I'd say it was downright friendly."

The casino man said, "You investigate all you want, Sergeant. You file for your little warrants and papers. I assure you, I won't stand in your way. But let me tell you this from the bottom of my heart. You are way off-base—"

"No, I'm not, Mr. Lewiston. As a matter of fact, I am so on-base I'm sliding into home. You're powerful, sir, but you're not invincible. I'm going to peg you for the murder of Sarah Yarlborough, *and* I'm going to nail you for the death of Honey Kramer. I don't know how long it'll take or exactly how I'll do it, but I swear as I breathe, I'll do what should have been done twenty-five years ago."

"I don't know what you're talking about—"

"Yes, you do."

"Now, son, don't you go interrupting me. I know *who* you're talking about, but I don't know *what* you're talking about. Linda Hennick committed suicide. She was a very sick woman. You, of all people, having had firsthand experience with lunacy, you should know what *I'm* talking about." Lewiston cocked a thumb over his shoulder. "You been hanging around that joker too long."

Down the hill, Poe regarded a distant figure. It was Y.

Lewiston shook his head in mock pity. "He's nothing but a lovesick old fool, Detective Sergeant Romulus Poe. Had I knowed what Linda meant to him, I would have never even bothered. She was one of many, boy. And like so many, she couldn't handle getting old. Looking back on it, she weren't worth the effort." He ran his tongue along the inside of his cheek. Then he tipped his hat to Rukmani. "Ma'am."

He turned, placed the Stetson on his head, and walked away, sandwiched protectively between his two goons.

Poe glared at the old billionaire, then whispered under his breath, "Son of a *bitch.*"

"Yeah, he's a piece of work," Rukmani answered.

"Trip, you *bastard*," Poe swore. "Fall flat on your fucking face."

Without warning, Lewiston suddenly lost his footing and tumbled with a smack onto the ground.

Rukmani gasped, put her hand to her mouth.

Quickly, his bodyguards were at his side, pulling him erect. His face was flushed, the knees of his pants were scuffed and dusty. He flung his arms out as if fighting his sentries off, then broke from their grasp. Casting a brief glance at Poe, he brushed off his pants in swift movements, then stomped off.

Poe let out a small laugh. "Son of a gun!"

Stunned, Rukmani said, "How'd you do that?"

"Do what?" Poe was still chuckling.

"Make him . . ." She stopped talking.

Poe was still smiling. "I didn't do anything, Ruki. I must have cursed the geezer a thousand times. Guess the odds finally played in my favor."

Rukmani couldn't answer, still taken aback by the well-timed coincidence. Poe had stopped laughing, was rubbing his arms. The gravediggers had finished the burying and had moved on to tamping the ground, packing the dirt.

Poe remarked, "Honey held on for two months. What's it like being in a coma for that long?"

"She probably didn't feel much of anything, Rom."

"Murderous bastard!" He shook his head, then took out a handful of loose yellow daisy petals from his pocket. He threw them over the freshly turned earth. "It ain't much, Honey. Then again, we never really had much of a relationship."

Rukmani said, "It was nice of you to come."

"I felt like I owed her something." He unhooked himself from Rukmani's grip. He took her freed hand and kissed it. "I've been meaning to tell you something."

She waited.

"When I told you what happened that night, thanks for not trying to convince me I was seeing things. Because I know what I saw, Ruki. I *know* what I saw."

"I know. I believe you, Rom."

Poe grinned. "You're one great liar. I love you for it." He kissed her cheek, brushed hair out of her eyes. "Y's waiting for me."

Rukmani wiped sweat from her face. "Are you about to embark on one of those macho male-bonding experiences?"

"It's a dangerous omen, Ruki . . . Y being up in the daytime." Poe lit a cigarette, waved to the old man. Y waved back. "I'll meet you back at the car."

Walking downhill was especially difficult, trodding through sheaves of grass yellowed by the unrelenting summer heat. At this time of year, the city threw all sorts of specials to boost tourism in the Mohave: three nights, four days at the such-and-such, complete with buffet breakfasts and including tickets to the popular blah, blah, blah all for the price of a dollar.

Anything to get them into the air-conditioned casinos.

Poe haltingly made his way down, meeting Y on level ground. In the sun, the air was oppressive, but the cemetery had the courtesy to provide shade in the form of canopied elm trees. Y brought out a goatskin of moonshine and the two men cooled themselves under one of the tree's lacy boughs.

"This stuff is terrible," Poe said.

"It's got a good aftertaste."

"Doesn't make up for its terrible beforetaste." Poe took a whiff of his smoke. "Sad state when you need nicotine to wipe out the taste of bad alcohol. Anyway, what's a bat like you doing up in the daytime?"

"I'm paying my last respects."

Poe inhaled the smoke, then chuckled. "So you were also one of Honey's? Good for you, old man."

Y glared at him. "I'm not here to be congratulated. I'm here because that son of a bitch you were talking to got away with it again. What are you going to do about it?"

"Me?"

"Yes, you. Aren't you a homicide cop?"

"So they say."

"Then investigate the goddamn homicide, Romulus. If you *do* something, Poe, then maybe you'll actually arrest someone!"

Poe dropped his cigarette on the grass and stepped on it. He picked up the butt and dropped it in his pocket. "You know, Y, you're one queer bird. When I tried to investigate the homicide of a woman you had loved, you shut down like an overheated engine. Now you're egging me on with Honey. So what aren't you telling me, old man?"

"Fuck you, Poe!" Y bolted off.

Poe caught up with him, grabbed the old man's buckskin shirtsleeve. "You self-righteous son of a bitch! You know damn well Lewiston didn't murder her—"

"Go to hell."

"Linda Hennick killed herself—"

"Let go of me!"

"Did you hear me, Y? She *killed* herself! She committed suicide—"

"You cops are a bunch of jokers."

"You want to bury your head in fiction or do you want to hear the truth? Because God forbid something should sully the image of your true love. You know, Chief, for once I agree with you. Linda Hennick *wasn't* crazy! Her nighttime jaunts weren't the psychotic rambles of a disturbed woman. They were Linda Hennick having a good old time. She was a good-lifer, Y—a bored housewife who willingly turned herself into a rich man's whore—"

Poe felt his head split open from the force of Y's fist crushing his nose. Blood gushed from his nostrils. Instinctively, he wiped his nose on his sleeve. He stared at Y, then at his bloodied shirt. He sighed with more pity than anger. "Lewiston was right about one thing. You are a lovesick old fool."

As Poe hobbled off, Y gripped his arm. About to speak, the old man opened his mouth, but no sounds came out. He clutched his shirt, then began to fall backward. Poe caught him before he hit the ground and carried him under the shade of a tree. Poe reached inside Y's pocket and pulled out a nitro capsule. He broke it open and held it under the old man's nose. Wiping Y's clammy face, Poe spent a few tense moments waiting for the medicine to kick in.

It seemed like hours. But, in fact, color quickly began to return to Y's cheeks.

"I'm all right," the old man said between gasps for air.

"Just relax."

"How's your nose?"

"My nose is fine."

"Broken?"

"Just bloodied. You're too old to do real damage."

Y managed a sick smile. Then the corners of his mouth turned down. As his eyes watered, he looked the other way.

Poe spoke softly. "Y, you know the suicide note that you said was planted? It wasn't."

Y didn't answer.

"It was her handwriting," Poe said. "She wrote the note. I'm sure of it."

"So what? He made her write the note! He probably had a *gun* to her head!"

"No, Y, I don't think so." Poe wiped the old man's brow. "I think you're right about certain things. I think that Lewiston did go to her hotel room that night. And he probably did beat her up. Probably because he wanted to scare her into silence. But the beating wasn't what did her in. According to the coroner's report, she died of *self-inflicted* knife wounds to her wrists. And I believe the report."

Again, Y gazed outward at nothing.

Poe said, "She took herself out slowly. She was punishing herself, Y, trying to attain . . . absolution or something." He took a deep breath. "Linda died because she had an attack of *real* conscience. She felt horribly guilty about what she'd done. Which is more than I can say about Honey Kramer."

Y looked at Poe questioningly.

"Same thing twenty-five years ago, Chief. An unknown mutilator/murderer called the Bogeyman took out a local girl named Janet Doward. The murder gave Parker Lewiston some mighty black ideas. I think Lewiston copy-catted the Bogeyman and killed his own unknown chickie— a kid who, like Sarah Yarlborough, died with *grass* under her fingernails. She was *found* by Linda Hennick, but paid for by Lewiston."

Y looked away.

"I believe that Linda, like Honey, had *pimped* for him—found him young playthings. And probably there are other women in between Linda and Honey who also pimped for Lewiston. And who's to say there aren't murders in between that I don't know about. What can I say, old man? Lewiston is in a rut."

No one spoke.

Then Y said, "Romulus, you told me you only found one Bogeyman case in your back files."

Poe said, "Y, this is where your song and dance about Lewiston paying people off carries weight. No doubt Parkerboy paid people off to quash the investigation. Hell, if he tried to bribe me—a police officer—I'm sure he'd have no qualms about paying off a petty bureaucrat to misfile a simple case. After all, the Jane Doe was an unidentified drifter."

Y said, "Lewiston tried to bribe you?"

"Offered me money to forget his sending out his goons. Same thing." Poe paused and licked his lips. "You know what, old man? I would never have known about that second case except for you. *You* were the one who told me that there were *two* cases accredited to the Bogeyman. You and Alison. And I believed you both, Y. So I kept looking for a second file . . . looking until I eventually found something."

No one spoke.

Then Poe said, "Linda Hennick brought Jane Doe to Lewiston because she was a nothing, like Sarah Yarlborough. He sent out his love-starved, aging whores to find throwaways for him. And that was Linda Hennick to a T—a once beautiful but quickly aging love-starved woman who had been forced to settle for Gerald Hennick."

A pause.

"Because the man Linda wanted had married someone else. And after Linda became pregnant by Mr. Married Gigolo, she had to take what she could get."

"Your father," Y said.

Poe focused his eyes on the old man's face. "You knew all along, didn't you?"

"You're not the only wiseass with an ace up his sleeve."

"Did you know when Alison and I were going together?"

"I had suspicions."

"So you stood on the sidelines while I screwed my half sister."

"I said I had my suspicions. I didn't say I was sure!" He grunted. "Besides, you weren't complaining."

Poe buried his head in his hands. When he lifted his face, he noticed his hands were all bloodied. He wiped his palms and nose with a handkerchief.

Y said, "You'd better be careful, Poe. Insanity is often inherited from your parents. And like you said a few minutes ago . . ." The old man's smile became wicked. "Linda Hennick wasn't crazy. So what does that say about *your* old man if he was Alison's father?"

"I'm quaking with terror."

But deep inside, Poe was uneasy.

What *did* it say?

The old man grumbled, "Help me up."

"Why should I help you?" Poe grumped. "You're an old, mean bastard."

"Romulus, I'm a survivor." Gently, Y slapped Poe's face. "Like someone else I know."

FIFTY-TWO

The same damn recurring dream. By now Poe knew it by heart.
As the sun blasted on the bleak ground, microbes began to
appear on the surface of the recently subsided crater. They were pinpoint,
teeny things that wriggled and squiggled and scampered over the sand's
surface, weighing next to nothing.

They made Poe itch. He scratched in his sleep.

It was the first time the bugs had seen sunlight. Within moments of
hitting air, long-dormant nuclear bodies began to waken as the mites
moved away from their anaerobic state into the aerobic process of con-
verting oxygenated air into energy.

They skittered across the desert floor to firmer ground. Once they were
planted on stable soil, they started to coalesce into a blob—shapeless,
formless, unrecognizable as anything. Soon more bugs joined the biolog-
ical soup, until it started to thicken in dimension. The gloop elongated
upward, grew toward the sky as if it were heliotropic. As if a sculptor
were working magic, the clump lengthened into something around two
or three feet tall and five feet wide.

Poe's eyes jerked spasmodically under his lids as he tried to follow
the motion.

The protoplasm cinched around the front part to form a grotesque neck
and head—embryonic in nature, with a mouth too wide and ears too low-

set. But then the form refined itself until small red eyes appeared, deep-set into bony orbs. Minutes later came a long, hairy snout that held sharp teeth. Then pointed ears covered with red fur.

He started trembling—looking at the same monstrous face he had seen at NTS.

Cellular divisions down below. The blob forming dense leg bones, then the musculature—thick haunches that were strong and developed. Outpouchings off the ends of the bones turned into paws that elongated and grew nails as keen as razors. Eventually hair covered the entire beast.

His heart pounding as he slept fitfully. Aware that he was dreaming, but unable to rouse himself to wakefulness.

The coyote shook out its fur like a wet dog.

Usually the dream ended here. But this time, the coyote looked him squarely in the eye. Then it opened its mouth and sound poured forth. Something about returning to him, that they were eternally linked, bound by love and blood. But for now, it had work to do in a city filled with angels.

Then the vision faded.

As usual, he woke up filled with dread, confused and disoriented. He forced himself to open his eyes.

The moonlight pierced through the open windows as the crickets chattered, clicked, and hissed. Naked and coated with sweat, he lay on his side atop his foldout couch, staring at the shadow of his kitchen, listening to the hum from his battery-operated fan as it pushed hot air from one side to the other. Every few seconds, he felt the relief of a passing breeze only to have it snatched away, leaving him mired in sluggishness.

Slowly, groggily, he wiped sweat and fear from his brow.

The usual routine, Poe. Talk it out, talk it out.

You're not crazy.

It's just a dream, it's just a dream.

Everything is going to be okay.

And he had logical reasons for believing that.

Because things had returned to their former states. Life had taken on a routine buzz. Jensen had been restored to the force, transferred out of Homicide and into GTA. They hadn't spoken much, but Poe had heard he was doing well.

That's good. See, even Jensen is doing okay.

You'll be okay, too.

419

And then there was Patricia. The brass had wanted to transfer her, but Poe had insisted on keeping Deluca in Homicide. She had been grateful, announcing that she'd prove him right. He had taken her out to dinner about a week ago to talk about that night . . . to make sense of it all.

At first, they spoke about physical, indisputable things. About Deluca's Saturn hidden in one of the many caves surrounding the city proper. Once it was in impound, Poe had searched the car and had found a needle and syringe that contained traces of some kind of knockout drug used by Alison to control Patricia.

But how Alison had been able to get the needle into Patricia was anyone's guess. Even Patricia had no idea, remember almost nothing until she had reawakened inside Alison's Explorer.

Between you and me, Patricia, do you remember anything that happened before you woke up, tied up in her car?

Patricia thought about the question a long time. She had become very uneasy in his presence.

I saw this big bird, sir. Like a hawk or an eagle swooping down on me. It must have knocked me down. A pause. *It must have knocked me out.*

A big bird? Poe questioned.

A real big one, yes, sir.

Like as big as a person?

Excuse me, Sergeant?

Was the bird as big as a person? Say . . . as big as Alison?

I don't think so, sir. Squirm, squirm. *But . . . but it was big.*

And you don't remember seeing anyone else?

It was getting dark. I don't remember seeing anyone.

Alison was nowhere in sight?

I don't remember seeing *her. But that doesn't mean she wasn't there. Obviously she was.* Patricia laughed. *She couldn't have come out of thin air.*

Of course not. Poe continued to press her. *Tell me about the feathered Indian headdress.*

Alison had this headdress in her car. She said something about me liking her bird bit, but I don't know what she meant.

Poe thought about the feathers he had pulled out of the sinkhole. Lots of feathers, more than would have been found in a headdress.

Patricia still talking. . . . *rambling, sir. Just talking nonsense. But real scary stuff. I'd only say this to you . . . because you went through the*

*same thing. But she was truly terrifying. I've never been more frightened
in my life.*

I understand.

Then she switched the subject. Poe relented, listening to her talk about
her current cases. When she spoke about them, her face took on an animated glow. Excitedly, she started her sentences with *Oh, let me tell you
about this one.* Or *You* won't *believe this!*

Whatever Patricia had seen, it hadn't freaked her out . . . not like him,
anyway.

Or maybe it had and she just wasn't talking.

Poe stared at the fuzzy outlines of the items on top of his kitchen
counter—a basin which contained soaking dishes, this morning's newspaper, a mug, a twelve-ounce bottle of sparkling water, a few pieces of
loose paper . . . maybe a pencil. Licking his chapped lips, he realized
he'd become very thirsty. His throat begged his legs to get up and
fetch that water, but the rest of his body was too bogged down in tor-
por.

He closed his eyes. A big mistake. The dream's image visited him, this
time stronger than ever, with a face detailed in its clarity. Again it spoke
to him, though this time he couldn't understand her words. Still, he answered her back.

"Alison, you fiendish waif," he whispered. "Did you know all along
about your mother and my father?"

He sighed.

Poe's father had always been a mystery to him. And he would probably remain an enigma. Certainly he wasn't going to broach the subject
with Emma. She had just finished her last bout of chemotherapy back
in Reno, back with Remus where she belonged. The therapy had been
pronounced a great success, and the doctors had cheerfully announced
that she was in full remission. Poe had promised to visit this weekend,
but Dad would not be a topic of conversation. Some stones were better
left unturned.

It was easier for Poe to think about quenching his thirst. So he thought
about that cool water, about moving his legs, getting up, and pouring the
clear liquid down that parched throat of his.

His mouth tasted like sandpaper—gritty, dry, and hot. If he didn't drink
something soon, his tongue would start flaking off. He stared at the evil
sparkling water bottle a few yards from his grasp. He stretched his
hand out.

C'mon, you little sucker. Just grow some legs and walk over to Papa.

At once, the house jerked and the bottle bulleted across the room and landed smack in the palm of his hand, his fingers encircling the glass. Poe was so startled he opened his grip and the bottle dropped to the floor with a clunk. Water started spilling out as he bolted up from the bed, bent down, and snatched the bottle from the floor.

His heart was hammering in his chest, his knees felt weak, and his head was sparkles of light. He had to sit down, drop his head between his knees.

He screamed out, *"Alison!"*

His response was the echo of his own voice.

Get a grip on it, Poe, get a grip on it!

Naked and clammy, he realized he was rocking like an abused child.

Stand up, you idiot!

He forced himself to stand on shaky legs. Slowly, he downed the remaining contents of the water bottle, then put on a pair of scrub pants, slipped a tank top over his head.

The house had jerked. Earthquake. Not uncommon here. Made the bottle fly. That was it, that was it.

With shaky hands, he reached for his cigarettes and stuck a smoke between his lips. Hunting for matches. Where were the damn matches? Probably on the counter. He snapped his fingers, but the matches didn't move.

He wiggled his fingers and said, "Fly to me, matches. Fly to me, fly to me."

Nothing happened.

Poe rolled his eyes, retrieved the matches, and sat down on the edge of his mattress. Lighting the cigarette, he inhaled deeply, letting smoke drift out of his nose and mouth.

What a *relief*!

He was imagining things. Just like that night. All in his head.

Or so they told him.

He stood up, went to his cooler, and downed a beer in one gulp.

A dream, Poe, simply a dream.

But *deep* down . . . in his heart . . . he knew that tonight *wasn't* a dream. Alison had appeared to him. And Patricia's ambiguity, coupled with her failure to find any rational explanation for her kidnapping, made it even clearer.

He hadn't imagined a damn thing, either then or now.

What Poe had witnessed at NTS—Alison's transformation from human to animal—had been *real*! And no one would *ever* convince him otherwise.

Of course, he'd never be able to convince anyone else otherwise, as well. They'd say things like . . . that his mind was playing tricks because he had been under such duress, that he was . . . imagining things!

Just like the water bottle flying mysteriously into his hand.

I know what I saw.

He was trembling now: uncontrollable spasms of his hands, arms, and legs. He couldn't move without shaking.

Alison, Alison, Alison.

What were you doing *to me out there? Were you trying to kill me? Or were you trying to* transfer *your powers to me by biting me?*

What powers?

Y's prescient words: *Insanity is often inherited. And like you said . . . Linda Hennick wasn't crazy.*

Going nuts, Poe, are you?

But that water bottle hadn't fallen off the counter. It had flown into his palm.

And Lewiston had tripped when Poe willed it. Both he and Rukmani had seen it.

Just pretend it never happened, Rom old boy.

Just don't try to *move* things by mental telepathy and you'll be just fine.

Don't ever, ever, *ever* try it again.

So that was settled.

It was just one big mistake.

Just don't try it again, don't *try it again.*

But he knew that eventually he would try it again.

Well, then, don't try to do it tonight.

He exhaled, snuffed out his cigarette, and threw it across the floor.

Eternally linked by love and blood.

Exhausted, he lay back on his bed.

In his heart, he knew what he'd seen.

In his heart, he knew she was alive.

But she had work to do in a city filled with angels.

So Alison was on her way to Los Angeles.

Out of his jurisdiction.
Let them worry about it.
He closed his eyes.
For once, the images didn't come.
For once, he slept through the night.